THE HOUSE OF SAINTS

Also by Derek Künsken from Solaris

The Quantum Magician
The Quantum Garden
The Quantum War
The Quantum Temple (coming 2024)

Flight From the Ages and Other Stories

The House of Styx

THE HOUSE OF SAINTS

DEREK KÜNSKEN

SOLARIS

First published in 2023 by Solaris
an imprint of Rebellion Publishing Ltd,
Riverside House, Osney Mead,
Oxford, OX2 0ES, UK

www.solarisbooks.com

ISBN: 978-1-78618-867-0

10 9 8 7 6 5 4 3 2 1

A CIP catalogue record for this book is available from the British Library.

Designed & typeset by Rebellion Publishing

Printed in the UK

For Beatriz,
who offered me a
new world.

CONTENTS

THE EVENTS OF *THE HOUSE OF STYX*

George-Étienne D'Aquillon lives with two of his sons, Pascal and Jean-Eudes, and his nephew Alexis, in the lower cloud depths, part of the new Venusian colony founded sixty years before by the Québécois. George-Étienne is bitterly estranged from the colonial government and the Bank of Pallas, which holds the colony's debt. The D'Aquillon family survive by herding—and living within—the native Venusian 'trawlers.' They have modified the strange, buoyant plants to collect metallic dust from the clouds to barter with the metal-poor flotilla, the main body of the colony living in the bright upper cloud decks. The family leads a hard life, but perhaps not for much longer. For years, George-Étienne has known of a strange stationary storm on the uninhabitable surface of Venus.

He and Pascal send down a probe built to survive the crushing pressure and melting heat, and they discover something inexplicable: the heavy Venusian atmosphere is flowing *into* a cave. Pascal, an aspiring engineer, suggests that they hook a camera to a cable on the probe, and lower it into the cave to see what could have created this pressure sink at the bottom of the Venusian atmosphere. The camera descends the contours of the cave and, in an eddy, glimpses a sediment-dusted, unnatural, triangular shape, where there should be no technology. There is also an elusive, repeating radio signal from deeper in the cave. But they can't learn more through the probe.

George-Étienne proposes that they go to the surface themselves and recover the mysterious device. The family has an old bathyscaphe that George-Étienne has used a few times to briefly salvage from the surface. They descend through the ocean of Venus's atmosphere to the eerie surface and anchor themselves outside the cave.

While recovering the triangular machine, Pascal extends the camera deeper, seeking the source of the mysterious radio transmissions. Buried in the silt of another eddy, the camera finds not just one of these strange wing-like devices, but a dozen of them, all inert. And in the darkness at the end of the cable's furthest extension, the camera, impossibly, glimpses stars…

Meanwhile, in the upper clouds, in the dirigibles of the main colony, live George-Étienne's other children: his ne'er-do-well son Émile and his daughter Marthe, who is the family's representative in the colonial *Assemblée.* The D'Aquillon family has long been a thorn in the president's side, and it appears that she has found a way to remove Marthe as a political actor. The colony intends to repossess the fraying upper-cloud habitat called *Causapscal-des-Vents,* where Marthe and Émile live. It will be disassembled and its parts used to sustain newer habitats. Marthe and Émile will be given bunks elsewhere in the flotilla.

Marthe descends to the lower clouds to consult with her father, who surprises her with the mystery of the cave only they know. George-Étienne wants to find a way for the family to profit from it. He is getting old, and Marthe and her brothers and nephew need a better future. They needn't be trapped on Venus by a short-sighted government and a grasping bank, when they might literally reach for the stars.

Pascal's filmed evidence of the apparent wormhole under the surface of Venus and the triangular probes they found in the cave gradually overcomes Marthe's disbelief. Pascal also shows her the probe they retrieved, which he's been disassembling. He's found radioactive power cells and complex circuitry unlike any technology that any nation of Earth has ever produced.

George-Étienne suggests that if they are going to lose the upper habitat anyway, why not steal it, for themselves, for the D'Aquillon family? Pascal has come up with a plan to cap the cave on the surface in layers, to simultaneously manage the pressure differential, cool the unsurvivably hot environment, and provide power through turbines. But they can't do anything without metal and other building materials, which can be retrieved from the family's doomed upper atmospheric habitat.

Marthe admits it's possible, but they wouldn't be able to succeed alone—they would need help from other families. They haven't the engineering experience to disassemble the habitat and refashion it into building materials that would survive the surface, nor the resources to catch the sinking habitat. George-Étienne trusts no one, but Marthe eventually persuades her father that they should contact two other families: the Hudon family who bioengineer, grow, and herd the huge trawlers they could use to catch the habitat's weight, and the Phocas family, whose son Gabriel-Antoine is a trained engineer.

Marie-Pier and Gabriel-Antoine accept invitations to talk, and romantic sparks fly between Gabriel-Antoine and Pascal. When they arrive in the cloud depths, Pascal shows what they found on the surface and George-Étienne offers to share it with the Hudon and Phocas families. Marie-Pier and Gabriel-Antoine are dubious, but like the D'Aquillon family, they have no future to offer their heirs. The three families agree to form a new political and social unit, the House of Styx. They begin planning to sink the D'Aquillon family's upper habitat *Causapscal-des-Vents*, disguising their theft as an accident.

In the meantime, the Bank of Pallas and the forces working for the president have found strange radioactive signals in the atmosphere where there should be none, from the probe that Pascal dismantled. Believing it evidence of a terrorist plot—or at best, proof that the colonial government is working with some other bank, in contravention of their investment accords—they lean on the president of *l'Assemblée*, who quietly mobilizes forces to find the radioactives, somewhere in the deepest clouds.

Marthe notices something off with Pascal and in a private moment, Pascal reveals feelings of dysphoria and depression, and that she might be trans. Marthe welcomes her new little sister and promises to help Pascale with the hormones and other things she'll need, although medicines are scarce. Marthe recruits Marie-Pier in this effort, appealing to her experience with the flotilla's black market. Marthe also recruits her disaffected older brother Émile to help her with the fiction they'll need to create to convince people that the *Causapscal-des-Vent*'s sinking was genuinely an accident.

In the deep clouds, the House of Styx has harnessed together four of Marie-Pier's big bioengineered trawlers to act as buoyant floats to support the *Causapscal-des-Vents.* In the clear air at sixty-five kilometers above the surface, Marthe and Émile at first fall behind the flotilla, claiming engine trouble. And as they drift further and further back, they finally declare a buoyancy problem and drop the habitat into the sulfuric acid clouds. Never meant to survive the wind and chemical stresses in the cloud deck, the *Causapscal-des-Vents* sinks fast. Marthe and Émile use radio transmissions to spin their ruse, and Marthe flies off, leading the repair and rescue planes away from the sinking habitat.

The scheme works, and Émile brings the *Causapscal-des-Vents* lower and lower, until Marthe runs into a sudden storm. Marthe's survival equipment is damaged and Émile abandons the *Causapscal-des-Vents* to try to help her. This makes catching the dropping habitat more difficult for the rest of the family, but they manage it in the last moments.

Émile reaches an unconscious Marthe and does his best to try to save her, going so far as to exchange his good helmet for her damaged one before passing out himself, both of them hanging beneath an emergency balloon. When Émile wakes up in the hospital, he finds out that only he was rescued; the emergency pilot never found Marthe.

The House of Styx have succeeded in their plan—they have stolen the *Causapscal-des-Vents,* and with it, they can try to reach the stars—but Marthe, their leader, did not survive to see it.

DRAMATIS PERSONAE IN 2256 CE

Ayotte, Réjean—a flotilla *Sûreté* constable, and a sometime artist and friend of Émile D'Aquillon

Copeland, Amanda—security chief for the bank branch office

Corbeau, Félix—son of Victorine, a *coureur*
Corbeau, Herman—son of Victorine, *a coureur*
Corbeau, Victorine—a *coureur* living in the middle cloud decks on the *Perchoir*, who partners with Narcisse Mignaud from time to time

Daigle, Yvon—a flotilla *Sûreté* constable

D'Aquillon, Chloé—daughter of George-Étienne, born 2229 CE
D'Aquillon, Émile—son of George-Étienne, born 2230 CE, a *coureur* now living in the flotilla
D'Aquillon, George-Étienne—patriarch of the D'Aquillon family and head of the House of Styx, born 2203, a *coureur*
D'Aquillon, Jean-Eudes—eldest son of George-Étienne, the only Venusian with Down syndrome, born 2227
D'Aquillon, Marthe—daughter of George-Étienne, born 2232 CE, deceased 2255 CE
D'Aquillon, Pascale—daughter of George-Étienne, born 2238 CE, a *coureur*
D'Aquillon Régnard, Alexis—grandson of George-Étienne, born 2245 CE, orphaned son of Chloé D'Aquillon and Mathurin Régnard

Ferlatte, Eugène—son of Orphilie, a *coureur*
Ferlatte, Toussaint—son of Orphilie, lives on *La P'tite Piouke,* a *coureur*
Ferlatte, Orphilie—matriarch, lives on *La P'tite Piouke,* a *coureur*

Gaschel, Angéline—*Présidente* of *l'Assemblée nationale,* Chief Executive of Venus

Gaschel, Mélusine—niece of Angéline Gaschel, works at the Bank of Pallas

Hudon, Florian—son of Marie-Pier, born 2247 CE

Hudon, Marc—a *coureur* botanist, born 2219 CE, brother of Marie-Pier

Hudon, Marie-Pier—a *coureur* bioengineer, head of the Hudon family, born 2215 CE, widow until she 'married' George-Étienne D'Aquillon and Gabriel-Antoine Phocas to form the House of Styx

Hudon, Maxime—son of Marie-Pier, born 2245 CE

Jeangras, Laurette—daughter of Lazare, black marketeer on the *Détroit d'Honguedo*

Jeangras, Lazare—father of Laurette, black marketeer on the *Détroit d'Honguedo*

Jetté, Thérèse—artist and mechanic, assigned to common bunking on the *Escuminac,* but almost nomadic, one-time lover of Émile D'Aquillon

Labourière, François-Xavier—Gaschel's chief of staff

Lalumière, Noëlle—Marthe D'Aquillon's former on-again, off-again lover, in an unstable long term relationship with Délia Bolduc

Malboeuf, Juliette—a *coureur* living on *La Reine des Fées,* one of the members of the House of Faeries

Mignaud, Angèle—cousin of Narcisse and Liette, sister of Angèle, a *coureur*

Mignaud, Fabienne—cousin of Narcisse and Liette, sister of Angèle, a *coureur*

Mignaud, Liette—sister of Narcisse, cousin of Angèle and Fabienne, a *coureur*

Mignaud, Narcisse—patriarch of the Mignaud family on *le Grand Platin* habitat, a *coureur*

Phocas, Gabriel-Antoine—independent flotilla engineer, one of the three 'spouses' heading the House of Styx, lover of Pascale, born 2232 CE

Phocas, Louise—sister of Gabriel-Antoine, born 2243 CE

Phocas, Paul-Égide—brother of Gabriel-Antoine, 2247 CE

Tétreau, Laurent—once a secretary to Lévesque's Resource Allocation Committee, a politically-minded junior engineer in industrial works and a police lieutenant, now attached to Gaschel's staff

Tremblay, Grégoire—missing from *la Passe-au-Chevreuil,* and believed to have been murdered

Woodward, Leah—branch manager of the Venusian branch of the Bank of Pallas

PLACES ON VENUS

L'Anse-à-Beaufils—the former trawler habitat of the D'Aquillon family, now used as storage, where Marthe and Pascale were born and Jeanne-Manse D'Aquillon died

L'Avant-Guardiste—a flotilla habitat of the mask artist Isolde Livernois

Baie-Comeau—a large, heavily mortgaged flotilla habitat containing government offices, a hospital and 200 inhabitants

Baie des Chaleurs—a welling of warm air above Guinevere Planitia

Batiscanie—a flotilla habitat

Branche-de-l'Ouest—a stable storm system powered by the winds deflected off Sif Mons east of Guinevere Planitia, and part of the same eddy system as *Trou à Mémère* and *Trou-à-Eudore*

Cap-de-la-Madelaine—a flotilla habitat

Causapscal-des-Profondeurs—the Venusian-grown habitat of the D'Aquillon family, floating in the middle and lower cloud decks, generally 36-50km above the surface of Venus

Causapscal-des-Vents—a former flotilla habitat of the D'Aquillon family, launched in 2221 CE and sunk in 2255 CE, believed destroyed

The cave on the surface—found by George-Étienne and Pascale D'Aquillon, located in the Diana Chasma in the Aphrodite Terra at sixteen degrees south latitude, one hundred and fifty-four degrees east longitude

Coucoucache—a flotilla habitat

Coureur des Tourbillons—the Venusian-grown habitat of the Hudon family, floating in the middle and upper cloud decks, generally 50km above the surface of Venus

Détroit d'Honguedo—a big, aging habitat on the outskirts of the main colonial flotilla, one of the last original habitats sent from Earth for the first immigrants to Venus

Escuminac—a flotilla habitat capable of doing machining work and repairs

Forillon—a larger flotilla habitat, a second generation dirigible housing about twenty people

Le Grand Platin—a Venusian-grown habitat of Narcisse and Liette Mignaud floating in the lower and middle cloud decks, usually about 45km above the surface of Venus

Grande Allée—a stable layer of atmosphere approximately 58km above the surface of Venus that is free of visibility-obscuring clouds, separating the middle and upper cloud decks

Jonquière—a mid-sized flotilla habitat

Lac-Aux-Sables—a flotilla habitat

Lac-Édouard—a flotilla habitat

Marais-des-Nuages—a flotilla habitat, the home of the Phocas family, and after the sinking of the *Causapscal-des-Vents,* Émile D'Aquillon's

La Marcotte—the Venusian-grown habitat of Fabienne and Angèle Mignaud, floating in the lower and middle cloud decks, generally about 48km above the surface of Venus

La Matapédia—one of the large, first generation habitats, which sank decades ago with much loss of life, becoming a byword for disaster

La Mitis—a flotilla habitat

Montée de Corte-Réal—one of the large, first-generation habitats

Mont-Joli—a flotilla habitat

Petit Kamouraska—a flotilla habitat with chemical labs and some detention facilities

Les Plaines—a stable layer of atmosphere approximately 52km above the surface of Venus, free of visibility-obscuring clouds, separating the lower and middle cloud decks.

Pointe-à-la-Croix—a small flotilla habitat of the same class as the *Causapscal-des-Vents*, launched in 2223 CE

Pointe Penouille—a flotilla habitat no one wants to be on

Les Rapides Plats—the rolling horizontal convection cells between the super-rotating layer of the atmosphere and the upper cloud deck at approximately 65km above the surface of Venus

La Reine des Fées—the Venusian-grown habitat of Juliette Malboeuf

Ruisseau-Creux—a small, steady lower cloud deck jet stream relatively free of storms

Saint-Jérôme—a flotilla habitat

Temiscouata—a flotilla habitat

Trou-à-Eudore—a stable storm eddy in the lower cloud decks connected by jet stream flows (like *Ruisseau-Creux*) to other stable storm systems like *Trois-Frères*

Trou-à-Mémère—a semi-permanent storm eddy in the lower cloud decks frequented by the Mignaud family

Venusian Branch of the Bank of Pallas—a large flotilla habitat containing living space and offices for some Venusians and thirty off-worlders who staff the branch office

ONE

Fabienne Mignaud banked her plane to port, tuning back and forth through a narrow range of the radio band, listening for some signal within the static filling the clouds of Venus. The black wings vibrated and hot sulfuric acid made trembling streaks over carbon nanotube fuselage. Vapour blotted out visibility. Faintly, she heard it again: the faintest of station-keeping radio signals, the kind that *coureurs* used among their trawlers so the herds didn't drift too far apart.

She'd left her trawler habitat *La Marotte* about ten kilometers higher in the cloud banks. She'd glided, following trails of volcanic plume down to fortieth *rang,* dragging filter nets behind her to collect floating ash, hopefully more metal-rich than last time. Her electric engines were off, so she could listen for the faint radio hum of a wild trawler's cable moving through the clouds.

Catching a signal from a domesticated trawler surprised her. No one expected to run into another family in the immensity of Venus's atmosphere at any time; and she didn't think any *coureur* families lived at this latitude, unless they were chasing the same volcanic plumes as her. It might be a domesticated trawler blown from its herd, which meant free metal salvage—with a little reprogramming, somebody's lost trawler could become hers.

It could get touchier, though, if she'd found more than just a lost trawler. Strictly speaking, nobody knew the Mignauds had a plane. She'd stolen it months ago during a storm, right out from under the workshop where old lady Orphilie had built it. She'd been flying it discreetly since then. If a *coureur* spotted her and she didn't identify herself, she'd be taken for a spy or a thief. If she *did* identify herself, explaining the plane became a whole awkward story. That said, in an engine-off glide with her radio on receive-only, she shouldn't be drawing attention. As she levelled her flight, she realized it wasn't just one signal—she counted three or four. She'd found someone's herd. A mid-sized trawler came into nebulous outline, floating dark in the spongy gloom. The hazy outline of an antenna and propeller assembly showed on its crown.

She wasn't sure of the directions of the others, and she didn't want to find herself suddenly doing a fly-by of someone's habitat—although if there was a habitat here, she would have expected more radio noise. Had she found a pod of lost trawlers with enough automation to keep them clustering?

She wasn't that lucky. She passed another trawler to starboard, dark, quiet but for its low-energy station-keeping transmissions. And then through the fogginess, a big shape loomed, bigger than anything she'd ever seen in the clouds, dark and totally quiet.

What the *crisse*? She banked to port, pulling a homemade spyglass out of its clip.

The contour was hard to resolve in the mist. It had component shapes she didn't understand: three or four big trawlers seemed to be floating in formation, like precision flying, which made no sense. She slotted a small camera attachment into the spyglass and started taking pictures. Between the four trawler cables she made out a lumpy shape, bigger than the trawlers, but it didn't have a hanging cable—or maybe it did, above it? Too misty to tell. It didn't even look like it had a proper head; the shape looked broken and fragmented underneath, like spikes and ribs hanging from what looked like the top of an umbrella. If it were a broken trawler head, how was it floating?

Fabienne heard more short-range station-keeping radio signals, and then caught a family identifier: D'Aquillon. Identifiers only transmitted from habitats, not the herds, so she was definitely in someone's yard, and she didn't like the idea of getting caught. With engines still off, she banked to port, bleeding off altitude. The mists above her swallowed whatever strange trawlers the D'Aquillons were herding.

She thought she was clear when her radar alarm sounded. *Câlisse*!

She'd been made. She didn't turn on her engines yet—its electrics would be heard in the radio bands, and sometimes the clouds were just enough to blur radar. She flattened and straightened her glide path before she got too deep, and made away from the herd. She reeled in the filter drag netting, no longer caring if she'd scored anything big. A kilo of ash wasn't worth getting caught with a stolen plane.

There was something funny, though. The radar signal hadn't been as loud as she expected. She noticed when her radar alarm went off again. It wasn't close. She didn't think it had come from the D'Aquillons. Was another one of the government 'mapping' planes nearby? Goddamn government. They'd been rooting around in the real clouds for months, instead of minding their own business in the flotillas. As far away as it was, there was a chance, even a good chance, that she was just a radar shadow, mistakable for a small trawler or a colony of blastulae, even a dense cloud.

The display screen in the radio rig was broken—*bébittes* had gotten in and she'd never gotten it to work again—but once she was back home, she could hook up the rig to her data pad and see if there was anything worth seeing in the reflected radar. Even if there wasn't, the pictures might be worth something to her cousin Narcisse.

TWO

PASCALE D'AQUILLON WAS breathing hard, beginning to feel the heat after hours in the oppressive clouds around the platform, floating forty-five kilometers above the surface of Venus. The yellow haze beyond her tools was motionless and patchy, like the chaos before creation. More and more they'd been guiding their habitats to this region of the atmosphere, where the hundred-and-twenty-degree heat broke the sulfuric acid into less dangerous chemicals.

She moved the next metal plate onto the worktable. Gabriel-Antoine had succeeded in making some construction robots, although this one was mostly dumb arms and grabbers, so Pascale still had to fit and feed the metal plates into position manually. On the one hand, it was tiring work, but on the other, it was the uplifting act of bringing a dream to life. As they finished shaping each piece of metal, she hung them beneath the gantry, like the clappers of a strange wind chime. The steel frames of two of the big disks that would cap the cave system on the surface already swung beneath her feet, beside the rudiments of electrical turbines. It was hard to believe they'd come this far, that the first parts of their dream were literally taking shape.

The half-disassembled *Causapscal-des-Vents,* the D'Aquillon family's old dirigible habitat, loomed above the gantry. Acid burns had opacified the habitat's plastic hull while she and her father had dismantled the underside, revealing the steel frame to the haze. The floors and walls and engine were gone, transformed for new purposes on a new world. What the old habitat had been before didn't matter anymore. Like a chrysalis, protecting the metamorphosis within, curtains of trawler cable scrap and dried epiphytic weeds hung over it, blunting radar detection. Pascale sometimes just stopped and stared up at it, feeling a nervous pang of sympathy.

Gabriel-Antoine was struggling with a heavy steel beam; Pascale's father George-Étienne took a side and helped heave it into place. Pascale's eyes lingered on Gabriel-Antoine. In the seven weeks since they'd sunk the *Causapscal-des-Vents*, Gabriel-Antoine's survival suit had transformed too, no longer sleek and pristine like the suits of the *colonistes* living above the clouds. Acid had etched it, dulled its finish. Colorless patches covered holes, tears and wearing. Gabriel-Antoine had begun to look like them, like a *coureur des vents,* the wind runners who lived within Venus's cloud decks. His body, already fit, had become more muscular and hard. And she knew from experience that his skin had felt Venus's lash, bearing new lumpy red acid scars. Still, Venus hadn't rejected Gabriel-Antoine or directed her full hostility against him yet. He was earning his place down here, within her cloudy skirts.

Pascale couldn't hear their words at the other end of the gantry, but the two men sounded cheerful when they finally got the heavy beam onto the bench where Gabriel-Antoine had installed another robot to shape it. It was good to see Pa… living.

Pa had lost so much that for a while, Pascale hadn't been sure that he was going to go on. He'd lost his wife to untreated sickness when Pascale had been small, and his daughter Chloé to Venus's caprice not too much later. His son Émile had become estranged, driven by whatever winds blew fathers and sons apart. The loss of Pascale's big sister Marthe two months ago had come closest to breaking the old man.

When *Maman* had died, Pa had a big family to support and raise—

the dream went on. The stepwise shrinking of the family came closer and closer to dissolving George-Étienne's dreams. Growing into social awareness as a teenager, Pascale had understood that in George-Étienne's mind, Marthe had become his heir—that she would lead the family after him. Her loss felt harder because he had so little left, of family or time. So Pa's odd new political marriage to Gabriel-Antoine and Marie-Pier Hudon was something meaningful, for Pascale and for Pa. A political marriage couldn't replace blood, but the dreams survived in a new kind of family.

Just visible from Pascale's vantage point, Marie-Pier was a tiny, foreshortened figure taking measurements, atop one of the four great trawlers from which the remains of the *Causapscal-des-Vents* hung. The *coureurs des vents* didn't use the dirigible habitats of the flotilla that were built in factories in the asteroids and sold to *la colonie* at usurious prices. Those sorts of thing wouldn't survive down here anyway. The *coureurs* domesticated and bred these floating Venusian plants. Oxygen filled their segmented, garlic-shaped heads so that they could drift through the atmosphere of Venus, collecting static electricity and lightning from the clouds. The *coureurs* of four decades ago had found mutant trawlers with double layers within the heads; with the addition of airlocks, they had been adapted for people to live within. Marie-Pier and a few other biologists had mastered the acid-thriving genetic materials of the trawlers and engineered much larger specimens with more buoyancy and more space for inhabitants.

Marie-Pier's four engineered trawlers bore the weight of the *Causapscal-des-Vents* as Pascale, Gabriel-Antoine, and George-Étienne disassembled and transformed it. They had to work fast, though—Marie-Pier's trawlers were adapted to neither this load nor this altitude. Once a week, the family wrapped the old habitat and everything they'd made of it tightly against the acid and rose to the cooler clouds at the altitude of fiftieth *rang*. There, Marie-Pier's trawlers fed on the lightning and took in moisture and acid.

Marie-Pier extended her wings and leapt from the crown of one of the great plants, gliding at first, achieving level flight before engaging her wing pack engine, which whined as she banked in a wide arc towards them. She wasn't as practiced a deep-cloud flyer *coureur* as the D'Aquillons, nor as elegant a flyer as Gabriel-Antoine, but the easy shifting of weight, the subtle angling of arms and legs showed the fluency that came with growing up in the clouds. She angled up, bleeding off speed before catching herself in the netting under the gantry. Pascale gave her a hand up. Marie-Pier regarded the robot arm busily welding under Gabriel-Antoine's fretting eye.

"I wish we could automate everything," she said with a kind of satisfied exhaustion. She sounded breathless. The glow of the displays inside her helmet reflected in the sweat on her forehead.

"You're still not used to the heat," Pascale said. "It's been hours."

"I can do it."

"We got a lot done today. Even *coureurs* don't work in this heat all day."

Marie-Pier slapped Pascale's shoulder playfully. "I am a *coureur.*"

Pascale smiled. There were many *coureurs,* but few families lived as deep as the D'Aquillons did. "Let's get you and Gabriel-Antoine inside."

Pascale moved two more steel plates into the reach of the robotic welder and covered up tools and materials. The sub-cloud haze was neither windy nor rainy, but they'd grown up with so little that it was instinctive to secure everything as if Venus were about to pour all her acid upon them. Sometimes she did, even down here. Pascale tuned to the common channel.

"Pa, we should call it a day and get Marie-Pier and Gabriel-Antoine inside," she said.

George-Étienne took a while replying, and Pascale imagined him grumbling to himself. This dream they had of going to the stars had swept him up too, and he probably could have worked outside another hour.

"*D'accord,*" he agreed finally.

Gabriel-Antoine and Marie-Pier must really have been wilting—there was little chatter as they all flew the kilometer and a half to the *Causapscal-des-Profondeurs.* It was smaller and dingier than the young trawlers holding up their engineering work, age- and acid-stained, overhung with the black creepers and vines that colonized any surface in the clouds. Beneath their home, ringing the thick base of the trawler cable, hung a gantry made of carbon fiber recovered from older trawlers. The four of them landed in the netting under the gantry and climbed up before neutralizing each other's suits with pads of bicarbonate paste.

When they opened the outer airlock door, they found Jean-Eudes and Alexis grinning nervously inside their helmet faceplates. Jean-Eudes wore one of Chloé's old, many-patched survival suits. Alexis didn't quite fill out the suit Pascale had used as a thirteen-year-old—it wrinkled and sagged around his smaller body.

"What's this?" George-Étienne said. "You can't come out now. Who checked your suits?"

"We did!" Alexis said fearlessly. During quiet moments in the last seven weeks, George-Étienne had been teaching his son and grandson how to put suits on and to take them off, how to neutralize acid, how to deal with failures big and small. Jean-Eudes and Alexis had each done exactly one walk around the gantry under their home, supervised by George-Étienne. Only ten years old, Alexis was young to face Venus, even for a *coureur*. And it had always been a question whether Jean-Eudes would ever go outside: he was good at making small repairs to the habitat and patching suits, but Venus intimidated and frightened *la colonie*'s only Down syndrome son. Marthe wouldn't have approved.

"I'll put them to work out here, Pa," Pascale said. "You take care of Gabriel-Antoine and Marie-Pier."

"I don't need taking care of. I can stay with you," Marie-Pier said.

Gabriel-Antoine sweated profusely behind his faceplate, smiling like he was going to throw up. Pascale clipped a safety cable onto the front of Jean-Eudes's suit and pulled his older brother out.

"Jean-Eudes and Alexis are ready for this," Pascale said, "and we need their help."

Pa snapped a safety cable onto Alexis. "Do everything that Pascal says," he said grudgingly.

Jean-Eudes and Alexis nodded earnestly, coming onto the gantry. They pressed their backs to the cage wall that separated the work area from the long, electrified cable beneath the trawler.

"They have to learn," George-Étienne said, guiding Gabriel-Antoine and Marie-Pier into the airlock. "We'll get you both water and cool soup."

"I hate the soup here," Gabriel-Antoine said, trudging into the airlock.

"I know," George-Étienne said, closing the three of them in.

Alexis was looking excitedly at Pascale, his gloved fingers wound into the grille of the cage. He kept rising on his toes, surveying the exterior of the *Causapscal-des-Profondeurs,* rather than the sometimes vertiginous yellow haze surrounding it. Jean-Eudes's eyes were wide. Pascale put a hand on her big brother's shoulder.

"All good?" she asked.

Jean-Eudes nodded jerkily in his helmet, knocking his forehead against the plate. Alexis giggled. Jean-Eudes smiled sheepishly.

Pascale led brother and nephew through a complete safety check of their suits again before they walked further around the gantry. Jean-Eudes stepped hesitantly, peeking over the railing into the ochre mist below.

There was drudging work to do. Metal was rare and costly on Venus, and the ubiquitous acid chewed through exposed machinery, so robotics and electronics were an expensive, losing investment in the clouds. But all those considerations had muted now that they had the cave on the surface, and its pathway to the stars. They'd been building all sorts of smelting, welding, and cutting machines, devoted to the construction of the big steel doors, the airlocks and the turbines they would need to cap the cave system. And despite this automation, a lot of finicky, boring work still needed doing.

Pascale gave Jean-Eudes a hard, homemade brush.

"Does it have acid on it?" Jean-Eudes asked.

Pascale showed the trunk where they kept their tools.

"All closed in," she said. "Your gloves will keep you safe most of the time."

"What about the rest of the time?" Jean-Eudes said.

Alexis made an impatient face behind his uncle.

"Venus will always touch us to mark us as hers," Pascale said. "If we're careful, she won't mark us often, and if we practice, her touches will be small."

In the low light it was hard to tell Jean-Eudes's expression.

"Remember all of Pa's stories of how Marthe burned herself?" Pascale said.

Jean-Eudes smiled wanly. So did Alexis.

"She didn't have so many scars, did she?" Pascale said.

"I miss her," Jean-Eudes said.

"Me too," Pascale said, and the world seemed heavier, gloomier as she said it. Marthe's absence was all-pervasive. The family needed her. Pascale needed her. "I'll teach you everything she would have, okay?"

Jean-Eudes took the brush and Pascale pulled a tarp off a bunch of scrap metal and parts they'd collected from the *Causapscal-des-Vents*. They brought smaller pieces into the habitat, but they had to be cleaned of corrosion and sorted, which was boring. Jean-Eudes and Alexis began scrubbing them with bicarbonate paste while Pascale busied herself with the more complicated business of finding which computer chips from the *Causapscal-des-Vents* were still good.

"We can't even see how high we are," Alexis said on the common channel, "because of the clouds. I'm not scared."

"Me neither," Jean-Eudes said.

"I wonder when they'll teach us to fly," Alexis said, putting one cleaned part on a tray.

"You're too small."

"Émile flew at eleven."

"Émile is big. He was as big as *Papa* at nine."

"No way," Alexis said. "Pascal, is that true?"

"Jean-Eudes was there. He would know. I was just a baby when Émile was nine."

"Émile was as big as *Papa* at nine," Jean-Eudes said earnestly.

"This is boring," Alexis said.

"We have to work hard. Family first," Jean-Eudes said.

"That's not what that means," Alexis chastened.

Jean-Eudes became quiet. It was harder now, for all of them; Alexis was very smart, and increasingly out-thought his uncle, but didn't always have the maturity to handle it. Sometimes he said things in a way that he later realized sounded like he was calling his uncle dumb. Pascale got ready to intervene, but Alexis peeked into Jean-Eudes's face plate.

"Sorry," Alexis said. "I won't complain anymore. I just want to fly."

Pascale tested three of the control chips they'd salvaged from the *Causapscal-des-Profondeurs*, and which they would need to operate the cap system on the surface. It had taken them longer than they'd wanted to recover these chips, and in the pressure and heat of the lower cloud deck, acid had slipped past the seals. The chips were unresponsive in every test. Glumly, she started putting them in her suit pocket when a radar ping sounded on her helmet display.

"*Merde*!" she said.

"What is it?" Alexis demanded. Neither his suit nor Jean-Eudes's was set to monitor radar frequencies.

"Get inside. Don't skip any steps," Pascale said. "It's another survey plane."

"What's it doing?" Alexis demanded.

"Come on!" Jean-Eudes said. "*Papa* said do everything Pascale says. Show me your checks."

"I want to see a plane," Alexis said. He mumbled more, but Pascale didn't hear as she leapt back into the clouds. The government planes had been flying for months, ostensibly making another cloud and surface map, but it was suspicious. Their radar pulses were sometimes lacklustre and weirdly timed, and from all that Marthe had said, *la colonie* didn't have the computers to process all the data of a real survey. And the planes flew an awful lot along wind routes the *coureurs* used. The House of Styx wasn't using typical routes, but this survey plane was closer than most and Pascale wanted to make sure that they'd covered everything so that their radar reflections looked like just another herd of wild trawlers.

THREE

Réjean Ayotte hated these stupid cloud dives. He imagined the sulfuric acid rain wicking through gaps in the seals and getting into the cockpit, or slowly corroding engine parts until the plane engine died and he was stuck until rescue could get him. He'd managed to get out of two shifts already, calling in sick for one and paying Yvon Daigle to take the other, but there just weren't a lot of constables who knew how to pilot planes in the cloud decks below sixty-fifth *rang*.

The dark yellow clouds, patched with brown, extended gloomily in every direction. Sometimes, he thought he saw spectral lights, but he was never sure. The bioluminescent bacteria growing in the clouds would apparently sometimes shine, but he'd never seen it in anything but pictures. When he'd been little, his brother had scared him with stories of ghosts in the cloud decks. He was grown now, but the stories of dead habitats emerging from the clouds, crewed by suffocated ghosts, looking for air to breathe… they never let go.

There were no ghosts.

But he was all alone in a poisonous ocean.

It was time. He switched the radar to transmit. His plane battery could only handle so many radar pulses, and the little plane computer could only handle so much data, so survey control had timed when and where he switched on the radar. The rest was just boring-but-scary flying in turbulent cloud decks of sulfuric acid.

Noisy radar data filled the crummy display screen. He wasn't a radar expert, but he'd been pressured into enough of these runs that he could do crude interpretations. He saw heavy clouds, storms and some harder reflections from what might be a field of blastulae drifting in a burning breeze. In the distance, some reflections looked big enough to be trawlers, clustered like they were calving. And he saw a radar echo of what looked like a plane? He was the only one on the survey team in the *Trois-Frères* wind system. Who was down here?

Crisse.

It was deep—too deep, he thought, below fortieth *rang,* deep enough to already be in the haze. That made no sense. He pinged the radar again, off schedule, and got a similar image. It was far, at the edge of detection in this cloud, but its profile didn't look exactly like the planes they used in *la colonie.* The plane was moving slower than it should, on a descending glide path. Why was it descending? It was already so fucking deep, gliding like it had no engine, which made no sense.

There are no ghosts. There are no ghosts.

Tabarnak. He wasn't going to draw attention to himself any more than he already had. He throttled up and lifted his nose, taking the plane up early. He was going to get in shit, but this wasn't his job. He wasn't a radar specialist. He needed to see the sun, and at best, it would take twenty minutes to get above the clouds.

"WILL THEY BE okay?" Marie-Pier asked George-Étienne. She was gently sliding a worn pad covered in bicarbonate paste over the seals of Gabriel-Antoine's suit in the airlock. "Hold still, you," she added.

"Pascal is a good boy," George-Étienne said. "He'll keep them safe. They have to learn."

Marie-Pier said nothing about Pascale's secret. It wasn't hers to tell.

She didn't know anyone who'd lived something like this. She hoped George-Étienne would react well when he found out.

"*Oui,*" she agreed.

She turned in the cramped airlock to neutralize George-Étienne's back and suit seals while Gabriel-Antoine's lethargic hands did the same to her. The D'Aquillon patriarch no longer intimidated her. In the months since she'd met him, she hadn't seen the reputed rages, although she'd seen the tough endurance of the man. They'd all withstood a lot, and had more to endure yet.

They have to learn. Would her children have to learn that same endurance? She hoped not. Not yet. Maxime and Florian were too young, although not much younger than Alexis. Children had to grow up fast on Venus, but she didn't want that for hers.

They cycled through the inner airlock door and removed their suits, piece by piece. The coolest the habitat could get at this altitude was about twenty-eight degrees. Whatever modesty they might have had before had been quickly shucked in the last weeks, not just from the tight quarters but the daily grind of using the suits. They stank of old sweat and new, of bodily processes, of breath soured by long hours with nothing but sipped water and bitter protein pills.

The *Causapscal-des-Vents* rationed and recycled its precious little water, so bathing was a wet cloth, after which she put on a light hemp robe, something that had belonged to Marthe. Gabriel-Antoine put on a pair of shorts. He had a beautiful, hard body, on display as he collapsed on a hammock and closed his eyes. She touched his hot forehead and held out a bowl of soup.

"You might have heat exhaustion again," she said.

"Not as bad as the other times," he mumbled.

She held the bowl to his lips. "Stay awake. Drink."

He sat sluggishly and made a face as he drank the soup.

George-Étienne appeared with soup for her. "Same for you," he said.

She patted Gabriel-Antoine's head and went to the table with George-Étienne. The patriarch of the D'Aquillon family—and the head of the House of Styx now, she supposed—had quiet moods she'd come to recognize. The staring at the cup. The eyes that no longer cried, but that still reddened at the edges. The slight quirk of a lip that had been a mannerism of Marthe's too. George-Étienne carried with him his pasts and his might-have-beens. She put a hand on his.

She didn't have words for his loss, there were none. She'd discovered that when her husband had died, when every day had been like sleepwalking through an oppressive darkness. Those around her couldn't carry any of the burden of grieving, only accompany her in some kind of solidarity, everyone hoping that the blackness would one day slough off like a scab. She squeezed and he squeezed back.

Gabriel-Antoine slurped his soup down, made a sound of disgust and shuddered at the taste, before staggering to the room he shared with Pascale. He didn't even turn the light on. The squeak of his hammock sounded through the hanging curtain doorway, and then silence.

"He said I killed her," George-Étienne said quietly.

"Who did?"

"Émile. When he called to tell me. He said I killed Marthe."

"What?"

He pulled his hand away slowly, and his expression tightened further. "Émile was never any good. He abandoned us."

"Marthe died of bad luck in the clouds," Marie-Pier said.

George-Étienne sat straighter and met her eyes. "Émile blames me for everything that's gone wrong with the family. His mother's death. His sister Chloé. Now Marthe."

Marie-Pier shook her head. "Venus," she said with the fatalistic realism all the *colonistes* shared. Venus hadn't killed her husband, but she knew the game they all played with the goddess, the cards they could be dealt, the stakes they paid. They each, in their own way, loved Venus, but Venus loved no one.

"Maybe Émile is hurting, like you, like Pascale," she offered. "Maybe he doesn't know how to handle it."

"He was lazy and selfish as a boy. He's just become worse."

"Did Marthe handle him? Take care of him?" Marie-Pier asked.

"Marthe didn't talk to me about Émile unless she had to."

In their silence, the habitat ribs creaked, low and arrhythmic, adjusting to pressure changes.

"Marthe risked herself for the dream of the stars, for three families she welded into one," she said. "There wasn't a storm when we started. We checked. The clouds blew bad suddenly."

"Venus pounced," George-Étienne said flatly.

She reached across and pulled his hand into both of hers. He wiped at his reddened eyes with his free one.

"Now is the time to mourn," she said, trying to smile encouragingly, "together. And then will come the time for the dream, for our family—and maybe, if we're lucky, our hearts will be lit by starlight."

He smiled wanly.

"You're right," he said softly. "About us needing more allies."

She'd mentioned allies over breakfast, starting a nascent argument they'd each retreated from. In the intervening ten hours he'd obviously given it some thought.

"You're right," he repeated. "The fucking bank and fucking government will eventually find out we've discovered a road to the stars. What do they do then? If the Axis only benefits these three families, it'll be easy for them to justify taking it away."

Maybe it was a little petty, and she knew she shouldn't, but she felt a need to assert some balance in their partnership.

"Now you agree we'll get found out?" she said.

He regarded her steadily for a moment. "You were right," he said finally.

She felt like she'd kicked someone who was down and regretted it, but he'd needed that admission. So had she.

"Marthe told me about your family's system of buying favors and votes from among the *coureurs*," Marie-Pier said. "I'll need to start that up again."

He nodded. She hadn't brought up the subject until now, worried that he might want to be the one to pick up Marthe's contacts.

"We need the allies," he said. "We'll need a lot of allies. And you and I will have to get them. Once we're found out, all the allies on Venus might not be enough. The Bank of Pallas holds all the cards right now: access to the solar system, access to shipping, the terms of loans."

"We've got our cards," she said.

George-Étienne's face began to brighten, as if he was ready to turn to other things, when the alarm on the radio went off.

"*Merde*!" he said, moving quickly to the little radio set just as it gave another pulse. A radar alarm.

"It sounds pretty far," she said.

"It's close enough. Goddamn government!"

He verified that the power on the transmitter was low, switched on the family mask, and tapped out a signal to Pascale. The *coureur* families had simple codes of long and short pulses, and they'd invented filters for their radio transmitters to mimic the natural sounds of Venus. Instead of clear tones or pings, their radios could simulate the crackles of trawler cable discharges or the staticky echoes of distant lightning. In a side-by-side listen, the *coureur* transmission masks wouldn't stand much scrutiny, but from a distance, even the more persistent listener wouldn't be able to tell that the sounds weren't natural in Venus's noisy radio bands.

Everything is covered, Pascale transmitted.

Bring in the boys, George-Étienne tapped.

Gabriel-Antoine appeared in the doorway to his bedroom. "What's wrong? Is Pascale okay?"

"Goddamn government flyers again," George-Étienne said. "Still radar pinging like idiots, looking through the clouds."

"We've got to move again," Marie-Pier said.

"Yeah. If there's any chance they noticed us here," George-Étienne said, "they'll follow the jet stream out of *Trois-Frères* and look through *Ruisseau-Creux*. Better for now to crank up the propellers. If we head north from here, we can catch the outer winds of *Branche-de-l'Ouest* and let the trawlers feed at *Baie des Chaleurs*."

Branche-de-l'Ouest was a stable if ragged storm system driven by the winds off the Sif Mons volcano, just east of the calm air above Guinevere Planitia.

"That's a long trip," Marie-Pier said.

"Better than them finding us."

She did some of the math in her head. Crossing the equator and slowing down at *Baie des Chaleurs* might mean getting back to her own habitat and her boys a few days sooner. "Let's do it," she said.

FOUR

Pascale brought Alexis and Jean-Eudes into the trawler. Some of the thrill and fear of being outside was wearing off as they grew accustomed to it. Pascale had noticed Jean-Eudes often checking his tether, and that Alexis didn't stray close to the railing or even look out into the clouds. Even in storms, they felt safer inside their floating home. It felt different outside, on a hand-made platform, forty kilometers over an inhospitable surface, surrounded by scalding poison gas.

They neutralized each other with bicarbonate pads, before the airlock and again within it. Alexis was so much smaller than his suit that they had to pull apart the wrinkles to neutralize the whole surface. All three sort of fell into the habitat from the airlock, Alexis and Jean-Eudes suddenly brave and excited.

"We cleaned the steel!" Alexis said. He'd been decidedly less enthusiastic outside.

"I brought in the pieces Pascale said to," Jean-Eudes announced, holding up a mesh bag of scrap and containers of chips they'd recovered from the *Causapscal-des-Vents*. He pulled it back as George-Étienne came close. "It's hot," he warned. "I'm hot."

"Don't cross the line, *grand-père*!" Alexis commanded with delight.

"Good," George-Étienne said proudly to them, and then to Pascale, "The survey sounded pretty far off, but they pinged more than once. They saw something."

Pascale had thought the same. It gave her a swimming feeling in her stomach.

"They didn't stay. They didn't follow it up," she said.

"In her clouds, take your luck and run," George-Étienne quoted.

Pascale smiled and nodded, the twist in her stomach not quite gone. Everything they were doing was so risky. They could be found out so easily.

Alexis and Jean-Eudes began the third and final neutralizing pass, the obsessive witchery all the *coureurs* did to defang the goddess inside their homes. Then, seals opened, helmets came off and brother and nephew were chattering about their experience. George-Étienne and Marie-Pier supervised them getting out of their suits.

"Soon it will be time to teach Maxime and Florian to do all this, and bring them down here," Marie-Pier said.

"They don't know yet?" Alexis said with the jaded pride of ten-year-olds. Marie-Pier brushed hair away from his sweaty face.

Pascale made out the shuddering churn of the propellers beneath the gantry. "Close to full throttle?" she asked. George-Étienne nodded.

Marie-Pier moved to admire the two atmospheric diving suits that Pascale and Gabriel-Antoine were close to testing.

She ran a finger over the chest plate of the ADS. Bone-hard carbon fibre and insulation on the outside covered thick steel inside. Each one was two and a half meters tall and filmed with an aluminized foil to reflect infrared. The suits were a challenge to Venus from her children, who wanted to walk on her surface. Alexis followed her, trying to turn one of the big forearms on the axis of its elbow, but it wouldn't budge.

"Everything has power assist," Pascale said, stowing her survival suit. "The joints can still move without it—it's just really hard."

Pascale and Gabriel-Antoine had built the suits together, based on century-old open-source designs for industrial diving suits used on

Earth. In these suits, they wouldn't look human anymore, foreign to Venus. In these disguises they would open up the surface. She felt a kind of elation every time she thought about it. She padded to her room, leaving the tired excitement of Jean-Eudes and Alexis. A whole day in her suit left her more dirty than hungry. She quietly washed, and shaved her face, chest, and arms while Gabriel-Antoine snored softly in his hammock.

She pulled out her little bag of crude, hand-pressed hormone pills. She'd only been taking them for six weeks and hadn't really noticed any changes in her body, but all the articles she'd read said that she wouldn't see any changes for months yet. She no longer avoided the mirror though; the young man's face staring back at her was no longer a strange experience. This wouldn't be her body forever. Knowledge of her true self was a lens through which she could glimpse a different future. She could almost see the path she had to fly, despite the unimaginable gulf of distance. She'd continued growing her hair; it was annoying in her helmet, but could now fall in a way to hint at femininity in the smoothly shaven face.

Some Venusian plants underwent metamorphosis. The deep *coureurs* sometimes observed the strange, slow rains of dying blastulae on their way to the surface, offerings to the goddess from the clouds, and not all of them were dead. Sometimes, their shells became harder, woodier, forming a chrysalis. It didn't stop the sinking descent, nor prevent destruction, but the unsightly pods cracked as they fell, releasing spores suited to the heat and pressure of the sub-cloud haze in ways the human *colonistes* did not yet understand. Something in Pascale responded to the fragile, reaching beauty of these spores, in their awkward stage of becoming, as she responded to the dying *Causapscal-des-Vents*. Their old home, shrouded in the vines and moss and detritus of Venus, was in its own chrysalis; soon it would become unrecognizable, suited for a new way of living on the floor of a great ocean of carbon dioxide.

Pascale was nervous about her change, though; it frightened her despite how badly she wanted it. And the pills were expensive. In a quiet moment, Pascale had asked Marie-Pier just how much she'd paid for them, and after some hesitation, Marie-Pier told her. Pascale didn't understand the black-market economy, but seventy-five kilograms of specially engineered trawler cable was a lot, *every month*. It was like slaughtering and processing a trawler every three months. Who had that many trawlers? Marie-Pier was culling four engineered trawlers per year, just for Pascale's medicine. It was too large a gift, from someone she hadn't known for long. Her unease ran deeper than her personal burden on Marie-Pier. Marie-Pier could have traded that special trawler cable for something the family could have used on the surface. What if the expense made the difference between success and failure? How could Pascale live with herself, if she'd cost their families their chance to reach the stars?

If Marthe's sacrifice had been for nothing?

Gabriel-Antoine shifted in his hammock and made cute snuffling noises.

"Are you shaving?" he mumbled.

"Yes," Pascale said a bit self-consciously.

"Is it for kissing?" Gabriel-Antoine said a little more clearly.

"Who would I kiss?" Pascale whispered.

"Come closer and I'll tell you."

Pascale took three steps and stopped. Her heart thumped hard and she felt her cheeks hurting with her smile. Gabriel-Antoine lifted his head.

"Closer," he urged in a hoarse whisper. The light from the main room reflected in his eyes.

Pascale slid one foot forward.

"Closer," Gabriel-Antoine urged teasingly.

She slid the next foot forward and Gabriel-Antoine leapt up, grabbing her. She shrieked and laughed as he dragged her back to the hammock.

"Shhh!" she said, giggling.

"You're the one making the noise," he whispered into her ear, tickling her with his breath. She couldn't stop laughing. She couldn't stop being happy. And when he pinned her under him in the hammock and pressed his rough lips to her smooth ones, she slipped her arms around his ribs.

FIVE

Suspicious of each other, suspicious of the government, the *coureurs* nonetheless needed companionship, a sense of belonging, the sound of a voice other than their own, more than just immediate family. Shortwave radio antennae didn't use much metal, the sets were easy to build, and the signals wrapped around the planet. The *coureurs* kept their locations secret by relaying transmissions via their domesticated trawlers, which might be floating dozens or hundreds of kilometers away from their homes.

Much of the time, the shortwave channels were just static, but Pascale had listened to hundreds of hours of *coureurs* speaking to the void, including her father. Most of it was pedestrian, even gossipy. Some of it was paranoid or misleading. Some *coureurs*—and some up-clouders in the flotilla—were trying to make a weird naturalist religion. Some *coureurs* had regular broadcasts where they tried to push Venusian-native herbal remedies. Many transmissions were amateurish skits and jokes. The flotilla habitats could pick up the broadcasts, so some of the *coureur* used the thick, quick-evolving *joual* dialect that was harder for the up-clouders to understand.

"Is it good?" George-Étienne asked.

Pascale had been setting up the maser connection to their shortwave transmitter a hundred kilometers away, running along steady equatorial winds while the *Causapscal-des-Profondeurs* continued to float in an eddy of predictable clouds fifteen degrees south. It was challenging to program antenna orientations on both trawlers.

"No one will find us from the shortwave," she said.

Marie-Pier was outside taking care of her big engineered trawlers. Gabriel-Antoine was sleeping. Her father took a few big breaths, centering himself as he took the microphone and stared at the ceiling. He began to transmit.

"This is George-Étienne D'Aquillon. I haven't spoken about it yet, but I lost my daughter to Venus. She was the second child Venus took from me. I love them both the same, but this loss hit me harder—maybe because I'm older. I had hopes for Marthe. She was going to be the one to take care of my family when I got too old. She was going to take over. That's gone now.

"My wife. Two daughters. A son-in-law. All gone. It's like a slow massacre, and we all feel it. Venus hunts us. This is the story of every *coureur* family. It never stops, so we don't stop mourning. Maybe loss would be easier in a place where the world lets memory exist, but Venus erases us after she's killed us. The bitch gaslights us.

"'Family?' Venus says. 'You had family? Prove it! Show me a body. Show me a grave. Show me pictures.' We're too poor to have pictures. And maybe our habitat went down in a hurry and we lost our mementos. Or maybe Venus snuck in, and dissolved our keepsakes and reminders. She erases us until we think we're crazy to be mourning."

Pa took an uneven breath, but his eyes traced along the ceiling ribs, as if looking all the way to the cold stars. He wiped his eyes with the back of one hand and Pascale did the same. He was a mirror to the little and big angers in her heart.

"I grew up in Trois-Rivières, on Earth. We had cemeteries going back to the 1700s. We had roots, centuries of stones and records to say, 'A family of D'Aquillons lived here. These were their names. The stones were erected by those who loved them.' The D'Aquillons exist on Venus, but we have no graves and no histories other than what we can remember, just what we can tell our children. Jeanne-Manse will exist as long as our children exist, and then she'll be truly gone. I wanted Marthe to live longer than my memory. If you hear my memories, she'll exist a little longer.

"My Marthe could swear up a storm. She was a good mechanic. She was a great flyer, both in the depths where she was born and in the upper clouds. She was also clumsy as fuck and couldn't have burned her hands more with acid if she'd tried. She could see through the government's bullshit and go toe-to-toe with the pencil-necked fuckers licking the bank's shoes. She could help people, more than I could. She begged me for oxygen to give to so-and-so, metal powder for someone else, and so on. And I couldn't say no, because she was right: *coureurs* have to stick together.

"I taught her lots of things, but she taught me too. That's one way I'll make her memory live. I'm going to help the other *coureur* families like she would have made me do if she were still alive. Our memory anchors us to the past, but if it's just a look backwards, it's a dead memory. We need to act on memories to make them live. I'm thinking about what Marthe wanted for me, and for our family, and for Venus. She wanted us to be a community, to work with other *coureurs*. I'm starting.

"And while you're out there, hearing about Marthe, and Chloé and Mathurin and Jean-Manse, and letting my ghosts live a little longer, listen to your own ghosts, and tell me. I'll listen too. I'll carry your memories of your loved ones as far as I can."

George-Étienne stopped transmitting and wiped his eyes. Pascale instructed the distant trawler with the transmitter to change altitude and break south, out of the equatorial winds, to rendezvous with them when next the winds brought them together, probably weeks from now. Pa turned off the maser, but left the radio on. Some small, crackling voices began speaking, some with sincere if impotent condolences, others commiserating over the tithes of Venus. After a few moments, some named other souls culled by the goddess. Others were encouraging, in a kind of solidarity that the *coureurs* found easier to express at a distance than in person. The ones that most haunted Pascale were the voices so distant that the names they spoke were ghostly and indistinct, as if truly forgotten. George-Étienne heaved himself away from the radio gear. Jean-Eudes stood in the doorway of the room he shared with George-Étienne.

"Don't worry, Pa," Jean-Eudes said. "I'll remember *Maman*. We danced together. She told me fairy tales. She liked tickling." He paused, face focused. "Sometimes I snuck up on her and she laughed so hard. I'll remember Marthe. She was smart. And she painted my toenails when I asked her, but she said wash your feet first, silly."

"*Maman* and Marthe would love those memories," George-Étienne said. "What's wrong, Pascale?"

Marthe had always swept in with a kind of magical presence, and… *changed* things. Marthe was hard to put into words, so the simplicity of her brother's words felt oddly right. Pascale tried to remember *Maman*, and Chloé too, as much as she could, but she'd been young and the memories had aged, becoming soft and patchy.

"Just remembering," she said.

SIX

The trawler was smaller than the *Causapscal-des-Profondeurs* and in rough condition. Its garlic-shaped head was dented, and one of the twelve segments seemed to be cracked. The whole habitat listed a few degrees.

"Is it safe to board?" Marie-Pier said.

"Safe enough, or old Orphilie wouldn't be in it," George-Étienne said.

Marie-Pier didn't think *La P'tite Piouke* was too long for this world. Its four-to-five-degree tilt would be putting stress on the cable follicle and the bulb ribbing. At the very least, they should be hanging more weight off the opposite side, to prevent the pinching of phloem channels, which were more fragile than people realized. The cable itself would eventually become less responsive to charge, which would affect its ability to capture electricity from the atmosphere.

Tangled epiphytic vines and mosses cascaded over its surface, filtering dust from the atmosphere, absorbing the scant water, cracking water out of sulfuric acid. And some of them glowed. The upper cloud decks rarely lacked for light—Marie-Pier was used to the constant brightness of scattered light, yellow during the day, reddened orange at night—and Venusian plants did not bioluminesce at those altitudes. But *La P'tite*

Piouke throbbed with blue and yellow organic light. The gently glowing plants seemed to have been cultivated among the snarl of epiphytes.

"This is the faerie light people talk about," she said.

George-Étienne turned awkwardly to look back at her. They were testing what he knew of the controls of Marie-Pier's airplane. He'd examined the wings and airframe she and her brother had carved out of trawler crown wood and familiarized himself with the wire pedal and stick controls that would have been at home at the dawn of flight. He'd flown them here without error and blown the oxygen float-bags, and was now completing the after-flight checks.

"The deep *coureurs* tell lots of stories," he said, "different from the ones you upper *coureurs* tell. We see things no one else sees. Sometimes we see faerie light."

"It's very romantic, in the older meaning of the word," she said. "Legendary."

"These are grittier romances than the French lords told themselves," he said. "We live in a more dangerous world than those dark primeval forests."

Someone outside the habitat flew out with a tether, landing long enough to tie a quick knot and jump off before the whole plane tilted from the unbalanced weight. Marie-Pier and George-Étienne dropped through the floor hatch, extended their wings and flew to *La P'tite Piouke*. A silent figure in a patched survival suit waited beneath the habitat on a small, mean gantry. Rather than radio, they used hand signals Marie-Pier didn't recognize; George-Étienne answered similarly. With a discernible lack of enthusiasm, the figure helped them neutralize and they returned the favor before they all cycled through the airlock.

The gloomy interior of the habitat smelled of sulfur and sweat, and the lights of the outer rooms, if any, were extinguished. Some shaved-headed figures waited at doorways, but no one spoke. The floor tilted noticeably. George-Étienne finished neutralizing Marie-Pier, and she him, and both of them the person who'd accompanied them from outside. George-Étienne snapped the seal on his helmet and pulled it off, and Marie-Pier did the same. After some moments' awkward silence, George-Étienne hefted a cable-weave sack.

"Some metals," he said, holding it out.

One of the darkened shapes in the doorways jerked a chin and the helmeted person behind Marie-Pier pushed past her and took the sack from George-Étienne. They opened it, angled so that their helmet light shone in, and poked a finger desultorily. They pulled the ties tight again and then slid and tumbled the sack across the floor to one of the doorways. A shadow took it and vanished.

"What do you want, George-Étienne?" a voice said from one of the other doorways. Low. Gravelly. Wheezy.

"I came to talk, Orphilie," he said.

"Who's the stranger?"

"My wife," he said. "Marie-Pier Hudon, from fifty-first *rang*."

"The trawler breeder?" Marie-Pier nodded. "What do you want to talk about?"

He slowly pulled a jar out of his bag. "I brought some *bagosse* to help us talk."

"Is this going to be a hard conversation?"

"You're cagier than you were ten years ago. You expecting trouble?"

"The world is getting dangerous for *coureurs,*" Orphilie said.

"I heard about Clément. I'm sorry."

"I heard about Marthe," Orphilie conceded. "But that's not what I'm talking about. Toussaint found *la Passe-au-Chevreuil* adrift at forty-eighth *rang*."

"Grégoire Tremblay's habitat," George-Étienne said.

"One of its airlock doors was open," Orphilie said warily, "and its radio equipment was stripped. But whoever it was, they left behind the secondary radio equipment under the gantry. And the airlock, of course. No one was inside, but he found four bullet holes in it, and blood. No one's seen or heard from Grégoire."

"You sure it was bullet holes?"

"Each hole in the interior wall had a matching hole in the outer wall. They were shot from inside by somebody they let in. Toussaint can show you the *Chevreuil*. We've recovered it. We're stripping it for metals."

"How long ago?"

"Five weeks."

"I saw Grégoire about ten weeks ago," George-Étienne said. "Not at the *Chevreuil,* but at one of his calving trawlers."

"What were you seeing him about?" Orphilie asked evenly.

"We were trading," he said with rising heat. Marie-Pier was getting a bad feeling about this. She wanted to somehow prevent George-Étienne from flaring up, but she was a passenger in this encounter. She didn't know anyone.

"Did anyone see him after you did?" Orphilie said.

"His daughters, I hope. They were off chasing down some strays."

"You don't know?"

"I didn't ask because it's none of my damn business. Just like this is none of yours. You think a *coureur* did this? Me? If any *coureur* had done this, would they have left the secondary radio equipment? Or the airlock?"

Orphilie Ferlatte stepped into the light. She was about sixty, sturdy, her bare arms and neck showing wiry muscle, under dry skin ridged with a topography of old acid scars. Blue eyes ready to accuse looked out from under wild gray hair.

"A *coureur* got himself murdered. Government planes are flying all over… mapping."

"I don't like those planes any more than you," George-Étienne said.

"You and I haven't talked in years, and now during all this, you show up."

"*Because* all this is happening."

"With a new wife," Orphilie continued, "bearing gifts, like the ones you brought to Grégoire? While your son is a cop?"

George-Étienne's face went through a series of silent, stupefied expressions, shifting from white to red.

"Émile is *what!?*" he exploded. "What kind of an idiot would make that good-for-nothing loser a cop? Where did you hear that?"

Orphilie's eyes narrowed, as if prying at his words, parsing them for falsehood. Then they softened, perhaps realizing that deception was precisely George-Étienne's weakness. He couldn't hide his feelings if he tried. One of his hands had curled unconsciously into a fist.

"You must be travelling deep winds if you haven't heard all this news," Orphilie said.

"Marthe was my eyes and ears," he said flatly. He held out the jar almost violently. "Are you going to drink with me, or tell me to get the hell out? It was a *crisse* of a long trip to find you."

Orphilie took the dark jar and considered it, before finally giving a *coureur* hand gesture Marie-Pier didn't know. The lights brightened slightly and Orphilie motioned them to a tilted table. George-Étienne peeled his suit down to his waist and sat in a huff. Marie-Pier did the same as Orphilie wiped at a few little glasses carved crudely from trawler shell joints. She unscrewed the jar and sniffed with distaste as Marie-Pier sat on a wobbly stool. Orphilie poured for George-Étienne first and he drank. Then she poured for all three. Marie-Pier was prepared for the taste; she had tasted the D'Aquillon family *bagosse* before.

"To your Marthe," Orphilie said. "She was a tough one." She drank the shot down, grimacing.

"Marie-Pier and I are married to Gabriel-Antoine Phocas as well," George-Étienne said.

"Oho! That must make the bed interesting," Orphilie chortled.

"It's a political alliance," George-Étienne said. "The D'Aquillon family has been standing on its own for twenty years, just like all the other *coureur* families, and we have no influence. The goddamn government can deal with us one-on-one, and the government always wins."

"I gave Marthe my vote," Orphilie said.

"And if you're willing, I think you should give your vote to Marie-Pier," he said. "I've given her my vote to represent us in *l'Assemblée*."

"Why?"

"So we can stand together. Stick it to the government."

Orphilie snorted. "You came all this way for my vote?"

"That's just part of it. Votes aren't going to get us far. All the flotillas and upper habitats still outvote us. No one cares about the *coureurs*. We need more alliances. The *coureurs* have to work together."

"Are you inviting me into your bed, George-Étienne, with her and the other one? What was he called?"

"Families are too small," George-Étienne said. "No one gives a shit about one family, and its four or five people, and its trawlers. If a *coureur* family sinks into Venus, does anyone notice? I made an alliance with two other families. We're going to share resources and share risks. We'll be harder to push around. You need to make alliances."

"I do?" Orphilie growled. "Is that a threat?"

"You named the threats," Marie-Pier said, cutting off George-Étienne's reply. "We didn't know about someone gunning down Grégoire and sinking his habitat. We do know the planes are all around, flying where they've never flown before, but we don't know why. The government is trying to take the habitats I grew with my own sweat. They're cracking down on black marketeering. I don't trust *la présidente*—Gaschel is a bitch—but she wouldn't be cracking the whip without bank cover. She might not even be holding the whip."

Orphilie looked dubious.

"My son Pascal is learning to be an engineer," George-Étienne said. "Gabriel-Antoine is an engineer. And Marie-Pier modifies and breeds trawlers. We're putting together skills that no individual family has on its own. We have our habitat homes and we have the Phocas habitat at sixty-fifth. As a house we're stronger than the families that make it up."

The old woman mused. Marie-Pier tried another sip of the awful *bagosse* as she watched them.

"Why do you care?" Orphilie asked eventually.

"Venus has to change," George-Étienne said. "The goddamn bank is taking us over. The goddamn government is driving *la colonie* into the ground. We've got no future if we don't make it ourselves. When you're stronger, so am I."

"We're all too poor to have a pot to piss in," she said. "It doesn't matter if we're allied or not."

"I brought some metals. Marie-Pier has trawlers, trawlers we know the government wants. Let's all get into a position to bargain from strength, and then see where we can go. I'm tired of being pushed around."

SEVEN

Émile sat in his survival suit on top of the *Marais-des-Nuages,* behind the low utility box. He needed space away from the Phocas family. The two cranky grandparents and the two bratty kids either didn't talk to him, or they talked too much. They sure as *crisse* didn't think trading Gabriel-Antoine for Émile was a good deal, not that he gave a shit.

The sun flared blinding white on the horizon. Fingers of clouds welled up over thermals, reflecting sunshine like a forest of diffuse ghosts beneath a star-dusted sky. He would have liked to believe in ghosts, to think that somewhere in that spectral landscape, Marthe might be wandering, flying, persisting. If she'd really been a ghost, she would have come back and haunted him anyway, maybe in a good way, maybe in a bad way. Her nagging and bossiness had come from a place of love—frustrated, angry love. But Venus dissolved even ghosts, leaving Émile clutching at slow-fading memories.

He sat with his back in the shadow of the box, with his legs stretched out in the sun. Between the two, he was just the right temperature. His data pad was linked to voice commands in his helmet. He had words in him somewhere, fragments of poems close to surfacing, aspiring to clarity, and maybe truth and insight. Words felt promising, germinal, but only when they floated unformed inside him. They never turned out right, but that didn't stop them from compelling their own birth, sometimes with all the poetic elegance and beauty of a bad *bagosse* hangover. He knew that if he could just make the words burble up, he would feel better and disappointed at once.

He wanted to work on *The Harsh Mother*, a growing poem about the Venus they inhabited, or *The Whirling Children of Cain*. He'd been working on both for a long time, and they were difficult births, products of old angers and resentments. *The Harsh Mother* had taken two of his sisters and his mother, and *The Whirling Children of Cain* lived out the consequences of someone else's sins. He needed both to exorcise his own hauntings, but instead of finishing them, he kept coming back to *The Weeping Muse*.

He hadn't seen Thérèse in months. She'd probably heard about Marthe. The spectacular loss of a habitat with some of its crew was big news. It had been a decade since anything like that had happened. *La colonie* had fallen into a kind of grudging armistice with their environment, and Venus hadn't regularly sunk their homes for thirty years. Thérèse hadn't reached out to say anything to him, though. Réjean had; Hélène had; hell, even Cédric had, and he was a tool.

He couldn't know Thérèse's heart, how much pain she must be in. Cutting was common. Drugs were common. Overdoses were accidental, until they weren't. If not for him, Thérèse would be dead right now, dissolved and incinerated in her fall from the clouds, like Marthe. He'd tried to save both, and had succeeded with Thérèse and not with Marthe. There was some meaning in there, some measure of the depth of his love for Thérèse. Between bouts of swearing off thinking about her, he daydreamed about her, and about some grand gesture that would reveal his heart to win hers. If she could see him with new eyes, realize that something special inside him was worth loving, he would feel… He didn't know. He didn't know.

But those daydreams were just invented ghosts, telling him nothing about the true Thérèse, the muse he was trying to write about. He didn't know her enough to do her justice in a poem—or to interest her in him, apparently. He flipped from shitty poem to shitty poem, his words constipated and unformed.

He lifted his head. The nearest habitat was a green marble a few kilometers away, drifting on the high winds just below the stars. Further afield, many more showed as startling emerald pinpricks, moving deceptively slowly in the jet stream. But one thing moved faster—a figure, he realized, riding wide wings. People hopped from habitat to habitat all the time, like boats passing on the sea, but the figure was definitely coming this way. Émile self-consciously closed the poem files and slipped the pad into an outer pocket as he sat on the utility box to warm his back. A few minutes later, the traveller slowed, swooped and flared, coming to a running stop on the flat roof. He furled his long wings and lifted the pack off.

Tétreau, the police lieutenant, shook gloved hands with Émile. They'd been talking on and off for a couple of weeks, and Émile was close to agreeing to be a sergeant in the *Sûreté*. He didn't love being a cop, but it was easy work; it beat fixing things. Although he still had to do that too. The constabulary was, like firefighting, a job that happened when it happened. In between, there wasn't much to do. The crackdown on black marketeering made things busier, though.

"When you want to move to someplace better, say the word," Tétreau said. "Your brother and his boyfriend can come live up here and take care of the family themselves. You don't need to do everything for everyone."

Émile shrugged. "Got another raid?"

"Running out of *bagosse*?" Tétreau laughed.

"We haven't confiscated anything yet that hasn't ruined my guts."

"I have a line on some whiskey," Tétreau said, "aged in real casks."

Tétreau had shared some really good stuff with him once. Émile hadn't been drinking much lately, but he wouldn't say no to something good.

"I've got something I think you can help us with," Tétreau said. "We're looking for a radiation source in the clouds."

Émile didn't show his confusion. Tétreau was looking at him like he was interviewing him, but Émile didn't really care about being in the *Sûreté*.

"How do you lose radiation in the clouds?"

"Somebody stole it from the bank," Tétreau said.

"How much radiation are we talking about?"

"Enough to make a mess."

"*Tabarnak,*" Émile swore. "Like terrorists?"

"We don't know. Nobody's made any demands yet."

Émile scanned the whole horizon of clouds. "It's a really big goddamn planet, Laurent."

"I know."

"What do you think I can do?"

"The radioactives aren't on any habitat or factory floater at sixty-fifth *rang,*" Tétreau said. "We checked everyone while doing a 'health inspection.' The material didn't leave the planet, and it's not on the surface."

"It could be if it was wrapped in lead."

"On the surface, lead would melt and run off," Tétreau said. "That means it's got to be among the *coureurs*. I don't know anything about them, but you do. You're an expert."

Émile didn't like being called an expert at anything, but he was a *coureur,* even if he hadn't been deeper than sixtieth *rang* more than once in five years. Where you grew up didn't rub off.

"So. If you were a *coureur* hiding radioactives from Geiger counters on government habitats," Tétreau said, "what would you do?"

EIGHT

Fabienne Mignaud's herd of trawlers avoided a storm and reached the rendezvous site only a day late. Many believed that Venus was a little sister to gas giants like Jupiter or Saturn, deep and chaotic, but in truth, prevailing winds and the major convection cells imposed coarse structure on her atmosphere. Experienced travellers could follow stable storms, eddies, predictable thermals and mountain waves like small rivers and deer paths through a dense forest. The *coureurs* knew many of these mercurial structures and the crossings between them. Every three to four weeks, the Mignaud family reassembled in a semi-permanent eddy they called *Trou à Mémère*.

From the half-built gantry under *La Marcotte,* Fabienne and her sister Angèle watched as *Trou à Mémère* took their carefully herded trawlers and began to string them into a line, joining her cousins Narcisse's and Liette's flocks. The eddy was broad, with few shear forces, but it could still scatter a herd if they were careless or unlucky. *Mémère* was a good place to stop and replenish the trawlers, though, especially if they'd gone deep for volcanic ash. This pocket of atmosphere was rich in the static electricity on which the trawlers fed. Flashes of arcing blue light popped along the vibrating plumb lines as the trawlers followed twisting winds. Sometimes *Trou à Mémère* temporarily caught wild trawlers in its circular currents. The Mignaud family had occasionally added to their herds here, when they had enough metals to domesticate new trawlers.

She didn't see Narcisse among the hundreds of trawlers, but recognized his habitat *le Grand Platin* about four kilometers away, nestled within the orange-red light of the storm wall at the far side of the wide transparency of the eddy. Fabienne was used to being surrounded by cloud, so open spaces gave her strange vertigos. She and Angèle flew in an arc across the wide hollow, until they could alight in the netting under the gantry at *Grand Platin*.

Inside, she found Narcisse, her eldest cousin, a stout man in his fifties, and his sister Liette. The pair had raised Fabienne and Angèle after their parents' deaths, but as soon as they were old enough, the sisters had moved into a crude habitat they'd fashioned from a wild, double-layered trawler. They'd started shepherding smaller flocks of Narcisse's herds, and gradually begun catching and taming their own. Eight years on, the Mignauds now had hundreds of trawlers, producing oxygen, collecting organics and water, and yielding acid-resistant building materials, and the younger sisters shared in that bounty. The family could have handled a larger herd, but every scrap of metal they had was doing something. They couldn't build more circuitry, or compressed air tanks, or capacitors, motors or control systems. They had what they collected from the skies, and some supplies from *la colonie*—things that were considered safety equipment, or things the family had inherited, or traded, or walked off with while no one was looking—but little else.

Narcisse was de-sulfuring what looked like a stew. Liette, a gray-haired woman in her late forties, had disassembled an electric motor all over the table.

"You're late," Narcisse said.

"Venus was a bitch again," Fabienne said. "She turned us around at *Branche-de-l'Ouest*; the herd nearly got split in two, so we had to cycle twice."

"I told you to watch your entry there."

He was usually sour-tempered with Fabienne and her sister; he had never wanted children. But he *had* warned them about the entry. It wasn't that they hadn't been careful. It was always tricky to use the outer edges of a storm for anything, and Venus laid traps for them. When they were lucky, she didn't draw blood.

Fabienne and Angèle shucked their suits, and Fabienne brought a durable memory card out of an inner pocket. "I have to show you something."

"What?"

"The D'Aquillons are up to something."

"What?"

"I don't know. I took pictures. They were in the old storm eddy at *Trou-à-Eudore*."

"Did they see you?" he said, the stew forgotten. He began rooting around in a cupboard for an old reader.

"Of course not."

"How do you know? That old goat George-Étienne is a tricky bastard, and suspicious. If he recognized you..."

"I was radio-silent, engine-off in the mist at fortieth *rang*. I drifted through, circled down and didn't turn on my engine until I was five kilometers gone, and even then I left the radio off."

She waited, but there was no reply.

"A survey plane was out there, though," Fabienne finally added.

Narcisse turned back to look at her, his face reddening. "Did you get pinged?"

She said nothing.

"How bad?" he demanded.

"Twice, but it was far off."

"So they saw you!"

"He was five kilometers away at least. The echo would have been nothing."

"Twice," he accused.

"If he'd noticed me, he would have followed and pinged more. He didn't. He just left," she said placatingly. She was still holding out the chip.

Narcisse's shaggy face was still sour as he found the reader and took the chip from her. Liette left the motor and came to see. The reader's internal battery was long-dead, so Narcisse had to wire it to a battery on a workbench. After fiddling with the connections, he finally got its screen lit. When he plugged in the card, he squinted at the images.

"What the hell is that?" Liette said.

"Have they… harnessed trawlers together?" Narcisse said.

Fabienne nodded.

"This isn't something we can do in the clouds," Narcisse said with a kind of resolute belief.

"What do you mean?" Liette asked. Narcisse grimaced before speaking.

"That harness—the D'Aquillons had help. Some special project that the government hasn't told anyone about." His fingers expanded the image to grainy blurriness, trying to see what hung between the four trawlers. He swiped to other images, then back.

"It's like they're building some disk," he said. "Out of metal. That's not carbon, or pressed trawler cable."

"Where would they get that much metal?" Liette asked.

Narcisse expanded a later image, one of the last Fabienne had taken, from about three hundred meters below, looking very near to straight up. The picture showed the four trawlers in the mist, and between them, the dark, confusing form draped in debris.

"Broken," Narcisse said. "Like an egg shell." Fabienne had never seen an egg, but she knew them from pictures, and stories her cousins had told of their childhood in Québec. He expanded the image bit by bit, until it was just pixels.

"Shitty picture," Liette said.

"We don't need to see anything. This is a straight line. This is a right angle," Narcisse said, tracing with his fingertip. "They aren't gutting a trawler. This is artificial. A habitat. I bet you it's the *Causapscal-des-Vents*. There was a big fuss a couple of months ago about the government confiscating the *Causapscal* for parts. Before the issue could be sorted out, it sank. D'Aquillon lost his daughter in it."

"Martine, or Madelon, or something," Fabienne volunteered.

"George-Étienne must have cut a deal. With the *Causapscal* written off, the parts could be sold on the black market with no one the wiser. I bet you that D'Aquillon is paying Gaschel a fortune in kickbacks."

Fabienne hadn't thought all of this through.

"How long ago did you take these?" Narcisse said.

"Twelve days."

"*Trou-à-Eudore* is a slow eddy," Narcisse said. "It isn't big enough to feed the trawlers or low enough for ash, but it's out of the way, and calm. This set-up of theirs, they probably don't want to try running it through a storm. They might be staying there."

"If they were avoiding storms," Fabienne said, "they could hop from *Trou-à-Eudore* to *Trois-Frères* and follow *Ruisseau-Creux* halfway around the planet." *Ruisseau-Creux* was a small, steady jet stream that rolled high and low over mountains, but was relatively free of storms. Poor feeding for trawlers, and relatively untravelled by *coureurs* who had herds to keep healthy.

"Could you find them again?" Narcisse said.

"Why?" Fabienne said.

"Because I don't have a plane and my herd is bigger," he said testily. "We need information. If D'Aquillon and Gaschel are scamming *la colonie,* there's something in it for us to keep it quiet. We need better pictures, and we need to tie this directly to the D'Aquillons."

"I heard their identifier," Fabienne said.

"Did you record it?" he said.

"Why would I?"

"Because no one will take your word for it."

"If we take our trawlers all along *Trois-Frères* and *Ruisseau-Creux* to try and find one floating workshop, it's going to take a while, and our trawlers won't feed," Angèle said.

"Liette and I can take half your herd for now. If you spread yours wide, they'll feed well enough. If you're spotted by the D'Aquillons, it even gives you an excuse to flying around: you're pulling your herd back together."

Fabienne didn't like the idea of leaving half her herd with Narcisse, and didn't like having to snoop around, and didn't like that they hadn't talked about what she was going to get out of all of this. But Narcisse had raised her, and she still owed him.

NINE

LAURETTE RUBBED THE grains through the little baggy, looking doubtful. She shifted her weight, putting a hand on her pregnant belly. Opening the bag, she sniffed experimentally, then rubbed the metallic crumble between thumb and forefinger.

"It's not a lot," Laurette said.

"I *have* a lot, though," Marie-Pier said, setting her pouch on the carbon weave table. "Three kilos. Mixed metals."

"Not iron or nickel or aluminum," Laurette said, half question, half accusation. Marie-Pier would have preferred Lazare Jeangras; he was a more relaxed barterer. They were deep in the hidden guts of the *Détroit d'Honguedo,* one of the big older habitats, where some of the best black-market trades could be made.

"Mixed metals," Marie-Pier said again. "This is good stuff. If you don't want it, I can offer it to Thibodeau."

"Thibodeau wouldn't know what to do with this," Laurette said dismissively, which was a lie. "*Papa* won't be back for two days, though. He's on the *Baie-Comeau*. His heart. He'll know if we can move this. Are you looking for something new, or is this part of the payment for the hormones?"

"Either way. Or credit. I'm going to need some chips very shortly."

"What kind?"

"Mid-performance processors, like for data pads."

Laurette gave her a dubious expression. "Pricey."

"I've got these metals, and more."

Laurette rubbed a knuckle along her jaw. She'd been part of her father's black-market dealings since she'd been in pigtails; now she was grown up and expecting her own first child. Only Lazare had the experience to move the weird stuff, though. No matter who eventually traded or bartered for this metal, it still needed to be smelted, and the few solar smelters in the flotillas would pick up Lazare's calls.

"Since when are you moving volcanic ash?" Laurette said.

"George-Étienne D'Aquillon and I are a thing."

"Don't know him," Laurette said.

"He's a *coureur*."

"You're a *coureur* too," Laurette said.

Marie-Pier waggled her hand, *comme-ci, comme-ça*. "I live too high for the *coureurs* and too low for the flotilla. No one counts me as theirs."

"I guess people will think you made your choice."

Marie-Pier pushed the pouch a centimeter closer to Laurette. "Can you take this?"

"I would rather *Papa* looked at it. Come back in a couple of days?"

"Okay," Marie-Pier said disappointedly. She fastened the ties on the pouch.

"And I'm waiting on the cabling," Laurette said. "*Papa* told me about your deal. Seventy-five kilos. End of the week, right?"

"It'll be here. My brother is processing it right now."

"Don't be late."

Marie-Pier put the pouch in the front pack of her survival suit as she left the black market. She slipped through the concealed door at the back of a government parts distributor. The government employee minding the shop nodded to her and went back to his cataloguing.

Marie-Pier had food chits; she grabbed a spicy noodle bowl from a kiosk before heading to a stairwell to the roof. Many of the lights in the stairwell had been burnt out for months, so she didn't see the guy on the landing until he grabbed her arm and held a homemade knife in front of her face.

"Keep quiet and nothing will go wrong," he said.

She nodded.

"What did you get in the market?" he said. "Show me the drugs."

"I didn't get anything." The man's face tightened in anger and she quickly added, "They didn't want what I had. I have volcanic dust. They said it wasn't good enough."

He started patting her down, hands hurrying into pockets, pulling out everything. He found the three kilos of metals she hadn't been able to trade and the small sample bag.

"This is metal," he said.

"They didn't want it."

He unstrapped her pack, the crude knife shaking in his hand.

"You stay here a minute," he said. "If you make a sound, my guy at the top of the stairs or my guy at the bottom of the stairs will be the only one to hear—and I'll be pissed."

PASCALE CAME OUT of the airlock onto the gantry. Hot winds gusted in the low light, flinging acid sideways. Drops glided down the round head of the *Causapscal-des-Profondeurs,* joining into streams, filling the sulfuric acid tank; after the downpour, they would use the electricity the trawlers collected to crack it into water and poisonous gases.

"You shouldn't be out here, Pa," she said.

He stood near the grounded cages, close enough to get inside in a hurry if the lightning rumbled closer. He slammed and pushed at something that wouldn't fit into one of the chests. Pascale neared. Pa held an awkward bundle of resin blocks they'd cooked out of blastula husks. They didn't even need to be in the chest. Pascale lifted one end of the bundle, but Pa set his down and pushed her hands away.

"Let it be," he snapped.

"Are you okay?"

George-Étienne closed the chest and leaned on it with straight arms. Pascale craned to peer into his helmet. She thought she saw tears.

"What's wrong?"

He lifted the lid a little and then slammed it down, just making noise.

"What are you angry about?"

He turned, showing the intensity that had sometimes frightened Pascale as a child.

"Aren't you angry?" he demanded. "This is my family! I was supposed to give my family everything. There's no more Marthe. No more Chloé. No more Jeanne-Manse. No more Émile. I was supposed to give them all a good life."

The rain slackened, but the winds kept shifting. *There's no more Marthe*. Pascale missed *Maman,* and Chloé, but those were old hurts. Marthe was... more important, more needed. *We know where you are, little sister,* Marthe had said to Pascale, in the way that promises are said. *You're not lost anymore. We'll come get you.*

"You can't control Venus, Pa. No one can."

"I chose to immigrate. Then I chose to come down here. I chose this for us."

"Those choices weren't wrong, Pa. You did the best you could. Jean-Eudes is alive and happy. So am I. So is Alexis. And Émile is too. He's got a girlfriend in the clouds. She seems nice."

"They all deserved more." George-Étienne sat on the chest, slumping dejectedly. "Sometimes I only see the dark, Pascal." She put her arm around his shoulders.

"We're finding our way to the stars."

"I would rather have my family back."

"I know."

Hot sulfuric acid whirled on contrary winds, tap-tap-tapping against their helmets. Pa's shoulders shuddered under Pascale's arm as he cried, and she squeezed. She felt helpless. She wanted to be honest with him—about her—but this didn't feel like the right time. And of all people, she didn't know how to tell him, and that made her feel worse, like she wasn't giving him something she should.

After a time, his breathing steadied. He sighed, but said nothing. The radio crackled in her earpiece and Gabriel-Antoine's voice spoke.

"*Chéri*, are you and your *papa* coming in? Marie-Pier just sent a message. She's all right, but she was robbed."

LOUISE KEPT BEATING on the door as Émile rubbed his eyes. Eventually she just opened it and came in.

Louise was twelve, the same age as Alexis, whom he hadn't seen in five years. She was tall, gangly and dramatic. He hoped to *crisse* that Alexis was less... Just *less*.

"Don't you wake up?" she demanded. "It's the comms. I'm not your message service!"

She didn't leave, though. She watched him turn in the hammock and put his bare feet down among all the neatly organized tools in Gabriel-Antoine's workshop.

"What's the message?" he said.

"It's not a message. It's your brother."

She lingered in the doorway, glaring at him judgementally.

"My brother's been gone a long time."

"I know," Émile said, drinking from a jar of water and standing up.

"I think they like each other."

"You saw them more than me," he said, padding to the doorway.

She stepped aside. "What did your brother say about it?"

"Nothing."

"Well, find out," she said.

Grand-père Phocas was off in his own bunk, but *Grand-mère* Phocas hunched over an alternator, slowly replacing parts. She'd gotten used to Émile, it seemed; since Marthe had died, something had turned. *Grand-mère* hadn't warmed to him, but the edge had come off her disapproval.

The comms set in the Phocas habitat showed signs of having been disassembled, stripped for parts and put back together with the minimum of flash. Louise stood close. Émile checked the readings: the maser scattering was less than four centimeters. No one would be able to intercept the call. The dish on the habitat was pointing about thirty degrees south of the equator. Where the hell *was* his family?

"*Oui*?" Émile said.

"Émile. It's Pascal."

Émile's first urge was to throw back something flippant, something half-angry. He'd stewed for days and weeks about being left out of the family's plans, brought in only at the end, only to the extent that they needed him, and not a bit more. That said everything that needed to be said about his relationship with Pascal. Pascal was in Pa's camp.

"Are you okay?" Émile finally said.

"I'm okay," Pascal said.

"I'm okay too. Thanks for asking," Émile said into an extended pause.

More light static and silence.

"Can you help with something?" Pascal said.

Of course. "What?" Émile said.

"Somebody robbed Marie-Pier," said the distant voice. "She's a bit shaken up, and it cost us. Can you help her?"

"What is this? Are we taking care of everyone but our own?" Émile said in a low voice.

"She is our own. Marthe picked her as an ally. She's family now, one of us."

One of us. Did Pascal's *us* include Émile? Pa's didn't. Even though Marthe had been a pain in the ass, when she'd been alive, they'd been a family, Émile and her. Louise rocked on her heels, close.

"Ask him if he's my brother's boyfriend," she whispered.

"He's not going to answer if he thinks you're listening," Émile said, cupping his hand over the microphone. She frowned, then backed away. Paul-Égide leaned out the door to their little room to see what was going on. Émile cupped his hand over his mouth and the microphone and said, "Did you guys steal radioactives?"

The fuzzy static lengthened.

"No," Pascal said finally. No surprise. Not 'What are you talking about?' Just no.

"They're looking for stolen radioactives, and it looks like they're pulling in the bank to help," Émile whispered.

"No one stole any radioactives," Pascal said. "Will you check in on Marie-Pier? And help her?"

Émile had something in his chest, something wanting to come out in words, to tell Pascal, to give Pascal, but he didn't know what it was or how to say it. He wanted back the moment of closeness they'd had, when Pascal had come to the upper clouds, when for a little while they'd just been brothers catching up, happy to see each other, rebuilding a bridge between them with enthusiastic awkwardness.

"Yeah, okay," Émile said.

The silence dragged on for a bit, and then Pascal said, "Send me more poetry."

Then the maser line ended. Émile held the speaker to his ear for a bit. Was it about holding this bubble of privacy for a little longer? Or had something been there? It hadn't just been business. Like so many things, what he'd been reaching for, feeling for, was gone.

He turned the dish back to equatorial and erased the last angle from the log so that no one could work out the location of the *Causapscal-des-Profondeurs*. It was a *coureur* habit, grown automatic. He rested the set in its cradle.

"What did he say?" Louise said. "Is he my brother's boyfriend?"

"He was too shy to say."

Louise grinned excitedly. "I knew it!"

TEN

Fabienne could not find the D'Aquillons. Venus was a planet-circling ocean of carbon dioxide seventy kilometers thick. She couldn't use radar; even if her equipment had been good enough to run constantly, it would have told everyone she was looking for something, like the government 'mapping' exercise that had been running on and off for months.

She and Angèle took turns. One stuck with their shrunken, ragged herd, and the other flew the plane. With the engine on, they climbed it into the acid rain layers at fifty-eighth *rang* and then powered off, gliding for hours through the clouds, catching lift in convention cells and wind upwelling from the mountains, listening to static on the radio. It was a boring, exhausting exercise, occasionally dangerous when she came close to a wild trawler or to a cloud of woody blastulae.

Fabienne flew the long, mind-numbing, featureless length of the *Ruisseau-Creux* jet stream, sometimes crossing it in wide zigzags in case the D'Aquillon installation was in the gentle turbulences off its edges. *Trou-à-Eudore,* a great, slow eddy of one-hundred-and-forty-degree mist, cottony and orange, was empty, as was *Trois-Frères,* a stable, leisurely eddy above three high mountains.

One day, at home in *la Marcotte*, as the ruddy red light of dawn gave way to the brighter yellow-orange glow of morning, Fabienne and Angèle put their heads together. They liked to make ink out of soot and had drawn a map of the middle and lower cloud deck wind systems on the inner wall of their trawler. The sisters had travelled many of the atmospheric rivers and tributaries over the last weeks, portaging at storms and eddies, but hadn't run into anything useful. Fabienne was cranky, sweaty, tired and accounting a trawler they'd lost in the back of her mind, including the metal they'd installed on it. They'd lost kilos of metal, while the D'Aquillons, if Narcisse was right, had gotten away with stealing *tons* of it.

How had they done it? To sink the *Causapscal-des-Vents,* the D'Aquillons would have needed Gaschel or someone in the government to turn off sensors or fake the readings while they sank it through *les Rapides Plats*. They might even have needed someone in the government to kill any follow-up investigations, or make fake reports. That was a big conspiracy for D'Aquillon to pay off. How were they getting the metal and parts back to the flotilla for the kickbacks?

Maybe that was what the radar survey planes were doing. Three or four planes could just be wasting their time, or maybe even conducting an actual survey. One of them—you'd want the same pilot doing all the pickups—was finding the D'Aquillons and picking up a load of stuff for the black market. Maybe that's why they needed to look with radar. It was kind of the perfect cover. And if Fabienne could get proof, Narcisse could blackmail them and get in on it. Fabienne would get in on it. She'd insist on a bigger cut from Narcisse; a finder's fee. Narcisse had figured it out, but she'd been the one to get the first pictures. And she and Angèle would get the proof.

Except she couldn't find the D'Aquillons.

Angèle was tracing her finger along their stylized map of the wind systems tattooed on the inner skin of their trawler. The *Ruisseau-Creux* jet stream, the spiral of *Trois-Frères,* the big winding circle of *Trou-à-Eudore*. And the 'x' they'd marked at *Trou-à-Eudore,* where she'd seen them. She didn't know George-Étienne D'Aquillon, but Narcisse did.

"That old goat George-Étienne is a tricky bastard, and suspicious."

"What?" Angèle said.

"Narcisse said old D'Aquillon is a tricky bastard."

"So?"

"So we've been looking all along where he would have floated next, following the currents."

"Yeah?"

Crossing the winds was hard. Winds at different speeds ground against each other, making turbulence and shear forces. And moving a herd tired them out, because the propellers had to be powered by the trawlers' living capacitor organs.

"Because maybe George-Étienne saw me or heard me," Fabienne said. "And if he's tricky he'd know that if *he* could follow the currents, so could someone else."

"So?"

Fabienne held her finger over the 'x.'

"We know when and where he was," Fabienne said. "We know how fast trawlers can travel, and for how long, before he runs them to death."

There were uncertain atmospheric patterns to the south, which could easily scatter a whole herd. The prevailing winds along the equator were low in static, which meant trawlers with bad luck could starve in those winds. North of the equator though was *Baie des Chaleurs,* above Guinevere Planitia. Not the best feeding, but not terrible. If the D'Aquillons had been able to swing around *Branche-de-l'Ouest* in time to avoid the shear winds off Sif Mons, they might have made it. Fabienne and Angèle had been looking for weeks: the D'Aquillons could have gotten to a lot of places in that time—or maybe not.

It was a long haul to get from *Trou-à-Eudore* to *Baie des Chaleurs*. If the D'Aquillons had done that, across the prevailing winds, the trawlers would need to rest and feed, maybe for weeks. Guinevere Planitia was a few hours away right now, a little less if Fabienne flew as high as *les plaines*.

"I've got an idea," Fabienne said.

ELEVEN

THE *CAUSAPSCAL-DES-VENTS* ROSE and fell gently, as if rolling over great waves in the clouds. Pascale didn't move, but Gabriel-Antoine, despite weeks in the depths, listened alertly.

"What was that?" he said.

"A thermal," Pascale said. "A small one, or we wouldn't have felt it so much."

Gabriel was sweaty and pensive. His body hadn't gotten used to the heat in the cloud decks, and often had a muscular shine Pascale liked to peek at when he wasn't looking. Like now.

"The herd will follow?" he said, looking at her. Pascale cast her eyes back down at the knee joint she was building. Whenever they got too hot or too tired to work outside, they came into the habitat. So they rested, building hard shells that could withstand conditions at the bottom of the atmosphere. Section by section, joint by joint, they each added to their atmospheric diving suits.

"We don't usually lose trawlers when we're just floating around. It's the storms that scatter them."

Gabriel-Antoine put down his tools, rose, and padded barefoot across the woody floor. He wiped himself with a towel and drank a handful of water.

"You need more than that, *chéri*," Pascale said.

"*Chéri?*" Gabriel-Antoine looked back, arching an eyebrow.

Pascale's cheeks flushed hot, but she didn't take it back. She focused on her work, smiling.

"Where'd the cup go?"

"Maybe Jean-Eudes washed it?"

Gabriel-Antoine rummaged in the little curtained cupboards carved into the hard wood fiber.

"Pascal?"

"What?"

"What's this?"

Gabriel-Antoine held up a little carbon-weave bag innocently, its neck open. He had one of her hormone replacement pills between his fingers. When he saw her blanched face, he looked at the pills with more suspicion.

"What?" he said. "Is this some kind of homemade rapture? Meth? You told me you don't take drugs!"

"I don't!"

"This is a shitload of pills, Pascal."

"It's not…" she said, rising. Her head felt light and a metal tool clattered on woody floor. Gabriel-Antoine's face hardened; he'd once told her that his father had used pills, and had one day just vanished. Gabriel-Antoine sniffed.

"*Tabarnak*. What is it? Does George-Étienne know? Did your brother give you these?"

"No! No," she said more quietly. "No."

He was holding her life in his hands. All that she wanted.

"Give it back. I didn't ask you to go rooting in my stuff. It's not rapture. It's not meth."

He dropped the misshapen pill back into the sack and then plopped it in her hand.

"What is it?"

She moved past him and put the bag on the bottom shelf at the back, where it was less likely to be seen. She took an unsteady breath. Her eyes were wet.

"What is it, Pascal?"

Venus was a world without solidity. They inhabited an ocean of precipitous drops with only tiny island footholds. Those perches could seem steady, for months at a time, but they never really were. At any moment a downdraft could tip them into the abyss. Equipment could fail. Gabriel-Antoine had fallen into her life, literally. She clung to that like a tiny island the two of them could stand upon. She gripped the bowl of the sink, against a dizzy flushing heat. He was everything her heart hadn't known it had wanted. He made her feel electric and excited and cool and pretty and loved. So much happiness seemed so easy to lose. She wept silently.

She rose and turned.

"What is it?" he said.

"I don't want you to be mad."

"Why would I be mad?"

She closed her eyes. She pressed her lips together. She heard him breathing.

"Why would I be mad?" he said, louder.

"I'm a girl."

"What?"

"I'm really a girl. I haven't known it for long." She gestured behind her. "The pills are hormones. Girl hormones. To go through girl puberty."

"You're already a man," he said.

She shook her head cautiously.

"You're..." Gabriel-Antoine said. His eyes narrowed, then his finger stabbed towards the cupboard. "These pills are going to change your body? Into a woman's body?"

"They can't do everything," she said. "Only partway."

"And then what?" he demanded. His face went red in blotches. His anger was hot, like the air of the lower cloud decks pressing against a face plate that couldn't cool it enough.

Like the way Venus killed.

"Doctors." Her voice sounded squeaky. This was all spinning the wrong way. This hadn't been the way she'd meant to tell him. She hadn't known how to tell him.

"You're going to be a woman?"

She lifted her chin. "I am a woman. In my heart."

"How long is this going to take?" he said heatedly.

She shrugged helplessly. "A year? Two? Three? I haven't talked to a doctor yet. I'm learning this all from textbooks and instructional guides from other colonies."

"I don't like girls," Gabriel-Antoine said.

Pascale swallowed a sob, making a weird strangled sound.

"When were you going to tell me?" he demanded.

"I was scared."

"Of me? I'm not the one destroying our relationship!"

"I didn't know how to tell you. I'm scared!"

"Then don't do it!"

"No… I was scared of you rejecting me. I'm happy. With you. But I don't have all the answers."

"I guess you have all the answers you need," he said accusingly. "You started the pills without telling me. I wasn't important enough to tell."

"That's not it. I'm sorry. I didn't know how."

"Yeah, well, now *I'm* scared," he said. He picked up his tools and the part of the suit he'd been building and stomped out of their room.

"Gabriel-Antoine, please!"

He didn't look back.

Pascale stood in their room, her throat painfully tight, her eyes burning and wet. The world closed in on her, feeling hot and lonely and black.

TWELVE

TÉTREAU HAD BEEN talking to Émile about a new berth, a big room on *l'Avant-Guardiste*—fitting for the role of sergeant, if he took it—but Tétreau wanted some help briefing his boss. They couldn't understand some *coureur* stuff. Émile thought he remembered the way to Labourière's office, but the *Baie-Comeau* was a big habitat and he got turned around somewhere in all the hallways of carbon-plastic, ending up on the same level as the hospital. He began to back away from the antiseptic smell of alcohol vapors and the associations he had here: his legs badly burned, Thérèse almost dying.

"Émile?" someone said.

He hadn't noticed the face looking up from a gurney. He approached the sheeted figure. It was Cédric, brown hair cut short since he'd last seen him, his shoulders bare.

"What are you doing here?" Émile said.

"Hernia."

"Ouch."

"Yeah. Won't be long, though," Cédric said and looked away. "I'm sorry about your sister."

"Thanks."

"I heard your Pa's transmission," Cédric said. "I tune into it sometimes. He speaks from the heart. You're lucky to have him as a father."

"He's actually a giant ass," Émile said.

"Oh. Um. What have you been up to?"

"I'm shacking up at a friend's place, looking after his family while he's working. And I write poetry," Émile said. And then hastily, "Working with the *Sûreté*."

"Ugh. That's too bad. A lot of meat heads. You're better than that."

Émile snorted. He wasn't better than anything.

"Can I see your poems?" Cédric said.

Émile shrugged.

"Hey, guys," someone said. Anne-Claude came up behind him. She kissed him on both cheeks in greeting and then put her hand on Cédric's forehead. Her eyes were clear and lucid. They'd all been stoned the last time he'd seen them, experimenting with breathing the air of Venus, an idiotic idea, one of Thérèse's manias. "Thérèse said good luck."

"She's around?" Émile said. A tiny elation rose in his chest.

"She's in the bay," Anne-Claude said.

A small nurse in a white uniform came over and told Cédric it was time.

"I gotta go," Émile said. "I have a meeting."

Anne-Claude followed the nurse wheeling away Cédric while Émile backed away. His appointment with Labourière was in three minutes and he still hadn't found the office, but he knew the way to the cargo area Thérèse and her followers used for their ceremonies.

He hadn't spoken to her in weeks. He'd broken something between them when he'd interfered with her communion with Venus. The one that had burned her whole chest. Whether it was a trust he'd betrayed, or some fear in himself he'd shown her, she'd found him wanting. It was as if, for a time, he might have been someone she was ready to love, but then she'd come to know the real him and been disappointed. He didn't know. These were just his theories, meticulously constructed of interdependent guesses and maybes. The larger part of him, the part still swept up in her, wondered if maybe he'd misunderstood the situation and if there might be a way to fix things. He'd resisted that last voice.

Until now.

He followed the black carbon weave stairs two levels into the belly of the *Baie-Comeau* and into a small, dreary cargo bay crowded with sealed boxes and a sliding pulley crane hanging from the middle of the ceiling. Thérèse sat alone in a nest of crates, her long legs crossed under her, eyes closed. She cupped a lumpy, guttering candle in her hands. It stank of sulfur and a kind of rancid grease the *coureurs* sometimes made out of plant parts. She had thinned, almost ascetically. Her eyelids had paled, revealing fine lines of blue veins. Her jumpsuit was zipped to the neck, hiding the burns. He stilled.

After a time, she gave an annoyed sigh, opened her eyes.

"What do you want?" she said.

"I remember once we'd talked about you seeing down-cloud."

"Do you have a way?"

"Not right now. If you gave me a few weeks to think about who could host, I could ask."

She cupped the candle, as if memorizing its shape.

"Are you okay?" he asked.

"Why wouldn't I be okay?"

"I was just asking."

She regarded him doubtfully. "Everything inside you shows in your face eventually, Émile. You want something from me I'm not offering. You want to be something you're not. You have the heart of a farmer and yet you're up here with machines and artists and orgies."

The words that would make this right, that would show her who he was, were somewhere in his mind, like a poetic turn of phrase that came only when it chose. But then the airlock door opened, echoing from the hard walls. People came in, speaking in hushed, reverent tones. He wanted to go, but it felt like the words were right there.

The people were around him now. Each of them held a lumpy unlit candle.

"This isn't for you, Émile," Thérèse said. "Venus doesn't know you and you're not ready for her. She wants honesty, not just going through the motions."

For a moment, he stood with words about to come before they evaporated and he was unarmed. He turned and pushed past some people, almost knocking down a small woman. She swore after him. He spun the airlock wheels angrily and made his way through the stairways, up to the dorsal levels of the *Baie-Comeau,* to where the office executives would be.

Going through the motions. Going through the motions! Who the hell was she to say he wasn't committed to knowing Venus? Her stupid empty ceremonies and prayers… reaching for a planet's heart, as if it had a soul, as if they all had souls. He knew more about the real Venus than they did. Marthe had told him what lay at the heart of the planet, even if he struggled to believe it. If Thérèse knew the truth, it would blow her mind. She would invent a pile of mysticism, and anthropomorphize what Pascal had found, attribute intent where the dumb stuff of the universe just moved unguided. Émile wasn't going through the motions. He'd been kind, humoring her, not telling her that she believed a bunch of bullshit. His chest ached and he wanted to punch something by the time he finally found the small office suite of the *présidente* and the wankers working for her.

Labourière's office had a frosted glass door and Émile stopped there for a second, willing himself to calm the *crisse* down. It wouldn't do to punch Labourière—wouldn't help him or Pascal or Jean-Eudes. He pushed the glass door open and walked in. The office was big, bigger than some whole apartments. The greenhouse layer within the envelope of the *Baie-Comeau* behind the desk made everything seem weirdly green and alive.

Tétreau was there. He introduced him to Labourière, who was really… clean. Clothes, hair, skin—they looked like they'd just been washed. Lots of people made Émile feel like they thought they were better than him, but they usually carried their own patches and scars. Not this guy. Labourière shook his hand, though, and seemed to take Émile seriously enough. There was a woman too, a bank cop, Amanda Copeland. She spoke French with a lumbering accent and tangled syntax, breaking into English often, which Tétreau and Labourière seemed to understand. Tétreau encouraged Émile to explain to Labourière and Copeland what he'd already explained to him.

"If I'm a *coureur* looking to hide stolen radioactives in the clouds," Émile said, "I have to mask the radioactivity first so I need some lead, right? Fortunately for me as a *coureur,* lead's not that hard to get a hold of. It churns up in volcanic ash. *Coureurs* make cooling radiators on their habitats out of lead. Once I wrap the radioactives in enough lead, the Geiger counter won't go off and the government can't find it."

"Then what?" Tétreau said.

"If I was suspicious? A lot of *coureurs* really follow the clouds. We pick our favourite prevailing winds and circle Venus with our herds. We avoid storms. The equatorial winds are steadiest, but ten or even twenty degrees north will be constant enough and you'll never run into your neighbour, especially if you play up and down the column."

"The column?" Copeland said.

"The air column," Émile said with a little annoyance. God damn Anglos. "Up and down. When I was growing up, when we weren't chasing volcanoes, we floated at every altitude from fortieth to fifty-fifth *rang.*"

"Why north? South isn't good?" Labourière said.

"My family found the northern winds steadier," Émile said. "And luckier."

"Luckier?" Copeland asked with a hint of judgment.

"We did both southern and northern routes when I was a kid. My mom died over Talakin Mons in the south, and my sister and her husband disappeared in a southern storm that blew the family all the way to Themis Regio. You can say luck doesn't exist, but shitloads of *coureurs* have stories about bad luck with south runs."

They looked a bit uncomfortable, even Copeland. "I'm sorry," Labourière said. "That's a difficult path for your family."

Émile debated how to respond. It wasn't all Pa's fault. It was also the government's. But he hair-split too long and Labourière began speaking again.

"So if you were looking to hide stolen radioactives, you'd pick a latitude and just bob along the prevailing winds?"

"If I was suspicious and thought you were looking for me, no."

"What do you mean?" Tétreau asked.

"I don't know all the *coureurs,*" Émile said, "but the ones I know don't trust the government to do anything more than screw them. So if I really wanted to avoid being noticed, I'd go further off the grid."

"Below fifty-second is off the grid," Copeland said, torturing her French syntax.

Labourière sat like a man about to take a math test; Tétreau was trying to look attentive; Copeland looked like her time was being wasted. They weren't getting it. Sure, they knew the size of the atmosphere, but they hadn't ridden it, hadn't been beneficiary and victim of it. Their questions hinted at a gulf of understanding they couldn't bridge. And they hadn't given any sign that they respected the cunning of the *coureurs,* their ability to survive, lonely in their floating islands.

"There's off and there's *off,*" Émile said. "*Coureur* trawlers circle Venus over and over. They avoid storms and eddies because those break up herds and mess with synchronization with the upper flotillas, and even conjunctions with other families we need to trade with. If you want to go further off the grid, you've got to look like a wild trawler. Wild trawlers get swept up in the skirts of storms and in eddies rolling off the mountains, away from the safe, stable volumes. It's dangerous, but I'd want to look like every other trawler, because in tens of thousands of cubic kilometers of clouds, how's your radar going to distinguish a single *coureur* trawler from a hundred thousand wild trawlers? *That's* going off the grid."

"So how do we find them?" Tétreau said.

"Your thieves?" Émile said. "I don't think you can. You couldn't even find every habitat, much less search them. Even if you could, maybe they'll have stored it on a supply trawler, dozens of kilometers away, at a different depth in the column."

"It would take forever to search the whole atmosphere," Labourière said.

"So cut a deal," Émile said. "*Buy* your radioactives back."

"Offer a reward?" Tétreau said.

"And amnesty, I guess," Émile said.

"You'd like that, wouldn't you?" Copeland said accusingly.

"What?" Émile said.

"You're a *coureur* yourself," she said.

"I was, but I'm here now, and if you don't want my advice, don't ask for it."

Labourière thanked him and Tétreau led Émile out. "That was really good," he said as he ushered him through the door. "Really useful. Come to my office tomorrow and let's talk about those sergeant's chevrons."

The Muse Weeps at Twilight, by Émile D'Aquillon

She weeps from broken
flesh,
tears trickling from tectonic
wounds.
Moist fascia trembles between the crater
lips
of scourged highlands, those blessings of
terrible
communion, the searing brands of
divinity.

She dreams many-colored
epiphanies,
a palette of pigments painting a
world
aching for poets. This muse,
enchanted,
loves with the deceived
hope
of a discarded doll, outgrown,
unloved.

The muse, soulful, longing, regards the
goddess,
who stares back, gorgon-faced.
Petrified
by misguided joy, the muse
cracks,
spilling tears unrequited,
misunderstanding
her stony face in the mirror's
reflection.

THIRTEEN

IN THE HALLWAY outside Labourière's office on the *Baie-Comeau,* Noëlle Lalumière had been about to knock on the glass doors, but drew back when she glimpsed Émile. Tucked inside the front zipper of her suit was the pad she'd taken from his room on the *Causapscal-des-Vents* months before. She'd gotten the pictures of the naked women off it and had been trying to decide whether she could trade it away without tipping off that she'd stolen it. Since the sinking of the *Causapscal-des-Vents,* she'd thought it might be valuable to Labourière. He'd been interested in Marthe and Émile. What if there was hidden information on this pad, in a code she couldn't recognize?

And now Émile was here?

Noëlle crept down the carbon plastic hall, slipping into a vacant office. What was Émile doing here? It hadn't looked like he was in trouble. *Merde.* If he found her here, he would be suspicious. She didn't have an excuse for being here. The hospital was two floors down. No one would believe she'd taken a wrong turn looking for a doctor.

The sound of voices briefly swelled and footfalls rang in the narrow hallway. Some men were talking in low voices. She couldn't make out the words, but through the gap between the door and the jamb, she saw Émile's unmistakably big body pass. She waited a bit longer, then edged the door open a bit further to peek out.

"Who are you?" a woman said. Noëlle yelped.

"I…" Noëlle's heart was beating so hard. She leaned on the door.

"Who are you and why are you skulking?" the woman said. Her French had a cumbersome English accent.

"I'm…" Noëlle faltered again. She was a terrible spy. "I'm here to see Labourière," she said in a thin voice. Inspiration struck: "That was my ex-boyfriend. He's a real creep. I didn't know he would be here and didn't want to see him."

The woman frowned, took hold of Noëlle's arm and dragged her towards Labourière's office.

"Let go of me!" Noëlle said, trying to yank herself free, but the Anglo woman was strong. She straight-armed the door to the office, and Labourière looked up, puzzled.

"Are you waiting to talk to her?" the woman demanded.

The man regarded Noëlle silently and finally said, "She has an appointment."

"Do all your appointments skulk in offices that aren't theirs?" the woman said, switching to English and releasing Noëlle. Noëlle didn't understand every word, but got the gist.

"I'll take care of this," he answered in French.

"You'd better. Your security is a shit-show," the woman said in English. Then she left.

"What are you doing here?" he said in a low voice when the door had shut.

"You offered me a berth on the *Baie-Comeau* or the *Forillon* if I spied on Marthe and Émile," she said.

"I offered you those things for the location of the *Causapscal-des-Profondeurs,*" he said. "You never got that and the D'Aquillon habitat sank anyway."

"I got you directions on their maser."

"We checked. The maser direction you found was pointed at a storm.

The D'Aquillons obviously reset the maser direction after they finished their transmission."

She pulled Émile's old pad out of her suit. "What about this?"

"This is Marthe's?" he said.

"Émile's. The guy who was just here. Why are you bringing him in here?"

He thumbed it on, swiped through a few directories. "Did you find something about the location of the *Causapscal-des-Profondeurs* on here, or *anything* incriminating?"

"Maybe there's stuff in code."

Labourière regarded her with fading patience.

"Look into it," she said. "Seriously." She pulled the pad closer and opened the folder of Émile's drafts. "All of these."

Labourière opened a few and then frowned. "Is this poetry?"

"He's not a poet. These could be in code."

"Do you have the cipher?"

"Don't you have computers or people to break codes?" she said.

Labourière opened a few more files.

"These are all poems," he said. "*Monsieur* D'Aquillon apparently writes poetry."

"What about a new berth for me? I tried. I risked getting caught."

He returned the pad to her.

"We didn't ask for poetry. If you can find out where the *Causapscal-des-Profondeurs* is, we can talk. Good day, *mademoiselle*."

FOURTEEN

THE TWO STORMS were small, but they lengthened Fabienne's trip by three hours. She'd climbed high, higher than the clear air at *les Plaines,* and in the turbulent upwellings over Eistla Regio, she'd powered off the plane and begun a long glide, riding the prevailing east-to-west wind, listening to the radio crackle for the sound of trawlers or station-keeping transmissions. Her chances were not good.

Venus was a volume, not a surface.

She might fly a few kilometers above or below something and never know it. Sometimes the sulfuric acid clouds packed tightly enough to soak up the reddening light, reducing visibility to a few dozen meters. At other times, pockets of clear air opened, widening her world to hundreds of meters, or even as much as a fuzzy kilometer. She took breaks to just close tight her eyes and blink away what the *coureurs* called *le travers,* a kind of disorientation that crept up after too many hours in a featureless fog.

The storms collapsed in the *Baie des Chaleurs,* and the clouds became a spongy world of burnt ochre cotton. In the first hour, she covered a hundred kilometers of the immense space, catching a few thermals, before inevitably dropping all the way to the bottom of the lower cloud deck and into the sub-cloud haze. Gliding any further at this point would only cook her. Reluctantly, she powered on the engine and climbed. The electric engine made so much of its own static that listening for stray radio sounds became futile guesses. She'd continued her line, riding the east wind as she climbed. She wanted to get to at least forty-eighth *rang* before she engined off again, but at forty-four kilometers above the surface, she thought she heard a distinctive crackle in the radio band.

She turned off the engine. As the propellers staggered to stillness, she banked, turning back the way she'd come. She hadn't quite risen out of the virga zone yet; a hundred and five degrees was too hot for sulfuric acid to survive. That was good for plane pieces not dissolving, but not great for visibility. The radio band was quieter in *Baie des Chaleurs* because the lightning static of storms was distant, and it was only that reduced background that allowed her to hear that distinctive clicking again.

It wasn't a transmitted signal; it was machinery. Equipment to direction-find radio signals existed, even in the *colonie,* but *coureurs* didn't have it. So she circled, listening to the strength of the sound, slowly triangulating that way. It took fifteen minutes and a few false turns and one period of climbing under power, but finally a single trawler came into view, floating in the sub-cloud haze.

She blew the float bags and cut the engines. Oxygen balloons inflated off the wing struts, nose and tail, jerking the plane to a halt and suspending it in the fog. On most planes, a little chip balanced the volumes of the balloons automatically, but they'd taken out the chip to run the nav drive on *la Marotte,* so Fabienne had to manually adjust them. The starboard wing was a bit finicky and finally she just gave up and left the plane floating on a twenty-degree cant to the left. She'd fix it another time.

She dropped the seat back, crawled sternward to strap on her wing-pack and open the ventral door. Hotter mist swirled beneath the plane as she dropped a rope ladder out the hole and climbed down. At the bottom of the ladder, swaying in the haze, she dropped off and flew on the wing-pack, spiralling to gain altitude until she was above the trawler. It was a nice one, young, about six meters in diameter. On its crown was a small tripod with a propeller and an antenna. Under it hung two small metal tanks. This was crazy luck. Whether or not the tanks held oxygen, the metal alone was a win.

She circled it twice before sweeping up and stalling, landing lightly on the woody roof of the trawler. The big plant tipped a bit, but by then Fabienne had a hand on one of the legs of the tripod and pulled herself closer to the center. It was so hot at this altitude that the usual puddle in the middle of the crown had desiccated into a brown sludgy slime.

She saw the problem right away. A gear in the propeller assembly had gone off true and stuck. Every couple of seconds, the little electric engine tried to turn the propeller shaft, but the grinding resistance engaged the auto-shutdown and reboot cycle. She opened the panel and hooked her suit into the rudimentary operating system of the trawler equipment to pause everything while she fixed the gear. She found a couple of D'Aquillon identifiers in the program. She had to take the assembly apart and take a small bend out of the gear shaft, and finally grind off one of the teeth. When it was back together, she turned it on and it spun properly. The gear shaft would eventually need to be replaced, and she would do that once this thing was in her herd.

Normally, the *coureurs* kept their trawlers together by setting the nav algorithms to cluster: too far away and the engine activated, bringing the trawler back to the herd. Basic sheepdog algorithms. The trawler control system had GPS, but most *coureurs* navigated by the clouds. The Mignauds, for example, returned their trawlers to the stable storm system at *Trou à Mémère*; if the trawler could get there, they would eventually find it, especially now that she'd rewritten the ownership addresses, putting her name where the D'Aquillon name had been.

She opened the GPS subprogram to give it a location to meet the rest of her herd, and found some coordinates in there already. She didn't recognize the numbers: fifteen degrees south by a hundred and fifty-five east. She called up the map on her suit computer. The coordinates mapped to the clouds above the rough, broken terrain of Aphrodite

Terra. She knew the zone; she'd passed through the volume once or twice. Sending a lost trawler there didn't make sense. It wasn't like the eddy at *Trou à Mémère* where herds might collect. The deep valleys and high mountains of Aphrodite Terra made weird, boiling upwellings that were hard to predict. They would certainly scatter a herd that stayed too long.

Then she smiled in quiet admiration. She didn't know George-Étienne D'Aquillon, but she knew Narcisse. And if Narcisse said D'Aquillon was tricky, then he was *really* tricky. This location hadn't been sloppiness, leaving an old rendezvous point in the lone trawler by accident. George-Étienne D'Aquillon had probably left a fake RV in the system to throw off any government people if his trawler went missing. It meant sacrificing a trawler for secrecy, which was hardcore.

She entered the coordinates for *Trou à Mémère,* closed the panels and turned the system back on. The propeller dutifully began to spin, the little rudder turning to steer towards the Mignaud rendezvous eddy. It would take weeks, but hopefully it would get there. She strapped the oxygen tanks to her chest and flew back to the plane. She didn't leave *Baie des Chaleurs* right away; maybe the D'Aquillons were still around—and maybe they'd lost more trawlers.

FIFTEEN

Pascale prevented herself from crying in front of anyone else, although she wept in the quiet of her hammock in the dark. Gabriel-Antoine had said nothing since finding her medicines. He wasn't speaking to her at all, unless someone else was around, and then only to keep up appearances. He was good at pretending that things were okay in front of the family, but he wouldn't speak to her about anything other than work, even outside in their helmets while they were working.

On the second day, Pascale was working on her atmospheric dive suit in the main room. Everyone else had gone to sleep except for her and Pa, who was fiddling with the controls of the shortwave. He rose for water but stopped at the table, where her hands had gone idle. He stroked her hair.

"Is everything okay, *mon cher*?" he said.

Pascale smiled and nodded.

"You can always tell me what's going on. I'm always on your side."

The feeling of blackness filled her whole world, ached in a way that made it hard to breathe. But if she shared it, she would make more problems, and be seen as herself in a way that she wasn't ready for.

"I know, Pa."

He went for his water, bringing her a cup too. Pascale was glad when he returned to the shortwave, because she felt like she'd crack open in front of him. She drank the sulfur-bittered water numbly. Her father began transmitting.

"Does anyone feel like the bureaucratic politics, the ill-fated economics, the drudging sameness of our future and our present, are working? Parts of this government feel like they're panicking. Other parts feel like they're sleep-walking. A vision is trotted out, like a magician beginning her trick on the stage. 'Look right here,' she says. 'Watch my hand carefully.' It's myopic in its detail, or fuzzy in its vastness, but it never addresses any of the basic questions about how we live.

"That's what the president's vision is worth, what the bureaucrats' vision is worth as the bank slowly disenfranchises us, day by day, as if it's destiny. This is not destiny. This is us repeating mistakes of the past. We've been here before. We have the songs from the last time we lived under the political and economic foot of another empire: '*On est pas maîtres dans nos maisons, car vous y êtes.*' We're not masters in our houses, because you are.

"We're surrendering what is ours, not because the magician has dazzled us with her sleight of hand, but because we've lost our imagination. We can't imagine a world or society that doesn't have banks and loan payments in it. We can't imagine a world where we live differently, outside the frames of fiscal years and taxation, without the soft, dull cages of life stagnating on Earth.

"Do you know how much we owe the Bank of Pallas? Every one of us? Divide the colonial debt by four thousand, nine hundred souls. That's what we owe. Did the government come to you and ask you to contribute? Did they ask for your consent? They call this representative government, but I didn't say 'yes,' and neither did you. They said that *l'Assemblée* voted on it, so it must be right.

"My daughter sat in *l'Assemblée*. She argued every minute she was there that the government was making one terrible bet after another.

And it wasn't their money. That's our money, but you don't have a dollar more than me, do you? Marthe was always voted down. And I'm angry with *l'Assemblée*, for voting one debt after another after another to fund their stupid investments. Have their investments changed the lives of the *coureurs?*

"I'm living off the grid. I'm using next to nothing. I graft together my own habitats out of wild trawlers. A couple of airlocks and some compressor tanks and some wings is a hell of a lot cheaper than buying the *Baie-Comeau*. I might even be a little less angry if their investments at least helped the up-clouders, but they don't. Are up-clouders living any easier because the *Baie-Comeau* is up there? The only people living on it are the government. Other than the hospital, the only people working there are people in the government, apparently paid not by me, but by taking out more debt in all our names.

"So, *crisse,* yes, I'm angry that I'm carrying a debt I didn't earn, wearing a debt I voted against, and not just because someday someone's going to come into my house down in fiftieth rang and tell me to pay up. I'm angry because every dollar we take is a bit more of our house that we don't own. They come in and put conditions on us, how we're supposed to spend our money, how much of it goes to their loan interest. We're not living any vision of the lives we want—we're living the vision of some investor's balance sheet.

"I'm mostly pissed because everything we're experiencing was decided long before we were born. I came to Venus thirty years ago because there was nothing in Québec for me. AIs and automation had 'surplussed' me. What a term, eh? Our lives weren't needed. We were extra. I grew up knowing that my life was a bother to people with power. The company presidents got rich, though, didn't they?

"Here, here I'm someone. I'm not rich, but I raised my family on my own sweat. I fed them without robots or AIs that would have melted here. We curse the *bébittes* of Venus, but they make sure automation'll melt too fast. If anything's going to be done, I have to do it.

"But sweat only goes so far. There's no way to really get ahead when we owe so much. Anything we manage to make, even the littlest extra thing, belongs to the bank. We get ground down so some CEO's bonus goes from ten million to ten million and one. We didn't write those rules. We didn't get to say, 'Where's my goddamn exclusion clause?' We're in. If we breathe, if we live here, we're in.

"Fuck those rules. I never took out a bank loan and I'll be damned if I'm going to pay for the *Baie-Comeau*. Let those who live on it pay for it. People hope to get a bunk on some good habitat, like it's the government's to dole out to the well-behaved. We made the government. And we have voices. And we have to be loud enough for everyone to hear us."

Pa shut off the shortwave transmitter, signalled the main transmitting trawler to set its receiving dish to neutral and change its course in the clouds. He came and sat beside Pascale and put his arm around her shoulders without saying anything. They just stewed there, the two of them, each with their endangered passions.

"We have a dream of a new life, Pascal," he said finally, and kissed her on the top of the head as he got up and went to his room. The blackness that seemed all around her hadn't receded, but it felt for a moment after he'd said those words that there would be stars somewhere beyond the gloom.

SIXTEEN

Émile's ribs hurt like hell, so he got out of the bed slowly. He could hear Paul-Égide talking in the common room of the *Marais-des-Nuages,* but couldn't make out the words. Émile rotated one arm experimentally, then the other, then pressed his palm gently against the angry purple-and-yellow patches on his ribs. He didn't think they were broken. He found his indoor pants on the floor and pulled them on before going to the cool dark of the living room. Only a few lights spilled a yellow glow around.

"Whoa," Paul-Égide said, getting up from where he'd been chattering at his grand-parents. He came close as Émile poured himself a plastic cup of water. "What happened?"

"I got into a fight."

Grand-mère Phocas tsked.

"With the Sûreté, *ma tante,*" Émile clarified. "Police business. Black marketeers were stripping parts from the *Escuminac*. They ran."

"You chased them?" Paul-Égide said.

"Well, I wasn't going to catch them if I stayed where I was."

The boy pressed his fingers into the muscle on Émile's forearm. "These are gross," he said of the ropy acid scars.

"So don't touch them."

Émile ladled a bean stew from the stove into a clean bowl.

"To look at," Paul-Égide clarified.

"So don't look at them."

"Can I punch you in the stomach?" Paul-Égide asked.

"Why?"

"When I'm with my friends, we flex our stomachs hard and then punch them."

"That's a stupid game."

"Punch me," Paul-Égide said.

Émile scarfed down spoonfuls of beans.

"Punch me," the boy repeated. "I'm flexing."

"I will if you wash my bowl."

"Okay," Paul-Égide said, taking the bowl and spoon and turning to the sink.

Émile visited the head, washed a bit, punched the boy lightly in the stomach, and went to get dressed. By the time he emerged in his survival suit, Louise was removing her pressure hood from the survival suit she used to visit the greenhouse between the inner and outer envelopes of the habitat. Shiny spinach, fat yellow peppers, small red tomatoes, assorted green beans and a few anemic grapes covered the table.

"Where are you going?" she said. "You need to help with the crops. We need to compost a bunch today and replant strawberries."

"Use Paul-Égide. I have to work," Émile said.

"He's useless," she said.

"I have a job," he said. "Do what you can. If I get back early, I'll help."

"You worked all night," she said.

"And now I've got to play bodyguard."

"Cool!" Paul-Égide said. "Are you protecting *la présidente*?"

Émile snorted. "I'd just as soon throw her overboard."

"Who is it?" Paul-Égide asked.

"You don't know her," he said, picking up his helmet and wheeling open the door to the airlock.

Louise raised her eyebrows curiously. "Oh, it's a girl!"

Émile closed the door and spun the wheel. He put on his helmet as the pumps removed the air and the outer door light turned green. Stars sprouted like mushrooms every Venusian night, and all of them, it seemed, had turned out tonight, along with Saturn, bright and high. He leapt from the roof of the *Marais-des-Nuages* and left the hard white lights of its roof behind.

Émile liked high Venus at night. The clouds beneath him darkened, but not all the way to black. Sunlight diffused all the way from the dayside of the planet, but this far to nightside, light became somber and attenuated, underlighting the clouds in patches of gray, with occasional glimmers of faded yellow or tired orange. Those glimmers of color appeared and vanished without rhyme or reason, and the *coureurs* told their children stories of fairies and ghosts. *La colonie* had a lot of ghosts. Venus had delivered unlucky ends to enough *colonistes* for the clouds to fill villages of the restless dead. There was nothing for them to haunt on the surface, so—the *coureurs* said—they haunted the clouds.

Ghosts didn't frighten Émile. If there were ghosts, *Maman* and Chloé were among them, and now Marthe. They might be pissed at him, but they would never hurt him.

He made some wrong movement and flinched from the pain, wobbling his flight. He corrected his angle of attack. Paul-Égide's admiration aside, his cocked-up police job was getting worse. The government had flipped its lid with the loss of the *Causapscal-des-Vents* and, as far as he understood it, was crapping its pants trying to make the next debt payment to the bank. Part of that was cracking down on black marketeers and confiscating anything people had that wasn't registered. People were as happy about that as anyone would have expected. He didn't pity the *présidente*, or *l'Assemblée*; if one 'accident' could throw off their whole fiscal plan, it was a pretty bad plan.

The *Sûreté* was the pointy end of a crappy government decision, and whatever goodwill he might have had from regular folk was evaporating. People were more likely to fight for their scraps and were willing to take punches. He'd taken a few last night, but others had gotten it worse. Two of the people they'd arrested had needed a doctor in the cells. He liked the fighting, but the situation was shitty, and he got closer and closer to just not showing up. Let the *Sûreté* fire him; he could do better. He still hadn't agreed to being a sergeant.

Against the distant moan of his wing-pack engine, he felt like the only person in the world, himself haunting a dark ocean of clouds, lonely, unheard and unseen. A cluster of lights finally resolved into the *Détroit d'Honguedo,* the big old community habitat where he'd met Marie-Pier last time. Yellowy spotlights lit the roof and colored LEDs marked the runways. He came down lightly and stowed his wing-pack in the lockers before threading through some of the dock workers to the airlock.

He made his way down through the corridors to a cafeteria on level four. The yeast and bean and garlic smell hit him before he got there. At other times, he might have lamented not having a ration card for the *Détroit*, but *Grand-mère* Phocas and Louise were good cooks, and their gardens abundant. He found Marie-Pier sitting alone at a corner table, nursing a coffee. Her survival suit was opened to the waist, showing a thermal shirt. She had a few visible scars around her left wrist and some spots on her neck. Her brown hair was pulled into a ponytail.

"You had any trouble?" he asked.

She shook her head, rising. She drained her coffee and dropped the cup into a bin on the next table.

"Where we going?" he said.

"Level four, stern. I'm meeting someone."

He wasn't sure he understood her. Molecular biologist, mother, more up-clouder than *coureur,* and yet involved in the theft of the *Causapscal-des-Vents,* and kind of hooked up with his father for a bunch of crazy hopes.

"Who're you meeting?"

"I talked with your father before I came sun-side. He's having a really hard time since Marthe died. He told me you said he killed her. That hurts him. A lot."

"It should."

"That's cruel."

"Disowning a child isn't? He can go fuck himself."

She stopped. Émile's hands twitched like he needed to do something, to act, to hit.

"What's between you and your father is your history," she said. "This was Marthe's plan. With your father. With Pascale. With me. With Gabriel-Antoine. The storm isn't anyone's fault."

Émile heard a grinding and realized it was his teeth.

"I know you love Pascale and Jean-Eudes. Whatever else you and your father have between you, they both need him. They put on brave faces, but they're scared and they lean on your father. Maybe you and he need to heal together."

A few months ago he might have told her to fuck off; he had told Marthe off over this very kind of conversation. But she'd told him off right back, because that's what family could do.

"You're not my mother," he said. "You're not even really his wife, are you, with Gabriel-Antoine in your little political alliance? Don't put your nose into things that have nothing to do with you."

Marie-Pier didn't say anything for a while, although her eyes didn't leave his. Then she pulled something from an inner pocket of her suit and held it out. It was a folded piece of paper, the crude kind that *Maman* had taught them to make as children, the kind he sometimes made now for the first scrawlings of his poetry.

"It's from Pascale."

He didn't trust himself to look at it now, in front of her, so he carefully pocketed it.

"Let's get going," he grunted. "I have crap to do for Gabriel-Antoine's family."

Marie-Pier led him along the echoing plastic hallways of the *Détroit d'Honguedo*. There were plenty of people, some police with badges showing on their suits, some black-market types he recognized from deals he'd made in the past, some people he recognized from the other side of raids. An embryonic and unsophisticated gang operated on the *Détroit d'Honguedo,* keeping news and problems in the family, so despite his promise to Pascal, it might be that he wouldn't be much use to Marie-Pier anyway. If they knew Marie-Pier carried stuff they wanted, they could always rob her again here. Anything he did would only make it harder.

She led him into an administrative area he'd never visited before and they stopped in a small hallway outside a door.

"What are you trading?" he said.

"It's mostly a political meeting, although trades might help."

"Why are you bringing a cop?" He shook his head.

"Pascale said you wouldn't snitch on us."

"Pascal doesn't know me."

"Are you going to?"

"Just go in. I'll wait here."

She knocked and then to a microphone in the wall gave a password he didn't catch. After a moment, the door slid open and she passed in. Émile leaned against the wall. He was still pretty sore from last night, but he felt like he'd been punched in his heart too. Marie-Pier played dirty in arguments.

Pascal's paper made a scraping sound as he pulled it out of his pocket. It was tied closed with homemade twine, thick and rough, the way Jean-Eudes twisted the fibers. He ran his thumb over the unevenness of the paper's surface. It felt different from the stuff he made at sixty-fifth *rang*, even though Émile still used *Maman*'s recipe of old blastula husks, pounded flat between soaks in a light neutralizing solution to raise the pH so it wouldn't disintegrate too quickly. *Maman* loved to draw and paint and write in pencil. She'd taught them all how to draw. He thought that's where his artistic urges came from; he couldn't draw or paint, but he tried and tried to paint with words. And although it had receded in his mind, every act of making his own paper and writing by hand was an act of remembrance to *Maman*. He'd replicated her paper recipe in the upper clouds the way he had as a child with her, but it never came out as supple as this paper of Pascal's. Émile untied the string, pocketed it to admire later, and then carefully unfolded the paper. Pascal wrote in a tight hand, using small, clear letters, dated a couple of weeks ago.

Cher Émile,

I miss you. I'm sorry the last time we saw each other didn't go the way we wanted. I was nervous and overwhelmed. I felt a little bit like I was a different person, but I found out that I wasn't different. I just wasn't seeing me as I was. I'd been feeling wrong inside for a while and didn't know what it was, until Marthe talked with me and we discovered that I'm a girl.

I'm not your brother. I'm your sister. This is hard to write down and I keep worrying that someone other than you will see this. Only Jean-Eudes and Marie-Pier know, and now you. You shared your poetry with me and not anyone else. You trusted me.

Gabriel-Antoine and Pa don't know. I have to find a way to tell Gabriel-Antoine. We're kind of involved and it's scary and amazing, but I don't know how he'll react. Pa has too much to deal with right now. I think he'll understand, though.

Marie-Pier got me pills. Knowing this is so big I don't know what to do with it. It changes everything. I know who I am now. I wanted you to know, so you could understand how sorry I am that our visit didn't go well. I didn't impress your girlfriend and I couldn't tell you everything, about me or what we were doing.

All the love, your sister,
Pascale

Émile wiped his eyes with the back of his hand. *Nervous and overwhelmed… Feeling wrong…* That poor kid. Émile had gotten angry with Pascal—Pascale. He'd told Pascale off. Émile was a fucking heel. And he was still one of just three people Pascale told. Pascale still felt honored that Émile showed his poetry to… her, as if not showing it to anyone else was an act of trust instead of cowardice. Émile was a giant tool. He didn't deserve his brother and sister. He folded the letter and stowed it. He leaned his head back against the wall and just breathed. *Tabarnak* but he could use a drink.

Pascal's letter… Pascale's letter… this scrap of crude paper was a fragile monument. Marthe didn't have a grave. It was like she'd dissolved.

But her name was still there on the paper, alongside his and Pascale's. Someday he and Pascale would be gone, and maybe this letter in other hands might be the only proof that they'd existed, that they'd suffered, that they'd reached out for one another. That they could be forgiven.

Footsteps sounded in the hallway, but no conversation. A pair of guys stopped and looked at him, frowned and then came down the narrow hallway to him. They had badges on their chests, but that didn't mean much.

"What are you doing here?"

Émile opened a pocket and showed the little plastic shield that was his badge. The older one frowned. The younger, a blond with buzzed hair, squinted. "You're, uh... D'Aquillon?" he said.

"Yeah," Émile said. "I don't remember your name. I think we raided some habitat together a couple of weeks ago."

"What are you doing here?" the older one said. "We didn't get any orders that anyone would be operating here. This is our territory."

Émile slipped the badge back into his pocket. "I'm not on duty. My 'step-mother,'" he said, putting air quotes around the word, "heard stories that the *Honguedo* was rough. She felt better with company."

"So what are you doing in the hallway?"

Émile hooked a thumb towards the door behind his shoulder. "Not my business. She does genetic work on trawlers and people always want to learn about that. I just wanted to fly a bit." Émile pushed himself off the wall. "Why all the questions? You don't want me here?"

The older one frowned and held Émile's stare, while the younger smiled nervously.

"If you're doing any trading here and we're not getting our cut, you're going to end up in the hospital," the man said.

"You can try," Émile said. He was a lot bigger than both of them.

"We're going to finish up our rounds and come back. If you're still here, we're bringing friends."

"Make sure to visit the *Baie-Comeau* sometime. I'll show you around."

The older guy looked tempted to force the issue now, but finally turned and stalked off, the younger constable following. Émile deflated once their footsteps had faded around the corner. He waited for a count of five and then softly knocked on the door. A minute later, Marie-Pier's face showed in the crack.

"We should probably go," he said. "I'm attracting attention."

She shut the door without saying anything. He couldn't make out the words of the raised voices. He waited another minute and almost knocked again when Marie-Pier emerged. Émile craned his neck, trying to see into the room.

"There are better parts of the *Honguedo,*" he said. "You should use those."

"The black market areas are usually fine," she whispered. "I was jumped on the way to them."

"This isn't those areas," he said.

She led him to a ladder, up two levels to a busy greenhouse, bright yellow lights shining on shelves and shelves of green crops. A few people tending to the gardens gave them suspicious looks as they emerged from the ladderway.

"Those were short-term rental rooms?" The *Baie-Comeau* had some glass-walled multipurpose rooms, but the *Détroit d'Honguedo* was older and crappier.

"Those rooms get used for a lot of things."

"And what were you doing?" He held the door for her into the back causeway, where he'd come a few times for low-end dental work and tools carved from trawler carbon weave.

"Politics," she said. "Some meetings can't be seen."

"For you?"

"For the whole family."

"You and Pa's weird marriage?"

She looked at him curiously. "Phocas too."

"It's weird," he said.

"A triple alliance?" she said.

"A marriage. Go with who you want when you want. Nobody marries anymore."

"Your parents were together a long time."

"Yeah, well, I loved *Maman*, but she might have hitched her wagon to the wrong horse."

She watched him in a way he found slightly unnerving. She wasn't threatening or even aggressive, but he didn't get the feeling she would easily fall for bullshit. He opened the door for her beside a little shop that repaired fabric and made new clothes out of carbon fibre grown on some of the big habitats. She stopped in the hallway on the other side, just before the stairs.

"Is something bothering you?" she said.

He let the door shut behind him and looked down at her.

"How is Pascale?"

"What was in the letter?"

"She told me you're getting her drugs."

"She's doing alright. She doesn't talk about it to me. She's shy."

"Pascale didn't tell Pa, but she told me. What's that about?" he asked.

"If you're looking for me to say she doesn't trust him, I'll never say that. Pascale obviously adores your Pa. Sometimes you don't tell your parents everything. Maybe it's easier for her to reach out to you because she's only got an image of you?"

"What the hell does that mean?"

"If you don't want to hear what I think, don't ask."

"I love Pascale, but she's been having to deal with this alone."

"So come home."

"It's not home."

"That's what Marthe wanted for you. She thought George-Étienne needed his son, and that Émile needed his father."

"It only matters what George-Étienne thinks," he scoffed. "That's the way it's always been."

SEVENTEEN

PASCALE, GABRIEL-ANTOINE AND George-Étienne mounted the third hinged disk to its frame in the gloom of night at forty-sixth *rang*. Their spotlights cast hard actinic glows and sharp shadows onto their work, but at even a short distance, the mists sponged up the light, making everything beyond feel darker. The first hinged cap, for the mouth of the cave, was under an acid-proof covering, ready to be installed. This second one, slightly smaller, would fit into a narrowing they'd found deeper in the cave system.

It took a lot of teamwork with winches and pulleys and clamps to get the pieces into position while bobbing in a mist of sulfur dioxide. The welding had to be precise, given the enormous pressure difference across the surface cap. That was where Pascale and Gabriel-Antoine had to work most closely, in testing the welds. Both said the words they had to say, but no more than that. In those silences, their dream of steel and stars and engineering continued to take shape, and in some ways, that balmed Pascale's heart.

If all tested well, tomorrow they could send all three caps down by balloon and drone. With the three caps, they could bring to life Pascale's idea of taming the winds in the cave, creating a station on the surface that cooled itself and made its own electricity. Completing the caps felt bittersweet, though. They'd done it without words, but they hadn't needed them—they usually anticipated each other's needs.

The whole family was tired as they broke for the day and went inside. A piece of steel had come apart early and hit George-Étienne in the ribs. Nothing was broken, but he was bruised. A bit of acid had burned through Alexis's suit and he was upset and brave and mad. Jean-Eudes felt terrible that the suit hadn't been good enough, but it wasn't that acid had dissolved a seal or a patch he'd done; the suit was just worn. Pascale wished Marie-Pier wasn't in meetings and negotiations at sixty-fifth *rang*. She made things feel smoother at home.

Pascale didn't think she could be around people right now. After stowing her suit, she retreated to their room with a bowl of cool soup. Indistinct voices in the main area faded, and after a while, Gabriel-Antoine came through the curtain. Pascale didn't pretend to be asleep and Gabriel-Antoine looked around, almost impatiently. His face was a bit red. He came to the inner rib of the trawler, to which Pascale's hammock was anchored. He leaned against it, bare sweaty arms crossed. He looked so good.

"I love you," Pascale said quietly, for the first time.

Gabriel-Antoine's expression softened.

"I love you," he said, for the first time, and Pascale felt a giddy elation. "As you are," he added. "I love everything about you, *chéri*. I love the way you fly fearlessly, the way you can take care of me in the clouds, and make a motor work with half the parts missing, and the way you get oil and dirt on your face, even when nothing is dirty."

She knew this was going to turn. She knew this was going to turn hard, but she could hold onto this moment, these words, store them in some place she could recite them over and over in the dark. Gabriel-Antoine left the rib and, a little uncertainly, took hold of the webbing of Pascale's hammock.

"You're a cute, smart guy," Gabriel-Antoine said. "I'm into cute, smart guys."

Something in her chest was melting, not the way fat melted for cooking, but the way machine parts melted outside, becoming soft and misshapen.

"I never thought I'd meet anyone in the godforsaken clouds. It's all muscleheads and potheads and old people and mystics. I was lonely and I was alone, and you flew into my life."

"I love the way you swagger," Pascale said, "especially when you don't know what you're doing. I love your brains. I love the way your ideas give me ideas. I love your stubbornness. I love the way your muscles move. But I'm not a guy."

His face hardened. "When did you decide? On the first kiss? Our third?"

"I didn't decide," Pascale said in a hard whisper. "This is something I learned about myself."

"Was it before we made the family deal?"

Pascale took a steadying breath. Gabriel-Antoine let go of the hammock and stepped to his own hammock, presenting his lithe, sweaty back to her.

"Why? Wouldn't you have joined?" Pascale said in a small voice. Gabriel-Antoine didn't turn.

"Maybe I would, maybe I wouldn't. But trusting you was part of my decision." Gabriel-Antoine met her eyes, challenging, daring. "I didn't know Marthe. Or your dad. Or Marie-Pier. I trusted you because my heart thought you were being honest with me."

"I'm sorry. I wasn't hiding anything," Pascale pleaded. "That's not how this works."

"How *does* it work?"

"I don't know! I didn't know this about myself."

"I feel tricked."

"How do you think I feel?" Pascale demanded in a low, urgent voice.

"How do you know this is it? How can you be sure?"

"I'm sure."

Gabriel-Antoine came closer, kneeling and lowering his voice.

"*Chéri,* you being sure is breaking my heart. I've never felt this way. I'm giving my heart to you, and you're stomping on it."

Pascale hopped out of the hammock and knelt with him, taking his hands. “I’m not stomping on your heart,” she whispered. “I want your heart. I want to protect it forever. I want you to hold mine.”

“How is this protecting?” he said, pulling his fingers away. “You’ve put a time limit on this. Two years? Three years? And then you’ll be a woman? I was offering… I was giving everything—I was looking at decades together. You didn’t have a right to make me believe I could fall for you if you were only in it for a while.”

“I want you forever,” she said.

He rose. The anger and pain in his expression was his response. His eyes were red-rimmed. She didn’t know how long her eyes had been wet. Her heart hurt so much. She didn’t know if she could stand it anymore.

“*Chéri,*” she said, holding her chest, “can we have a time-out?”

“What?”

“It hurts to fight. I don’t know how to do this. Can you please hate me tomorrow? Just not now?”

“I don’t hate you.”

“I love you.”

“Love isn’t enough for everything.”

“You love me now. And I love you now. Right now, can we not fight? Can we just hold each other? Just for an hour? Just pretend we’re happy?”

Gabriel-Antoine wiped his eyes. His lips trembled. He collapsed beside her, and after a few moments, he put his arm around her shoulders. They slumped together on the floor and they were both crying. After a while, their hands became less comforting and more urgent and reaching. Without breaking their embrace, they struggled up to fall into Pascale’s hammock together.

EIGHTEEN

"WHAT IF THE rendezvous point wasn't a trick?" Fabienne asked again.

"I don't know," Angèle said.

They sat in *la Marcotte,* on piles of old trawler ribbing they were eventually going to carve into something. A bare bulb swung in an ellipse, reacting to the slow drift of the habitat through the clouds. They were both tired from a long day of herding, and Angèle was nursing a new acid burn on her forearm where her suit had failed.

"Everyone makes a mistake sometimes," Fabienne said.

"But setting a rendezvous over a bunch of tesserae and coronae and chasmata doesn't make sense," Angèle said. "It's just wind churn."

"We'll be north of it tomorrow," Fabienne said.

"I'm not doing the herding again by myself!" Angèle said. "You have to work instead of flying around."

"The last time I went out, I brought back two oxygen tanks and a domesticated trawler, chips and all!"

Angèle crossed her arms. "You got lucky."

The idea of maybe finding other trawlers, other computer chips and other salvage was seductive now, even though it was a long shot.

"I could get lucky again."

Angèle made a derisive sound, turned off the light and climbed into her hammock.

La Marcotte reached the dense clouds over the Haasttse-Baad Tessera, just on the northern edge of the continental highlands of Aphrodite Terra. Fabienne got up early and flew south, climbing high to take advantage of faster windspeeds, and to get altitude for a long glide. She found the clouds calm today, once she'd shut off the engine. Periodic thermals lifted her from time to time, extending her glide. She listened in on the radio bands, keeping an eye on the barometer and thermometer. The atmosphere was about ten degrees cooler today, so after an hour and a half of gliding, when she got to fortieth *rang*, she decided to give it a bit more time.

She pushed her luck, her glide falling one kilometer after another, and she'd dropped to thirty-sixth *rang*. She'd never expected to break through to clear air, but the bottom of the sub-cloud haze flexed and wobbled with different convection effects. Today, the very bottom of the haze was high and Fabienne abruptly found herself looking straight at the naked, rocky Venus. She was an ugly bitch, but seeing Venus was always breathtaking—all that hard, open rock was so strange and compelling and powerful in its perfect stillness.

Except that something was moving. Way below, something floated, round and pale, tiny in the distance. Not natural. Not Venus. She lost it, first in a clot of haze, next when she fumbled to point her telescope down. It took ten minutes to find the thing again with her naked eye and then another couple to train the narrow field of the telescope on it. By then it had shrunk to a speck, but in the telescope she made out a parachute, or a balloon.

She thought it was descending over Ceres Corona, near the wide field of Rusalka Planitia. GPS was shit down here, but she was good enough at navigating that she jotted down *twelve degrees south of the equator* and snapped a picture. She hadn't planned on looking quite this far with the telescope, but she did have another, stronger eyepiece lens. As she rooted in the pocket compartments for it, she scanned the clouds, looking for anyone else at her altitude. Thirty-sixth *rang* was empty, a dark diffuse haze making a lonely fuzzy ceiling to the world. She changed out the 4× lens for a 10× one and laboriously found the object again.

It had dropped a lot further. She saw a grimy balloon. Hanging beneath it on two cables was some kind of disk. It looked like metal, like the disk she'd seen hanging beneath the harnessed trawlers. Where was it going? What were the D'Aquillons doing? She'd come all this way, trying to get a second glimpse of their secret project, and instead had found they were dropping stuff to the surface?

It didn't make sense. *La colonie* hadn't put any structures on the surface. The crust had few useful metals to justify the expense and effort; computer components that could survive four hundred and fifty degrees were hard to build, and no one could survive those pressures. Even thirty-six kilometers above the surface, she would slowly roast if she stayed much longer.

The thought made her back itch. She'd been working in the sub-cloud haze a few years ago, a dozen kilometers from the habitat, trying to recover the equipment and metals from a dying, sinking trawler. They couldn't afford to lose anything. She hadn't kept track of time or depth in her frantic disassembly. Her glove had failed and holed. In the lower hazes, the heat dissociated even sulfuric acid, but that only meant that Venus burned in other ways. Fabienne had gotten most of the equipment back in exchange for a permanent scalding scar on her hand.

She could understand the will-o'-the-wisp lure of undiscovered resources on the surface, but the idea of seeking anything below this altitude felt dangerous, transgressive.

Heat alarms flashed yellow, surprising her. The plane wasn't meant for this altitude. They would go to red soon. Attaching the camera to the telescope, she snapped pictures as quickly as she could. As different dials reddened, she started the engine and set a climbing path through the clouds, away from her own habitat: *coureurs* always left false paths to keep their locations secret, and she was too close to the D'Aquillons. Narcisse would be pissed she hadn't stayed to get more 'evidence,' but he hadn't been the one beneath the damn haze. Fabienne hadn't even meant to go that low; Venus had moved aside her own skirts to reveal someone else's secret.

NINETEEN

MARIE-PIER AND ÉMILE winged their way to the *Petit Kamouraska*. The cloud ridges ahead of them throbbed bright white, casting long gray shadows. She didn't often have occasion to visit the *Petit Kamouraska*. It floated gently on the wind, the hydroponic gardens in the bow reflecting a lively green. Thirty souls lived there, labouring at the small, overworked chemical plant. It used to have factories, but one broke down and *la colonie* had re-used the parts and pieces for other things. The freed space had been repurposed for detentions.

Her ID check on the roof was cursory. The constable seemed more interested in the food she'd packed, some for the guards, most for one of the detainees. Émile's badge seemed to smooth things out as well, but she wasn't sure of the details; the constables talked on their own channel.

She and Émile made their way to a large, dorsal bay that had been caged off into a few big cells using trawler cable heartwood. Some privacy curtains segregated the cages for men and women. Most faces had listless expressions, even the bored guards. Émile stayed and talked with the constables. Detainees looked up as she scanned them. She signalled one man, who seemed puzzled. They met at the bars. Lazare Jeangras was thinner than she'd last seen him.

"What are you doing here?" he said.

"This is a step down from the *Détroit d'Honguedo*," she said. Lazare and his daughter Laurette had run their black market operation from there.

"Not by choice," he said.

"I want to try to get you out," she said. "On parole, probably, but if I can get the charges dropped, all the better."

"Really?" he said hopefully. Then, his expression changed. "Actually, get Laurette out. She's got a baby in here. I can stay in the cells until the trial."

Marie-Pier grimaced. "I think the only way I can get you out is to offer to keep you in my habitat in the cloud decks."

"I can't leave my daughter in here."

"I'm doing what I can."

He swept back his lengthening salt and pepper hair.

"Why do you want me out? Why the cloud decks?"

"I need help on my habitat, and you can work hard," she said in a low voice, as she casually eyed who might be watching them. "There are a lot of trading opportunities in the depths, too many for me to keep up with. And I need to be better plugged into the trade network up here. When they caught you, they put a dent in the whole market."

"Which is why it won't be so easy to get me out. Laurette can learn to live in the depths, and is a good trader."

"I've had babies in the cloud decks. It's a full-time job keeping them alive. She and your grandson are safer here. You can send her more from the outside. Start by giving her this."

She handed him a shoulder pack through the wooden bars. Inside were vegetables, little tasteless cakes, a sack of water and powders to mix in to make little puddings and pastes. It was a couple of days of good enough food, probably better than what they got here.

* * *

PASCALE AND GABRIEL-ANTOINE had each done three hours of test drills in the atmospheric dive suits, checking every joint, the computer chips, and the insulation. With some modifications and refits, the hard suits had passed every test except the final one: pressure. They couldn't simulate ninety atmospheres of pressure in the clouds. They could only test pressure by descending. At five kilometers above the surface, they could challenge the suits with seventy atmospheres of pressure and about four hundred degrees, and if they did it slowly enough, they could rise before any failures turned catastrophic.

They floated downward, within a kilometer of each other, under brown and slate balloons of oxygen. Each of them huddled in an awkward shell. Pascale tested out the arms and legs. In the distance, Gabriel-Antoine was doing the same. Above them, the sub-cloud haze glowed a sullen orange, the sun glacially setting in the east. The light colored the empty world, the crags and fragments and ridges of Venus's ugly skin spread wide beneath them. They were the only two people in this world.

"How's your suit?" she asked, the wattage of her transmission dialed down to carry only a few kilometers.

"It's fine."

They hadn't talked about what had happened two nights ago. They'd made love like it was their last night, holding nothing back. An energetic desperation had gripped them. It wasn't just strong hands and hard muscles holding them together; gentle fingertips and stroking palms and tracing tongues and brushing lips said things they couldn't. Sometime during the night, Gabriel-Antoine had retreated to his own hammock.

Since then, he'd been distantly friendly and she supposed that she'd matched his tone, afraid of what she might give away, afraid that she might, without understanding, burst the fragile bubble made in the alchemy of sweaty, wanting bodies. When she was alone, she was so frustrated with herself for maybe seeing more meaning in the act than Gabriel-Antoine had intended, for interpreting it with all the aching hope in her heart. She didn't know anything about love, and she wished someone were here to tell her anything. In these days she most missed Marthe, who would have known what to do.

"I liked what we did in my hammock," she said.

Time stopped. The world was windless, soundless. The low sharp mountains and volcano domes and fractured black stone were frozen. She and Gabriel-Antoine hung in that stillness.

"I don't know if I can pretend," his voice came back with a tiny crackle of static. "I saw I was hurting you. I wanted to make the pain stop for a bit, but the pretending felt cheap. I don't know if I can just do this, knowing it will end. My heart isn't that tough."

"I'm sorry," Pascale whispered.

"I've been wracking my brain, day and night, to see if I could love a woman. The idea leaves me cold. I like guys. I love one guy. I'm just trying to be true to myself, like you are."

"I love you," Pascale said without transmitting.

"For now, I think we should stop this," Gabriel-Antoine said. "We should say to ourselves that we tried it out, but it didn't work. And it hurts."

Pascale pressed the transmitter, but had no voice.

TWENTY

"Good morning," Gabriel-Antoine said two days later. Pascale opened her eyes. The ribs of the trawler framed his bright expression. She sat up in her hammock. He held out a cold tea.

"Good morning," Pascale said blurrily. Normally she woke up first. Gabriel-Antoine was already dressed. She took the tea. He'd sugared it a little too much, but she wasn't going to turn her nose up at it.

"I set out your razor," he said. "I would have washed your clothes, but didn't want to wake you." He wore his lazy half-smirk, half-smile.

"How long have you been up?"

"I couldn't sleep." Gabriel-Antoine shrugged and pulled their sweaty clothes from the sack to wash them. "I did a lot of thinking. I guess I realized that things could be okay."

"Really?" Pascale said, sitting up, almost spilling the tea.

"Yeah. You want… to change into a woman. I'm starting to accept that, but…" Gabriel-Antoine look away, almost shyly. "I don't want you to be hurt or disappointed, but I don't know how we can afford the pills for long on the black market, or even how long *la colonie* will still be able to afford drugs. Who would do the surgery? We don't have enough doctors. Sometimes we want things that aren't possible. I don't know how we can get you what you want."

The words at first bewildered, but then felt like a slap, someplace deep. Her words tangled and didn't want to come.

"You're trying to sabotage me?"

A wash of heat rose in her face. Was Gabriel-Antoine accusing her of being selfish?

"No! It's just, in the middle of the night, I realized we're fighting over stuff we don't have to. You shocked me and surprised me. It hurt. I love you. I want to be with you. But if you aren't going to change anyway, then I don't care if you want to change your name to Jeanette or wear dresses or want to be called *mademoiselle*."

"Don't make fun of me."

"I'm not making fun of anything. I'm dealing with this. Pragmatically."

"This is important! I need this. I know who I am now. When I found out, I told Marthe I felt like a princess trapped in a tower. She said she would rescue me. But she's gone now, so I'm rescuing myself. If you can't even hold my horse while I sneak out of the tower, why are you with me?"

Pascale hopped out of the hammock and stomped out of their room. The rest of the day was washes of angry and sad. She worked outside in a survival suit, so if she started crying no one would notice. Pa's private questions while they worked with Gabriel-Antoine were probing, like he'd heard something.

After a punishing ten-hour shift in the heat outside, finishing some of the last tools they would bring down to the surface, they flew back to the *Causapscal-des-Vents*. With understandable exhaustion, Gabriel-Antoine went in, while Pascale lingered on the gantry. Pa did too, supervising Jean-Eudes scrubbing corrosion off pieces of metal.

"Is everything okay?" George-Étienne said on a family channel, just the three of them.

"Yeah, it's all fine, Pa," she said, putting false cheer into her voice. "It's coming together."

"Is he treating you right?" Pa said.

Her eyes were hot, but she said, "Who? Gabriel-Antoine? Yeah. Of course."

Pascale and George-Étienne had never spoken about her romance with Gabriel-Antoine—he didn't ask questions, and she'd felt shy and exposed about it from the beginning.

"You can talk to me," he said, and Pascale felt awkward and uncomfortable.

"Everything's good, Pa."

"Okay," he said, and she could hear him wanting to push more, but deciding against it. "I'll check the rigging on the trawlers."

When Pa had flown off, Pascale stared off into the clouds. Faint, ethereal lights shone behind curtained layers of mist. Many of the plants floating in the clouds of Venus bioluminesced, although no one had figured out why. Early colonial biologists had come up with unpersuasive reasons for why blastulae and protists might luminesce after some pressure waves and not others, why they might remain dark to one rise in temperature and not another, why they appeared to glow faintly, in quiet sympathy to one another, on some still days but not on others. The theorists had gradually given up—keeping *la colonie* alive and well was more pressing.

Living in the middle and lower cloud decks, the *coureurs* liked the mystery and proposed no theories.

They called the glows faerie lights. *Maman* had particularly loved them and, like many *coureur* parents, had stitched them into the backdrops of dozens of *contes de fées* she made up for her children, fairy tales that belonged to the *coureurs* alone. Stories of the wisdom of the quiet blastulae rafts, stories of lost baby trawlers, stories of witches emerging from haunted mists, tales of brave princes and princesses questing, rescuing one another from the dangers in the clouds.

In most of *Maman*'s stories, the characters were named after her children, so some of Pascale's earliest memories were stories of Jean-Eudes and Chloé rescuing small Pascale from cloud dragons and trolls living in misty castles. Or, just as often, Pascale would be the prince saving Émile or Marthe or *Papa* and *Maman,* which made them all laugh; even as a five-year-old, Pascale would squirm with the thrills of the worlds *Maman* would create. The faerie tales made Venus so much bigger, and yet more comprehensible; Venus's teachings could be grasped even by a child. Lessons of survival in a harsh world became magic spells and nursery rhymes and folk wisdoms.

Now Pascale was big. She'd grown to know herself and she'd become a questing knight, pitting her wits against everything that all the witches and trolls of Venus might throw at them. And she wasn't alone. Pa and Jean-Eudes and even Alexis were with her; and Émile, at a distance. None of them could do what she could do in designing and building a new world on the surface. Gabriel-Antoine could, but in the most important quest for Pascale—in becoming her real self—he was not with her. That solitude felt bigger than any dragon or misty troll or trawler-living witch.

The gantry rocked slightly and Jean-Eudes was beside her. He hugged her sideways instead of waiting for her to turn.

"Jean-Eudes…" she said. "Don't get a burn." Pressure and squeezing didn't really help or hinder the little holes acid burned in their suits, but they all said it did, and they usually avoided adding any wear. After a moment, she awkwardly hugged his arm until he let go.

"What was that for?" Pascale said.

"I don't want you to be sad."

She wanted to reassure him, but didn't have the energy anymore. They both stood there, silently, hands at their sides, puffs of wind gently stirring the hundred-degree haze around them. She checked that the power on her transmitter and his was too low for anyone else to hear.

"I don't know what I'm doing," she said with a shaky voice.

"Gabriel-Antoine can show you," Jean-Eudes said. "He showed me."

"This isn't about building the caps," she said. "I don't know what I'm doing with a boyfriend."

Jean-Eudes watched her patiently.

"We thought we had the same dream, but I changed it, I guess. I'm going to be a woman and he doesn't want to be with a woman."

"Why not?" Jean-Eudes said.

"He only likes boys."

Jean-Eudes was pensive for a while and Pascale took up a piece of metal scrap and scrubbed off the rust. "Oh," he finally said.

"I'm hoping he'll see some way to be with the me I want to be, the one I am. He's hoping that I either change my mind or don't get what I want."

"You should get what you want," Jean-Eudes said.

"We should all get what we want, but what do you do when two people don't want the same things?" She stopped her scrubbing as exhaustion melted over her again. "I love him. I want him, but I want me too."

Jean-Eudes held her shoulder.

"*Papa* would help."

"He wants to," Pascale said finally, "but that's the problem."

"What?"

"Of course Pa loves me. He'll want to fix all my problems—that's who he is—but this is a problem only I can fix. I can't handle him trying while I'm barely holding this together myself."

They stood there in the gentle gusts for a while, blooms of yellow and ochre rolling beneath the grille under their feet.

TWENTY-ONE

FLORIAN, THE YOUNGER, didn't want to get off, and he whined. Marie-Pier hugged him hard and lifted him with her as she stood and he laughed. She set him down on the table. The naked lightbulb attached to the rib of the trawler cast white light onto his face, making him look pale and transparent.

"Don't go," he said.

His older brother Maxime watched them guardedly. Their uncle Jean-Marc was brushing his teeth, keeping an eye on both nephews. Jean-Marc was increasingly raising them, which wasn't what she wanted. She'd only been home for a week, and it felt harder and harder to leave them. Sometimes when she'd been in *l'Assemblée,* or selling goods in the upper clouds, she'd leave them for a week at a time, but her absences were now longer. She was doing her own job and Marthe's.

"I'll be back soon," she said. "Take care of your uncle."

Maxime sighed, but didn't near. Marie-Pier pulled Florian close.

"I've got a dream of the future," she said to all three. "Someday we'll explore space together. And one day, you'll inherit the stars. It means I have to work hard, far away, but it's all for us. Clouds and stars together. We'll have it all." She didn't know how to convince someone of a secret hope she held tight. Time would make things clear. She pulled up her suit and sealed it all, minus the helmet.

"Okay, boys," she said to them at the airlock. "Big kiss."

Florian darted back, hugging her survival suit and kissing both her cheeks. Maxime came more sheepishly, hugging her like it wasn't a big deal to him. She grabbed him and planted a kiss on the top of his head as he protested. Then she put on her helmet and entered the airlock.

She wouldn't need her plane today. She and George-Étienne had timed this meeting by the winds. Her habitat, the *Coureur des Tourbillons,* survived best at about fiftieth *rang*, in winds that moved faster than the ones buoying the *Causapscal-des-Profondeurs* in its construction yard eddy. The different wind speeds brought their habitats close enough every few cycles around the planet. Today both were relatively close to *Le Grand Platin,* Narcisse Mignaud's habitat. Marie-Pier had only met Narcisse once. He was a deep cloud, volcano-chasing *coureur* like George-Étienne, and could be a good trading contact, or even an ally.

Her home must have stumbled upon a thermal; when she emerged from the airlock, she found herself looking out onto *les Plaines,* the kilometer of clear air between the lower and middle cloud decks. The view extended hundreds of kilometers, as if she were in a pane of glass. She admired the sight of the billowing burnt ochre cloud tops for a moment before diving into them.

Le Grand Platin floated about ten kilometers deeper, forty kilometers north and twenty kilometers ahead of them in the winds. Driving her wing-pack hard, she reached the approximate location of *le Grand Platin* in about half an hour, but navigating in the clouds of Venus was always a process of narrowing down volumes. She'd reached the region, but now she had to find the herd. She listened carefully, picking out two low-wattage radio signals.

George-Étienne's was the first; the telemetry showed that he was only a few minutes behind her. The second was a herd nav buoy transmitting an automated set of instructions for finding the habitat. She'd lose the signal if she drifted very far from it, so she boosted her transmitter wattage and signalled her location to George-Étienne.

Her path and George-Étienne's met at an old trawler, heavily overgrown with black epiphytic plants. It displayed the misshapen symmetries of a trawler domesticated from the wild. A third of its lower gantry was torn and missing, but boxes had been stacked and tied down in places to rebalance the weight. She circled it once out of caution, then banked, flared, and landed in the black netting. George-Étienne, an expert flyer, landed moments later. Two figures emerged from the airlock. When Marie-Pier climbed to the grille floor, they offered hands to help, but didn't make any move to invite them inside. A salt-and-pepper-bearded face peered from one visor and a middle-aged woman watched from the other: Narcisse and his sister Liette.

"George-Étienne," the man said.

"Narcisse," George-Étienne said. "Liette. This is Marie-Pier Hudon, my wife."

Narcisse nodded curtly to her, but Liette gave her a good stare and came closer. She had a bit of a stoop and as she looked up, Marie-Pier saw graying hair framing her face. Her expression was inscrutable.

"We got your messages," Narcisse said. "You're making houses in the clouds, eh?"

"The House of Styx is working out," George-Étienne said.

"Three cooks make a confusing kitchen," Liette said.

"But not so much that we won't try it ourselves," Narcisse said, "with two families, not three. Victorine Corbeau is giving it some thought." He smirked. "She's got to pick between being my wife or Liette's. Not much choice for her, eh? Still, Corbeau is an interesting name. House of Crows has a nice ring to it."

"This will make us all stronger."

"Or maybe it's shuffling the plates without putting any new food on them," Narcisse said grimly.

"We're deep cloud families, Narcisse. Phocas brought engineering know-how to the depths. He's helping with automation. More hands."

Narcisse stomped to a wooden box, pulling aside its cover. He thrust at George-Étienne a rusted metal rod that might once have been a screwdriver. "Metal doesn't do well down here, George-Étienne."

"We're trying to make more and more things out of trawler wood. Marie-Pier has been isolating acid-resistance proteins and oils from trawler DNA to protect machinery better. We want to prototype some drones soon."

"So take over the clouds." Liette waved her hand dismissively. "Be the big man."

The conversation seemed unable to gain any altitude. Marie-Pier stepped forward.

"We're just one collection of families, working to keep the government's nose out of our business. I like safety in numbers."

Marie-Pier wasn't as anti-government as George-Étienne, but she was a *coureur.* 'Safety,' to the *coureurs,* meant safety from thieves and safety from the government, and Liette and Narcisse would know what she meant. They all just scraped by, shadowed by the collective fear of having even less. Hope for any sense of security tempted even the most jaded of them.

"Why Victorine Corbeau?" George-Étienne asked.

"She's the only one who'll work with us!" Narcisse said, barking a laugh. After a moment, more quietly, he added, "The Corbeaus grow beans like a sonovabitch. I don't know how she does it. She needs minerals all the time, though. We can find some. No computer geniuses among us, though."

"That's where the houses work together," George-Étienne said. "My boy Pascal has made processing chips, really simple ones that don't wear out at eighty and ninety degrees. He's teaching my grandson to make them too. Small fingers."

Behind the faceplate, Narcisse's eyebrows rose. *Coureurs* needed computer chips for every trawler they domesticated. Chips managed battery performance, radio transmissions to other parts of the herd, propeller direction and speed, and so on. Storms scattered domesticated trawlers, but more were lost when chips stopped working at high heat. Then the trawlers just drifted away, batteries, metals and all. George-

Étienne pulled out a small bag of carbon nanotube weave and handed it to Narcisse.

"Three of Pascal's homemade chips are in there. You can test them."

Narcisse turned on an extra light on his helmet to examine one of the chips as he turned it in his fingers. It was big, palm-sized. Ugly and uneven on some edges. Its ceramic finish shone in the light. Compact and neatly laid out layers of metal filled the surface.

"What's the difference?"

"Pascal figured out how to make silicon carbide from scratch to package the chip," George-Étienne said. "The interconnects tolerate higher temperatures. We've been using them on my trawlers for months."

Narcisse handed the chip to Liette without taking his eyes off George-Étienne.

"Fail rate?" Liette asked Marie-Pier as she eyed it. Interesting that she didn't ask George-Étienne.

"None yet," Marie-Pier said.

"They're primitive," Liette said, taking the bag from her brother and comparing one to another.

"For a trawler sheepdog control system, we don't need more," Marie-Pier said.

"What are you doing with all your normal chips?" Narcisse said, with a fishing tone Marie-Pier recognized as an opening for bargaining.

"Gabriel-Antoine is building things that need more sophisticated chips. It's one of the reasons we're here."

The shallow tolerance in Narcisse's expression evaporated.

"Pascal and Alexis are building these chips. Each takes a week or two to make. These three are a gift. If you like them, I can get you more. I would trade you six of these for one regular chip."

"My good chips, that I had to trade or steal from the upper clouds?" Narcisse scoffed. Liette stiffened.

"In the end, if you get six chips instead of one, you'll be ahead. You can domesticate more trawlers."

"So will you!" Liette said.

"If you don't want to trade, don't trade," Marie-Pier said. "It's an offer. We can see if other families would be interested."

"You came to me first, eh?" Narcisse said.

"Yeah, we did," George-Étienne said, and then to the unspoken question he added, "We're all *coureurs*, and the government is trying to fuck us. We're scattered and suspicious, which helps the government, not us. Gabriel-Antoine is going to need chips he can't make from scratch. Marie-Pier needs chlorine salts. I need scrap silicon. There are a thousand things we each need, and trades can make things happen."

Narcisse seemed pensive. "Sorry to hear about the *Causapscal-des-Vents*," he said. "I hope you'd already scavenged the shit out of it before it went down."

"Marthe had taken some stuff," George-Étienne said.

Marie-Pier felt like Narcisse was baiting George-Étienne, but she didn't understand the nuances. George-Étienne watched Narcisse coolly.

"We'll try out the chips," Narcisse said. "We'll see what we think. If we're selling chips to you, it won't be for six of these little homemade things. It'll be for a piece of the pie. We don't have a Gabriel-Antoine. And the House of Crows needs metal for our own ideas."

"Let us know what you think of the chips," George-Étienne said. Marie-Pier watched him, looking for the signs of anger or distrust or any of the other emotions that seemed to come so easily to him. If anything, he seemed guardedly cheerful to her. She really didn't know him yet.

Narcisse and Liette were quiet. Narcisse was a weird one. Marie-Pier had never been to a *coureur* habitat without being invited inside. She hoped George-Étienne had other possible trading partners in mind too.

Marie-Pier and George-Étienne moved to the edge of the gantry and extended their wings. They leapt into the thick yellow haze and powered up their engines. The clouds swallowed *le Grand Platin* as they began the long flight back to the *Causapscal-des-Profondeurs*. She had a day in the depths to check on her big trawlers before she had to be back at the flotilla altitude for trading and *Assemblée* work.

Goddess in Repose, by Émile D'Aquillon

The model reposes,
adjusts her skirts
in afternoon light,
to be painted in ephemeral oils
or graven in brittle stone
to be dissolved if she
dislikes the likeness.
Through diaphanous clouds,
the artist glimpses her charms:
puckered, tectonic sores, stiff crags
jutting between cracked chasmata,
bleeding poison.

On canvas, the titan rises
from bubbling
slag and volcanic
foam on a scallop shell.
Demurely, she conceals cooling,
brittle flesh. Her fingers caress
creased skin
seductively. Angels of Spring
wrap vapors
of poison around a beauty,
alien and unfathomable
by duped painters.

The poet descends
through her crushing skirts,
beneath her biting rains,
to gaze upon a beauty
of cracked basalt,
of blighted

seeping stone,
a rite of passage,
to a manhood
to be snuffed out,
if the goddess
dislikes the words.

TWENTY-TWO

Émile arrived at the kitchen court on the *Baie-Comeau* early. When he'd been seeing Thérèse, they'd often met here. It was seven floors of industries, living spaces, the hospital, government operations and some recreational spaces for those with community credits to spare. Sometimes, when she was late or he was just getting away from the *Causapscal-des-Vents,* he'd found the kitchen court anonymously welcoming, if he could find a one-person table near the back. The ceiling was high and one wall was clear dirigible envelope: two layers with plants between them, bright with sunlight during the day, lit by battery power during the night. The food smells tempted him, but he rarely had dining privileges here. So he would sip from a flask while playing with words. Today, he found his old table, wiped off dried spatters of stew, and sank into the chair. The dozens of people talking over each other made a white noise that could help him focus. It was playing with words; calling it 'writing' felt presumptuous, and he didn't want to claim more than his due. He sometimes felt like phrases and snippets came together for some effect, but it took more than fragments to make a poem. Poetry was a language of the heart and mind. A poem had to begin with a leap, propelling itself forward. A good poem had a strength, a consistency, its own unique voice and message that both justified its existence and provided the momentum for it to glide through thought. A poem landed with an economy of effort, a conclusive ease, a heart-hitting shock of revelation and textured meaning.

Thérèse might have been his muse, if muses existed, if he deserved one. Muses were divine servants, and in the court of Venus, even muses needed to be consecrated with blood. If he hadn't yet suffered enough to deserve a muse, he wouldn't survive waiting much longer. Maybe his muse was incompetent. Or he was. Try as he might, nothing he wrote felt inspired. Somewhere between his soul and the page, the transcendence slipped away.

He'd lost his data pad of poems, and he felt the loss. It was all shit, but it was part of him, something he'd made. He had the ambition, the unreasoning belief that if he kept at it, he might become good. Last week, he'd decided to try rewriting his lost poems from memory. He'd begun rewriting *The Goddess in Repose*. It wasn't coming out badly yet, although there were good bits he couldn't remember or recreate. They'd been moments of minor inspiration, and inspiration never struck twice in the same way. He had some new poems he wanted to try too—*This Is All There Is, I Am Made of Skins,* and *Florets in Bloom*—but none of them were clear enough yet to start. And his early ideas felt too shallow, too dependent on styles and conceits from three or four centuries ago. He was afraid to leave the shadows of Apollinaire and Éluard, and afraid of being seen in the scaffolding of their voices.

He wanted to write about Marthe, but he didn't know how, couldn't even frame a title. She was too big an experience and too complex a soul to capture. Or maybe a poem for Pascale, his new little sister, to encourage her? He held his cheek in his hand as he tried to put pencil to paper for some time, but the words felt presumptuous and pretentious, because Pascale was new to him—he didn't know her. The white noise fell away for a while and words started to form in his mind, but after a time, he realized that someone was standing in front of him. It was that pretty woman Marthe had been scoring with sometimes. She stared at him, crossing her arms nervously.

"What are you doing here?" she said.

"What do you want? You're... Noémie?"

"Noëlle," she said, then ducked a bit and pulled a stool from another table. "Are you writing poetry?"

The page he had in front of him was empty. He hadn't touched it yet. "Why do you ask?"

She shrugged. "I'm being polite."

"Marthe told you I wrote poetry?"

She looked mystified, then a bit alarmed. "I guess."

"You guys were closer than I thought." He watched her, but she didn't seem to know what to say. He was busy. "Do you want something?"

"I'm... Was Marthe involved in something criminal?"

He gave her a dubious look he'd learned from the cops. It rarely worked—on anyone—but she started to fidget.

"I just heard talking," she said.

She must have expected him to start talking at some point. She apparently hadn't expected to have to carry the whole conversation. She wiped at her forehead.

"Black marketeering," she said. "I know she must have traded away stuff from your habitat. I saw the inside of that sty. And I caught her once on the *Détroit d'Honguedo*."

"What does this have to do with anything?"

"Well," she said, "if she did, I think I should know. People saw us together. Sometimes in public. Maybe they'll be out for me, for something she did or owed."

"That seems unlikely."

"The police might come looking, depending on what sort of stuff Marthe got into. I didn't know everything about her."

"No one's investigating her. I'm with the *Sûreté*."

Noëlle gaped. "You're a cop?"

"What, I don't look like one?"

Her expression answered his question, which didn't surprise him, but it happened so often that it was starting to get annoying. He blandly zipped down his suit, revealing a badge and a short baton that wasn't really a police tool; Réjean had lifted it off a black marketeer they'd arrested and had given it to Émile. Her eyes widened.

"So... nice to see you," he said, pointedly. "Catch you around, I guess."

She didn't move. The moment drew out, increasingly awkward. What did she want?

"I'm kind of busy with something," he added, indicating the blank paper in front of him.

She leaned closer, looking like she'd had to screw up her courage. "Things weren't always good between Marthe and me, but I really liked her. There aren't a lot of people like her."

Remembrances of Marthe, from annoying bucktoothed little sister to know-it-all adult, came to mind, more strongly than he'd expected. Marthe had been robbed. Maybe Noëlle had been too. "No. There weren't."

"I'd like to call your father to express my condolences," she said. "And your brothers. I wanted to say a few things to them I thought were really special about her."

"Give me a message and I'll send it down."

"I'm not as good at writing as you probably are. I want to talk, not just send a message."

Émile couldn't imagine anyone in the depths being happy with a call from a stranger. This was a weird request. No one from up-cloud had messaged the family when *Maman* had died, or Chloé and Maturin.

"They won't be in comms range for a while. And Pascale and Jean-Eudes are really shy. And my Pa's a dick."

"I'm grieving!" she whispered fiercely, leaning in. "This is hard on me too. You're not the only one who thought Marthe was special!"

Finally, across the length of the kitchen court, he saw Marie-Pier walking by. She was with someone he didn't recognize, and she wasn't looking his way. He folded his pages. Noëlle's expression became bewildered.

"Write a note. Don't force them. You don't know what they're feeling."

"Can you ask them quickly?" she said.

"You're getting weird."

"Wait!"

"Look, I'm really busy."

Marie-Pier was almost at the forward exit, and he shadowed her along the edges of the kitchen court, tucking his papers into an inner pocket of his suit, scanning the crowd casually. A couple of guys rose suddenly from their meal and set a purposeful pace towards the exit. The second guy looked around, but Émile kept his eyes forward and walked steadily. When the guys slipped out, he followed them, picking up his pace and scanning the dining area one last time. No one paid any attention to him except Noëlle, who was still lingering uncertainly by his table.

When Émile got to the corridor, he slowed to a saunter and pulled the papers out of his pocket to seem to be reading while walking. The hallway was always busy, and he didn't know where Marie-Pier had been going. She had a lot of contacts, political as well as black market, and she could be on the *Baie-Comeau* for either reason. Along the left were offices, classrooms, and multi-purpose rooms of different sizes benefiting from window views of the hydroponics growth. Along the right were workshops, storage areas, bits of small industry, computers, labs and other crap. Émile was tall enough that on tiptoe he could see over pretty much everyone's heads. About twenty meters ahead, he saw one of the guys by a stairwell leading to the less fancy, less frequented parts of the *Baie-Comeau*: the cargo bays, the engines, the yeast tanks, the atmospheric scrubbing equipment.

A few people complained as Émile shoved past. He looked back in case anybody was following him. He didn't see anything suspicious, but it didn't mean he and Marie-Pier didn't have other tails. He reached the stairwell door and, as casually as possible, shouldered it open. It only went down, and through the lightly rusted metal grille of the landing, he saw one of the guys' heads two levels below him. The face looked up, but Émile didn't wait—he took the stairs briskly and loudly.

Two levels down, the dark-haired guy stood at a partly open door. Émile recognized him, a *coureur*: Herman or Hermès or something, from the Corbeau family. He was the same age as Émile—they'd traded pot once or twice in the depths. The other guy had a bird's nest of red hair and his suit's patches and discolorations screamed 'deep cloud decks.'

"Corbeau," Émile said. "Long time no see. You're far from home."

"*Coureurs* aren't welcome in the flotillas?" Corbeau said.

"Come anytime," Émile said. "I live here now."

"Yeah, I heard you went soft," Corbeau said.

"I'm looking for my stepmom. You seen her?" Émile pushed past Corbeau and the redhead. From this angle, he could just make out Marie-Pier walking away, far down the hall. "Oh, there she is. She got jumped a couple of weeks ago. Someone stole her shit. I told my family I'd keep an eye on her. What are you guys doing down here?"

"You got a smart mouth, D'Aquillon," the redhead commented. Both men looked uncomfortable about something.

"Do something about it." Émile was bigger than either, but there were two of them.

"Maybe we will," Corbeau said, "or if you give us something for our trouble, we'll let you walk away."

Corbeau's fingers moved to a pocket and closed on the handle of something. Émile's fist shot forward, bouncing Corbeau's head off the door frame. The redhead's fist glanced clumsily off Émile's chin. It hurt, but could have hurt more. Émile rolled with it and pulled him stumbling into the stairwell by the arm.

Corbeau glared at Émile, blood pouring from his nose. He had a small blade that looked carved of trawler cabling—sharp enough to cut and kill, and cheaply replaceable. Corbeau's partner was in the way, though; here at the bottom of the stairwell, no one could move much. They shoved him against the wall, which gave Émile leverage, and he landed some hard rabbit punches right through the redhead's blocks. Émile kneed him and launched an uppercut under his jaw as he crumpled. A crack sounded: maybe teeth, hopefully bone.

Corbeau stood on the other side of the slumping redhead, his shiv held less certainly. He only came up to Émile's chin, and he'd only talked trash when he'd had backup. Émile pulled out his short baton. Corbeau swung his knife in a figure-eight, defensively. Émile feinted and then rammed the little baton into Corbeau's hand, and the knife dropped. Then he pounded his fists into Corbeau's kidneys until the *coureur* collapsed.

Émile was panting over them. His face was bleeding from somewhere—Corbeau or the other guy must have gotten in a punch he hadn't tracked. He closed the door to the stairwell so they wouldn't be disturbed and patted down Corbeau. Then he propped him against the wall with his hand around Corbeau's neck. For his own safety, he put his foot over the redhead's neck, ready to apply pressure.

"What made you go after Hudon?" Émile asked at Corbeau's ear. There was no reply, so he punched Corbeau hard in the stomach and the man gasped, almost puking. "I can't hear you. What put you after my stepmother?"

"*Maman* told us she might have something worth taking..." Corbeau groaned.

"Take what? What's she got? I know my family is poor. She hasn't got shit. You after her trawlers or biotech?"

Corbeau wasn't forthcoming, so Émile rammed his knee into the guy's balls. Corbeau gagged.

"Take what, *tabarnak*?" Émile demanded.

"Anything!" Corbeau gasped. "Anything she's selling. Any electronics too. Sticks. Datapads. Chips."

"Why? For selling?"

"Not for sale. *Maman* wants the electronics," Corbeau gasped.

"Victorine is your Ma, right?"

Corbeau nodded painfully.

"If Marie-Pier sees either of you two losers *anywhere* again, I'm going to put both of you in the hospital. You got it?"

Émile squeezed his fingers tighter and Corbeau nodded, wincing. He punched him once more for good measure, and this time the *coureur* did puke on his red-headed friend. Émile shoved Corbeau back on the stairs, opened the door and headed into the passageway Marie-Pier had taken, puzzling. Why the hell would the Corbeau family target Marie-Pier?

TWENTY-THREE

PASCALE AND GABRIEL-ANTOINE dropped gradually out of the sub-cloud haze in their atmospheric dive suits, hanging from partially inflated oxygen balloons. They still didn't know how quickly they could safely ramp up the pressure or temperature, so they took things slowly for now. Propeller drones, clipped into harnesses midway up the cables, steered their descent.

Pascale stared at the majesty of Venus from twenty-nine kilometers. East-to-west winds blew them over webs of radial fractures running down the tan and black shoulders of Khabuchi Corona. They drifted, sinking, crossing the lowland basaltic fracture fields between Khabuchi and concentric fracture patterns at the jagged heights of Miralaidji Corona. In many ways, Venus's stark angularity was off-putting, hostile, inhospitable; but through the right eyes, the tumbled scarps of black and gray basalt had their own kind of beauty. The wrinkle ridges scouring the broad plains of Rusalka Planitia on Pascale's right had to be taken on their own terms. Further north, the hard, broken ground rose to meet the hundreds of volcanic shield domes pocking the surface and Pascale tried to see them with Venus's own eyes, to understand the natural processes that had made this celestial body. Directly west, along the path of their descent, one of the arms of Diana Chasma began, the Hadean bed of an immense river that had scoured steep valleys right out of the hard skin of Venus, the sign of a living planet.

Pascale would have liked to share the experience of the vast, stark beauty of Venus with someone, to validate that the beauty she found was... That someone else also saw it. Gabriel-Antoine floated a kilometer south, maybe feeling the same awe, but valleys separated them too, valleys she didn't know how to cross. In a way, though, she wasn't alone. Even without speaking, they were seeing the same things, crossing the same coronae and chasmata. If in the future they could cross the space between them, they could talk and share this moment with each other. And they were about to spend days and weeks together, working side by side, on a common dream. Maybe in all that building, they might make a bridge.

At just fifteen kilometers above the surface, thirty-three atmospheres of pressure squeezed the suit shells. Their suits became buoyant, an effect that would only increase. To continue descending, they gradually pumped oxygen out of their balloons and compressed it in their tanks. Venus became more real. Pascale had been to her surface twice, but both times in a steel eggshell. This felt tactile, visceral.

In another ten minutes the slide zones and fracture lines at the bottom of the chasma came into sharper detail. The jagged ridges and rockslides seemed endless. The shield tops of Nuahine Tessera came level with her eyes and then the light changed as the upper edges of the chasma rose above them, becoming redder and dimmer. The pressure, already at eighty-six atmospheres, kept rising. Their suits were heavy enough to sink even in the supercritical carbon dioxide at the bottom of the atmosphere, but not by much. Fortunately they each carried construction materials, tools, and tanks of compressed gas, all of it serving as ballast.

The cave mouth became visible, a dark patch on the uneven dirty gray basalt of one wall of Diana Chasma. The terrible wind was invisible, but existed as a thrumming roar. The three caps rested on the slope, a hundred meters above the cave mouth, where their drones had set them before anchoring themselves to solid outcroppings. The steep rock face was so big that it was its own tipped world, speckled with ledges, ridges, lava caves, and outcroppings. Pascale and Gabriel-Antoine alighted between the cave mouth and the caps. This close, they heard the wind entering the cave as an endless roll of thunder, so powerful that it vibrated through the rock.

"We're on Venus," Pascale said.

Gabriel-Antoine was silent, but not in a bad way. She made out his expression through his faceplate. This moment was marking him as well.

"It's so big," he finally said. And it was. The cliff face rose for kilometers. The chasma was a broad cut in the stone, touched with fallen scree, fracture lines, and boulders, extending beyond vanishing points. "We should start," he added after a time, as if distracted.

They found good outcroppings to anchor their equipment bundles and then paid out cable to descend to a small side-cave, east and uphill of the main mouth. This one channel was the only other significant flow into the cave, no bigger in some spots than their outstretched arms, and it was going to be their emergency exit. They needed to block it before blocking the main entrance. They tied themselves to new outcroppings and lowered themselves into the small branch cave.

Gabriel-Antoine and Pascale had built a pair of airlock doors and customized frames fitted to this tunnel. Gabriel-Antoine had constructed and programmed special robots to bring these airlock doors down and pre-position them. The robots weren't smart enough to seal the seams, though, nor verify their emplacement. They needed human brains for that.

The frames fit well enough, although their mapping had missed some protrusions, and some gaps were too big to be filled with cement. The former they chiselled away and the latter they pre-filled with smaller rocks before cementing. The airlock became the first permanent structure on the surface of Venus—there was little ceremony, but Pascale didn't lose the significance of the moment.

They moved back up the rock face, using buoyancy and the muscle assist of the dive suits to reach the anchor points for the three big caps. These steel disks, housed in hinged frames, contained wind turbines that would tame the four hundred and fifty degrees of heat and ninety atmospheres of pressure. They hung from the cables that had carried them down, on winches strong enough to hold them on this slope, but not nearly enough to control them through the terrible wind of the cave mouth. Using the tools they'd brought down, they locked together several more cables to each winch and anchored them to rock outcroppings, distributing the weight against the horrific forces that would soon try to tear the caps free. If they made a mistake now, one of the caps could be swept down the cave mouth and wedged further in, where it might take weeks to get it free.

"Will they hold, do you think?" Pascale said.

"We've done everything we can. That's ten kilometers of cable."

"You can lower the last cap on your own?"

"With the winch, yes," Gabriel-Antoine said.

"I'll go in the cave, then. Good luck."

"Good luck," he said.

Things almost felt normal. When they worked together, they each knew the other's needs, they could finish each other's sentences. It gave her hope, as much as Venus herself. The tumbled, craggy, remorseless beauty of Venus, her boundless vertical space, her endless mountains and valleys, created a place that made anything possible, so much so that they'd found a doorway to the stars pulled straight from fairy tales. Magic existed here, an ineffable kind that had shared none of its secrets yet.

With slow bouncing steps, Pascale made her way down the rock face to the side channel where they'd set up the airlock. Gabriel-Antoine had already lowered the third cap, the one that would be closest to the wormhole, halfway down the rock face. Two cables dangled below it, their tips only a dozen meters from the central mouth of the cave system. Invisible turbulences made them dance. Pascale compressed the oxygen from her buoyancy balloon and stowed the empty sack in a pouch hooked to the waist of her ADS.

"Entering the airlock," she radioed.

This crude, person-sized airlock would not pressurize or depressurize completely, with its imperfect seal, but they didn't need perfect. They needed a place to briefly shield themselves from the winds while they installed the caps. She cycled through the airlock and entered Venus, her helmet lamp lighting the underworld.

The airlock blocked almost all the wind pressure in the side tunnel, and she stepped down to the main cave with only a little hunching and twisting. Erosion, a force rarely seen on the surface of Venus, had smoothed the side branch in many places, but Pascale found a few outcroppings solid enough to anchor her safety lines. She hammered a pair of pitons in and tied herself securely. Where the side branch met the main cave, she paused, as if standing on the edge of an invisible, raging river. She had to get into the main channel of the wind. If she'd misjudged any of her anchor points, the current would sweep her away, probably smashing her against a stone wall before carrying her lifeless body through the wormhole and into space.

Two cables flapped from the top of the cave mouth.

"I can see the cables," Pascale said, "about three meters of each one."

"The bottom edge of the cap is about ten meters from the top of the cave." Gabriel-Antoine's voice crackled in the static. "Are you safe?"

The question made her chest hurt a bit, in a wishful and hopeful way. She discovered she was smiling.

"I'm anchored in a few spots," she said. "I'm going to lower myself into the wind and see how the suit handles. Keep paying out the cable."

"Be careful."

"You too."

Pascale put a hand into the main channel and felt the pushing of the current. Ninety-three atmospheres of pressure, the weight of a column of Venusian air seventy kilometers high, drove supercritical carbon dioxide through this relatively small hole and out into space. In the context of all of Venus, the leak was a minor thing, insignificant; but to a single person, it was like standing in a fast current at the bottom of the deepest ocean on Earth. Pascale tested her cables and eased into the flow. The dense stream buffeted her, lifting her from her feet. The cables strained as she bobbed. She let out more cable and her suit began to vibrate; she let out even more and let herself hang against the full force of the only cataract on Venus.

"Everything is holding," she transmitted. "I'm in the main cave. Play out more cable."

She could see about twelve meters each of the two cables attached to the bottom of the cap. They fluttered and whirled about one another against the roof of the cave. She and Gabriel-Antoine had planned for her to reach them before lowering the cap into the cave so that they would have two sets of hands to handle it. The cables shivered about five meters from her outstretched hand along the ceiling. She could pay out another five meters of her own anchoring rope, but the wind would keep her from the ceiling.

"I can't reach the cable from here," she transmitted. "I'm going to increase my buoyancy and try to walk across the ceiling."

"There's too much wind resistance on the balloon," Gabriel-Antoine replied in a crackling voice. "You'll be blown away."

"Not the way I'm going to do it."

Pascale had various mesh sacks of tools clipped to hooks on the hard outside of her ADS. She pulled an unused bag free and clipped it to her chest. Then she put the buoyancy bag into it and slowly filled it with compressed oxygen until it tugged her up towards the cave roof.

"I got to the ceiling," she said.

"How? Are you safe?"

"I'm climbing across now."

She'd intended to clamber around the ceiling like a spider, but despite the handholds, the current pushed her back. The cables stayed out of reach.

"Can you pay out any more cable?" she said.

"A few meters. Hold on."

Slowly, they snaked longer and longer until the wind-braided ends fluttered only a meter from her hand.

"Any more?"

"Any lower and the cap itself will be in the wind."

She was dangling at the end of one of her cables, but still had a little more length available in the other three.

"I can probably reach the ends if I release one of my cables," she said.

"No!"

"Don't worry," she said, although she was far from sure.

"Don't be stupid."

"This is smart," she said as she put one glove around the release clamp for the shortest cable. "Not *wise*, but smart." Her fourth cable fluttered away to slap into the cave wall. "I'm okay with three."

She paid out more from the remaining three cables and crawled along the ceiling. Each new handhold against the current was a fight. Every centimeter towards the middle of the cave dragged her a centimeter downstream. She didn't think about where she was, or what would happen if the cables failed. She crept closer and closer, until she stretched one hand against the current—needing the suit's powered muscle assist—and the hard fingers of the glove caught the wriggling ends. Then something snapped and her heart lurched as she slipped almost a meter downstream. But she'd kept a hold of the cable from the cap.

"What happened?" Gabriel-Antoine demanded.

Pascale looked down the body of her suit.

"*Maudit,*" she swore. "One of my cables snapped."

"Are you okay?"

"There's a lot of strain on the last two," she said. "They're holding my weight *and* the weight of the dive suit against the current. And I'll have to go back against the current."

"I'll come down!" he said. "I'll get another rope to you and pull you in."

"Stay there! I've still got the two cables holding me to the wall, and now I'm holding on to two more from the cap. Lower the cap and I'll use all four to pull myself back."

"As soon as the cap gets into the stream, it could shake in any direction. It could fling you into a wall."

"Lower it slowly and we'll see. I've got to tie the cap in somewhere anyway."

"I don't like this."

"We knew we needed to take some risks."

After a moment he finally said, "Holler if you want me to stop or pull back."

Pascale tied the ends of the cables from the cap to eyelets in the dive suit so that they bore some of her weight. As Gabriel-Antoine lowered the cap, she winched the branch tunnel cables shorter. Very slowly, she pulled herself along the ceiling against the terrible wind, back the way she'd come.

The cap appeared first as a curving, smooth-edged silhouette peeking from the top of the cave mouth, and then as a growing crescent, an advancing eclipse, scraping the stone. A painful subsonic thrumming sounded, as violent eddies became visible where the supercritical carbon dioxide cavitated, forming little bubbles of low-pressure gas swirling with stone grit.

She'd nearly reached the tunnel wall when she missed pulling in the slack on her safety lines, and the cables from the cap suddenly bucked, smashing her into the wall. She held on to an uneven, rocky projection about a meter below the branch tunnel while Gabriel-Antoine's voice shouted over the radio.

"Pascale! Are you okay?"

Holding on with one hand, she pulled in all the slack on her safety cables.

"I'm okay," she said breathlessly. "I got knocked against the wall."

"Is your suit damaged?"

"I don't think so. I'm not dead."

"This is no time for joking around!"

"I'm not joking."

She really wasn't. If her suit had cracked, the pressure would have squashed her. The current by the walls ran slightly slower and she pulled along the ropes to climb into the branch tunnel. The cap cables trembled in the current and tugged at her. If some accident carried the cap away now, she would be pulled with it.

"Are you steady?" she asked.

"Everything is holding, but I'm a bit nervous about the anchors," he answered.

Pascale detached the cables to the cap and got into the branch channel and its still air. There, she wound the cables to the cap around outcroppings of rock and hammered in pitons to tie the ends down. Then she reattached her third and fourth safety lines.

"I've tied the two lines to the wall," she said. "Keep going."

Pascale watched the silhouette of the cap grow against the shape of the cave mouth. The turbulence rumbled like a coming storm as half of the cap showed in the opening. This was the most dangerous moment for Gabriel-Antoine. If any of the anchor points let go, if a cable caught him as it whipped by, even the armoured suit might not protect him.

"Careful!" Pascale said.

The thrumming grew loud and painful. She could barely hear him say, "I'm going to speed this part up."

The cap and frame tipped slowly inward, scraping against rock, and as it angled slowly into the cave it acted like a rudder, changing the flow of the atmospheric torrent, disturbing indentations and hollows that over centuries had collected sand, dust and pebbles. Silt sprayed into the middle of the current. Pascale picked up the slack by wrapping new coils around the outcroppings until the cap and its frame came to a kind of rest, bucking and bobbing horizontally in the current.

"We did it!" Pascale said. "We got one in." She'd helped make the plans, but so many things could have gone wrong, and still could, that just getting the cap into the cave against the current had seemed impossible.

Venus had not rejected them.

TWENTY-FOUR

Fabienne hadn't been on Victorine Corbeau's trawler since she'd been a teen learning to fly. The *Perchoir* at that time had felt brighter, one of the first trawlers she'd been on other than Narcisse's home. Fabienne hadn't grown any since then, but the *Perchoir* felt smaller, dirtier. Habitats aged; the woody parts cured in the acid while the rind darkened between hardening veins that eventually cracked and bled.

Victorine had long ago booted out her husband; for all Fabienne knew, he'd fallen into the clouds. Victorine's sons, Herman and Félix, had their own families and trawlers and herds, but Félix had come for today's meeting. Narcisse had brought Fabienne along, with Liette. They'd brought gifts. A sealed jar of stew—the jar being more valuable than the food. A bundle of trawler cabling, not their best. Some pain pills, which were always hard to get.

Victorine as host didn't need to give gifts, but she had to feed them, and her food was actually good. They ate crusty barley bread, with a vegetable paste made with spices and herbs Fabienne didn't know. More importantly, they almost disguised the omnipresent taste of sulphur. Angèle was going to be mad she missed the meal. Neither of them were great at leaching the sulphur out of food.

The five of them talked shop for a while, mostly Victorine and Liette, who knew each other from younger days. Félix was a sullen man, and Narcisse seemed to have trouble knowing where to break into the conversation between his sister and the host. Félix pulled out the *bagosse* and filled cleanly carved little cups. Gradually, Narcisse's cheeks reddened and he became more talkative, but it was Victorine who brought them to business.

"My boy didn't get to the Hudon woman," Victorine said. "She had protection."

"Government?" Liette said.

"Herman said it was the big D'Aquillon boy," Victorine said. "He's a *Sûreté* constable."

"George-Étienne D'Aquillon has his hand in everything," Narcisse said. "This house he's building with these political marriages… Having a cop in the family gives him someone to warn him about raids and investigations, maybe even get him out of fixes. The *Sûreté* are all corrupt thieves."

He took a sip.

"He's making computer chips," Narcisse said, "or his boys are. The chips work."

"Good," Victorine said, refilling his cup.

"He wants my real chips, my upcloud ones, in trade."

"Tell him to fuck himself," Félix said, his cheeks pinkening too.

"He'll give me a handful of his chips for one of mine. I can use them all to domesticate new trawlers. Then I get more ash, more oxygen."

A silence settled on them. Fabienne drank. The *bagosse* had a skunky undertaste.

"If he's making the trade, there's more in it for him than for me," Narcisse mused. "This house of his… It's got an engineer, it's got the Hudon woman and her special trawlers." Narcisse gave Fabienne a keep quiet look and then said, "And he's getting metal from somewhere. A lot of it. I think he's in cahoots with the government."

"We don't have an engineer," Victorine said. "We don't have a lady growing trawlers. And we're not making computer chips."

"We're being cut out of something big," Narcisse said. "If D'Aquillon's house idea takes off, anybody who doesn't join a house gets left behind. He's been talking to a lot of *coureurs*. And he's ahead of us already."

"Maybe he needs to be taken down a peg," Victorine said.

"They all do," Narcisse said. His expression tightened. "If he's getting metal from Gaschel, what's in it for her? It has to be something she couldn't say openly to *l'Assemblée*."

"How do you know they're dealing together?" Victorine said.

Narcisse hesitated.

"I saw it," Fabienne said. Her cousin's face swivelled to her warningly. Victorine noticed his reaction. "I was scouting and collecting ash and I stumbled onto the D'Aquillon habitat. I saw stuff being built."

"You landed and climbed onto their gantry?" Félix said dryly.

"It was a lot of metal," Fabienne said. "It didn't fit on their gantry. They were building something hanging under some trawlers."

"A plane out of trawler wood?" Victorine said.

"It was metal. A big disk. I don't know what it was for."

Tight-faced, Narcisse pulled out his data pad and opened an image and showed Victorine. Her eyebrows rose. She frowned and sipped at her *bagosse*. She almost said something, but stopped and looked at the image more closely. Félix leaned over her shoulder.

"There was no appropriation vote for that," Victorine said sarcastically. "*Crisse!*"

"They would have had to have melted down every black-market tool and part they've ever confiscated to make all that," Félix said. "Could Émile have been taking from the *Sûreté* evidence lock up?"

"Maybe it was funnelled through him, but to do drops like this," Victorine mused, "they would have been doing drops at night with emergency balloons, at times when they knew there would be less radar. The government had to have been in on it."

"So why is the government in the clouds looking around with radar anyway, then?" Félix said. "Did D'Aquillon double-cross them?"

"It's making the rest of us more cautious," Narcisse said. "Maybe they're keeping our heads down."

"If he double-crossed Gaschel, she's looking for her investment," Félix said.

Victorine frowned. "Whatever D'Aquillon is doing, he's got to sell or trade to someone, and with this amount of metal, it won't be to one of us. We can't afford it. Gaschel is his only customer, whether she's dirty or not."

"Maybe she lowballed him?" Fabienne suggested. "Now he wants more and maybe he's blackmailing her?"

She'd never said this before—it hadn't occurred to her before—but a lot of pieces fit better if she was right. It's what she would do, if she had Gaschel over a barrel.

"If they're hiding something together, there are things *we* can do together," Narcisse said. "Hush money at minimum, but probably more, depending on how important the secret is to them. But my family alone and your family alone are too easily picked off if we crossed an alliance of three families."

"A house..." Victorine said.

"Yeah," he said. "Other people are getting the idea too. Orphilie Ferlatte is talking with someone, I don't know who. Léo Bareilles is talking with Cédélise Deschênes to make a House of Ghosts."

She nodded slowly.

"Houses are an interesting cover too," Victorine said.

"What do you mean?"

"I know Willy and Juliette are in the House of Faeries, but maybe not everyone does," she said. "Suppose we do something, or steal something, and leave the blame on the House of Faeries, or the House of Styx, or the House of Ghosts. Who's to know? And D'Aquillon talks big and dreams big, but if he's partnered with Gaschel, he's eventually going to flame out."

"We'll be in a position to sift through the ashes and pick up the pieces," Narcisse said.

"I'm more interested in getting our cut before the fire. And maybe a House of Crows will get us there."

Narcisse lifted his glass, and Victorine echoed the toast.

TWENTY-FIVE

MARIE-PIER FOUND HER way to Tétreau's small office on the *Baie-Comeau*. Tétreau was a middling-height blond man in maybe his early thirties who gave the impression of officiousness, of someone who had things to do and places to be. She'd never met him, but had known of him as a bureaucrat in *la colonie*'s powerful engineering department. He was now associated with the president's office.

"*Mademoiselle* Hudon," he said, shaking her hand. "Water?"

She never said no to water. Talented fingers had carved the cups from trawler wood and polished them smooth to reveal the grainy vasculature. The water was leached of sulfur and tasted sweet.

"D'Aquillon said you wanted to talk about parole of some kind?" he asked. "Are you in trouble?"

"I need help in the upper cloud decks, to grow trawlers to replace some I lost in a storm. I need someone who knows their way around some biochemistry. Everyone is busy and the Labour Office doesn't have anyone to offer."

"What does this have to do with me? The loss of your trawlers, just when *la colonie* needed them, was bad luck for everyone. I'm not the

Labour Office."

"I can grow more with help. Lazare Jeangras is a pharmacy tech, but he's sitting in the *Petit Kamouraska*."

Tétreau pursed his lips and raised an eyebrow in gentle disbelief. She waited. He sighed.

"The *Petit Kamouraska* is holding the people who've been stealing parts from their habitats, medicine from stores, and falsifying documents," he said. "Our bank loans are in danger because these people got greedy."

"Jeangras will have his day in court. I'm not asking for him to be absolved, but right now he's a drain on the flotillas, just like everyone else in there. I can feed him, give him oxygen, and he can help me grow more trawlers. My brother and I can't do it all. You're a police lieutenant. Let him go for a bit."

"Judges give parole," Tétreau said, "and the judge overseeing the black marketeering cases is throwing the book at the lot of them."

Now it was her turn to show her dubiousness.

"I didn't approach the judge. I came to you. Let him go for a while."

"Release him?"

"You control a lot of stuff. Release him for... medical care. Or because he's in danger of getting beat up. Or just lose his paperwork, I don't care. *La colonie* needs those trawlers to handle overcrowding. I can get a couple more ready in two years, but if I don't have to do all the growth factor biochemistry myself, we can cut that to a year, and probably grow an extra trawler to boot."

"You *had* your trawlers ready, and the moment *la colonie* was going to take them, you lost them."

She didn't know where he was going with this. Did he suspect something?

"Am I responsible for the weather?" she demanded with heat. "On *Venus?*"

"I'll take up your idea with the Labour Office and the judge."

"Meaning 'no.'"

"Meaning I don't have control in this case."

"I think the *Sûreté* has as much control as they want to take in any situation."

Tétreau put away the jar of water.

"My big trawlers make steady oxygen," she said. "I give most of it to *la colonie,* but I can come up with the occasional tank for you. And the same with trawler cable. A few dozen kilos a month is nothing to sneeze at."

Tétreau looked up something on his pad. He read and she waited, finishing her water in the awkward silence.

"I knew I remembered Jeangras's name," he said. "He's at the center of a lot of black market activities."

Tétreau put down the pad fussily, and shut it off. His straight-spined officiousness was back.

"I'm not stupid. If Jeangras is down there, he and you will be moving black-market goods around."

"Through the upper cloud decks?" she said with all the derision she could muster.

"You're setting up something off the grid," he said. "But *this* isn't going to be off the grid, and it isn't going to be free. I'll take a forty percent cut of everything moving through your habitats."

"That's not—" she tried to say, but he wasn't done talking.

"I need to know where your habitat is at all times. And I'll check in personally every couple of weeks and inspect everything to make sure I'm not getting short-changed. If at any time I can't find him—*or* your home—there'll be two arrest warrants going public."

"This is ridiculous!"

"Take it or leave it," he said.

TWENTY-SIX

Fitting the frame of the first cap into place took Pascale and Gabriel-Antoine twenty-three hours. Pascale had done hard work all her life and had invented solutions to problems for years. She thought she'd been ready. But her aching body, the frustration, the failed and repeated tries, the moments of hopelessness had overwhelmed her. Gabriel-Antoine was a dynamo, solving many of the problems she couldn't, or coming up with workarounds with her. It was a reassuring, replenishing kind of closeness.

After a lot of small modifications, the frame fit snugly into the outer rock face, blocking the cave's main current. Wind still whined and moaned through small branch channels, around the edges of the main cap, and through the wind turbine embedded in the cap, but the pressure in the cave was more than eighty atmospheres lower than outside, steadying between ten and twelve atmospheres. The decompression worked exactly like in any refrigeration system, and the apparent temperature of the atmosphere dropped more than three hundred degrees to around the one-fifties. They'd hoped it would drop below a hundred degrees, but the cave walls radiated heat like an oven.

They'd accomplished something extraordinary. They'd cooled the cave, set up the first wind generator for electricity, paying for it in bruises, bumps and exhaustion. Venus had not tithed them. Did the goddess welcome the company? Did she, like Pascale, want someone to see her as she really was?

At the end of those twenty-three hours, Pascale and Gabriel-Antoine clipped their suits to cables from the ceiling and slept for a few hours, while their suits recharged on the wind turbine. Pascale had strange dreams. Her fitfully sleeping mind turned the moan of wind into something haunted and lamenting and reaching without touching.

They woke to find their suit batteries full again, although more than a few fuses had tripped. The wind turbine generated electricity, but the current was dirty, rising and falling. The turbines were homemade, although the trawler cabling they used for wiring might also have been damaged on the way down. Eventually they would have to build real transformers and fuses, but that was for later.

That second day, they lowered the other two caps deeper into the cave, and installed one into the throat of the cave. When it was in place and its wind turbine off, the pressure beyond it fell almost to zero. They hadn't gone to the wormhole yet—there was too much to build and too little time to look at the stars—but a cold vacuum enclosed them from the second cap onward. The cave walls creaked and crackled and occasionally even popped explosively as the stone outgassed.

They hadn't talked much during the day, beyond the diction of their strange technical communication, helping each other in the right moment, passing work from one to another like jugglers. It was a kind of closeness, but not the closeness they'd had. They ended the second day eating the last protein paste in their suits, sleeping suspended off the baking floor in the space between the first and second caps, twitchy from stimulants and hunger. They could recharge the oxygen in their suits every five to six hours, and their suits could carry two days of food, but they couldn't open them to resupply until they reached a safe habitat. They'd known they would have to go without food for a day or two, and it wasn't pleasant; and any longer than that would be dangerous.

While they'd been working on the complex installation problems, two of Gabriel-Antoine's little robots had been building a simple heat-resistant, pressure-sealed box—a single room. Gabriel-Antoine and Pascale had considered all the habitat designs in open-source engineering texts, comparing each one against the materials they had on the surface, which were few, and their needs, which were very different from those facing the authors. Habitats on the moon or the asteroids had to deal with intense cold and zero pressure, while Pascale and Gabriel-Antoine had the opposite problem; habitats in space environments needed to protect the inhabitants from radiation, but that wasn't a concern here. They'd adapted blueprints as best they could, optimizing for ease of building with dumb robots. By the end of the second day, the robots had finished welding and sealing the walls, but activating the airlock and the environmental systems was slow, finicky work that didn't get done.

Pascale woke on the third day crusty-eyed. It was exciting to be under the surface of Venus, to be building a bridge to the stars, but the groggy tiredness, the waning strength of her arms and the loss of intimacy with Gabriel-Antoine made the world feel prickly. She thought he was getting testier too, but couldn't even be sure if she was hearing right. They installed the third cap, losing two hours when they found that their survey had missed a small outcropping that they had to laboriously chisel down.

While doing this, a finger-sized stone was driven by outgassing into Gabriel-Antoine's helmet, hard enough to chip the heat-reflective aluminum. They tried to repair it, but found that he needed to take it off first, which they couldn't do until they'd finished the habitat.

At the end of their third day, the third cave-blocking airlock had been installed and their rudimentary habitat was pressurized with breathable air. They would eventually expand it, but for the foreseeable future, this space—enough for two people and all their tools, work benches, and life support—would be all they had. This would be where they would repair their suits, do work that required fine control, and rethink any plans or designs that fell afoul of the reality under the surface.

They opened their suits. The cool air contrasted with the rank, sweaty smell of their bodies. Pascale felt the long stubble on her face self-consciously. This was the longest she'd gone without shaving, and where once she might have been repelled by it, it was temporary—she knew who she was now. Gabriel-Antoine watched her out of the corner of his eye. She swallowed hard and pulled a bottle of water from their supplies. Her hands shook with hunger, as did Gabriel-Antoine's as he rifled for food—real, solid food, after the paste of their first two days.

Pascale went back to her dive suit. Inside the torso shell were a few inner pockets. She pulled out the bag of handmade pills and took one. She hadn't been able to for three days. She hoped it hadn't slowed down any of the changes. She found his eyes on her as she put down the water bottle. She frowned and went back to uncrating the food.

Pascale eventually drifted to the corner, hung her hammock and collapsed into it. Hoping for his acceptance felt hopeless. After a time, Gabriel-Antoine followed. He looked at her stretched out on the hammock, then looked away, and she realized she'd been crying. She felt like she had nothing left to give or fight with, and that the pills hadn't done anything. She desperately wanted them to have some effect. She was losing Gabriel-Antoine, in trade for something she believed in but couldn't see. She wiped her face and sat up, as if to speak to him in a way they hadn't in a while.

"I was saving up a joke," she said, "to tease you with when we got the suits done, but I didn't say anything because I hadn't felt like laughing."

"What was it?" he said. He stood with his back to her as he put paste on his toothbrush. On the *Causapscal-des-Profondeurs,* while he brushed his teeth, she used to sneak up behind him and hug him and they'd both laugh, like it was really funny, when really it had only been a transparent excuse to grab each other.

"It wasn't very good. It's actually only a little funny if you were in love."

"I still want to hear it."

"I was going to say that you're finally my knight in shining armor."

She'd meant to make it sound light and funny, but her voice broke on 'shining.' Gabriel-Antoine leaned on the little table.

"I would have laughed," he said finally.

She wiped her hot eyes and looked away.

"And I would have been happy," she said. "Stupidly happy."

He wasn't doing anything, not brushing his teeth, not going to his hammock. He just stood there with his back to her.

"It hurts all the time," she said softly. "I'm lonely. Not *alone*—I don't want anyone else—but it feels like my heart is suffocating." He hadn't moved. She swallowed and wiped her eyes with her shirt sleeve and pressed on. "I understand that who I am is a brick wall in the middle of our road. I understand you're mad about it. And I'm slowly... understanding the idea that maybe you're not my forever knight in shining armor, and that maybe I shouldn't have dreamed fairy tales."

She hugged herself and then tried to dry her wet cheeks on her palms. She needed a deep, shaky breath.

"But if you're not my forever knight, maybe you're still the hero for me for right now, and maybe I'm the princess for you for right now. And maybe at the end of the adventure, you'll find someone right and so will I. And maybe if we're lucky, we'll look back on right now and we'll remember it and smile. Maybe you're the first love that got away from me."

He turned and neared, close enough to touch. She wanted to.

"I'm not going away," he said.

"You already have, *chéri*."

"You left me!" His cheeks were wet.

"I'm sorry," she said, taking his hands. "I'm sorry I wasn't what you wanted... what you needed."

"You are."

She shook her head. "The real me is someone else, and you already said you don't want her."

He rested his forehead against hers. His shoulders were shaking. She stood and reached around to hug him. He held her tight.

"We're just ghosts now," she said, "hugging in the dark."

TWENTY-SEVEN

In the lots for order of speeches in *l'Assemblée,* Marie-Pier had drawn a time near the end of the session, which was still weeks away. But the little quiet place where her hunches came from told her that events were moving quickly, and if she didn't make a move, events would overtake her. So she talked to Maëlle Guillot from the *Escuminac*. Maëlle wasn't particularly friendly, but her habitat needed more oxygen because of an envelope leak that wouldn't be patched for months. For several hundred litres of oxygen, Maëlle gave Marie-Pier her scheduled spot.

Each week, rows of folding seats, little ceremonial fences, tables and benches, flags and bunting came to fill the assembly hall, turning it from a sports gymnasium into the seat of legislative authority for Venus. It smelled of sweat from whatever teams had been using it a few hours before, despite the vents churning near the high ceiling.

Marie-Pier knew most everyone: Barnabé Chambeau represented the *Petit Kamouraska,* Casimir Daigle spoke for the *Montée de Corte-Réal,* Ovide Dubé from the *Lac-Édouard* looked bored already. The clerks who kept the official minutes and the order paper readied the front table. The bank had an observer in the public seating, an Anglo man called Nasmith; interestingly, Tétreau was sitting with him. He spotted Marie-Pier and their eyes held for long moments before breaking off. Gaschel entered with her chief of staff Labourière, and Marie-Pier found herself half-smiling. *The bitch* came to mind now whenever she thought of Gaschel; George-Étienne's habits were rubbing off on Marie-Pier.

The session began with tedious financial reporting prior to a vote on Gaschel's quarterly budget. The finances never seemed convincing, and *la colonie* always seemed a couple of quarters away from disaster. Their whole Venusian project, all the blood and sweat and death they'd spent to get to the precarious here and now, always seemed to be reduced to mortgages and ownerships and near-defaults.

And while George-Étienne was sometimes overwrought in his resentments, she didn't think he was wrong about what would happen if the Axis Mundi became known. The bridge to the stars could be a priceless piece of collateral for *la colonie,* a magic ticket out of their current financial problems, but without the right vision, it would work once or twice, buying them some more habitats and medicines, without ever changing the essential situation of Venus. Their fragile little nation wouldn't be suddenly self-sufficient. It wouldn't run differently. People wouldn't *think* differently, not the way the House of Styx thought about it, struggled to think about it. Very dimly she could see a new way to be a people, even if the details were hard to make out. There was a passion to release. They'd each immigrated to this new world for a reason, for their own dream. Venus was more than a tragedy and it was more than today's order paper.

The items proceeded, one by one, and just before the first break, Marie-Pier was finally called. She rose and went to the nearby lectern. The looks she received from colleagues and acquaintances were a mix of curiosity and boredom. Gaétane Bolduc idly recorded everything—she recorded a lot of things, and transmitted them later like news if they were any good.

Fingers crossed that Marie-Pier had a show for her now.

"Thank you, Mister Speaker. I want to ask *la présidente* about a growing crisis in the flotillas," Marie-Pier began. "*La présidente* has for some months been pursuing a policy of widespread incarceration, and we now have over a hundred in detention."

The hall went silent in most parts, with soft grumbling from some quarters. Gaétane sat straighter, focusing her camera on Marie-Pier.

"Every person in detention right now is a mouth to feed, but they don't grow food, or fix solar cells, or build new machines. *La présidente*'s policies make sure none of them can contribute anything, because the government decided to attack the symptoms of a crisis of shortages. We *know* we're short of parts, we *know* trading amongst ourselves is a temporary solution. Is it the best? Of course not. But the policies of this government brought us to this point, and the choice to incarcerate so many is not going to fix the root causes.

"*Madame Présidente,* I've heard you use that word, 'detention,' but that's a word for a short-term, administrative process. What we have now is long-term incarceration without justice. *La colonie* doesn't have the judges to try so many people in good order, nor do we have lawyers to make sure everyone is fairly tried. Everyone you've labelled a detainee will be there for a long time, will be a convict in all but name, while *la colonie* misses out on everything they could have made or built or grown."

A rumble of voices grew, some supportive, most objecting. She had another forty seconds before her microphone would be cut off.

"This is a social crisis created by government overreach, by austerity policies not endorsed by the people. Large scale, industrial justice copied from Earth doesn't work here. For that matter, neither does the police force the government has been building. We've lived within a system of social consent for six decades, and yet Gaschel is taking us down a path guided by the way the rest of the solar system works—or doesn't work. I call on my fellow representatives to demand the release of detainees on parole. We need them today."

She finished with one second to spare as the clamour of voices, against and for, rose over her.

TWENTY-EIGHT

Pascale and Gabriel-Antoine walked through the near-vacuum of the last cave chamber; the one containing their habitat and the wormhole. They wore their regular survival suits from the cloud decks. Discolored and patched, they could nonetheless handle several atmospheres of pressure difference in either direction, and the gloves were more dextrous than the mechanized ones in the hard suits. The key modification was an additional layer of heat-resistant soles to their boots; the survival suits could routinely withstand a hundred and twenty degrees, but the floor of the cave, despite the vacuum, had not cooled much below four hundred yet. One day, if all went well, they could install insulation on all the cave walls, but that was a luxury for the future.

The dark circle of the wormhole mouth and its smoky, eye-watering borders loomed at the end of the cave. Even under powerful spotlights, they saw only faint shimmers of a dark, indefinite surface. They marvelled at it, each wrapped in their own feeling of wonder. Weeks ago, they'd talked long into the night about it. Gabriel-Antoine had been fascinated by what its existence said about the cosmos. Pascale was fascinated by what its existence said about Venus. And their passions were both right.

They opened the valves of the turbines so that a gentle carbon dioxide wind tumbled out the Axis Mundi. Gabriel-Antoine had taken a small parachute and attached a compact camera to its top, along with a Geiger counter and a small radio antenna. The parachute flowered in the steady wind, billowing towards the inscrutable face of the Axis Mundi.

"Give it a little more," Gabriel-Antoine said.

Pascale opened the valve on the turbine until the wind in the chamber created a pressure of about one atmosphere. The parachute bloomed wider, its suspension lines tightening enthusiastically, pulling at the eyelets on floor and ceiling. Slowly, Gabriel-Antoine paid out line and the parachute inched towards the wormhole. Pascale pulled a pad from an outer pocket of her suit and plugged it into the cable from the camera.

The top of the parachute entered the wormhole and vanished, as if sinking into water. A circle of darkness appeared to pool on the interior of the parachute, and grow. Gabriel-Antoine stopped paying out line, his voice thick with excitement.

"Get some pictures of that. We can analyze them later."

Pascale neared the wormhole until she reached the end of the cable anchoring her suit. Secured, she took pictures of the strange effect with a camera and then retreated.

They watched the camera display on the pad together as Gabriel-Antoine paid out more cable and the surface of the wormhole swallowed the parachute. The pad still showed only darkness from the camera feed on the front of the parachute. The antenna heard smears of radio and microwaves, and the Geiger counter detected pattering x-rays, but otherwise not much more radiation than they would have detected beyond Venus's ionosphere. Something fluttered in Pascale's stomach, the anticipation of uncovering a wonderful secret, the promise of seeing a dream confirmed. She held her breath as the time lengthened and a small but hard fear grew that the bridge to the stars was gone, that there was only darkness.

Then, light.

"Stars!" Pascale said, grinning and tilting the pad to Gabriel-Antoine.

Points of light spattered the screen. The view wavered as the parachute trembled gently from the buffeting of escaping carbon dioxide.

"It's all true," Gabriel-Antoine said.

"You knew it was."

"I knew in my *head*..."

Pascale had lived through Marthe's disbelief, through Pa's reluctant acceptance. She didn't begrudge anyone time to accept the impossible. The idea of a wormhole came with its own cognitive dissonance—how couldn't it? Pascale herself didn't know what to do with all the philosophical, scientific and political baggage. But she'd *believed* from first sight. Maybe she had an easier time understanding that Venus had a secret heart made of stars, a hidden self that needed to be found and understood.

"It can't be natural," Gabriel-Antoine said. "Someone built it." She could hear his long, pregnant breath in her helmet earpiece. "We're not alone in the universe."

"We're not."

"Even if the builders went extinct, just knowing that intelligent life existed once changes everything."

"I hope they're still alive," Pascale said softly, "and that they're still out there, and that they'll be happy to see us use their lost wormhole. *Maman* used to tell stories about faeries in the clouds; what if we find faeries in the stars?"

"They bent space-time, Pascale. We don't even have good *theories* for how to do that. They might be able to manipulate negative mass, negative energy, exotic matter... Whoever made this wormhole is so far beyond us that we're like cavemen."

Pascale laughed a bit and then when Gabriel-Antoine realized what he'd said, he chuckled too.

"We're not alone in the universe," he breathed in a marvelling exhalation.

Pascale wanted to take his hand, to be together for this moment, for this proof, but she didn't feel she could anymore. There was too much between them now, and there was something profoundly sad in that, the blow cushioned only by the vastness of her awe. Then, tentatively, she felt Gabriel-Antoine's hand brushing hers, clasping it. He didn't look at her, but they breathed there in silent contemplation, soaking in the moment, neither of them alone.

TWENTY-NINE

WHEN THE PAPERWORK was done—or lost—by Tétreau, and the *Tourbillon-des-Vents* was within flight range, Marie-Pier and Lazare found themselves in their survival suits on the roof of the *Petit Kamouraska* at dusk. Tétreau was there too, not speaking, but watching them from a distance with crossed arms, as if to suggest *if you both aren't in the cloud decks soon, you'll both be in jail.*

"We'd better go, Lazare."

Marie-Pier had brought him a set of the stubbier wing-packs designed for the hotter, higher pressures of the cloud decks. Behind his faceplate, Lazare's skin had visibly whitened as he attached the harness. Marie-Pier had known Lazare Jeangras for a long time, but they were not close. The entirety of their relationship was based on the economics of trade, and that they each trusted the other not to rat them out. His tightly pressed lips might have been resolve or fear. Lazare had been in the cloud decks before, when he was a pilot, but he'd reminded her again and again that that had been decades ago.

With furled wings, they dropped from the overhanging platform at the edge of *Petit Kamouraska*'s roof. If Lazare made any sound, she didn't hear it. She gave small directional instructions as they fell, at sixtieth *rang* they extended their wings, biting the wind deeply, creating weight again as they levelled out and glided down through the red-brown acid clouds.

"Are you alright?" she asked within the wide stretch of clear air at *Grande Allée*.

After a moment, his thin voice came back. "Okay."

"We're close," she said encouragingly.

The *Coureur des Tourbillons* floated four kilometers higher today than normal, bobbing in stately stillness at fifty-fourth *rang,* wrapped in the browned cotton of the middle cloud deck. Other trawler heads were fuzzily visible in the distance, their cables invisible in the mist.

Lazare wasn't a bad flyer for the depths. It was often challenging for upclouders to adjust to the sensitivity of their wings here, where every shift in angle bit deep into thick cloud, compared to the thinness of flotilla height. Lazare swooped in, stalling a bit too far away from the netting beneath the *Coureur des Tourbillons.* He caught himself painfully in the net only after falling a couple of meters more than he should have. She swept in and landed beside him, catching the netting with hands and feet at the same time.

"Good?" she said.

"Just need a second."

"The decks aren't friendly to those who don't choose to live here."

"That's not promising."

"I didn't mean it like that. You're here now."

"I didn't choose it."

"I know. Come on. The pressure change is easier to get used to in a habitat."

They clambered up the netting to the neat, railed gantry, and cycled through the airlock to her home. Maxime and Florian, initially wary of the stranger, nonetheless darted in to hug Marie-Pier as soon as she was out of her suit. Marie-Pier's brother was out measuring the growth on the next generation of experimental trawlers, so the boys had a lot to say and were excitedly awake. They brought Lazare and Marie-Pier food and water. Lazare seemed gloomy and made a face as he ate. Maxime took the hint and pulled his younger brother back to their room.

"Nice kids."

She smiled.

"How long am I going to be here?" he asked.

"I can't see how the judges could see every case in less than months, but I also don't know how *la colonie* can keep so many people detained."

"Not really an answer."

"I didn't make this situation," she said, pulling away their empty plates and refilling his water. "Gaschel wants to break the black market."

"Fuck that bitch."

"We're out now."

He stood. He was taking deep breaths and sweating, as if he wasn't getting used to the thickness and closeness of the air. "Great!" he said, swinging his arms to take in the habitat interior. "Here I am in the dark."

"You're out and I'm out and we can rebuild the black market," she said. "We have to. Stuff will start falling apart if we don't."

"From ten kilometers beneath the flotillas?"

"Deeper, if we have to," she said, opening a cabinet where mildly corroded oxygen tanks were neatly rowed, connected by homemade hoses to the vasculature of the trawler. "We've got oxygen to trade, and a lot of trawler fiber for people to build their habitats with, so that they can free up metal for other stuff."

"That'll only go so far. You were trading that with me already."

She signalled him to come closer, to another cabinet that Marc had lovingly built with hand-carved panels and a door with wire hinges. Inside were rows and rows of sacks. She hefted one and took it to the table where he grumpily opened it. He stuck his hand in and drew out fine, shiny grains.

"Is this that volcanic ash you were selling me with metals in it?" He frowned. "How did you separate it out? You ground it?"

"Some of the deeper *coureurs* have found ways to get this metal-enriched ash," she lied. George-Étienne and Jean-Eudes had been busy grinding those probes, finer and finer, to separate out the metals. "They're willing to trade. Kilos and kilos of it."

"Kilos I could trade to some of the shops that do work on the side. They can melt and recast it. But getting it ten kilometers straight up… Hell, how do you do a trade with no one noticing, or the wind not blowing your stuff away?"

"*Coureurs* do drop-and-rise trades all the time amongst themselves, using balloons with semi-dumb drone engines," she said. "They do it on trust and reputation. If you short-change someone, it gets around fast."

"It's going to look suspicious if black market trades happen every time your habitat is in range of a good glide path."

"I've got a big herd and can run trawlers far ahead or behind," she said, pulling a flat, hard box out of the cabinet. She opened it on the table. Ugly, vaguely misshapen squares were tied down with twine. "We're also making computer chips. They're crude, but they'll run repetitive processes—simple steering, altitude control, pressure maintenance and so on."

Lazare untied one and eyed it skeptically. "How reliable are they?"

"Good enough for down here. They keep herds from dispersing. I also use them in my habitat. We've made enough of them that on critical systems, I've put in redundant ones."

"If they're not reliable…" he began, but his voice trailed off, as his eyes narrowed.

"Are you thinking of where you could use some extra chips?" she asked.

He grimaced, made to put the chip back, and then looked at it again. "Why not give this to the government?" he asked.

"You think any *coureur* would trust or trade with the government after the way they've been treated? Or that Gaschel and her kind would give anything to the *coureurs* that they actually wanted? She's more likely to just commandeer the chips. The *coureurs* are like anyone else in the black market; they've just put a lot more distance between themselves and the government."

He turned the chip in his fingers.

"I can't make you love it down here, Lazare, but this is a chance for us to cash in while we make something bigger for people. Used to be there were a dozen black market nodes—now, I think only Graveline and Couillard didn't get arrested yet, and they've gone pretty quiet. We have a chance to take as much of the market as we can handle, and I've got some protection."

"What do you mean?"

"Tétreau, the police lieutenant. He let you out. He knows that you'll run another black market node, and he wants a cut. So we run an operation that looks like what he'd expect, and give him his cut from that. In the meantime, we run something bigger out of sight. The *coureurs* can't be busted by a police raid the way you could up there. We can stash stock in any trawler, at any distance from where we are here."

"You're thinking big."

"We have to. And we can. Connections between the flotilla and the *coureurs* require people who walk in both worlds. My marriage to George-Étienne D'Aquillon makes me one of them. Now you're here too."

"And my daughter?"

"If we can bribe Tétreau, maybe we can get her down here to help."

He was pensive. He had only the one daughter, and the one grandson.

"You raised yours down here?"

"Their whole lives. It's not easy, but you saw them. They're good boys. And happy."

"Let's see, then."

THIRTY

Présidente Gaschel stood at the transparent wall, looking out through a meter of hydroponic gardens between the two envelopes of the *Baie-Comeau*. The watery white sunlight felt cold today. Labourière was late. The report was late. She wriggled her fingers and opened and closed a fist as she massaged her wrist. Her joints were sore, probably the beginnings of arthritis. She hadn't bothered seeing her doctor about it. She could diagnose it as well as he could, and there weren't treatments here anyway. Her assistant Cinthia's voice sounded from her desk.

"*Monsieur* Labourière to see you, *Madame la Présidente*."

She waved her hand and the glass door opened. He entered with a guardedly optimistic expression. She let herself feel some tentative relief as they sat by a small meeting table. When the door closed, he grinned and handed her his data pad. It was the latest loan progress report from the bank. All the indicators she needed to be green were green, especially the collateral inspections.

"They bought it," she said in a low voice, shoulders slumping in relief.

"It felt close, but we probably had another hour or two."

She snorted. An hour or two. That was cutting it real close. The *colonie*'s loans were heavily leveraged. The last round of loans had only been approved by putting up as collateral almost everything left floating in *la colonie*. And things still broke down. And black marketeers took parts out, to trade for other things, like oxygen she couldn't always provide. And the *Causapscal-des-Vents* had sunk with all its metals and equipment. The quarterly loan review could have triggered an interest rate increase, and *la colonie* had no reserve. And they couldn't pass the review, not without cheating. It had been her idea, but Labourière had pulled it off by secretly moving equipment and parts from habitats that had already been inspected to ones that had not, making it look like more habitats were functioning as they should. She slumped in her chair.

"*Tabarnak*," she said softly. "We have three months to find replacements for all those missing pieces."

He shook his head. "Even if we got everything back from the black market, we ourselves have repurposed so many things that there just isn't enough. We'll have to do this shell game again in three months."

"Every time there's a bigger chance of getting caught."

"Too bad Woodward isn't bribable."

Gaschel laughed derisively. "I'm sure she has a price. We just can't afford it. We're holding together a dream with string and tape and wishful thinking."

"In fifty years, Venus will be shipping exports across the solar system. Immigrants will be knocking on our door."

It was a good dream. A beautiful dream. Neither of them would live to see it, but they could do everything in their power to propel Venus into the future. They could midwife history.

Gaschel heard the disturbance outside her office and looked up.

"You don't have an appointment," her assistant Cinthia said loudly. "*La présidente* is already with someone."

A man with wild salt-and-pepper hair, in what looked like a *coureur* survival suit, made his way around the assistant's desk. Cinthia was on the phone, calling for help. The man beat on the clear plastic doors, pointing at Gaschel. He looked back and yelled at Cinthia.

"Tell her that if she doesn't see me, I'm going to the press to blow her whole scheme wide open!"

Gaschel stood, as did Labourière. She buzzed the lock on the door and it opened.

"I can hear you, *monsieur,*" Gaschel said. "What can I help you with?"

The man was of indeterminate age, forty to sixty. Sweat, oil and dirt grimed his face over blotchy acid scars.

"I knew you'd cave once you were discovered," he said. He pointed with his data pad.

"Who are you?"

"Your secret slush fund," he said. "Embezzlement with the D'Aquillons."

"I don't understand a word you're saying." She looked helplessly at Cinthia, who held up two fingers. Two minutes until security could get here. "Why don't you tell me what you think is wrong?"

"I want to know what it's worth to you."

"I don't know what you're talking about, so I can't say. But I don't have a slush fund, so it can't be worth much."

The man's lips tightened.

"With whom am I speaking?" she said.

"Narcisse Mignaud," he said. "I have copies of all my evidence hidden away with people who will release them if I don't make it out of here safely in the next hour."

"Of course you'll leave safely. The sooner you do, the sooner I can get back to my meeting."

Mignaud turned the pad to her, but then thought better of it, and pulled it back.

"You might not want him here, listening in," Mignaud said, nodding to Labourière.

"He can hear anything you have to say," she said.

"It's your political funeral." Mignaud swiped open a grainy picture before turning it to her.

She couldn't make it out.

"Are these trawlers?" There were shapes beneath them, like plates or pieces of construction material, hanging in the mist.

Labourière craned his neck to look with her. "Why are they so close together?"

"Don't play dumb," Mignaud said, reaching over with a dirty finger to swipe, showing the subject from a different angle. The scale was hard to make out, but it looked like four big trawlers in formation. As she toggled between pictures, she saw something like struts between them, like a harness. A confusing shape hung beneath it.

"What is this? When were these taken?"

The first glimmers of doubt began to show in Mignaud's expression. "*You* know."

"When were these taken?" she repeated.

"Is this part of the layout of a D-class habitat?" Labourière asked, tracing a finger over the image.

"Like you don't know it's the *Causapscal-des-Vents*," Mignaud said irritably. "It couldn't have survived if you hadn't help them drop it."

"Of course I didn't drop it," Gaschel said sharply. "It was collateral on a loan."

She shook her head in wondering anger. She pulled out a small ruler and compared some lines across the blurry images.

"The ratios fit a D-class frame," she said to Labourière. "If this is the *Causapscal-des-Vents,* then they caught it—which means they knew when and where it was going down. And if they knew that, then they must have sabotaged it."

"What are they doing down there?" Labourière said. "They aren't just stripping it for scraps, they're building something. What?"

Mignaud withdrew the pad and held it close to his chest. He stroked his moustache as if trying to tame it into his beard. His look was confused calculation.

"I need coordinates and time, *monsieur,*" Gaschel said. "You've caught someone committing a crime."

"Either you're a good actor, or you had the wool pulled over your eyes," Mignaud said. "The *coureurs* figured it out without all your fancy expensive equipment and now you're just 'give me coordinates'? I don't think so."

Two beefy constables of the *Sûreté* appeared in the doorway, batons in hand. She held up a hand. Mignaud followed her eyes, but his expression remained defiant. His greasy forefinger punctuated his next words.

"You're either in cahoots with the D'Aquillons and need to find out how much I know before you shut me up," he accused, "or you're clueless and need me to lead you to them. Either way, it's going to cost you."

"What are you looking for, *monsieur*?" Gaschel said.

"I think a few cases of engine parts, food, and heat-resistant circuits will do me just fine for the information I have," he said. "But if you want me and my insurance to keep quiet, we're talking medicine, water, nitrogen. And if you need coordinates on the surface? Well, make me an offer."

"Why would I need coordinates on the surface?" Gaschel said.

Mignaud's face twitched in a smile that looked like it couldn't decide between doubtful and gleeful.

"'Why would I need coordinates on the surface?'" Mignaud repeated mockingly. "I hope you're a good actor, because if all of this really happened behind your back, *la colonie* is truly and rightly screwed."

"What could the D'Aquillons make out of the *Causapscal-des-Vents* for the surface?" Labourière said. "None of the computer hardware *or* software can work long at those temperatures and pressures. Humans can't either. And there's no reason to go—there are no useful metals."

"Duvieusart went to the surface," Mignaud said.

"One crazy *coureur* doing an hour of extreme tourism isn't what I'm talking about," Labourière said.

Mignaud looked close to losing his patience.

"You have more information," Gaschel said placatingly. "Let's see what it is and we'll see what we have to trade. We might not be able to provide everything you're asking for, but I think we can meet you somewhere in the middle."

Mignaud shifted his attention to her again. Then he flipped through images on his pad and showed her another. A grainy picture of the surface showed sharp lines of shadowless basaltic stone, broken and fragmented by hundreds of millions of years of expansion and contraction of the crust. It could have been anywhere. But something quite obviously unnatural and out of place was there too—it looked like boxes, metal beams, some kind of metallic disk.

The picture had been cropped so tightly that even if he'd given it to her, no one on her team would be able to figure out the location on the surface. And looking for it with radar and infrared wouldn't work unless someone down there was stupid enough to transmit radio or do something much hotter than four hundred and sixty degrees. But *la colonie* didn't have that many cameras, nor any way to put them into place if they had. Was this where the radioactive signals were coming from? Had the D'Aquillons found a vein of radioisotopes, its emissions maybe shielded by lead sulfide snows?

"Who else knows about this?" Gaschel asked.

"People I can buy off for the right price," Mignaud said.

"Get them to shut up and make sure this goes no further," she said. "We can talk about a price for that, the information and the coordinates."

They haggled for a few minutes more, then Labourière signed requisition orders for Mignaud for a third of what they'd agreed to, with the other two-thirds to come when Mignaud brought better resolution copies of the pictures. When he'd finally gone, Cinthia cleared an hour of Gaschel's schedule and Labourière closed the door, returning to the meeting table.

"*Câlisse*!" she swore. "*Câlisse de crisse de tabarnak*! Those idiots! Those goddamn idiots. They stole from all of us. They did irreparable damage to every piece of metal and electronics on that habitat. People don't even have enough *oxygen*, and these goddamn thieves stole *tons* of metal."

Labourière regarded her. "D'Aquillon's own plan killed his daughter."

"How do we even know Marthe is dead?" Gaschel demanded. "She could be down there right now, laughing at all of us. I'm going to nail all of them to the goddamn wall, in front of everyone. They risked all of us, the whole *colonie*."

A silence fell on them. Labourière sometimes doodled when he thought, and he began now to sketch the structure on the surface. She pulled it towards her and looked at it for a while.

"What's down there?" she asked.

"Steel will survive forever, but all the squishy stuff, including computer chips, will melt or cook. Stirling engines can only cool things for so long. Refrigeration systems need a power source and a sink for the excess heat. Maybe they know enough to make a crude reactor for electricity? Better that than weapons."

It had been a rhetorical question, but Labourière had his own way of thinking things through, which she appreciated.

"Marthe D'Aquillon represented the Phocas family in *l'Assemblée*," Gaschel said, "and now Marie-Pier Hudon is representing the Phocas family and the D'Aquillons. Your sources said the Phocas engineer is gone and that Émile D'Aquillon is staying on his habitat. The D'Aquillon family doesn't have the engineering skills or tools to disassemble a habitat and make something else. They're mechanics, I thought. Phocas might, though. Something certainly illegal—and possibly treasonous—is happening."

"What are we going to do, go down and arrest them?"

"Damn right we are. Mignaud can't survive down there. We can't either. The bank probably has some drone equipment that could do the job."

"The D'Aquillons might just have automated stuff on the surface, or remote controlled machines," Labourière said. "Wherever they are, the D'Aquillons can't survive forever in the clouds without resupply."

"With that much metal, they can trade on the black market among *coureurs* for months. Years. And buy loyalty."

"We have to find out where they're getting their supplies and hit them there," he said. His eyebrows rose, he became more animated. "Émile D'Aquillon told Tétreau that if he was looking for something in the clouds, that *coureurs* preferred the northern hemisphere because the southern hemisphere is unlucky."

"Then when we get the coordinates from Mignaud, we'll have a good sense as to whose side Émile D'Aquillon is on."

THIRTY-ONE

After another fitful sleep and another round of excited planning, Pascale and Gabriel-Antoine found themselves in the last chamber, examining the wormhole again. Its surface seemed two-dimensional, without depth. Peeking behind it revealed only hot, black rock. The cave itself was not perfectly circular, so some of the Axis's edges intersected the walls in a way that looked like they were penetrating the gray-black basalt. They wondered if that was why the wormhole didn't move. There were gaps between the ceiling of the cave and the highest edge of the wormhole mouth, but neither of them dared touch the edges yet. The wormhole must be robust, but they didn't want to risk damaging it in any way. Gabriel-Antoine's magnetometer gave inconclusive readings near the surface and weirder ones at its edges—sometimes they detected a magnetic field and sometimes not. A faint hint of additional gravity around the edges showed itself too, pulling a pendulum bob off the perpendicular. But many other scientific tests gave nonsensical answers, or none at all. It might take decades to even begin to understand the Axis Mundi. They would have better questions to ask once they'd seen the other side.

So they stood in front of the wormhole mouth, clipped by long cables to steel eyelets in the cave floor. They'd already affixed two little tripods to the floor to anchor cables when sending parachutes through the wormhole. The cables pulled taut would be their handholds through the microgravity within the Axis Mundi, and in the naked space beyond. Pascale's hands tingled with excitement.

"You can go first," Pascale said.

He looked at her curiously. "Why?"

"History," she said. "You can be the first person to leave the solar system."

"History," he said, as if tasting the word. His smile appeared pale in the harsh shadows in his helmet and he seemed tempted. "No. You should go. You and your Pa discovered it."

"It belongs to all of us now."

"The House of Styx."

"Yeah."

Gabriel-Antoine looked her in the eye for long moments and she looked back, defiantly.

"You deserve it," he said finally. "I'll be right behind you."

She returned his wan smile, and then took a nervous breath and neared the wormhole face. From different angles she sometimes glimpsed faint, transient light, a blotchy orange, a stuttering yellow or a doubtful blue. She lifted a gloved hand and pressed it past the apparent surface. There was no feeling, not when she sank her glove in, nor when her whole arm passed through. Holding tight to the cable, she looked back at Gabriel-Antoine, then turned forward and stepped in.

A feeling of weightlessness came over her, like she was falling. There was no footing—she floated with the gentle wind blowing on her back and her hand on the cable as her anchor. Helmet lamps cast white light on the cables as she tilted. She put both hands on the cable, forced her feet upwind and caught her boots on it. Hand over hand, she inched along the cable, following the wind.

What they thought of as the 'wall' of the wormhole, or the throat, should have been about five or six meters from her to the right, but her helmet light didn't pick anything out. The throat appeared as featureless as the mouth itself. Gabriel-Antoine had argued that since the wormhole mouth had been here for years or decades, they couldn't damage it, but they'd agreed not to touch it yet anyway, just in case.

Moving like an insect along the cable in the still, eerie space, Pascale felt the weight of the moment: in all of humanity, in all of history, no one had ever been here. Pascale was crawling through proof of the existence of other kinds of life, of other intelligences. This tunnel burrowing through space had certainly been the roadway by which those triangular probes had come to Venus, even though they'd only crashed into a subterranean dead end. In some past, recent or deep, some non-human lifeform had built this Axis Mundi as a bridge. This proof of other life was spiritually humbling.

Gabriel-Antoine followed on the second cable, feet first, slowly catching up with her. She felt a smile on her lips. She still wouldn't have wanted to live this adventure with anyone else.

The quality of the empty darkness changed as she advanced, until the cable she held seemed to vanish centimeters from her hands. This was the other mouth of the Axis Mundi. The cable swayed softly with the wind and her own movements, making that weird end-spot move like a spoon lazily stirring dark coffee. Pascale held a hand out and it disappeared into that inky horizon.

She took a deep breath, creeping forward, one hand vanishing, then the other, without any associated sensation, like it was an optical illusion. Then the fluid blackness of the horizon pooled in her faceplate like a surface of dark water. She pressed forward with open eyes, almost anticipating the feel of a strange liquid. That dark film proved insubstantial, without tactile experience, ephemeral magic belonging more to the imagination and to expectation than the world of stone and cloud.

Then stars appeared, thousands of them in a sky of a deeper black than anything she'd ever imagined. Her cable and Gabriel-Antoine's ended ten meters ahead of them, in a pair of old, stained parachutes, quietly quivering in the last escaping breath of Venus, something from home and the past, set against a new firmament. She felt very small in this vast sky and yet important to the immensity of this new world. Gabriel-Antoine's neck craned beside her, mouth wide, as he took in all the stars.

"I believed it," he transmitted, his voice feeling close, "but..."

Pascale looked back at the wormhole mouth. The dark circle seemed to float freely in the vacuum, its edges hard to see. It appeared to be nothing more than a negative space marked by the absence of blackness-stippling stars, accented by the occasional flicker of transient color.

"Look at the radar," Gabriel-Antoine said.

Pascale's radar display had been minimized—the suit's computer could only do so many things at once. She closed other displays and opened the radar readings. A powerful radio source pulsed every zero-point-two-two-three seconds, acting like a repeating radar ping. The pulsar. Radio and microwaves bathed them, but that wasn't what Gabriel-Antoine meant.

Radar echoes bounced from every direction, a kind of fuzz that suggested scattering off many small objects. Pascale's suit could handle the calculations on a few radar objects, but there were countless pings. Gabriel-Antoine's suit had a much better processor, one he'd used for testing wing designs in the upper clouds. He shared his display with Pascale showing a sea of objects, some as close as a few kilometers, others dozens or hundreds of kilometers away.

There were soft and hard hits. Soft meant that either the surface was irregular or the material was radio-absorbing. Hard reflectivity meant either a smooth surface or a rigid one. The hard radar reflective sources were too many for even Gabriel-Antoine's processor to sort out easily. None of the radar-reflecting objects appeared to move—the radar didn't show them nearing or retreating, nor even moving across their field of vision.

"We're in a cloud of objects?" Pascale guessed.

"A really big cloud."

Pascale's faceplate couldn't magnify enough to resolve whatever floated out there.

"It's all too dark," she said.

Pascale watched the displays change as Gabriel-Antoine ran different analyses. She didn't understand them all. The flotillas used a lot more radar than the *coureurs* did.

"The closest object is about four kilometers that way," he said, pointing shakily in zero-g.

Living in the clouds, everyone on Venus worked a lot with the vague concept of *that way*, but Gabriel-Antoine laid the radar calculations over the visual feed of the background stars and highlighted it. After a moment that sounded like hesitation, he said, "Asteroids are usually so dark that they look black."

"You think they're asteroids?"

"Maybe. Pulsars are remnants of supernovae. If there had once been a supernova here, it would have smashed any planets in this system to rubble. I never expected anything to be close to the wormhole mouth. Whatever's out there, we might be able to turn it into building materials if we can get to it."

Pascale turned that idea over in her head. They'd brought down lots of tanks to carry reaction mass in case they needed to move around the vacuum, but they'd only been thinking of moving themselves and maybe antenna equipment. They hadn't expected to find anything worth travelling *to*.

But Pascale had an idea, and she began to explain it to Gabriel-Antoine.

THIRTY-TWO

Something poked at Émile's ribs.

His head throbbed. It had been a few days since he'd gotten wrecked, and he hadn't been intending to, but during a raid last night, they'd confiscated a cache of pretty good *tord-boyaux*. They couldn't carry all of it out, so they'd drunk as much as they could there. He vaguely remembered leaving with a couple more jars? In the quiet creaking of the *Marais-des-Nuages,* while the Phocas family slept, he'd continued to drink himself blurry.

The fingers poked again and he swatted at them. He pulled the sheet over his head, uncovering his feet.

"Hey!" Louise said. "You're not supposed to hit a girl."

"I'm hungover. Go play with your grandparents."

"They're napping. You've been asleep all morning."

"I'm not done. Go away."

"Have you been to Earth?"

He groaned.

"*You're* here in Gabriel-Antoine's place. I need someone to talk to."

He rubbed at his face. He dimly remembered what it was like to have a little sister. Chloé had annoyed the shit out of him. She'd been a good little sister. She'd always been good to him. *Crisse.* He rubbed his crusty eyes.

"Gimme ten minutes," he said and sighed, waiting for the throbbing in his head to stop.

The sheet was pulled from his face.

"You haven't been to Earth, have you?" she said.

His eyelids cracked open into aching slits. At least she hadn't opened the blinds. The sun was out there, throbbing too, trying to break into the cool shadows in here. Louise sat on a stool beside his bed.

"Do I look rich enough to go to Earth?"

"All the romance books are set on Earth," she said. "It must be something to just walk around outside. I want to ride a bicycle."

He pulled the sheet back over his face.

"I'm talking!" she said.

"You're hard to ignore…" He might not just be hungover—he might still be a little drunk. The world had the faintest dizzy spin. That *tord-boyaux* must have been pretty strong. If he didn't move, it didn't matter, though. The world became a gloomy pink again, behind closed eyelids.

"Do you have a girlfriend?" Louise asked.

He sighed. "She doesn't love me, so—no," he said.

"Why not?"

"Am I in hell?" He groaned. Getting upset wasn't a hangover cure.

Quiet settled for a time and he could have drifted back to sleep.

"Why not?" she said.

"Good question. Ask her." He rolled over, putting his back to her.

"What's her name?"

The pause lengthened.

"You wrote her love poetry."

"Are you rooting around in my stuff?"

"It's not rooting around if you leave it on Gabriel-Antoine's workbench."

"I don't leave it on the workbench for just anyone to read."

"It's heart-breaking," she admitted plaintively. "It's better than any of my romance books. If she doesn't understand your heart, she's stupid."

He scratched at his cheek, then his chest. He wasn't going to sleep again. Did they have any aspirin?

"She's really not."

"Get someone else."

"That's not how love works."

"I don't understand how someone could say no to a love poem," she said mournfully.

"Don't get worked up. She was my girlfriend, not yours."

"She dumped you?"

He wanted to laugh bitterly, but his headache stabbed and he just groaned.

"Is that why you're drunk?"

"How do you know I'm drunk?" If he pulled the cover softly over his head, there was less light and his head hurt less.

"*Grand-mère* said you're a drunkard."

He sighed. "Aren't you a little young for all this? Go read a book."

"I'm twelve," she said defiantly.

"And I'm sleeping."

"Can I hang off your arm?" Paul-Égide said. Émile put the pillow over his aching head.

"Let me sleep, *câlisse*."

"What are you doing?" Paul-Égide said to Louise.

"You're too young," she said. "We're having a conversation."

Someone got into bed with him.

"Can I hang off your arm?" Paul-Égide said, lifting part of the pillow.

"No."

"How come you're so big?"

Paul-Égide poked. Pascale used to poke and tickle and bother.

"I just came this way."

"Is your *papa* big?" Paul-Égide pressed.

"Just me," Émile said, pushing aside the boy's hand and clasping the pillow to his ear.

"Can you teach me to fly?" Louise said. "We have the suits. Gabriel-Antoine made us wings."

"Me too!" Paul-Égide said.

"No," Émile said. "Close the door on your way out."

After a time, the kids stopped talking and must have left. Or they stayed while he slept another hour. He woke to the smell of onions and spinach and soy with spices. The splitting of his head had dulled. He emerged to find Louise cooking and fussing. Her grandparents swayed in their hanging chairs.

"After this, you can teach me how to fly," she said over the noise of clattering bowls.

"*Non,*" her grandmother said softly.

"*Grand-mère* said no," Émile said as he entered the tiny head.

He could just turn against the toilet bowl to make the door close and then bend his knees enough to get his face close to the sink. He looked like shit. His hair needed a trim, and his beard. Blue crescents underlined the bloodshot eyes that stared back from the mirror. The *Marais-des-Nuages* had much better water reclamation than the *Causapscal-des-Vents,* so he could use a bit of real water to wash.

Émile didn't like thinking of Earth and of might-have-beens. When Louise thought of Earth, she thought of love stories and bicycles. Émile would have settled for water: streams and lakes and waterfalls and even just sinks where he could turn on the water and let it run through his fingers. The romance of Earth was different for each person; everyone dreamed of something they couldn't have.

He emerged slightly less hungover. The vegetable stew would help. Louise brought him his bowl. Paul-Égide shovelled heaping spoonfuls into his mouth. The grandparents chewed slowly, looking across thousands of kilometers to the horizon of clouds beneath black, starry sky. Louise sat straight, like someone twice her age.

"*Grand-mère* said you can teach me to fly."

Émile groaned.

THIRTY-THREE

In the habitat, Pascale and Gabriel-Antoine chewed rubbery, pasty rations distractedly. Pascale's new idea of bringing some asteroids into reach had seized them both. They talked excitedly and suited up quickly to get back out, to examine the edges of the wormhole mouth. They should have been building other things in the caves—they had a thousand things to do to try to make the surface safe and self-sustaining—but the chance to get materials from space was too big an opportunity to ignore.

In the near-vacuum of the last chamber, Pascale and Gabriel-Antoine measured the axis mouth with every electronic meter, Geiger counter, spectrometer and magnetometer they'd brought down, trying to figure out if the Axis Mundi was stable. Accidentally damaging or destroying it would not only be a crime against humanity, but might also blow up the cave system—or perhaps all of Venus. The Axis was bent space-time—the kind of thing that crushed stars and made black holes.

None of the instruments gave them any more insight than they'd had before. Pascale and Gabriel-Antoine just weren't equipped to ask these kinds of questions. No one on Venus was; *la colonie* was poor and newborn.

"We have logical evidence, though," Gabriel-Antoine said, standing in front of the wormhole mouth. He moved his finger within centimeters of one of the exposed sections of the edge. "Three-quarters of the edge of this throat is embedded in basalt. That could only happen if the Axis mouth had been here when this rock was still molten. Aphrodite Terra has been solid on the order of millions of years. It's possible the Axis mouth has endured this heat and pressure for all that time."

"You think the Axis will hold?"

He considered her and smiled. "If thousands of millennia of Venus's grinding geology and burning atmosphere didn't hurt the wormhole, your cable probably won't either."

"Let's try it."

The eager grin in Gabriel-Antoine's faceplate mirrored hers.

They ferried equipment and supplies through the wormhole throat, including all their trawler cabling. They'd brought down almost every bit of cable, old and young, from the *Causapscal-des-Profondeurs*. They'd known they might end up working in a vacuum, which needed lots of safety lines. Attaching all the segments together made a rope seven kilometers long.

As expected, their survival suits were poorly designed for long periods in zero-g. Neither had air jets, which risked them twisting and rotating in space. To align the world on the other side of the wormhole, they opened the wind turbines a little more, so that the escaping atmosphere pressed harder on the parachutes. This tautened the lines, which gave Pascale and Gabriel-Antoine semi-rigid anchors in the empty space.

Gabriel-Antoine played out a length of cable to float several hundred meters from the wormhole mouth, taking radar readings as he went, trying to get better measurements to the nearest objects. Repeated parallax readings sharpened his estimations: the nearest object floated just under five kilometers away. His readings suggested that the Axis Mundi mouth was floating in a dense debris field. A dozen objects over ten meters in diameter orbited within a hundred kilometers, and although he became less certain further away, Gabriel-Antoine estimated about another thousand such objects within five hundred kilometers. His processing chips couldn't do the math on objects smaller than a few meters, but there must have been many orders of magnitude more tiny objects, some of them metallic, for all the radar scattering they were detecting.

Pascale and Gabriel-Antoine now floated in the vacuum, holding onto the cables in the light breeze. He watched her through her faceplate, her face lit by the in-helmet light. Against the stars it felt like they were entirely alone—and they were. They didn't know how many light-years separated them from the Earth and all of humanity. Without the wormhole, the magical Axis Mundi, Venus and Earth were unimaginably far away, more than many lifetimes. Gabriel-Antoine had wanted to be the one to go to the nearest asteroid, but he massed more than Pascale, which meant more fuel to move his body. Also, whoever went would need navigational instructions and she didn't have his radar interpreting skills. Gabriel-Antoine seemed to be struggling with what to say. She liked the frown of concentration he sometimes had in these moments. He sighed softly.

"Be careful, Pascale. Watch your meters. Mind the oxygen. Don't get tangled. Don't go too fast."

"Eat my vegetables too?"

"You're going five kilometers through deep space on tanks that weren't made for jet propulsion and your safety line is made of plant fiber whose properties might have changed going through the oven of lower Venus. Be careful."

"You're in as much danger as I am out here. We'll both be careful."

"We'll both be careful," he repeated.

Almost sheepishly, Gabriel-Antoine knocked the top of Pascale's helmet, where he'd tied a curved piece of plastic. Pascale wouldn't be moving very fast, but Gabriel-Antoine worried about heavier debris, especially anything that could strike Pascale's helmet.

"Turn around," he said.

She complied and he checked the metal piping he'd jury-rigged into an improvised jetpack. He'd installed two additional air tanks filled with compressed carbon dioxide to the regular tank on her back. Then he'd used two pieces of long metal tubing that arched above her head before curving back towards her feet. When carbon dioxide was released through them, the tubing would drag her forward. Smaller curving tubes affixed to her ankles, with the nozzles pointed up towards her head, let her brake or change her orientation. Two simple hoses ran to her wrists for more delicate station-keeping, although the limited practice they'd done didn't inspire confidence in either of them.

"All good?"

He tugged at her harnesses. After some final adjustments, he turned in the zero-g to face the path towards the nearest asteroid. He slipped an additional telescopic lens in front of the ones built into his helmet's faceplate and rechecked the radio bands against the stars, verifying his navigational fixes.

"Are you ready?" he said.

Gabriel-Antoine was sharing the last layer of his navigational display with her suit, showing a line drawn from here to the asteroid. Her job was to stay on that line.

"Ready," she breathed, with less certainty than she'd expected.

They could do this. Corporate workers in the asteroids did this all the time, just not with homemade equipment, or with training quickly skimmed from sixty-year-old open-source manuals. She could do this. People had been doing stuff in space for almost three centuries.

She activated the cold jets with a three-second burst and began to follow the line. She gave another burst, longer, accelerating, but it wasn't that fast. Actually, she was always slowing. The seven-kilometer cable trailed behind her and as she moved away from the Axis Mundi, she pulled more of it with her. Its mass acted as a brake.

"You're good," Gabriel-Antoine said over the pulsar's loud radio static. "You're travelling six kilometers per hour. Is it okay?"

A quiet hiss sounded on her shoulders and helmet, like a faint rain of falling sand. Occasionally, something a little bigger bumped softly against her.

"I'm okay," she said. "I'm going to boost to ten or fifteen."

She thrusted, briefly reaching twelve kilometers per hour. The dragging cable slowed her more now that she was pulling a hundred meters of it.

"You're drifting," he radioed.

She wasn't far off the navigational line. Her body was straight—she was flying well. Torsion and inconstant flexibilities in the cable itself might have been pulling her off course. She held her hands in front of her and gave those cold jets a little burst, and her body backed onto the nav line again.

"Half a kilometer," Gabriel-Antoine said, his voice part of the static. "Ten percent of the way there."

Pascale laughed a little nervously. "Is that meant to be encouraging?"

"Yes." She imagined she could hear a smile in his voice amidst the static. "Go ahead and speed up if you feel you're ready."

Pascale gave another burst of air jets and felt the gentle acceleration. It was too dark to see the dust, but when she held out her hand, the tiny white running light on her wrist seemed to be almost fuzzy. She could make out some fine grains passing between the light and her eye. Some of it clung noticeably to her sleeve, a gossamer layer of soot falling towards her with static attraction.

"There's dust everywhere," Pascale said into the crackling.

"It's a dead solar system," Gabriel-Antoine said with a bit of reverence. The radio static rose until Gabriel-Antoine's voice resumed, soft and distant. "The human mind has a hard time imagining a whole planet. We certainly don't have a way to really understand the size of a star. And a star exploded here and blasted every planet and moon to dust and pebbles. The supernova probably smashed dozens of nearby solar systems too. We can't conceive of something that big, and yet we're here in a sea of ashes. Maybe all that's left of the people who made the wormhole."

"I thought my brother was the poet," she said. Pebbles tap-tap-tapped on Pascale's helmet as she applied more thrust against the drag of the cable. "If they built the Axis Mundi millions of years ago, they must have known their star was going to go nova. Maybe they all got out."

"To the bottom of Venus's gravity well?"

"It doesn't make sense that people who could build a wormhole would get it stuck on Venus," Pascale said. "They probably crossed to wherever they needed to go, and abandoned the Axis."

"Aliens in our solar system, millions of years ago?"

The static made it hard to hear his tone, to hear if he were teasing her.

"It's fun to think about."

"Yeah. Watch your course."

They were back to business. They needed to be. She'd covered about three kilometers. Each puff of air jets accelerated her less as she dragged more of the cable's weight behind her. She had to thrust near-continuously.

"How much farther?"

"It's looking like two kilometers," he said.

"My carbon dioxide tanks are three-quarters exhausted," she said. "Will that reach?"

He didn't answer right away and she stopped thrusting. After a few seconds, the tinkling of dust on her helmet quieted as the cable mass dragged her to a stop. She did her own calculations. The CO2 tanks weren't enough. Every hundred meters she travelled added another hundred meters of cable inertia.

"I can use my oxygen," she finally transmitted.

"That's for breathing, dummy."

"We can't stop here."

"Let me think," Gabriel-Antoine said. "I didn't think the cable would slow you down so much."

Pascale waited in the stillness of space, hearing her breathing and the scratching of the empty radio channel. The heart of Venus was a bridge to the stars, but it was a dark wreckage too, debris from a past too old for them to know. Pascale imagined that this is what Pa had meant when he'd talked about visiting a cemetery with all the signs of lives lived, memories made visible through time. They needed all this wreckage, though. There might be as much metal, as many silicates and volatiles, on this side of the Axis Mundi as in humanity's entire solar system.

"We need this."

"I haven't given up," Gabriel-Antoine said through the crackling. "I was doing calculations."

"Which ones?"

"I'll use my cold jets and accelerate half the cable."

"You're navigating," Pascale said.

"I might be able to do both. We know the star fixes we're aiming for. Can you see the asteroid yet?"

She peered into the darkness, looking for a dark object lit only by starlight. "No."

"On a three-count, thrust for ten seconds towards your star fix," Gabriel-Antoine said. "I'll follow and drag the line. Ignore the nav line once I'm moving."

"Okay."

This felt risky—both of them space-walking kilometers away from the Axis Mundi, with improvised equipment and a cable whose strength hadn't been meant for the hot depths of the surface *or* the cold vacuum here. She activated her cold jets on three. The kilometers of cable made acceleration slow, and she didn't notice any difference with Gabriel-Antoine helping.

"Too slow," she said at the end of ten seconds. "We've got to keep thrusting to get there."

"I've moved about five hundred meters up the cable," he answered. "I should be carrying half the weight and you the other half."

"Let's go," she said. "Twenty seconds."

They kept thrusting and it still seemed to Pascale that they made little headway.

"Is it going?" she said in frustration.

"It's going," he answered. "Can you see the asteroid? Try again."

"Can't see it. Thrusting for twenty seconds."

It might have been in her head, but it felt like the acceleration was easier, the drag genuinely reduced. The dust and pebbles tapped at her suit. She cut the thrust.

"Keep it up! It's working. I'm coasting!"

"I'm down to about a minute of thrust," he said. "I only have one CO2 tank and it's half-spent."

"Save it. For safety."

"Can you see it? You should have crossed four kilometers by now."

"We'd know if you'd kept navigating," Pascale teased. "I can't see it, but I've got about two minutes of thrust left. If I push hard, I should get there."

"Wait a second," Gabriel-Antoine said.

"What are you doing?"

"I'm crawling back towards the wormhole mouth along the cable."

"Why?"

"The cable is loose right now," he said. "Every meter I crawl back is a few meters I push towards you in the zero gravity. I can advance you a lot of slack to lighten your last push."

She waited, squinting into the darkness, trying to see the asteroid. She should at least see the occluded starlight, a dark shape against the starscape, but even though her star fix was right, she saw nothing. The dust and soot was thick enough that even a few hundred meters might be too much. In some ways, it was like being in the sub-cloud haze.

"Go ahead," Gabriel-Antoine said.

Pascale activated her cold jets, watching ahead of her, with one eye on the CO2 levels. She hadn't told Gabriel-Antoine that she was on her last twenty seconds of thrust.

Suddenly, she hit something and cried out.

"What is it?" Gabriel-Antoine was shouting into the helmet radio.

It felt like one of those times where she'd landed wrong under the *Causapscal-des-Profondeurs* and jarred herself in the nets with the last of her forward movement. Or when a capricious wind or miscalculation had stalled her two meters too high over a trawler cap and she'd come crashing hard into the woody shell. It was utterly dark. She moved, and felt grinding.

She pushed away and found herself floating in space, surrounded by a thick cloud of dust and pebbles, some of it refracting the distant white starlight. An unrelentingly black shape obscured the stars in front of her. She checked her suit's status readings. Her oxygen pressure was fine; no sounds of leaking or telltales warning of pressure loss.

"I'm okay," she said. "It's so dark, I couldn't see it even right before I hit it."

"Is your suit okay?" he demanded.

She checked again.

"Yeah. I wasn't going very fast and the surface is crumbly. Like dust and gravel."

"Lots of asteroids slowly collect dust and debris over millennia."

"I know what regolith is."

"Sorry. Your crash freaked me out."

A tiny elation bloomed in her chest at his worrying.

She couldn't tell the composition of the asteroid from here. Sooty dust covered it everywhere, almost soaking up her helmet light. "My impact made a cloud of debris. It's going to take millennia for it to settle again in such faint gravity. There'd better be something solid in the middle, or this has been a wasted trip."

"Can you get the cable wrapped all the way around?" Gabriel-Antoine asked.

She looked at her CO2 reading zero pressure. She let out her breath slowly.

"I'm out of reaction mass," she said. "I'm about five or six meters from the asteroid and if your radar is right, it's about a kilometer in circumference."

"Crawl back along the line," he said. "We'll refuel and jet out to tie it without the weight of the cable to carry. We finished the big part of the job."

"If the cable drifts relative, it may be kilometers away by the time we get back."

"There's nothing else we can do."

The fine, night black dust and grains dimly reflected Pascale's helmet light, or eclipsed into transient visibility as they drifted across tiny stars. It was a magically weird view of the world.

"I can use my oxygen as reaction mass."

"No!"

"Not all of it," she chided. "I've got sixty-three minutes' worth. Two-thirds of that might get me and the cable around the asteroid. Then, I'll have twenty minutes to climb back."

"You can't crawl five kilometers of cable in twenty minutes."

He probably wasn't wrong. "How much oxygen have you got?"

"What? Eighty-two minutes," he said.

"Meet me halfway and share."

Ambient radio static crackled for long moments.

"Try," he said reluctantly. "Running out of air isn't the same as running out of fuel."

"I can do it."

Pascale wasn't calculating numbers. She wanted this. She *needed* this. *They* needed this. All of them: the family, the people living in the flotillas, even the people who worked in the government. The beauty and true self of the real Venus of the stars had been hidden from humanity for all of history. Venus needed to be seen and known as she was. Pascale and her family had descended through the underworld to a stellar grave to rescue the soul of a goddess. Venus wouldn't have revealed herself to them only to dash their hopes, and hers, with failing oxygen. There had to be more to all of this, some meaning.

Pascale detached the improvised jet pack tubes from the CO2 tanks, shucking the dead weight, and for good measure, tied them to the cable. The feed to the secondary oxygen tank clicked in easily and the jet pack tubes pressurized. She took a deep breath… while she could.

"Ready," she radioed.

"Two-thirds is a lot."

"We can do this."

She activated her cold jets. Puffs of oxygen gas froze into tiny white crystals behind her. She corrected her path using gentle thrust from her wrists, and then opened the thrust wide. Her helmet weakly lit the surface of the asteroid. It was the dustiest, dirtiest thing she'd ever seen, giving no hint as to what was beneath. The little magnetometer they'd used earlier to examine the mouth of the Axis Mundi picked up magnetic fields from time to time—a good sign.

She corrected her attitude, following the curve of the asteroid. A weird vibration shuddered along the cable—her flight path was dragging it along the surface. The friction slowed her so much that her oxygen wouldn't carry her much farther, and the drag of the cable around the surface of the asteroid was also slowly swinging her towards the regolith.

"The cable is dragging across the surface, but I've got an idea," she radioed.

"What?"

She used her wrist jets to turn herself so that her back was almost parallel to the approaching asteroid surface.

"Inertia is swinging me into the surface," she said. "I'm going to see if I can use the tension in the cable to hold me enough to use my feet."

"What?"

"Hang on," she said.

Her drift to the surface was slowing. She corrected her posture relative to the regolith, leaning back. Her boot heels crunched into the gravel and dust, and the cable tautened in front of her. She carefully dug her heels in. The tension of the cable held her there for a moment, until it slowly began dragging towards her over the surface.

If she'd been standing straight up, any flexing of her legs would have launched her into space. So she leaned backwards into the cable's tension and held. She slowly stepped back, carefully digging new heelholds with each step. Sometimes her boot found something hard enough to push against, but often, her feet found only dust and loose, weightless gravel that silently drifted into the void.

"It's working," she huffed into the radio.

"Have you got enough oxygen?"

"So far!" she grunted as she heaved the cable along.

She wasn't sure, though, so she pushed until her legs and arms tired, dragging kilometers of cable. After about ten minutes, Pascale found herself staring up at the cable stretching all the way back into the dark and the axis. She'd dragged herself and the cable all around the asteroid. Her walking-dragging idea had probably saved her about half the oxygen she would have used flying. A hundred meters separated her from completing the loop.

"Almost there."

"How's your oxygen?" he said.

Her oxygen levels were way down. "Thirty-six percent," she lied, "but I can't drag this farther. I'm tying this end down for now. I'll fly to the rest of the cable. Maybe I can bring it over here."

Nearby, a craggy stone emerged from the regolith. It didn't move when she shook it. Promising. She pulled the cable and wound its end several times around the thrusting rock.

"I'm going to push off and grab the cable floating out there. There should be enough slack."

"Be careful."

She leapt gently off the asteroid, floating upward, mostly in the right direction. The cable showed only as an indistinct gray line. As she neared, she realized that her angle was off and she'd overestimated the strength of jump she'd need. She had to burn through more oxygen to arc her trajectory towards the free-floating cable and catch it as she floated past.

"I got it," she radioed.

"How's your oxygen?"

She was at twenty percent. "Thirty percent."

"We agreed to use only two-thirds."

"*We* didn't agree to anything. We made some plans we knew I might have to rework on the fly. I'm okay. I just have to drift back to the prominence where I tied the other end and then we'll have fished a *really* big fish."

Pascale's motion had stopped. Her momentum had dragged the free-floating cable slightly away from the asteroid. She oriented herself with her wrist jets and then activated her main thrusters, dragging the cable with her.

Twelve percent oxygen. About twenty minutes.

She was close. She could make out the prominence anchoring the end of the cable. One more thrust ought to do it. She thrust for twenty seconds, dropping her oxygen to ten percent.

She drifted to a stop, only a dozen meters from the surface.

Merde.

She knew what she and Pa and Marthe and Émile would all do now. Venus didn't care for cowards. Venus didn't care for the timid, for those who didn't commit to her. Pascale thrust the last few meters, catching the prominence with one hand and the cable in the other. She wound it around the rocky outcropping and tied it down. The asteroid belonged to the House of Styx now, the way a wild trawler could be caught. This was the new world.

And she had six percent oxygen. If she hurried down the cable as fast as she could, she could probably make it to the Axis mouth and their reserve supplies.

"What's happening?" Gabriel-Antoine's voice sounded through the static in her earpiece.

"It's tied up. Coming back now."

"Just a sec."

A light shone on the rocky outcropping, creating a shadow for her. She turned. Gabriel-Antoine was twenty meters away. He landed on the asteroid beside her, crunching silently in the loose gravel, thickening the dust and pebble cloud around them as he held tight to the rock.

"What are you doing here?"

"What's your oxygen really at?"

She was quiet for a second. "Ten percent."

"You're a lousy liar."

He produced a hose to connect his oxygen tank to hers.

"Wait. I'm actually at six percent."

"I figured four."

She waited in still, quiet gratitude as he attached the tube to her tank and equalized them.

"Do you have enough?"

"Does it matter?"

"Yes," she said, moving her hand to the spigot that controlled the flow, as if to turn it off. "I only need enough to get back to the Axis."

"We're in this together," he said, pushing away her hand.

THIRTY-FOUR

LOUISE WAS AS excited as Paul-Égide was jealous. She rocked on her heels in the airlock of the *Marais-des-Nuages*, obliterating the faux grown-up attitude she cultivated.

"Gabriel-Antoine said the wings have some autopilot, to help me learn," she said.

He wheeled open the airlock and they stepped into the gasping wind on the roof. Émile hefted her wing-pack; her brother had built it for her smaller body.

"Maybe in the asteroids, or on Earth, they have good AI to fly everything, but with *bébittes*"—the *colonistes*' word for the many technical failures when sulfuric acid got into things—"something always goes wrong."

"What does that mean?" she asked as he jerked and pulled at her harness, making sure the wing-pack straps weren't loose. "That's too tight," she complained.

"It won't be too tight when you're hanging over sixty-five kilometers of clouds." He tugged harder and she made another wordless protest. "If you expect something to go wrong, you live longer."

"You're not dead. My brother isn't dead."

He held back a cutting response. Pa would have cut loose, but teenagers were teenagers. He got a long cable from a tool cabin and clipped it to the front of his harness, tugging to test. Then he clipped it behind her, on the top of her wing-pack, and repeated the checks.

"I don't need that. Gabriel-Antoine wasn't going to teach me with a tether. I'm not seven."

"This is the way my Pa taught me and my sisters. This is the only way I know how to teach flying."

"I've got the autopilot!"

"I shut it off already."

"Why make it harder? I feel stupid."

"And I feel hungover. You shouldn't have woken me up."

He called up her system in his helmet. The controls seemed very sophisticated. The normal battery charge, flight speed, angle of attack, and GPS graphics were there, configured differently than he was used to. There was a lot more here, though: mechanical data, torque and stress data, a lot of it way over his head. He tried to slave her system to his, but their softwares didn't match.

"Damn. It's not going to work. I can't take control if I need to."

"I can do it!" she said, turning to punch his chest. "Stop treating me like a kid!"

"Whoa. Fine. I had little sisters. I know you're not a kid."

"Let's go. I've practiced on simulators."

He scanned the horizon. They floated a kilometer above the clouds today, on a thin, steady east wind.

"We'll try level flight first," he said.

She snickered and moved to the edge of the roof. He tugged lightly on the cable.

"How are you going to fly with a rope?" she said. "We're going to get tangled, or our wings will get fouled."

"When you're more experienced, you'll see."

He stood beside her on the roof with the cable loose in his hands. He extended his wings. She turned and extended hers. Their motors idled.

"Do we jump at the same time?"

"I jump a split second later. When my Pa taught me, we jumped together with a longer rope, but the atmosphere is thicker down there, easier to fly in."

"Yeah, yeah. That's really interesting. Can I go? Count of three?"

"Yeah. One-two-three," he said unenthusiastically.

She bent her knees and leapt. He followed. Their wings lengthened, catching the thin air. She wobbled, but swooped down about three hundred meters before getting into a glide path and then a gradual climb. He was a strong flyer and matched her movements closely enough to leave some slack in the cable between them.

Her balance was pretty good. First flyers often didn't get the hang of how to shift center of mass with subtle movements of arms and legs. She wasn't using her body's own drag to adjust, but he wouldn't even try to teach that until later.

"Turn to port," he said, "shallow at first, and then tightening up to a one-eighty."

Her turn began a bit jerkily and he followed about fifty meters higher, the cord hanging slack between them.

"Throttle up and as you come out of the turn, gain some altitude," he said.

"See?" she radioed back. "I told you."

"You're good," he said. He hadn't taught Chloé to fly, or Marthe, although he'd seen both fly many times. Louise looked like a beginner compared to them. Chloé was gone and sometimes he couldn't get the last hours with Marthe out of his head. She'd never woken up again, never even known that he'd been there. He wished she hadn't died thinking she was alone.

Maybe that didn't matter. Dead was still dead, no matter who was there with you.

"I don't need the tether," she said.

She probably didn't. When Pa had taught him, it had taken him ten minutes to get to a wobbly, level flight. Pa had had to drag him along on the tether to keep him from falling into one stall after another. Pa had sworn. Émile had sworn. And every time Pa had taken Émile's full teen weight, they'd done a three-count and then both dived to get Émile's airspeed up. They might have lost five kilometers that day; the rest of the lesson had been learning to climb. They hadn't removed the tether until they'd both hit the nets, Pa with his feet, Émile with arm, leg and wing. So far, he hadn't needed to pull even once to support Louise.

"Have you done simulated landings?" he asked.

"Of course! Just cut the tether. I'm not a baby."

She was climbing well and her level flight seemed steady. They cruised at the same altitude as the shiny green of the *Marais-des-Nuages,* passing it westward, towards a horizon bruising from yellow-white to orange against the starry black of the sky.

"You've got your parachute and, if need be, you can blow your oxygen bag. Getting caught in a spin is the most dangerous thing, but you can get out of it if you retract your wings. You just have to be okay with falling for a bit."

"Let's go, chicken."

Louise wasn't his sister. He would have given Chloé or Marthe an earful and let them take their own damned risks.

"Okay. Get ready," he said. He transmitted a command and the hook on her end of the cable opened, to trail behind him.

"Woooo!" she cried in his earpiece, throttling up and zipping ahead.

"Slow down!" he said.

He wound the cable as he accelerated. She banked right, throttling up to climb during the turn. Her engine was powerful, probably too powerful for an inexperienced flyer. Wind moaned past his helmet as he tried to match her, but his sub-standard-issue piece-of-crap engine complained at the effort. He jammed the cable into a pocket and dove in pursuit. Her laughter sounded in his helmet.

"Slow down!"

"Catch me if you can!"

"That's dangerous!"

Something was weird. He'd never taught anyone to fly, but he'd seen Pascale learning, and Louise wasn't flying like a learner. In fact, he didn't think he could catch her.

"Liar!" he finally said. "You already knew how to fly!"

She laughed louder.

"They don't let me fly alone," she said. "Tag now. Gabriel-Antoine and I played."

He was glad no one could see him being outclassed by a twelve-year-old. He throttled up as she tried to circle behind him. She was a lot lighter and her engine was newer, but he hoped his longer wingspan could give him some advantage. If he hadn't been hungover, some tricks might have occurred to him. She turned tighter than he could and came close to him before he dove straight down, getting his airspeed up before swooping to level flight and rolling into a tight turn to port. She buzzed on a path that crossed his, zipping behind him like a homing missile. In the open, she had the advantage. He flew straight towards the *Marais-des-Nuages*, arcing tightly around and under it, trying to lose her until something slapped his foot.

"You're it!" she taunted.

He was about to try to figure out how to catch her when his radio squawked.

"Constable D'Aquillon. Report to the *Détroit d'Honguedo*."

"Can you land?" he said to Louise.

"No!"

"I gotta work. I just got called."

"You just got tagged, loser."

"I'm landing. I'll help you stow your pack."

"Fuck," she said with the earnest gravity of a woman three times her age.

THIRTY-FIVE

Gaschel had received the terse invitation the evening before and had slept poorly. The meeting subject, 'Discussion of Clause 176,' could only refer to the loan subsection about *la colonie*'s interest rate. Had the bank discovered how they'd cheated the quarterly inspection? Any change in interest rate risked bankrupting *la colonie*. Out of respect for Gaschel's position as head of state, official meetings with the Branch Manager of the Bank of Pallas usually occurred in Gaschel's offices on the *Baie-Comeau*. This one would be in Woodward's office. She'd almost called Labourière in the middle of the night, but decided that one of them should be well-rested. He'd worried appropriately once he woke in the morning, and they'd set out.

The cloud tops of the upper deck were high and dark today, only a kilometer below the flotilla, looking like a choppy ocean. Most of the worst weather swirled and thrashed beneath the flotillas, but every so often, Venus reminded them of her reach, just like the bank did. The branch office floated, bright green with hydroponics growth in its outer envelope. Some surfaces reflected the orange dawn light behind Gaschel. She and Labourière touched down on the roof's wide landing pad. Unusually, someone was waiting for them on the roof: Gaschel's niece, an employee at the branch office.

"*Madame la Présidente,*" Mélusine said formally.

"Hello, Mélusine," Gaschel said. "What should I expect?"

"She's upset," Mélusine said. "She had two ad hoc meetings with Head Office."

"About clause 176," Gaschel mused. "Well, let's not keep her waiting. Tell me anything that might be helpful."

While they cycled through the airlock and stowed their helmets and survival suits, Gaschel tried to gauge how bad the situation could be. *Présidente* was a big title, and perhaps a bit premature, but she, and *la colonie,* had wanted some trappings of political legitimacy, even if their substance was still aspirational. Venus would someday be a mature state, part of the community of nations extending across the solar system, but nations had limits, sometimes sharp ones. Money, supplies, trade. Only the largest nations ever really got to do what they wanted. Most states, including Venus, were beholden to those who held their debt.

Woodward rose from behind the big desk in her office and had a tight smile for them. Her security chief Amanda Copeland rose more slowly. Woodward indicated the seats in front of the desk and offered tea, Earth tea. They accepted with pleasantries as Gaschel tried to get a read on either woman. Copeland was often taciturn. Gaschel had seen her CV on the bank's public site: a graduate of an old American military college, followed by specialist training at the Bank of Pallas's lunar base, then various postings in the asteroids. She was older than Woodward and seemed to be a competent officer.

"I have some news you're not going to enjoy," Woodward said in English as they set down their little painted ceramic cups.

Gaschel smothered the sinking feeling in her gut. There were ways to fix every problem. "Best to give it directly," she said. "That's what I learned in medical school."

"The Bank of Pallas is invoking its right to conduct a security assessment, pursuant to subsection 5e of clause 176 of the colony's loan," Woodward said. "We don't do these often, or without cause.

These assessments inform the risk analyses for our investments. I'm required to remind you that if the security assessment is downgraded past a certain threshold, it triggers an automatic interest rate adjustment on your existing loans. If that happens, the future loans currently awaiting approval at the head office would need to be reassessed. That includes the loan for purchase of automated mining equipment for the exploitation of asteroid 3554 Amun."

Woodward waited as Gaschel processed this. Gaschel didn't look at Labourière because she didn't trust that Woodward wouldn't see him sweat. This was far, far worse than anything she'd expected—it was, in fact, catastrophic. All her political promises and policies, all her ambitions for Venus, might be dashed.

"As branch manager," Woodward added in a less formal tone, "I had the authority to waive the loss of the *Causapscal-des-Vents* as collateral, which I did. Looking the other way on the growing political and security instability isn't my call, though. The fund managers at head office decide."

"Four months ago, you and I signed off on this," Gaschel said with the barest touch of heat. "Where did this sudden crisis come from?"

Woodward gave her a patient, condescending look and Gaschel seethed.

"You have a hundred and sixty people in detention right now for black marketeering," she said. "The trade in black-market goods keeps worsening the government's books, and one of the main sources of black-market materials is the very habitats you've offered the bank as collateral. Your deep *coureurs* talk like they're organizing themselves into political opposition units, and you don't even know where they are. And"—Woodward raised a hand like a teacher calling a class to order—"you haven't found the source of the radioisotopes in the clouds."

"You're exaggerating," Gaschel said. "When will the assessment take place, and what evidence are you really using?"

"The terms of reference for the assessment are being approved at the head office today," Woodward said.

"We weren't consulted," Gaschel said.

"It's not your assessment."

"You need information from us, though."

"Absolutely. Miss Copeland will be leading the assessment, with the help of our branch auditor. She'll give you lists of documents and information she'll need."

Some problems had understandable, predictable solutions. Others were tosses of the dice. Gaschel didn't feel in control.

"I can save you some time," she said. "We've sighted the *Causapscal-des-Vents.*"

"What?" Copeland blurted in English. "It sank!"

"It's in the lower cloud deck," Gaschel replied in accented English. "It's with the D'Aquillon family, and a couple of others that appear to be helping them. They caught the habitat as it sank. They seem to have hung it under four engineered trawlers. They've been dismantling it to build something on the surface. We're getting that location too."

"You're kidding me!" Woodward said. "It was intentional?"

"We're assembling teams and we'll be making arrests shortly," Gaschel said. "That will put an end to this political instability you're worried about. The arrests will serve as an example to black marketeers and put the metal back on our books as collateral. It also takes off the table your invented nonsense about us or one of the *coureur* families playing footsie with another bank. The D'Aquillon family obviously found a vein on the surface of something rich in radio-isotopes."

"That's a lot of political instability," Copeland said. "And this doesn't *nearly* cover everything in the scope of my assessment."

"A healthy government isn't one that doesn't have problems," Gaschel said. "It's one that solves problems. We'll police our own state, including on the surface."

Copeland looked like she wanted to add something, but Woodward gestured and the security officer pressed her lips into a thin line.

"By the time these kind of security assessments are triggered," Woodward said, "we already know the fundamentals are trending away from good."

The smothering anxiety, so long under control, now felt like it might slither out of Gaschel's throat.

"You're not the first colony mortgaged to the Bank of Pallas," Woodward continued. "Some colonies strike it big after a few decades: ore resources, volatiles, gravitational advantage. Something helps them leap from poor to rich.

"The bank partnered with Venus decades ago," the branch manager said. "It was a long shot, because Venus had so few things going for it. With the right collateral, though, we could afford to take some long bets. The problem is that those bets are getting longer and longer."

"Because of the *Causapscal-des-Vents*?" Gaschel said.

"Your misplaced habitat is a symptom. Most people still believe in your dream of building an enduring state, but more and more aren't. Differences of opinion are healthy, but actively undermining the core mission isn't. I can run all the economic projections I want, but the loans really come down to one thing: Do I believe you'll win, or that these criminals will? Other colonies have seen insurgencies like this. They don't all survive."

"This isn't an insurgency," Gaschel said. "It's black marketeers. Criminals."

"It's a well-understood developmental pattern," Woodward said. "Colonists start with one set of expectations. Reality impinges. Most adjust. Some don't, and they resent those who make the cut. The resentment builds, year after year. If they have a leader, the sparks become a fire."

"D'Aquillon."

Woodward shook her head. "Your insurgents don't just have one leader. They're organizing into 'houses' you can't police. This kind of structure of closed cells is notoriously effective for an insurgency, even if it takes them a couple of years to realize it."

"We don't have terrorists."

"You think your opponents will stop at ideas?" Woodward spread her hands and shrugged. "They have radioisotopes. It doesn't take a lot of tech to make dirty bombs. You already have a tough-to-stamp-out black market. You've got a flotilla you're struggling to keep floating. At the rate they're being cannibalized for black-market trades, it'll be months, not years before they start raining into the clouds."

"We're enforcing the laws. Behaviour will change."

"You can only enforce those laws across a very narrow slice of a very big planet. Where a state can't enforce its own laws, is it really sovereign? There's never a perfect solution. You can have a model state or immaculate principles, but not both. I am curious as to how you're going to police the surface."

"We have some old surface sample return equipment," Labourière said.

"I've seen your asset listings," Woodward said. "Your surface-capable equipment is small and unarmed."

"The *coureurs* have to come up at some point," Labourière said.

"Laying siege is hardly a robust demonstration of sovereignty. And you might have trouble working whatever mining vein the D'Aquillons have discovered," Woodward said. Her expression softened. "The bank has drone equipment hardened to surface conditions. Some rental or service agreement could be worked out. We have a lot invested here, and if some kind of partnership could be sustained…"

"Why don't we meet again tomorrow?" Gaschel said, rising, trying to take back the initiative. Labourière rose too, followed by the two bank officers. "By then, we'll know what information you need and we'll probably have news on the police investigation."

"We'll see you tomorrow, *Madame la Présidente,*" Woodward said, extending a hand. With guarded relief and draining adrenaline, Gaschel shook it.

Mélusine escorted them from the office back to the roof, and Gaschel gave her niece a summary of the meeting on the way. Presumably Mélusine would have a similar conversation with Woodward. Mélusine's role, treading the line between government and bank, had always been a complex one, intended to prepare her for more political responsibility in the coming years.

Gaschel and Labourière leapt into the sky, above sullenly rumbling clouds. She activated an encrypted tight-beam radio link with him.

"This is bullshit," Gaschel said. "It's a play to destroy Venus as a nation, to keep it permanently under bank control."

"I don't know," Labourière said. "We drew up the loan renewals, including money for 3554 Amun, without all of this. If they'd wanted to spring this on us, it would have been easier *before* we'd gotten as far as drafting paperwork."

"Maybe," Gaschel conceded irritably, "but it would be very easy now for them to crank up the interest rate so high that we'd never get into the black. We have to be spotless on this, François-Xavier. Don't give them a chance to make a single complaint, even an unfounded one. We have to come down hard on the D'Aquillons, the Phocas, and the Hudons, and we need to do it yesterday."

THIRTY-SIX

PASCALE HELD HER breath as Gabriel-Antoine pressed the button on his controller to start the winch. They floated in space, just beyond the mouth of the Axis Mundi. The radio static in their earpieces was a soft buzz, the anthem of this place, just as the moaning winds were the choir of the clouds.

Gabriel-Antoine had run more wires through the Axis Mundi, including a controller for an electric winch back in the cave. For the first try, he'd set the winch motors to a low gear for ten seconds. She and Gabriel-Antoine hovered clear as the cable tightened, and then slowly, the Axis mouth began to tilt in the direction of the asteroid and creep forward. When the winch stopped, the mouth stopped too, silent, apparently undisturbed by these humans and their tools.

"Ha!" Pascale said with the sudden elation of a released breath.

Gabriel-Antoine whooped.

At first Gabriel-Antoine hadn't known how to react to her idea. He had a great mind for engineering, and he learned astronomy and asteroid industrial processes quickly, but Pascale sometimes surprised him with her intuitive leaps. She'd thought of their problem in terms of moving the Axis to the asteroid rather than the other way around. The Axis Mundi mouth floated freely, appearing to weigh nothing, and they had no reason to think it had any preference of location or orientation. If she was right, they could just move the Axis to the asteroid, and maybe eventually the immense debris field that, for all they knew, circled the entire system.

"More!" she said.

Gabriel-Antoine signalled the winch to power another twenty seconds. The cable tautened and the Axis mouth moved forward again, following the tongue of Venusian plant fiber that extended into the vanishing dark.

"It has some inertia," Gabriel-Antoine radioed her.

"What?"

"The Axis mouth," he said. "When we accelerate it, it moves forward, but it doesn't keep its momentum."

"Friction with the dust?" Pascale asked, activating her cold jets for a few seconds.

"Its position relative to the dust cloud was stationary, so it was orbiting the pulsar in a completely normal way, responding to gravity as we would expect," Gabriel-Antoine said. "But the way it's moving now is strange. It doesn't seem to keep the momentum we give it."

"It's made of bent space-time," Pascale said. "It might not have regular inertia?"

"I can't imagine it has one kind of inertia for gravity and another kind for mechanical forces," he said doubtfully.

"This whole system will be like a laboratory for experiments on gravity and space-time," Pascale said. "Think of what we can learn. For years."

For a time, radio static crackled in her earpiece. "That sounds really cool," he finally admitted.

He powered the winch for another twenty seconds and the Axis mouth crawled up the cable. The equipment they'd brought through with them followed on cold jets. Gabriel-Antoine had set his robots to building two wide frames, each forty meters wide, with fine wire mesh stretched across them. These rectennae absorbed the pulsar's microwaves, converting them into electricity. Enough of them could power everything they wanted to do in this system, starting with strong lamps. The blaze of white light gave them the impression of drifting through a dark, still fog. The experience was eerie; nothing was ever still in the clouds of Venus—Pascale had never seen stillness, nor really heard silence, until she'd come here. Briefly turning off her radio, Pascale spread her arms, as if flying through the quiet.

Gabriel-Antoine set the winch to a slow, steady pace, and the Axis plowed through the dust cloud for long minutes until the big spotlights began outlining the approaching sooty asteroid, about half a kilometer away.

"This is crazy," he said with wondering admiration.

It was crazy. Where they were. What they were doing. Two fragile human beings had just dared move a piece of ancient technology to reach a wealth whose full measure their minds might not be able to process. They were claiming their own asteroid, their own mine, for their family and whoever they wanted to trade with. It felt electric.

"It's a good crazy," she said.

They would find all they needed here. Planets had shattered in this system. The rubble of worlds lay all around them, resources enough for not just the House of Styx and the other houses, but for a Venus much, much larger than the current *colonie*. They had enough to try anything, to *become* anything. It was a wonderful crazy.

They crept the Axis Mundi closer and closer to the asteroid. Now that the whole operation was starkly lit, Pascale was reminded of nothing so much as a frog's tongue drawing in a fly from one of *Maman*'s fairy tales. At a hundred meters, Gabriel-Antoine shut down the winch but didn't untie it. They didn't need to keep the Axis tied to the asteroid anymore. In theory, they would co-orbit the pulsar now, and with just a few puffs of cold jets, they could move from the mouth to their floating mine. But they'd brought the Axis mouth this close because Pascale had had another idea that, for all its simplicity, had still surprised Gabriel-Antoine.

"You sure about this?" he said.

"Aren't you?"

"We're making it up as we go along," he said with a little laugh.

"We sure are."

"Okay. Opening in five seconds."

The dust in the microgravity around asteroids was a well-understood problem in the asteroid mining and vacuum-industry operations beyond Mars, as well as on the moon and Mercury. Over millions of years, most mineable objects in the solar system had collected layers of dust, finer than anything on Earth, that got into equipment, clouded vision, interfered with metallurgy, and introduced contaminants into foundry operations. The particles often acquired a static charge, clinging to everything. Worse, dust got past seals on vacuum suits and became a health problem in the lungs. Various companies had come up with all sorts of fixes: magnetic dispersal, creating charges on the dust and then pushing it away with electric fields—even just clearing the dust with aerogels. Pascale and Gabriel-Antoine didn't have any of those tools yet. They only had the vast ocean of Venus's atmosphere.

"Three, two, one," Gabriel-Antoine said.

At first, there was nothing to see. Gabriel-Antoine's command travelled by wire through the Axis, where, beneath the crust of Venus, the wind turbine valves would be opening. Pascale had suggested starting with a light wind, in case her idea was destructive or dangerous. The cable between the Axis mouth and the asteroid began to flutter very gently as a growing breeze of carbon dioxide sprayed from the wormhole, freezing into snow. In the hard glare of the spotlights, the dust on the surface of the asteroid trembled, then started to jostle and fly away, visibly thinning.

Pascale held her breath, as if uncovering a treasure, waiting for something to go wrong. The gravity of the asteroid was so faint that the wind might be too strong—the pebbles and gravel, whose composition and value she didn't know, might blow away with the dust. The asteroid might not be solid all the way through; the wind might scatter the whole thing. So they'd kept the draft slight for now. Retreating dust revealed screes of pebbles that also began to blow away, exposing bright patches of higher-albedo surfaces beneath.

"Stop?" he asked.

"It's not breaking apart yet. A bit more."

A meter of dust and gravel had been blown away, exposing a craggy surface of odd colors and reflectivities that looked solid. The spotlights lit up a dark tail, like a comet's, beyond the asteroid, as Venus cleared the volume for them. Venus had no light of her own, but she could dispel the darkness here.

Gabriel-Antoine shut the turbine valves and Venus held her breath.

On gentle puffs of air, Pascale descended to the asteroid to a newly cleared circle maybe a hundred meters in diameter. Little hisses of attitude adjustments from Pascale's improvised wrist jets sounded as she neared. Gabriel-Antoine was a better flyer, even without an atmosphere, and he landed first, gloved fingers gripping a lumpy ridge that reflected his helmet light back at him.

"It's cold."

"Is it metal?" she asked.

He shifted so that he could hold a slight ridge and hit the glittering surface with a little hammer, breaking a few chips off. He let go his handhold, shaking his fingers. "Goddamn, that's cold. We need better gloves."

Without a sun, this system had been cooling for millions of years, every object in it gradually radiating its heat into space. The vacuum itself mostly protected them, but everything they touched conducted heat, and was two hundred degrees below zero. At this temperature, water ice was as hard as concrete, and if not perfectly pure was opaque, which made telling metal from water by sight difficult. They each caught some of the bright chips. They seemed like flakes of metal to her. She couldn't see through them. Gabriel-Antoine more usefully attached alligator clips to both sides of one of the chips and applied a current. It didn't melt with the current as water ice might have, and a little number on his voltmeter glowed.

"It's metal," he said, touching the vein of ore almost reverently. This was it. Iron and nickel and aluminum was better than gold on Venus. "There's a lot more in here." He turned to her excitedly. "If this is what even a fraction of this asteroid is made of, we've found thousands of tons of metal!"

"Would it all be metal?" she said, suddenly, inexplicably afraid of hope. "Maybe it's just on the surface."

"If the Earth's sun went nova, Mercury, Venus and Earth would be pulverized, but the rubble doesn't go away. Earth is mostly liquid phase. So is Venus. A supernova would burst them like water balloons. The magma and liquid iron cores splash into mountain- and continent-sized droplets, gradually freezing in the cold of space. This might be just a frozen drop of a planetary core. We've…" Words failed him.

She gripped his arms. His helmet lamp showed a grin in his beard.

"We can build anything!" he said.

They hugged and laughed.

THIRTY-SEVEN

EXHAUSTION SOAKED ALL the way to Pascale's aching bones, but she was still riding an adrenaline high, one that seemed to have been carrying her for days. She and Gabriel-Antoine had been surviving on three- and four-hour naps, as they built a new world from scratch, partly within a subterranean hollow, partly out among the naked stars.

Without morning or evening, they soldered new chips and assembled new robotic builders in their habitat. In survival suits in the vacuum of the last chamber of the cave, they sealed the edges and airlock of the new hydroponics cabin. They planted spinach, bell peppers, kale, chard, and various kinds of beans. Pascale whispered the French word for each sprout as she placed it in its tray. *Épinard, poivron, bettes, fèves*. It would be weeks—in some cases months—to harvest, but they were bringing life to the heart of Venus.

On the other side of the Axis Mundi, they worked deeper into the asteroid, finding that although it was solid, it wasn't one piece. It was a collection of heavy masses of metal and minerals and dust, welded together by delicate, crusty snows and hard, porous ices. They dug and melted their way in, freeing manageable chunks of metal. They used robot arc welders on the bigger fragments, powered by the microwaves of the pulsar, simply heating outer layers to bubbling liquid droplets that cooled and solidified in the vacuum.

The caves beneath the surface of Venus were perfect for processing metal ore. Carbon monoxide gas—a byproduct of cracking carbon dioxide into breathable oxygen—when mixed with metals at high pressures and about two hundred degrees, made gaseous and liquid carbonyls that could be handled relatively simply and then induced to deposit the metal on a surface. This became the start of making beams and sheets of steel.

Telling the different metals apart was challenging. Gabriel-Antoine didn't have a whole diagnostic chemistry kit, but they both knew how different metals reacted with sulfuric acid. With crude acid tests, they roughly identified in their asteroid a lot of iron, significant fractions of nickel, some platinum and some heavy metals they could only guess at. Their Geiger counter reacted to a mix of radioisotopes that they collected and stored in lead boxes.

Tired and often hungry, Pascale learned so much, and tried to help Gabriel-Antoine automate what they could. Venus was poorly automated, not because they didn't know things, but for *bébittes*. Venusians had learned not to rely on complex machines for life or death, but the rules were different here. She and Gabriel-Antoine had passed below the layers of acid. This was a new world with new rules. They had open-source software and design specs for industrial and construction robots, and each robot enabled the building of others, and their little brood of robots grew. Pascale loved learning it all, but even more, she loved the excitement in Gabriel-Antoine's voice, the light in his eyes as they talked about what to build next. When they were like this, in this creation dream, she felt connected to him, in a profound way entirely separate from her body—just two minds making a new world.

Gabriel-Antoine really was an inventor and a dreamer, but everything came in steps for him. His mind thought in priorities: first the rectennae in space that converted microwaves into electricity, and the turbines to give them power within the cave; then the robots. And as often as not, the robots were tasked with building other robots. They needed pairs of working hands as much as they needed ideas and brains.

They needed to build tools too, mostly from scratch. At first they would be crude. Everything that would have stocked a decent machine shop had to be built down here. They were limited by the speed at which an exhausted Pascale could make more of her simple, homemade computer chips for their primitive robots, stinking up the habitat with lines soldered into ceramic. The chips were not advanced, but even primitive chips, working together, could do repeated tasks well.

And they began laying down the frames of larger dreams. They didn't know whether to call them submarines or spaceships or airships—they wanted something capable of moving through all three environments. The lower atmosphere of Venus was so hostile that it was almost an impassable barrier. They could cross it in the atmospheric diving suits, or when they dropped equipment down with the bathyscaphe, but those methods didn't scale well. Everything else had to pass through crushing pressure and oven heat—unprotected medicines, food, and people couldn't cross.

The kind of heat-insulated vehicle that could operate in a vacuum, be buoyant in the middle atmosphere, and survive the surface wasn't easy to design—there was no single plan from last century they could turn to. Its rigid steel skin needed to be about a centimeter thick, like the bathyscaphe, but couldn't be very wide, or it wouldn't fit through the caves, which erosion had widened to about the diameter of the Axis Mundi. Gradually, designs took shape beneath their fingers, each adding elements, each finding pieces and short cuts the other had missed. Pascale and Gabriel-Antoine were making ships that could sail by starlight, through carbon dioxide ocean, or nestled by biting acid.

Having only two pairs of hands made everything slower and harder. While they worked, they talked by disembodied radio about who they needed here next, what skills they would need. It was a tough puzzle, because they were just two. Pascale kept circling back to bringing Émile to the surface, but the idea made her feel shy. Did she want him seeing her during her change, seeing her while she and Gabriel-Antoine… drifted apart? Broke up? She was feeling her way through everything and the idea of doing it with an audience made her cringe.

She had pried loose a big section of metal from the asteroid, two meters long, maybe twenty to thirty centimeters thick and wide. It was weightless in the vacuum, but it massed a few hundred kilos. Just pulling it out made her struggle with her footing. Gabriel-Antoine jetted close to steady her and the chunk of ore.

“That’s a big one! This alone could make a whole hull panel.”

“There’s more,” she said, indicating the hollow she’d pulled this one from. Metal glinted among ice aggregates.

She tied the ore chunk to a length of cabling. Gabriel-Antoine was getting into the hollow to chisel at the loose grains of ice and put them into a bag. They didn’t know what the ices were. Carbon dioxide, water grains, solid methane and ammonia snows all looked the same, so the best they could do was collect the snows and try to separate them on the Venus side. Gabriel-Antoine held up the newly filled bag a little triumphantly and floated away from the asteroid, where he’d been holding himself by wedging his feet against it. He rubbed his feet.

“Who would believe we have to worry about frostbite beneath the clouds?” he said.

“Regrets?”

He stopped moving and peered into her faceplate. She suddenly regretted the question—it was too bold of her. But he was smiling, maybe a bit wanly. She felt her cheeks heating.

“No,” he said, and he briefly stroked her shoulder and kept on smiling.

***The Harsh Mother*, by Émile D'Aquillon**

Suckling
her children on
volcanic ash and brimstone,
she caresses her brood with fingers
of nettled rains, scarring them
with pitiless, indelible
kisses.

Children
of a harsh mother
cling to apron strings,
paying dearly for love, crying out
when she finds them wanting,
and even when they are
good.

Urchins
know the mother's severity, learn to love in desperation,
fitfully, under the rod, resigned
to endure her caprices, for
nothing.

THIRTY-EIGHT

ÉMILE LANDED AMONG the roof lights on the *Baie-Comeau* for another meeting with Tétreau. The cloud tops glowed faintly in the starlight. In the west, the crescent of the horizon smouldered red with approaching dawn. Columns of altocumulus clouds reached high enough to be painted with yellow-white sunshine at their tips. The vastness of Venus and her works made human reaching seem small and presumptuous.

Tétreau had not stopped bringing up the idea of Émile becoming a sergeant, but he might be running out of patience. Émile hoped it wasn't that. If push came to shove, he could try wearing the chevrons for a while. He had a few thoughts about how being a cop could help him, in spite of Marthe's judging voice carping from the back of his head. Or maybe not. It wasn't just that the police work didn't interest him. He really wanted to *think*, to write, to make something real of his poetry. He'd even been drinking a little less.

He hung his wing-pack in the roof lockers and cycled through the upper airlock. He put his helmet on a shelf, pulled the netting across, and then went down towards the police offices. He found Tétreau and a few of the boys in the ready room. It had once been a meeting room, but for some reason had lost its table, so it had become an informal ready room where they could close the door, crank up the exhaust fan and light up. When he opened the door, everyone turned to look, like he'd interrupted something serious.

"I can come back."

Tétreau shook his head and signalled him in. "We have an op to do. Warrants and everything."

"Sweet," Émile said, closing the door behind him. "Who's the lucky bastard?"

"You are. I have a warrant for your arrest."

Émile looked around. Tétreau didn't seem to be joking. Émile suddenly realized that the guys here weren't random—Groulx, Jalbert and Daigle were the biggest constables. Daigle alone was as big as him. Émile lifted his hands placatingly.

"What for?" Émile said.

"The theft of the *Causapscal-des-Vents,*" Tétreau said.

"It sank, jackass."

Émile considered his options, then threw a punch at Daigle, who deflected it like a boxer. Then all three of them pounded him until he was on his back on the floor yelling, "Alright! Alright! Alright!"

They bound his hands behind his back while his lips and nose bled pools around him. It took two of them to lift him to his knees and then to get his feet under him. They patted him down for weapons or tools. Tétreau didn't say another word as they took him away.

They headed down several flights of stairs, which meant they were going to one of the bays, probably to transport him to a brig in a shitty habitat like the *Petit Kamouraska*.

Tabarnak. This meant everything was going south, for Pascale and everyone. The *Sûreté* could be a bit slapdash, but a search warrant took evidence, which meant they were all fucked. The clouds were big, but eventually someone would be bought off who could say where the D'Aquillons were. Stars or not, maybe one of the new 'family' had decided to turn Pa in.

They turned down a hallway near the stern, towards a bay he knew well, the little one used to lower five- and ten-meter bundles out of the *Baie-Comeau* for drone shipping. He'd been in this bay with Thérèse and her friends, taking off their helmets for their stupid communions with Venus. *Crisse,* but he felt like an idiot for… everything. Groulx keyed in a code and the door unlocked. The ten-by-eight-meter bay was bare except for Marie-Pier and a bucket. They shoved him in.

"Hey, hey!" he said. "Cuffs!" He turned his back to them and held his wrists out.

They paused noticeably and Jalbert said, "If you do anything stupid, we'll break both your legs and cuff you again."

"Yeah, yeah," Émile said. "You still brought three of you."

Someone opened his cuffs while he held still. Then the door closed, followed by a mechanical locking sound. Marie-Pier's expression was ashen.

"Still happy with your new husband?" Émile asked, wiping the blood on his face.

****** Special Bulletin ******

The *Sûreté de Vénus* made several arrests today after an extensive investigation into the sinking of the *Causapscal-des-Vents*. Constables today charged Émile D'Aquillon, formerly of the *Causapscal-des-Vents,* with the theft of that habitat. It was reported to have sunk two months ago, but new evidence emerged that it had been stolen and disassembled for parts to be sold on the black market.

Constables also arrested Marie-Pier Hudon as an accomplice. Still at large with warrants for their arrest are George-Étienne D'Aquillon, a *coureur* known to live in the trawler habitat *Causapscal-des-Profondeurs,* and Gabriel-Antoine Phocas, of the *Marais-des-Nuages*. Wanted for questioning is the minor Pascal D'Aquillon, also of the *Causapscal-des-Profondeurs*.

Any information regarding the locations of George-Étienne D'Aquillon, Gabriel-Antoine Phocas, and Pascal D'Aquillon leading to an arrest will be subject to a reward.

Alain Dussault
Inspecteur
Sûreté de Vénus

THIRTY-NINE

Émile paced the cargo bay. It was small for a bay, but big for a detention cell. The bay door, taking up the entire outside wall, had small porthole windows. The red-orange cloud tops fluffed themselves up like birds keeping warm before dawn. Émile felt like he wanted to lift something, hit something, or run.

Marie-Pier sat statue-still, looking ahead with glazed eyes. In their first hour, they'd spoken a bit. She was terrified of what would happen to her children without her. Apparently her brother was a good uncle, but he hadn't asked for this.

"This wasn't the deal," she'd said. "Marthe said that the whole family would work together."

Émile had been ready to say that when you get close to Pa, that's what happens, but he couldn't say the same about Marthe. Thinking about her made twisting feelings of hurt rise in him. Marthe had been just a little sister who'd loved him, when he'd been a big, clumsy brother making up games with her. She'd grown into a hard woman, with a spine that couldn't be bent. But despite the fighting and arguing she'd gotten good at, she'd never lost the hopefulness at the core of her.

"Marthe meant it," he said.

"Maxime and Florian were supposed to come down, to grow up with Louise and Paul-Égide and Alexis." She wiped her eyes. "They're all about the same age. Alexis has no one to play with."

"They caught us for stealing," he said. "We'll need to be punished, but that doesn't change that the whole *colonie* is an all-hands-on-deck place. We'll lose privileges. They'll still need me to fix things. They need you to make bigger and better trawlers. And they sure as hell need you to raise your kids. Pa and Marthe stuck it to Gaschel, so the bitch will have to do something visible and symbolic, but once it's clear that she won and we lost, she'll need all of us working."

Marie-Pier took a shaky breath, then rubbed her eyes.

"The kids are probably scared shitless right now," she said.

Émile tired of looking at cloud tops. They were always different, but they were always the same. He sat and pulled a few tightly folded sheets of paper from a pocket, and a crude, stubby pencil from another. He held them for a long time between his knees, his thoughts jumbled, slowly turning in the same direction as Marie-Pier. Émile's sister was dead. His Pa would get arrested, and maybe even Pascale too. Who would take care of Jean-Eudes and Alexis? They didn't have an uncle in the picture the way Marie-Pier had. Émile was in jail, and despite what he'd just said, he would get it as bad as Pa. Émile had been on the *Causapscal-des-Vents*. He'd been the one to sink it. Maybe at trial, he could say it had all been his idea, and that he'd forced the others?

He was the most disposable. He didn't take care of anyone. No one needed him. His head told him his love for Thérèse had been a mistake, an exercise of breathtaking denial and wishful thinking, but his heart wouldn't let go of its hope for something with her. Was he any different from Marthe? Marthe dreamed big and innocently, against all common sense. Her dream of stars had killed her. How was he different, except that his dream was narrower, less ambitious, more selfish? His hard anger, turned inward, was familiar footing from which he could write a new poem.

'Soul Rendered in Stone,' as a title, felt right and amateurish at once. He could fix it later. The words spilled in rivulets and channels of scratched letters filling one folded side of paper. He unfolded and refolded to reveal a blank space, filling that one, and moving to another. He was still scratching and rewriting words when he noticed Marie-Pier's attention. He angled the paper away from her.

"What are you doing?" she said.

"Poetry."

"Just like that? In here?"

He shrugged. "I got nothing else to do. They haven't offered us a lawyer."

"Pascale told me you're a poet."

"Pascale doesn't know a lot of poets."

Her regard was penetrating, intent, but her voice remained soft. "What are you writing about?"

He didn't like answering questions about his writing. Actually, he barely tolerated them, but dismissing Marie-Pier didn't feel like something he wanted to do. She was important to Pascale. She had been important to Marthe.

"I was with somebody," he said. "At the beginning, I didn't see what she was. Now I know she's vain, pretentious and absorbed with cultish bullshit."

Marie-Pier raised an eyebrow.

"She's one of the religious nuts that think of Venus as a goddess in more than a metaphorical way. Acid artists, chanters, trying to touch Venus," he added dismissively.

"So you turned a corner?"

"Maybe life would be better if I'd never met her, but the moments were real for me, even if they weren't real for her. There aren't enough real things in the clouds."

"Is that what you wrote?"

He shook his head. "This one may be just my resentment. It's an indulgence."

"Therapy?" she said.

He shrugged.

"Their pain is real," she said.

"Whose?"

"Those religious people, the ones who really take it somewhere," she said. "My brother Jean-Marc had trouble when he was younger. He got suicidal for a bit. He joined one of those groups. I don't know how much hope he got out of it. Maybe it was just a shelter from the storm for him."

"Pain is a badge to show off, for them," Émile said. "They're proud of feeling sorry for themselves."

"What did you call the poem?"

His cheeks warmed.

"Can I read it?" she said.

"It's bad. Everything is bad when you first write it down."

Without looking at her, he handed her the paper. She read quietly for a long time and it seemed to him that she was a slow reader, or was trying to think of something kind to say. Then, she folded the paper and handed it back. He put it in his survival suit and sealed the pocket.

"There's a lot of your father in you," she said after a moment.

He didn't know how to respond; he felt vaguely insulted.

He was about to begin with something flippant when yellow lights started flashing on the ceiling and he scrambled up.

"*Tabarnak*!"

Marie-Pier was also on her feet, immediately realising what was happening.

Émile slapped on the porthole window on the door, and looked through. No one was in the hallway. Marie-Pier tapped at the control panel, but it wouldn't turn on. Émile had done safety briefings, but he couldn't remember how the manual switches in the *Baie-Comeau* worked. Nothing ever broke on the new habitat. Marie-Pier opened the mechanical access panel. There were two levers inside, one for the outer bay door and one for the door to the hallway. The yellow caution lights on the ceiling strobed more quickly, and the outer door clanged as the locks disengaged.

"I'll pull," he said.

He gripped the manual bypass for the door into the *Baie-Comeau*, but it didn't budge.

"There's got to be a release," he said.

Marie-Pier's expression was horrified, blood-drained certainty.

"They must have blocked it," she said with a kind of stunned calm. "The panels shouldn't be off either. This isn't an accident."

"What?" He didn't quite follow her logic.

"We're not getting a trial. They don't want these questions answered in public. This is an execution."

The bay door began to swing up on its hinges along the top edge, like it had when he'd been here to touch Venus with Thérèse and her clingers-on. His pencil, forgotten where they'd been sitting, skittered along the floor on a breath of escaping air. Its clicking, rolling sound became distant, then muted. Pain stabbed Émile's ears and eyes and he let the air leave him, in an exhalation so powerful that his chest ached. Marie-Pier collapsed to her knees, her mouth wide, her eyes beginning to redden. She beat on the door silently, and jabbed at the dead pad beside it. No answer.

Marie-Pier's words sank in, and despite the panic he was getting mad.

He wasn't going to die staring at metal and plastic. He staggered along the wall, to the edge of the bay. Venus, the bitch, was below them in her finery, her skirts of clouds in late dawn splotched with amber and rust and carrot over grim shadows. The naked sun, which he'd never seen except through glass, stared back at him at eye level, painted in bloody gold.

Marie-Pier slipped to the floor, bleeding eyes lidding as she passed out. He wouldn't be far behind. People had maybe thirty to ninety seconds before passing out in a vacuum. This wasn't a way to die. It felt cheap and dismissive.

Fuck them! Fuck them!

The bay door had yawned open completely, and Émile didn't know what to do to make his last moments meaningful, to say, *Émile was here. Émile existed*. No one cared. His heart hammered. He could jump, ending it his way, dying as *coureurs* died, just him and Venus.

He staggered to the edge. His fingers curled around the icy edge of the wall… and felt a rung. He looked around the edge with the beginnings of dizziness. It was a ladder following the curving line of the habitat's envelope, maybe thirty meters to the roof. A habitat of this size probably had eight or twelve ladders along the outside. But he was still too far away from help.

Exposure to low pressure didn't kill right away, but unconsciousness came fast. They'd found that out with Thérèse and her followers, looking on Venus's clouds with unprotected eyes. He was going to pass out soon. His vision blurred under black speckling. He took a step towards Marie-Pier, but would never be able to lift her in this condition. He wouldn't even make a dozen rungs himself. He was sorry to leave her there, but this was between Venus and him now, about how to die. He pulled on his gloves, gripped a rung of the ladder and stepped out, his chest aching. Little bubbles tried to freeze at the edges of his eyelids. He looked one last time at Marie-Pier's still body, memorizing her death, and then climbed the ladder as fast as he could.

The *Baie-Comeau* seemed immense from outside, and time seemed to lengthen as his legs churned painfully, rung by rung. His arms and legs weakened as black spots stippled the edges of his vision. His mouth swelled and dried, and he couldn't swallow around his seizing throat. As the slope eased, the ladder led him to the low net around the edge of the roof. Two port workers saw him as his vision blackened and narrowed. He tripped over the netting and fell.

He was aware of his body being dragged to the airlock, but distantly, like something happening in a movie. He could no longer move. His eyes seemed to freeze at some middle focus in which the blurred rooftop ghosted by. The world narrowed to a cold, painful pressure on every part of his body. Then the sun went away and he was inside. Sound returned in stages of painful hissing as the airlock pressurized. His lungs didn't work. The pain made them feel shredded. His heart pounded, hadn't stopped hammering all this time. His ears heard nothing but ringing. His muscles cramped and ached like he'd overused all of them.

The workers dragged him out of the airlock and into the *Baie-*

Comeau. He knelt on all fours, trying to breathe. Someone had tried to kill him—probably the *Sûreté,* but maybe someone else. They'd killed Marie-Pier, and if they found him here, they would arrest him again and find some other way to fix their loose ends. He still couldn't hear much. He pressed his gloves to his aching ears and both palms came away bloody. Someone put water in front of him. He drank, but his tongue and throat didn't work; water spilled onto the floor. He sat, tried again and managed to drink a bit. It burned all the way down.

He heard, "How did you get out there, man?" and, "A doctor is on the way."

He crawled to the wall and leaned on it heavily to get to his feet. His helmet was still on the shelf where he'd left it before his arrest. He pulled aside the netting and drew it out. Every muscle in his body hurt and he wanted to lay down, but if he stayed here, he would die as certainly as if he'd never left the cargo bay.

"What are you doing?" someone said. "Hey, stop!"

Émile shook off their hands.

"I gotta go," he croaked. "They tried to kill me."

He put his helmet on and locked the seal, then turned the oxygen up as he stumbled back into the airlock. The dock workers hung back, looking spooked. The airlock door closed and he ran the sequence. Air traffic control had probably already been alerted, and if they weren't, they soon would be. Whether it was cops, the bitch, or someone else who had tried to kill him, they would check on their handiwork, see he was missing, and come looking for him. He opened the outer airlock door. No one else was on the roof right now. He uncased his wings and pulled them on, voicing some commands to his suit.

"Switch comms to passive," he wheezed through a burning throat. "Turn off ID transponder."

His HUD flashed various nag messages at him, asking for override permission. He gave it, gasping in pain. He spun up the engine on his wing-pack, staggered to the launch board and leapt. He flew, not terribly. As long as he kept his body straight, the wing-pack did a lot of the work. He banked along the port side of the *Baie-Comeau*. The cargo bay door he'd just nearly died in was closed. It made sense. Whoever had killed Marie-Pier wouldn't have wanted a bay door suspiciously open. They would have had it on a four- or five-minute cycle, just enough to suffocate and freeze the two of them.

He trembled now, and he didn't think it was the decompression or the adrenaline drop. He'd just witnessed a murder he couldn't stop. Marie-Pier had been kind to him, to Pascale. And because of this stupid dream of the stars, she was dead, and her kids were orphans. Shit, shit, shit. Marie-Pier was dead. His body shivered worse. Shit, Marie-Pier.

He needed to think this through. There was way more shit going on here than he'd thought. How had the bitch president found out about the *Causapscal-des-Vents*? Venus was too big to find a single habitat floating in the immensity of the atmosphere. Someone had ratted. It hadn't been Marie-Pier or Marthe. It hadn't been him, or Pa, no matter what he thought of the old bastard. Had it been Gabriel-Antoine?

Even with the theft of the *Causapscal-des-Vents*, why execute Émile? Or Marie-Pier? The only way to connect her to this, other than politically, was if they knew she'd used her big trawlers to hold the construction site afloat. The number of people who knew that was real small, and might include Marie-Pier's brother, Jean-Marc. It still wasn't worth killing over, though. Was it radiation? Tétreau had been nervous about that, but Tétreau lost his shit for small stuff.

The one thing worth killing over, though, was Pascale's wormhole. Émile had never exactly believed it; it was too big an idea to really buy. He'd only helped because Marthe was sure. Marthe had been sure of a lot of things that he wouldn't have swallowed or understood. And if Pascale's wormhole was true, then its value was… Well, people would stoop to killing for it, probably a lot of people.

And they'd be looking for him in the flotillas. They'd never find Émile in the lower decks, and if his math wasn't wrong, there would be a not-terrible glide path to the *Causapscal-des-Profondeurs* in six or eight hours. He would need to really calculate to see if it was possible, but he couldn't do that while flying, not in this condition. He also needed some wings for the cloud decks, not these up-cloud ones that would eventually melt. Man, he felt like shit. His gorge kept rising. His shaking got harder and he wouldn't be able to fly very far like this. He needed a place to lay low.

The last he'd heard, Thérèse and her sycophants were crashing on the *Avant-Gardiste*: one of Isolde Livernois's brothers had been shacking up with a girlfriend somewhere and the other brother was doing work on the *Forillon*. The *Avant-Gardiste* was only twelve kilometers northwest.

He set his course and flew against the sun as its light lensed sharply through watery eyes.

FORTY

Tétreau had been on his way to his office when multi-component alarms started buzzing on his notifications. Depressurization. Safety system failures. Offline alerts. He ran the last two floors, accidentally knocking over an accountant. Past the glass doors, he found Labourière, standing over Tétreau's smart desk.

"What's happening?" Tétreau asked breathlessly.

Labourière was oddly calm. "Taking care of problems."

Tétreau came around his desk. The display was already set to the alarms, the image windows flashing red. A camera showed Marie-Pier Hudon and Émile D'Aquillon in Cargo Loading Bay E. They looked panicked, and Tétreau was stunned to see the bay door opening, the line of bright sunlight overexposed, temporarily blackening the rest of the image.

"*Câlisse*!" he said, reaching for the controls to close the bay door.

Labourière shoved him.

"What the *crisse*?" Tétreau demanded, with a suspicious dread. The bay door rose fast, filling the bay with light. Another camera showed both of the detainees suffocating. "Get the fuck out of the way!"

Labourière gripped his arms. "We need to get rid of them quietly. No one will know."

"*Tabarnak*! The alert systems are linked to maintenance and ops! Everyone will know."

"I shut those feeds off," Labourière said. "I couldn't shut yours off because I couldn't get through the police encryption."

The images showed Hudon collapsing to the floor. D'Aquillon had staggered to the edge of the bay. He was going to pass out and fall into the clouds. Tétreau shoved Labourière, but the older man resisted. Tétreau freed a hand, punched him away, and began manipulating the desk.

D'Aquillon had vanished from the display, and Hudon lay still on the floor. Tétreau set the bay door closing and reactivated the safety systems, triggering a new wave of alarms. The door was fast, but big. It would be another dozen seconds to seal and then thirty to sixty to repressurize the bay, even under rescue protocols.

"You don't get it," Labourière said with hot disappointment.

"D'Aquillon and Hudon are problems alive, but they're bigger problems dead!"

"We're two steps from the interest on all the colony's loans being dialed up. *That* will kill us! That will kill the whole colony, everything we've sacrificed for. Two traitors vanishing buys us time."

"Does Gaschel know?" Tétreau demanded.

"Of course not, and if you're smart, you won't tell her. I've just given her a deniable accident. With a bit of work on the record-keeping, Hudon and D'Aquillon were never here."

"Three of *my* guys arrested him and threw him in that bay!"

The bay door was closed. Emergency repressurization began.

"You can't keep your own men quiet?" Labourière demanded.

Another alert sounded on his system. Port Ops was signalling. A message came through: *Depressurization incident—unidentified man climbed to the roof port of the Baie-Comeau without a helmet*.

"*Tabarnak!* Arrest him," Tétreau called through.

Labourière came to the display and saw the message. "What? How?" He'd gone ashen faced.

"You just dropped *all* of us into hot water," Tétreau said. Labourière collapsed into Tétreau's chair.

"He doesn't need to survive. He might not."

"Word of a guy without a helmet climbing to the landing pad will be all over the flotillas in an hour," Tétreau said.

"News of you re-apprehending a saboteur will be."

Another message came through his desk: *Unidentified man cycled out already with a helmet.*

"Congratulations. You just released D'Aquillon back into the flotillas," Tétreau accused.

"You can't catch one decompressed man? He just left!"

Tétreau issued new arrest instructions. He hoped some constables were nearby.

"You'd better hope D'Aquillon isn't using his radio to tell people what just happened," Tétreau said. "And so much for keeping Gaschel out of this. We *have* to tell her now."

STABBING PAIN SHOT through Marie-Pier's head in time with her racing heartbeat. Her eyes wouldn't focus properly. Hard lights shone in them. Vomit was bitter on her tongue and lips, which were also vaguely numb. Spasms knifed her muscles. She smelled her own waste. She remembered the depressurization and blacking out. The light flashed away from her eyes, replaced with a blurry ceiling.

"Can you hear me, *Madame* Hudon?" a woman said.

Marie-Pier's breath was watery in her chest, like when she'd had pneumonia, and she hadn't the breath to talk. She closed her eyes tight against the pain. Her suit was open to her waist and a cold stethoscope touched here and there.

"The gas-exchange tissues are probably torn," the woman said. "I've got to monitor her oxygen levels. She'll have bubbles in her veins that could block blood flow to the brain and kill her."

Marie-Pier tried to take a deeper breath, but it rattled below her throat and fire needled beneath her ribs.

"She's a seditionist leader," a second voice said. "Leaving her here will just endanger others in the hospital. I have to take her to a more secure location."

"Three minutes is a long decompression," the woman said. Marie-Pier's head hurt too much to move, but at the bottom of her blotchy vision was a blonde woman she recognised, Doctor Phaneuf. "She might not even survive. Until we run some tests, we won't know how much cognitive damage there is."

"Half an hour," the man said. "After that, the *Sûreté* has to take her into custody, for everyone's safety."

Marie-Pier tried to speak and rise, but her body was too beaten.

ÉMILE TOUCHED DOWN on the roof of the *Avant-Gardiste* and collapsed. The rising sun became whiter and more painful. His bones hurt in their marrows and the vision in his left eye was definitely screwy. Every muscle in his body hurt like he'd overworked them. His lungs ached, and even his tepid, cautious coughing spattered tiny droplets of blood onto the inside of his faceplate. He crawled, then stood, racking his wings before going through the airlock. He'd been listening on the common band and what police channels he could unscramble, but no news about him or Marie-Pier was out yet.

He hesitated before leaving his helmet in the entrée, but set it firmly on a shelf.

The *Avant-Gardiste* was a clean, newer habitat, decorated by someone who'd spent some time on it. The entry-hall had a mirror, and he took a moment to look at himself. Weird purple blotches bruised his face and the white of one of his eyes was pink and reddening. He pulled a rag from the inside of his suit and wiped at blood hardening to flakes beneath his ears and nose. His hands shook.

Crisse. Tabarnak.

He descended the stairs, leaning heavily on the railing. He heard voices through a door and pressed on to a larger galley than the one on the *Causapscal-des-Vents,* better organized and a lot less cannibalized.

Thérèse sat at the table, smoking. Réjean was there, and Hélène, and Lucette, and two guys he didn't recognize. Thérèse's expression shifted quickly from laughing to irritated, and still Émile had a stupid pang of longing. The others regarded him with cool disdain.

"Can I talk to you for a minute?" Émile said into the new quiet.

"No."

"My stepmother is dead."

Thérèse took a bored drag on her cigarette. "Sorry to hear that," she said without a hint of sympathy.

"I need a radio to tell my family," he said. They all still watched him.

"There are lots of radios in the flotilla."

"They tried to kill me," he said finally. "Okay? They did kill my stepmother. I'm on the run and I need to warn my family."

Thérèse's careful poise finally broke. She put down her cigarette. "The radio is over there." She waved a hand. "Who's 'they'? Black marketeers?"

"Come on," he said scornfully, striding to the radio. It was near the sleeping rooms, a couple of meters from the table. Not privacy, but better than nothing.

She rose, scowling. Near the radio, he said in a low voice, "I didn't know where to go. They arrested us and put us in the same cargo hold we used to look at Venus with our naked eyes. They opened the bay door. Marie-Pier suffocated. I found a ladder on the outside of the envelope to the roof."

"Who did this?" she said. "How do you know it wasn't a system error? What were you arrested for?"

"A system error, after being thrown in the bay instead of a brig?" he whispered.

"Are *we* in danger now?" she demanded in a low voice.

"I turned off my transponder. No one knows I'm here, because why would anyone think I'm coming here?" He needed to support himself on the counter. "I came because I thought we shared something once, because I thought you might have some kindness left."

"I'm not throwing you out."

"Yeah, I guess," he said. "I wrote a poem about you."

Her expression briefly softened.

"I need to lay low, maybe for a few hours."

"And make us accomplices? I don't think so."

Réjean looked up sharply. "Accomplices to what?"

"Sit the fuck down, Réjean," Émile said, but Réjean was on his feet and moving to the stairs to the roof. "Calling someone?" Émile demanded.

"No," Réjean said. "I've got a taser in my kit. If I need it, to get you out of here, I want it on hand."

"You're a tool, Réjean."

Réjean took the stairs two at a time as the pressure door closed behind him.

"They just tried to kill me, Thérèse!" Émile whispered.

"Why would anyone try to kill you?"

"You have to trust that there are some secrets that aren't mine to tell." He pulled the folded piece of paper from his pocket and slapped it into her hand: his poem, scrawled, unpolished. "This is for you. I'll use the radio and go."

She returned to the table and upended a shot. Émile pulled up the controls for the transmitting antenna. He couldn't remember exactly where the *Causapscal-des-Profondeurs* was in its cycle in the eddy. The last check-in had been at *Trou-à-Eudore* and they'd been planning to follow the *Ruisseau-Creux* jet stream to *Trois-Frères*. What day, though? He had coded notes on the *Marais-des-Nuages,* but didn't want to risk going there. Not yet.

He set the maser transmitter on a slightly wider angle towards *Trois-Frères* and signalled the *Causapscal-des-Profondeurs* with his personal code. He let it try to hook up for a few minutes. In the meantime, Réjean appeared from the stairs, hard-faced and holding his police taser. Réjean had always been a fucking loser. A light on the radio greened—the signal had received a response, carrying his father's code and some metadata for narrowing the beam to increase privacy. Émile entered passwords they'd agreed to and put on the headset. He'd only talked to his father once in five years, and that had been to accuse him of killing Marthe. He flipped the switch to activate voice transmission and reception.

"Where's Pascale?" Émile said.

"What do you need?" his father said.

He couldn't say it right away. It took some breaths. He felt, again, like he was going to puke.

"Marie-Pier is dead," he said in a low voice.

"What?"

"She and I were arrested. For... the theft," he said, looking back at the people straining to hear his words. "I don't know how they found out. They put us in a cargo bay on the *Baie-Comeau* instead of with other detainees in a brig. I thought it was because they'd run out of space because of all the black marketeer arrests. They opened the bay door to suffocate us. That's how she died. I almost did too, but I found one of the external maintenance ladders on the outer envelope and climbed to the roof."

"*Calvaire,*" his father swore in a punctured voice.

"We were in police custody when it happened," Émile said. "I don't know how the government found out about the habitat, but you better think hard about whether Phocas is really on your side."

"He's on our side," his father said with heat. "He's on the surface with Pascal."

"Well, it wasn't Marie-Pier who told anyone, and no one else knows."

"*Crisse,*" his father swore. "Did *you* give it away?"

"I didn't fuck anything up," Émile said, almost raising his voice, and looking cautiously at Thérèse, Réjean and their friends. "I'm not safe up here. I'm coming down. If it wasn't Phocas, then the government might go after his brother and sister to blackmail him. I may need to bring them down."

"Be careful with them."

"I know how to be careful."

"You haven't been in the lower decks in years."

"I'm *coureur,*" Émile said.

"You're... twelve degrees away. You'll have a drop window in a few hours."

"Yeah, if I was coming down on wings by myself. With the kids, I'll have to calculate it different. I gotta go. Marie-Pier's kids may be in danger too. She was really worried. You get them somewhere else."

Émile flipped the transmitter off, swivelled the antenna to station-keeping, and erased the log of his call so no one would be able to calculate the location of the *Causapscal-des-Profondeurs*. In all the time he'd been talking, Thérèse had not unfolded the paper. It sat on the table between her hand and Helene's. He didn't want anything unsaid between them, but maybe he'd said all he could. Maybe Thérèse's hardened heart was as distant from him as Marthe, or Marie-Pier, or his mother. Some messages could never get through.

FORTY-ONE

"WHAT HAVE YOU done, François-Xavier?" Gaschel demanded, with a feeling of falling hopelessness. "I have to address *l'Assemblée* in a few hours. What am I going to tell them?"

She, Labourière and Tétreau were in her office. Her assistant Cinthia had stalled a number of people in the waiting area to fit the two men in.

"I'm sorry, *Madame la Présidente,*" Labourière said, "but D'Aquillon will be back in custody shortly—or if we're lucky, he'll be killed resisting arrest."

Gaschel put her forehead between two hands.

"The bank is ready to cut us off at the knees because we don't have control of the colony," Labourière argued, "but now we've found the *Causapscal-des-Vents.* The whole D'Aquillon plot is so alien to everyday life that people will believe us. And so will the bank. Marthe D'Aquillon dying in that storm was a godsend. Dead people don't argue back. This almost worked."

"That's not what we have now," Tétreau said. "We now have two live people who know this government tried to kill them."

"Marie-Pier Hudon doesn't need to talk to anyone right now,"

Labourière said.

"Solitary confinement doesn't stop our bigger problem of Émile D'Aquillon running around," Gaschel said.

Tétreau was steady and quiet, but his tense body language betrayed a deep anger. She eyed him questioningly.

"My people can get him, *Madame Présidente,*" Tétreau said. "I just hope it's before he talks to anyone."

"Talks to anyone who believes him," Gaschel said.

"There is that," Tétreau acknowledged.

"There's more than that," she said. "I don't want this pointing at us anymore. Make it clear that D'Aquillon broke out of the bay, that he deliberately depressurized it to escape. Whatever happened to Marie-Pier Hudon is on him."

"That's not what the evidence will show," Tétreau said.

"François-Xavier will make sure the evidence shows precisely that," she said with finality.

"I'll begin immediately," Labourière said, standing. Tétreau stood too.

"Laurent," she added, "after managing your constables, why don't you see Cinthia and take a look at modifying my speech to *l'Assemblée* this afternoon? Make it work in light of all this."

Tétreau stood a little straighter. Labourière pursed his lips tighter, but did not object.

GASCHEL ROSE IN the special meeting of *l'Assemblée Nationale.* Gaschel had kept such meetings rare, and many representatives had made the effort. Not everyone could reach the main flotilla in just a few hours, but representatives in secondary flotillas had tuned in by radio. Most of the key members waited patiently in the chamber, though, including supporters of her governing coalition: Barnabé Chambeau from the *Petit Kamouraska,* Casimir Daigle from the *Montée de Corte-Real,* Maëlle Guillot from the *Escuminac,* Ovide Dubé from the *Lac-Édouard,* among others.

"Thank you, representatives," she began, "for joining us on such short notice. I bring sad news. It was important to me that you hear it right away."

Beside her, Labourière transmitted the photographs of the half-disassembled habitat hanging in the clouds, draped in radar-blunting epiphytes. Representatives began squinting at their data pad in puzzlement.

"These images are a few weeks old," she said. "This is the *Causapscal-des-Vents,* suspended from engineered trawlers at about forty-eighth *rang.* It's being disassembled. It's taken us the intervening time to confirm that these are not fakes, and to piece together the major parts of the story. It's clear now that ten weeks ago, the D'Aquillon family stole the *Causapscal-des-Vents* by sinking it."

A white noise of murmurs and cursing astonishment rose.

"The fake distress call was convincing," she said. "It mobilized, at great risk to life and equipment, extensive rescue efforts that in the end saved the life of one of the conspirators, Émile D'Aquillon. It is unknown if another conspirator, Marthe D'Aquillon, really died, or if her death was faked to cast aside suspicion."

A low tide of whispers and notes of disbelief bubbled. Several members signalled that they had questions.

"The D'Aquillon family could not have done this alone," she went on. "You may have heard short-wave chatter about the *coureurs* forming new political groups called 'houses.' The D'Aquillon family formed a house with the Hudon family, and the pictures show four engineered trawlers of a size that are grown by Marie-Pier Hudon. Some of those trawlers had been requisitioned by *l'Assemblée* six months ago, to provide extra storage space, and possibly even living space. Hudon reported them lost in a storm around the time the *Causapscal-des-Vents* was sabotaged. There they are in the pictures."

The exclamations grew.

"The other party involved in the 'House of Styx' is the Phocas family," she said. "Gabriel-Antoine Phocas is a talented engineer who for two years has been burying us in lawsuits to hoard tools and metal scrap, which he has traded on the black market. We know that there are other *coureur* families involved. We're tracing other leads right now to these *coureur* 'houses,' and through them to black-marketeering criminal groups among the flotillas."

She gavelled the noise from *l'Assemblée* to a low, affronted murmur and signalled to Labourière to show the next images.

"This isn't just a chop-and-sell criminal enterprise," Gaschel said. "The D'Aquillon, Phocas and Hudon families have been building something. You can see this in images six and seven. We don't know what it is, but they've been transporting tons of steel to the surface. Radar searches located the drop site as a cave mouth in the Diana Chasma."

The volume of questions and side conversations grew and she waited to let it ebb without the gavel, only holding up a hand.

"It has long been a dream of *la colonie* to set up industrial operations on the surface," Gaschel said over the noise, "for the benefit of *every* family. We were waiting for the right opportunity on which to risk our scarce resources. The D'Aquillons, the Phocas, and the Hudons have found an idea and have cut out everyone else. In the process, they stole from all of us, putting our loans at risk.

"It is also clear now why Marie-Pier Hudon, four months ago, tabled a bill in *l'Assemblée,* proposing some mineral claim rights for individuals. Ostensibly this was for trawler design, but its wording is open enough to cover mineral resources the D'Aquillons seem to have found on the surface. The motives behind the legislation are now clear."

Representatives shouted questions over one another. She held up her hands.

"Let me finish telling you all I know and then we'll discuss."

L'Assemblée quieted, only a little.

"We know they've found radioisotopes on the surface, which would be invaluable to everyone in *la colonie,* for medicine, for industry, and for propulsion in near-Venusian space. It's known to everyone that radioisotopes have to be carefully shielded, for everyone's health. Instead, the D'Aquillons, Hudons, and Phocas have been circulating radioisotopes among the *coureurs* for reasons unknown. At best, they're hoarding minerals they think they can later sell on the black market. At worst, the *coureurs* may be building dirty weapons. Even in the best case, people are going to get sick from improper handling of toxic materials. What could have benefited everyone is now endangering a few—or many, possibly all of us.

"A crisis was narrowly averted, recently, when the Bank of Pallas detected radiation in the clouds. They thought that *l'Assemblée* had broken the terms of our loans and were buying resources from another bank. If I had not investigated and explained to them what had happened, they might have used any number of loan clauses to demand back their investments immediately, with catastrophic results for every man, woman, and child in *la colonie*. Thieves and saboteurs and black marketeers have brought us to this point."

She let the cries of outrage rise for some moments, watching them with even calmness before finally gavelling.

"This is more than grand theft, or the possession and movement of dangerous materials," Gaschel said. "It also includes attempted murder."

Some of the murmuring voices in *l'Assemblée* quieted, while others spoke louder. Someone gave out a frustrated, "*Crisse de câlisse de tabarnak*!"

"The *Sûreté* apprehended Émile D'Aquillon and Marie-Pier Hudon this morning. To avoid placing them with general detainees and convicts, who might have assisted them in some way or spread misinformation, the inspector chose to detain them in a cargo bay of the *Baie-Comeau*. Barely three hours later, Émile D'Aquillon succeeded in opening the outer door of the cargo bay. He climbed to the roof of the *Baie-Comeau* without a helmet and managed to get aid from two dock workers who hadn't heard of his arrest. In making his escape, Émile D'Aquillon left his co-conspirator Marie-Pier Hudon in the bay to suffocate. We managed to save her, although her injuries remain severe."

Gaschel gavelled several times over cries of astonishment.

"We have a conspiracy of smuggling, of theft, of sabotage, of reckless endangerment, of possession and transport of dangerous goods, and of gross negligence, or possibly manslaughter," Gaschel said. "The *Sûreté,* reinforced with Bank of Pallas security staff, is moving immediately to capture all of the conspirators in the lower cloud decks and on the surface. Likewise, *Sûreté* constables are making raids on black-market partners of the 'House of Styx,' using warrants received this morning.

"This is not the news I had wanted to give you," she said. "For decades, we've been working not just as a community, but as a family, to lift one another up, to protect one another, to sacrifice for each other. That hasn't gone away. We're moving towards our dream of true economic independence, and the acquiring of a steady stream of affordable metals from 3554 Amun. The dream is nearing. It's unfortunate that our society has also developed dangerous criminal elements, but this is no different from any other society. How we act today, the resolve we demonstrate now, is what will define us and determine our destiny."

George-Étienne sat heavily at the dining table in the *Causapscal-des-Profondeurs*. It was covered with different scraps they were turning into tools and equipment. Jean-Eudes and Alexis were still asleep. It would be an hour yet before they would be at the correct angle to radio Pascale and Gabriel-Antoine to tell them, and then only through the small antenna on the surface that failed as often as it worked.

He'd radioed Jean-Marc Hudon to tell him about the death of his sister. It hadn't been a pleasant conversation, but George-Étienne had gotten through to him that it might not be safe for him and his two now-orphaned nephews, and that they should go to Juliette Malboeuf at *La Reine des Fées*. The House of Faeries would take care of them.

He rubbed his face and blinked. He was going to cry—he just didn't know when. A curtain moved. Jean-Eudes stood there, blinking. Now that Pascale and Gabriel-Antoine were on the surface, Jean-Eudes and Alexis had been excited to take their room. It made George-Étienne's room feel lonely and quiet. Jean-Eudes came closer groggily and stood by the table, puzzling at him.

"What are you doing, *Papa*?"

George-Étienne realized that he wasn't doing anything with his hands. He didn't have anything in his hands. That must seem strange to Jean-Eudes, after all their hurrying over the last months. When Jeanne-Manse had died, Jean-Eudes had been young, but surrounded by Chloé and Émile and Marthe. He'd understood. Everyone had helped explain. When Marthe and Chloé had been taken by Venus, it had been harder to tell him.

Now he was wiping at his eyes. Now was when he was going to cry. Jean-Eudes froze.

"*Papa*?"

George-Étienne took Jean-Eudes's hand and sat him down. "I have some bad news."

"What news?"

"Marie-Pier… She died. A few hours ago."

"I…" Jean-Eudes began, but there was nothing more than that. George-Étienne put his arm around his son. "She's never coming to see us again."

"I'm sorry, Jean-Eudes."

Jean-Eudes's expression twisted. "I liked Marie-Pier. She was really nice. She said she liked me."

"She loved you. Even though it had only been a few months, she loved all of us and we loved her."

Jean-Eudes squeezed his eyes shut in long, deliberate blinks. He pursed his lips. "I loved her," he whispered.

George-Étienne kissed the top of Jean-Eudes's head. "I know. So did I."

"It hurts," Jean-Eudes said.

"That means the love was real."

Jean-Eudes began to cry softly, and so did George-Étienne. Jean-Eudes wrapped his arms around George-Étienne's torso and clung hard.

"She was so young," Jean-Eudes said.

"I know."

"They were all so young. Chloé was younger than I am now."

The broadness and subtlety of this statement surprised George-Étienne. "I know, *chéri*."

"Venus shouldn't have taken them," Jean-Eudes said in a tight voice. "Venus shouldn't… She's…"

"It wasn't Venus," George-Étienne said quietly. "Someone killed her."

Jean-Eudes let go to look up at him in bewilderment. "Who?"

"*La présidente*'s people."

George-Étienne didn't know the expression in his son's face.

"How do you know?"

"Émile just called."

"Émile called you?"

George-Étienne faltered on his answer, but then finally said, "Yes."

Jean-Eudes was processing it, thinking it through at his own pace and route. Jean-Eudes had his own wisdom. George-Étienne had thought only a father could see it, but he was sure Marie-Pier had recognized it too. They held each other.

FORTY-TWO

****** Special Updated Bulletin ******

Suspected saboteur Émile D'Aquillon has escaped police custody. It is unknown if he is armed, but he is dangerous, and his whereabouts are currently unknown. He may have confederates helping him elude capture. If you see Émile D'Aquillon, call the *Sûreté* immediately.

Alain Dussault
Inspecteur
Sûreté de Vénus

Émile had taken a couple of rests by landing on the roofs of other habitats, to listen to radio chatter, including the public alert for his arrest. He finally made his way to the Phocas habitat. He hadn't seen anything suspicious on his approach, but that didn't put his mind at ease. He landed under the *Marais-des-Nuages,* at the emergency stern exit near the engines. Landing *under* something was always challenging, but it was a lot like the landings they did in the depths, except with less air pressure and lift, and with wings made for different stall angles. That was why he'd done it—it wouldn't occur to most flotilla folk to land this way.

He hung there for a minute, scanning and listening, before slowly opening the small outer airlock door. Inside the airlock, he removed his wings and hung them up before cycling the airlock manually, as quietly as he could. After a minute, the air pressure equalized, and he carefully turned the wheel. Gabriel-Antoine must have kept the doors well-lubricated; they made almost no noise. The inner airlock door opened onto the back of the small engine room. He removed his helmet and set it on the engine block.

He heard nothing, not even voices.

The kids didn't always make noise, and *Grand-mère* and *Grand-père* didn't either, but this was unusually quiet. He cracked the door open. *Grand-mère* and *Grand-père* sat in their hanging chairs in the living area. Louise and Paul-Égide sat miserably at the table. Also sitting at the table, waiting, was a man with a *Sûreté* patch on his survival suit. Émile couldn't see the guy's face—he was facing the main door leading to the stairs up to the roof. From the guy's seat, he could see the whole of the forward view. There was probably another guy at the top of the stairs.

Grand-père saw the opened door. This was it, if the Phocas family had sided with the government. Émile showed his face and put a finger to his lips. Old *Grand-père* Phocas's watery-eyed expression didn't change, but he stared at Émile. Idiot. Look away! If the cop didn't soon notice where *Grand-père* was looking, he was an idiot, and it was never good to gamble on somebody else being dumb. Émile stepped into the main room.

The hinge creaked, and Émile's foot sounded on the floor too. Everyone looked then, and the *Sûreté* guy half-turned, but Émile got him in a headlock before he could rise. The guy wasn't small, and he knew some pressure point stuff Émile had heard Tétreau talk about. He tried to jab his thumb behind Émile's jaw, but the lower half of Émile's helmet seal kept him from using all his force. Then he went for Émile's eyes.

Émile scrunched his eyes closed and tightened the choke hold. He lifted and dragged the guy back, then slammed his head into the floor. With his weight on him, Émile pulled the guy's head back, giving him no way to strike. He held on and held on until the guy passed out, and then waited a bit more, because the guy was probably faking. Louise and Paul-Égide were on their feet, but they didn't seem to know what to do. Both grandparents struggled out of their hanging chairs. None of them were running to the radio, or the door to the roof. Émile put his hand to his lips again. When he was mostly sure the family wouldn't lose their shit, he loosened his hold on the guy, taking his taser and night stick.

"Louise," Émile said in a hushed voice, "your brother has some electrical cable in his room. Go grab it."

She stood nervously, then bounded for Gabriel-Antoine's room. She came back with two different kinds. Émile took the thinner one and hogtied the cop. Rolling him over, Émile had a vague sense that he'd seen this guy somewhere, but couldn't for the life of him place the face. It hadn't been at parties, nor in any *Sûreté* meetings with Tétreau. He opened the guy's survival suit and, in the pockets, found little cards with English writing, which he couldn't read. What the fuck? This was a bank guy. Why was he wearing a police badge? This was some serious espionage or next-level stuff Émile didn't get. Opening a knife, he cut strips off the guy's undershirt and gagged him with them.

"Talk quietly," Émile whispered to Louise. "What happened? Did you let him in, or did he force his way in?"

"He has a warrant for Gabriel-Antoine's arrest. He wanted us to call down to Gabriel-Antoine."

"I told him to fuck himself," *Grand-mère* Phocas said in a defiant whisper.

"Good," Émile said. "This isn't a cop. I think it's a bank guy."

"His French is bad," Paul-Égide added in a tight voice.

"There's some serious shit going down. They arrested me and Marie-Pier Hudon and tried to kill us both. I got away. Marie-Pier didn't."

"She's dead?" Louise said.

"Yeah. I called the *Causapscal-des-Profondeurs* and warned them. Gabriel-Antoine is safe. They can't find him. He's with Pascale. I think we gotta get you out of here."

"He can't travel," *Grand-mère* said, nodding to her husband. "I shouldn't. And Paul-Égide can't fly."

"I can take Paul-Égide and Louise and bring them down to Gabriel-Antoine."

Paul-Égide's eyes widened. "I can't fly," he said, looking at his grandmother.

"You've got a survival suit. I'll take you both down in a safe sack and a balloon."

"I can fly," Louise whispered loudly.

"Flying upcloud is one thing. Flying in the lower decks is another," Émile said, hushing her with a gesture. "The wings you learned on will melt down there. Both of you go get your survival suits on, but stay quiet."

Both children ran to their room. Émile went into Gabriel-Antoine's workshop. Phocas had a lot of great shit, including experimental wings for the lower decks. They were a bit small for Émile, but he'd flown on smaller wings a couple of times. It meant less lift and more wobbling. There was a pair of lower cloud wings that Louise could grow into, but nothing for Paul-Égide.

There were tools big and small and scrap metal. Émile grabbed a sealable carbon-fibre bag and tossed in as many small tools as would fit, then filled in the spaces with scrap and electrical cabling. He slung the wings over his shoulder, grabbed some of Gabriel-Antoine's old shirts, and went into the main room. He blindfolded the unconscious bank guy with a shirt.

"I'll take Louise and Paul-Égide down-cloud to Gabriel-Antoine," he said to *Grand-mère* Phocas. "I'll keep them safe. The bank may think you were my accomplices."

"Fuck that," *Grand-mère* said.

"If I tie you and *mon oncle* up, you can say I overpowered you. They can't charge you with anything."

"I have to go pee first then," she said. "So do you," she added to her husband. They shuffled off. Émile loaded all his stuff into the back engine room. By the time he came back, the kids were suited up.

"Put your helmets on now," he said. "Seal check each other."

The bank guy started to struggle. Émile put his finger to his lips again for the old folks and then kicked the guy hard in the kidneys. The guy stilled. "Stay the fuck down and shut the fuck up," Émile said.

Grand-mère was done in the head and Émile gestured for her to lie down. The kids went wide-eyed and he gestured for them to go into the engine room, silently. He tied up *Grand-mère* gently. The old man shuffled over uncertainly, and Émile repeated the process and blindfolded them both.

"I'll take care of the kids. If it's safe to call, we will," he whispered very quietly in *Grand-mère*'s ear.

The bank guy hadn't moved. Émile knelt by him. "Nod once if there's a guy in the stairwell. Shake your head if no one's there."

The guy did nothing. Émile rammed his fist into the guy's nose, breaking it.

"Nod or shake," he said.

The guy nodded around his pained gasping.

"You're a bank guy? Nod or shake."

Hesitantly, bleeding a shitload from his nose, the guy groaned and nodded.

"The cops know you're doing this? Nod or shake."

Slowly he nodded.

Tabarnak.

"I'm taking the gag off. If you make any sound that makes me nervous or angry, I'm going to break your jaw."

Émile unwound the gag. He put his big hand around the guy's neck and tightened his fingers very meaningfully around the guy's windpipe—not enough to cut off breathing, but tight enough that he could choke off a scream if the guy was that dumb.

"I know what President Bitch wants out of all this, but what does the bank want me for?" Émile whispered. "Anything louder than a whisper and you're going to like me even less."

"You stole the *Causapscal-des-Vents,*" the guy said in his brutally accented French.

"The bank didn't lose their shit over other habitats getting lost," Émile whispered. "How much of this is about radioactives?"

"I don't know. Maybe some," the guy said in a choking whisper. He trailed off and Émile punched him in the stomach, tightening his fingers over the windpipe to stop him crying out.

"You fuckers killed my stepmom and framed me for it. Talk now."

The guy groaned. "I heard people talk about some of the *coureurs* having radioactives, so maybe they were secretly getting into bed with another bank. Or some terrorist smuggling. We found a place on the surface."

Merde. So Pascale and Gabriel-Antoine weren't safe. Émile gagged the guy unceremoniously and kicked him one more time. Émile was really scared for Pascale. Paul-Égide and Louise watched him from the engine room, helmets on, eyes wide. He pushed them in and closed the door. It would be very tight in the airlock. He carried the wings in and then clipped both kids to a cable attached to a balloon chute—basically a balloon and oxygen tank that could be inflated at a signal. Then he mounted the lower-cloud wing-pack to Louise's back, the safest place to put it for now. He pulled out the safe sack and got it ready on the cable attached to the two kids. He checked their neck and wrist seals and then did a radio check. He turned the power way down on all their transmitters, so their conversations wouldn't transmit more than a few hundred meters.

"This is going to be a wild ride," he said. "We're going to free fall straight down for about two or three kilometers. Maybe more. The winds will be bad, but if we go fast enough, nobody can catch us. I'm going to put the safe sack around you now, and you both hug until I tell you to stop. Okay?"

Paul-Égide had tears in his eyes. He breathed hard. Louise looked like she was going to puke.

"Where are we going?" she said.

"Somewhere safer than this."

He began draining the air from the airlock and twisting awkwardly to look out the little window in the door. No one was flying around. Yet. The real danger would be the exit from the airlock. That's when they'd be sitting ducks.

The pumps stopped and Émile crowded against the kids to open the outer door. Escaping air made a vanishing hiss. Émile stepped on the little ledge beside the airlock and harnessed his wing-pack. In his helmet, he heard some squawking on the police band. Suddenly someone flew by, fast, and his helmet speaker sounded.

"Émile D'Aquillon, stay where you are or we'll shoot. You're under arrest."

Émile ducked into the airlock, grabbed both kids in a hug and threw all three of them backwards, out into the upper-cloud morning. Paul-Égide screamed, loud enough that Émile heard it even through the faint air. Louise made some sound. Then they all froze rigid as Venus grabbed them hard and yanked them downward.

FORTY-THREE

PASCALE HAD BEEN in the sub-surface habitat, building more of her computer chips. Primitive as they were, enough of them together could run simple building software, the kind used in asteroid mining a century earlier. Across the Axis, nearly a dozen robots were digesting their asteroid, building more robots, and welding the plating onto the vehicles they were prototyping. She'd grown used to the habitat's creaking, wheezing and snapping in response to shifts in pressure and temperatures and had been happily working, but Pa's message had broken her from her focus.

They didn't have a good antenna yet, so it was just brief coded text messages. Pa's news about Marie-Pier and Émile hit her in the chest. She sent a reply and a request for more information, but he hadn't answered back, nor even acknowledged receipt, leaving Pascale with a feeling of doom, around which she could not concentrate. That was how Gabriel-Antoine found her later, when he came back with another armful of delicate work that could only be done with ungloved hands. It was only once he'd shucked his helmet and was opening the seals on his survival suit that he noticed her expression.

"What's wrong?"

She didn't know how to say it. Gabriel-Antoine kept removing his suit. It felt strange to her that they were in a place where they didn't need to neutralize acid. *Coureur* habits died hard, because Venus punished little missteps so severely. Maybe that was why she didn't know what to say. For their whole lives they were raised to be ready for Venus to turn on them; murder was different.

"Émile called my Pa. The *Sûreté* arrested Émile and Marie-Pier. They somehow found out about the *Causapscal-des-Vents*. They're looking for all of us now."

Gabriel-Antoine climbed out of his suit a little woodenly and came to the table. He sat heavily in the only other chair. "*Ostie de câlisse de tabarnak.*"

"They put Émile and Marie-Pier into a cargo port in the *Baie-Comeau* and then opened the outer door. Émile managed to get to the roof by an outside ladder and get help."

"Marie-Pier is dead?" Gabriel-Antoine demanded.

Pascale nodded sadly. Gabriel-Antoine's head dropped into his hands. "*Crisse,*" he swore. "Poor Marie-Pier. Her poor children."

"Pa is getting Jean-Marc to move her kids to one of the *coureur* habitats—Juliette Malboeuf's."

Pascale's voice sounded wooden to her ears. Gabriel-Antoine's expression hardened with narrow-eyed anger.

"What's the danger to the children? What about Louise and Paul-Égide and my grandparents? What's the danger to the children?"

"Émile has gone to bring Louise and Paul-Égide down to the *Causapscal-des-Profondeurs*. Pa and Émile don't know if the government will go after the children, but they don't want to risk it."

Gabriel-Antoine leaned back, staring at the ceiling, arms lifted helplessly. "*Câlisse*. Damn it!" he said, loudly knocking over his chair as he rose. "This for a goddamn dream of chasing stars!"

"Émile will keep them safe," she said, rising too, but afraid of touching him, of how he would take it. She tried anyway, but he knocked away her reaching hand without noticing.

"Your sister and your Pa didn't think Émile was worth helping with anything, and now we've got to hope he's sober enough to take care of *my* brother and sister? Is that what I'm hearing?"

She stepped back, without anything to offer him. His eyes were red-rimmed.

"*Crisse.* I don't want anything to happen to them. I don't even want them coming to the cloud decks. It's too dangerous."

"Émile will take care of them," she said. After a hesitation, she pictured the way she'd seen her brother above the clouds, the day she'd first seen the sun. She added, "I promise."

His shoulders slumped. "*Tabarnak,*" he said with soft exhaustion. "Poor Marie-Pier. Her poor kids."

They stood awkwardly before he opened his arms and they hugged for long seconds.

"She was so good," Pascale said.

She felt his head nod silently beside her ear. After a time, he released her and stepped back to get some water.

"This... She was..." he said. "You got your hormones from Marie-Pier?"

"She was cutting up her own herd to pay for them." After a moment, she added challengingly, "I felt bad that she was paying so much, but she thought I was worth it."

Gabriel-Antoine stared blankly ahead, holding his water.

"We're metal-rich," he said finally. "We've got more than enough to pay for whatever you want. Whatever you need."

Pascale was a bag deflating unsteadily, ready to tip over. Her gratitude for the barest acknowledgement that in this one moment, he seemed to have really seen her... It was overwhelming. She hadn't realized how much she just wanted to be seen as she was. By him.

"Thank you," she said softly.

ÉMILE PLUNGED THROUGH *les Rapides Plats* like a stone. For a few moments, he'd seen winged flyers approaching the *Marais-des-Nuages*. One had chased him, but couldn't keep up, or even follow—their wings wouldn't survive more than five or eight kilometers down into the clouds. He would have given them the finger, but it was hard enough just holding onto Louise and Paul-Égide.

"*Câlisse!*" he swore.

The winds of *les Rapides* felt like they came from all directions as they crossed the great rolling convection cells. Paul-Égide whimpered. Émile remembered Marthe and Pascale being scared by big storms, especially after their mother died. He remembered the way his annoying little sister had crawled into his hammock for comfort in the middle of the night, the way he'd reluctantly yet somehow gratefully protected her then. It had felt good.

"It's going to be okay," he said in the radio. Maybe they heard him, maybe they didn't. He held onto them tighter. Even he felt breathless from their speed. They'd probably reached terminal velocity. The clouds raced upwards all around them as the gloom deepened. It wasn't raining yet, but it was getting warmer.

"Hang on!" he yelled.

The safety balloon shrieked as it hit the wind. He couldn't hear the hiss of compressed oxygen inflating it, but a sudden drag reimposed a welcome *up* and *down* to the world. The gray and black fabric thrummed and flapped above them. They slowed, but a safety balloon was designed for the weight of one adult. Right now, they probably massed close to three.

"I'll be right back!" he said, and let go.

He dropped away, watching them rise far above him. He extended the wings he'd taken from Gabriel-Antoine's workshop and started pulling out of his dive. If he did it too fast, he would snap them out of their housings. It took about thirty seconds to safely go to level glide. He banked and turned directly back and into a climb.

For ten minutes, he pinged on low wattage, looking for the children in the clouds. Finally, he got a response that fed him a direction. He flared, stalled and landed on the little bar beneath them, bumping into them hard enough to send them swinging, as they began to sink quickly again. Paul-Égide screamed.

"It's okay. It's okay," he said, not through the radio; about half an atmosphere of pressure hugged them now, so their voices carried. His helmet said they were dropping briskly at about fifty-seven kilometers above the surface. Through the wet plastic of the safe sack, the kids looked miserable.

"Take us back," Louise said.

"Somebody came after us. I'm taking you somewhere safe."

"The clouds aren't safe!" Louise said.

"We'll get burned," Paul-Égide said.

"Your brother has been down there a bunch of weeks," Émile said. "I'm taking you to him."

"Can't he come up?" Paul-Égide said.

"We're all safer down-cloud. Don't worry. I grew up there."

They were silent for a while, and then they emerged into *Grande Allée,* the immense layer of clear air around fifty-eight kilometers above the surface of Venus. The view was almost as wide as that from the flotillas, but sandwiched flat between two cloud layers, one reddish-umber above, one brown and inscrutable below. The *coureurs,* when they first saw *Grande Allée* and its deeper cousin *Les Plaines,* felt the vertigo of all that wide, sudden space, but Louise and Paul-Égide squirmed with a different discomfort; flotilla people often described a weird, vertiginous claustrophobia in the cloud decks.

Their descent was too fast for the glide path he'd calculated. He popped his own emergency balloon and it inflated restlessly above him. He stopped its inflation before it would give him any serious lift, and then, serenely, the three of them sank into the middle cloud deck and into a misty, gloomy half-rain.

"What are we doing?" Louise said. Her voice was tight, higher than normal.

"The *Causapscal-des-Profondeurs* is a few hundred kilometers west," he said. "I might be able to fly there all the way, but not with you two as cargo. The higher the wind, the faster the wind. So if we stay at this altitude, the winds will carry us closer. Then we can drop."

"I don't like this," Louise said.

"You get used to it," Émile said. "*Coureur* children get exposed to the clouds around this age."

"I don't want to be a *coureur,*" Paul-Égide said.

The boy stalled on his next words and then said nothing. Émile could imagine what they might have been. *Dirty coureur. Smelly coureur. Poor coureur. Ugly coureur.* He'd heard it all. At least Paul-Égide had stopped himself from saying it.

"No one becomes a *coureur* because they want to," he said, as if apologizing without knowing why.

FORTY-FOUR

Marie-Pier was kept in a windowless room with a single dim bulb and a crude bench that did well enough for sitting, but not for laying down. She didn't know which habitat she was on. She'd been brought in a balloon, the way they moved children, detainees and people who couldn't fly on their own. The decompression pains persisted. There was a bucket, a sack of water, and a small plant fiber washcloth. She washed away the decompression accidents as well as she could. After a time, a pimply eighteen-year-old brought her a small tray of cold food, more water, and a new bucket. She tried to talk to him, but he ignored her and took away the first bucket.

She washed again. The smell was mostly gone, or maybe she'd gotten used to it. The effort wiped her out, though. She laid on the floor and dozed without time. Between waking and sleep, she worried about Émile. Someone, someone in the government, had tried to kill both of them. She'd barely survived. He was dead. She couldn't blame him for trying to get away, but he would only have blacked out on the hull of the *Baie-Comeau* and fallen to his death.

She didn't know how to break the news to George-Étienne and Pascale.

If she ever saw them again. She didn't know what had stayed the killer's hand the first time, but they could try again now and she was in no state to do anything about it. Maybe no one outside the government knew she was here.

As she drifted in a half-lucid wakefulness, Labourière came in. His brown hair was combed back and he wore the clean gray work suit that most bureaucrats on the *Baie-Comeau* favoured. He sat on her bench. She rose stiffly to her elbows and then sat. The aches all over her body were still bad, sometimes blooming into sharp points of pain.

He shook his head slowly. "I can't believe you betrayed everyone," he said.

"How did I do that?" she asked, tamping down a queasy feeling.

"We know about your little gang disassembling the *Causapscal-des-Vents* in the depths. We know you're building on the surface."

She felt as if her bones were melting, incapable of even holding her up. She locked her elbows.

"We know you struck a vein of radioisotopes on the surface and that some people in your network are looking at how to build dirty bombs," he said.

He didn't know about the Axis Mundi. That small relief was a sliver of hope, almost completely smothered by the horror at the accusation. She didn't know whether to deny just the dirty bombs, or to deny everything. Or keep quiet. She was no savvy conspirator. She was a botanical engineer and a black marketeer. He stared at her as if her thoughts were plain on her face.

"You managed to get most of it wrong," she said with all the bluff she could muster.

"We have photographic evidence of all of it."

"Did you keep evidence of you killing Émile?"

"The big bastard got away after the lock malfunction."

After a few moments, Marie-Pier felt herself gaping. Malfunction? Émile alive? Labourière was a good liar.

"You opened the lock," she said. "The controls and the safeties were off. That's not how a malfunction works."

"Our investigation found that someone had removed parts from the control mechanisms. The serial numbers will turn up on the black market soon enough and then we can work our way back to the saboteur. You and Émile D'Aquillon nearly died."

She didn't believe it for a second, but his explanation would sound plausible to anyone who hadn't been in the bay.

"I saw Émile go out the bay door without a helmet. He's dead."

"He surprised all of us. He climbed dozens of meters over the envelope while decompressing. He made it to the roof. Some dock workers dragged him through the airlock. He grabbed a helmet and ran. We'll catch him soon."

This felt like quite a stretch. She'd watched enough Earth police movies that she knew her captors should be trying to get her to rat out Émile. That would be easier for them if she thought he was dead. Could he really be alive?

"I need you to come clean, Marie-Pier."

"There's nothing to come clean on. And if you have photographic evidence, you don't need me."

"There are gaps."

"I want a lawyer."

"The lawyers are busy with all the *other* black marketeers. At this rate, one should be available in three to four months. That's too long, of course, for your children to be on their own. We'll have to foster them somewhere."

"They're with my brother."

"There are gaps, and the only person we see bridging those gaps is one Jean-Marc Hudon, another suspect in all this. *Sûreté* officers will be going down to the *Coureur des Tourbillons* as soon as it comes into glide path range. We'll bring your children up at the same time, and impound your habitat and experiments while the investigation is going on."

"My brother isn't involved in any of this!"

She struggled to her feet against all the pain in her muscles.

"We have to work with the theories we have until someone gives us a better picture," he said. "We'll have Émile D'Aquillon soon. I expect him to be more forthcoming, and I doubt it will show you in the best light. He's not the sharpest knife in the drawer, so we know he didn't plan the sinking of the *Causapscal-des-Vents,* its disassembly, or the black-market trading of everything you stole."

He stood.

"Anything to say?" he said finally.

They glared at each other.

"Since you're the only one we've got so far, most of this is going to fall on you, then, and your brother," he said. "I'll try to find someplace good for your children. Mathieu and Florian?"

"Maxime," she said in a dull voice.

Labourière had got the name wrong on purpose, of course. He was the government, and she wouldn't have a trial for months, years. She wouldn't even have a lawyer for a long time. Labourière could put her children on some habitat where they'd be a burden, where people wouldn't care what their names were, where people were given one extra ration to take care of two more mouths. And there was nothing she could do about it—or Émile, assuming he *was* still alive.

He pulled a sheaf of paper from an inner pocket and handed it to her. The pages were blank. He gave her a pencil too, of the kind Émile had used to write his poetry. "They're going to throw the book at you," he said. "The theft and mutilation of the *Causapscal-des-Vents* screwed the whole *colonie.* Our loans are in danger. What you did means we're not sure if we can buy medicine in six months. I think you're in the middle of this, but even if you aren't, you're the one in custody—and someone needs to take the blame, in front of *la colonie,* in front of the bank. If you were the mastermind, a confession will make this go easier on you and us. If you weren't, telling us how it all went down might be the difference between seeing your children in five years or fifteen."

He held her gaze for a long, expectant pause, but she didn't trust herself to speak.

"All the choices are yours," he said finally.

He left. When the door closed, Marie-Pier crumpled painfully onto the bench and the papers slipped from her fingers. The pencil rolled on the floor.

ORANGE-YELLOW LIGHT SHONE through the blinds in Gaschel's office, laying luminous stripes onto Labourière and Tétreau, who were bringing bad news.

"How the hell did your people fumble capturing or shooting him in the *Marais-des-Nuages*?" Gaschel said.

"We had two bank security officers in the habitat," Labourière said. "D'Aquillon somehow landed on the little ladder by the engine airlock."

"*Coureurs* land like that on their own habitats," Gaschel said.

"There's more pressure down there," Labourière said. "I don't know a person in a hundred who could do it in the flotillas."

"And now he's gone," Gaschel said. "If we're really lucky, he'll get taken by a storm like his sister, but if he links up with his father, you can bet he's going to be on the shortwave and we're going to have another narrative destabilizing things."

Tétreau turned away from the conversation, pressing a finger to his earpiece and standing up. His eyes widened as he said, "Transmit the frequency to me." He grinned. "Good work. Keep this quiet."

He rejoined them as his pad pinged with a message.

"An hour ago," Tétreau said, "before D'Aquillon's escape from the *Marais-des-Nuages*, Réjean Ayotte saw him on *l'Avant-Gardiste*. Réjean ducked out and took one of the *Sûreté*'s bugs that we were going to use to track black marketeers and put it inside D'Aquillon's helmet. It's good enough to transmit ten to twenty kilometers for a couple of days, and it's transmitting right now."

"You know where he is?" Labourière asked.

"He's going to lead us to the *Causapscal-des-Profondeurs*," Gaschel said. "Get your people ready, Tétreau."

FORTY-FIVE

THE WINDS BELOW *Grande Allée* pushed them steadily west for three hours. Louise and Paul-Égide had not warmed to the clouds, nor to the situation. They'd begun asking what would happen to their grandparents and when they could go back up. Émile didn't have answers and didn't try to make any up. He could really, really have used a drink. He didn't have the shakes or anything, but the punishment he'd received was piling up and he needed to take the edge off.

His left ear had stopped ringing, but it still felt full and plugged. His chest hurt like pneumonia; his lungs rattled when he breathed. He needed to cough, but was afraid to. He knew the watery pressure and the dull ache behind the sternum—his lungs had been damaged by depressurization. The damage might never heal.

He did the math and figured them to be about fifteen kilometers higher than the *Causapscal-des-Profondeurs* and about ten kilometers south. Louise still sounded nervous and asked too many questions, which he didn't really answer. This was tricky. Mostly he said, "Keep quiet for a minute."

He could spare about sixty meters of cable, and deflated his balloon a little to get them sinking. He extended his wings, dangled beneath the twin balloons like an ornament in a mobile, and ran his engine. He never got up enough speed to actually fly on his own lift, but the wing-pack engine had enough thrust to drag them northward as they sank. It was awkward and uncomfortable and hard as hell to keep his balance, but Gabriel-Antoine's down-cloud wing design worked better than he'd expected. They drove steadily southward through the gloomy mists.

The air heated and they sank through a pelting rain of sulfuric acid. Émile was still getting some satellite positioning signals, which told him he was getting farther from the global jet stream the *coureurs* called *Ruisseau-Creux*. *Ruisseau-Creux* had no meaningful volcanic ash, nor much electrical static for trawlers to collect, so the coureurs tended to avoid it, which made it a good place for Pa to lay low. Satellite positioning said to go south.

Even after years in the flotillas, he wasn't convinced about satellite positioning. The atmosphere was a big fluid. It had its eddies and turbulences and flows that constantly changed shape. Sometimes it was best to go by feel. His gut said *Ruisseaux-Creux* was westward. If it were only him, he'd just do it—he knew how to survive for days if he were lost in the clouds—but not with two passengers.

On the other hand, while his Pa was a tool, he'd taught Émile never to second-guess his gut.

Émile drove west without telling Louise and Paul-Égide what he was doing. The winds picked up; the clouds cooled a tiny bit. They had the feel of a slow flexing or throbbing. Though place was a very notional thing in the clouds and there was no visible change, these hints suggested they'd probably entered *Ruisseau-Creux*. He hoped to have more luck break his way, to maybe hear some transmissions from the D'Aquillon trawler flocks, but static frothed in the radio channels. The old bastard was so suspicious that he'd turned their transmitter power way down. Not that Émile thought that there was any such thing as 'too suspicious' anymore, but it didn't make finding the D'Aquillons any easier. The awkward flying, dragging the balloon, was exhausting him. His muscles hurt, and he wasn't actually sure how much more he could do. He shut his wing-pack engine, folded down his wings. Then he painfully climbed the cable to the safe sack and clipped his harness to rest. The air outside his suit had climbed to ninety degrees and one and a half atmospheres.

"You guys okay?" he said.

Through the plastic of the safe sack, he saw their hair plastered to their foreheads.

"Your suits can handle more heat than this," he said, "but the inner temperature won't get below thirty. You'll get used to it."

"I don't like this," Paul-Égide said.

"I'm sorry," Émile said, and there was feeling behind the words. He felt soft inside. He wanted to see Pascale again. And Jean-Eudes. And Alexis. "I wish you guys didn't have to run with me. I grew up down here, though, and deeper. We might see some trawlers soon. I haven't seen one in five years."

"Why not?" Louise asked.

"I've been in the flotillas."

"Why?"

"My Pa and I don't get along."

"Why?" Louise asked.

"He's a dick. And maybe I am too."

"We're going to see him?" Louise said.

"That's where we'll find out how to get you to your brother."

"You don't know where he is?" Louise asked in surprise.

"Venus is a big place, and your brother is smart—he's being hard to find." Émile didn't have the heart to say that the bank had an idea of where Gabriel-Antoine was. One thing at a time.

"Why do all this?" Louise said plaintively. "What's wrong?"

"My family and yours found something on the surface of Venus that might make us and the whole *colonie* rich. The government and the banks want to make *themselves* rich, I guess."

"What did you find?" Paul-Égide asked.

"Let's get to your brother first and then we'll see if they have pictures."

"You don't know?"

"My family doesn't tell me everything."

Louise's sweaty expression, through the faceplate and safe bag, was still judgy.

From time to time the cloud cover broke beneath them, revealing new depths. A crosswind blew north to south in uncertain gusts. Émile leaned around, looked down, up, side to side.

"What is it?" Louise asked.

"I think we're at *Trois-Frères*."

"What's that?" Paul-Égide asked.

"Some storm systems on Venus have been around for centuries. Others just decades. Sometimes a big eddy never gets violent enough to be a storm, but is just as stable. *Trois-Frères* is a small eddy that's older than me."

"I don't see anything," Louise said.

"It's not the kind of eddy that clears clouds."

"How do you know if we're in the right place?" Paul-Égide demanded.

"I come from here."

"What if you're wrong?" Louise said.

He didn't say that if he was wrong, he and two kids in a safe sack were going to float around the middle cloud deck until they ran out of air. Venus's threat was always a low humming background accompaniment to life. He might have gone a bit soft up in the flotillas, where Venus couldn't really reach them, but though you could take the boy out of the clouds, you couldn't take the *coureur* out of the boy. Fifty kilometers above the surface felt like home, in a way that the last five years had not.

"*Merde*!" he swore.

"What?" demanded Louise.

Émile pulled out his upper-cloud neutralizing kit. He opened the sealed bicarbonate paste pad and slathered it quickly over the tiny puncture in his suit where he could feel burning, scrunching it so some of the high-pH paste would go inside. He wiped and sealed the hole.

"What?" Paul-Égide asked.

"Venus gave me a welcome home kiss."

"You burned?" Louise asked. "Your suit isn't good against acid?"

"No suit is perfect. I'll teach you what to do."

"I know what to do," Louise said with nervous defiance.

"When will the acid burn me?" Paul-Égide asked.

"Wait! Shut up," Émile said, listening. He thought he'd heard something on the frequency the family used. It might be nothing, or he might have just brushed the edge of the outer range of one of their transmitters. "Stay here a minute."

"Where are you going?" Paul-Égide said.

"I'll be back in five to ten."

He hung upside down in his harness, extended his wings and unclipped. He plummeted, the two kids and the two balloons vanishing into the mists above him, then pulled into a glide, started his wing-pack engine and levelled into a wide circle. Every so often, he transmitted a low-wattage query code the family had developed. The radios of the trawler herd normally kept their transmitter range down to just far enough to catch the next trawler, but in response to a family query code, they would turn up the wattage and send a challenge code. If Émile got one of those, he could answer the challenge correctly, be recognized, and get some nav info.

It took ten minutes for his search pattern to find a signal from the unseen D'Aquillon herd. After a quick back and forth, he got a set of coordinates to decode, then throttled up and flew back towards Louise and Paul-Égide. They'd risen about fifteen hundred meters while he'd been hunting. They looked lonely and small and miserable, floating in a vaporous forest of burnt orange. He caught the dangling cable, and despite protesting muscles, managed to clip himself in. Then, hanging below the sinking balloons, he throttled forward and dragged himself and his cargo towards the herd.

THE BANK OF Pallas kept a plane for collecting meteorological and geological data, with a payload compartment jokingly called 'the bomb bay' that carried bigger atmospheric experiments. Laurent Tétreau had known of the plane and, in his old position in Industrial Works, had sometimes been involved in coordinating experiments and drops. He'd never expected that one day he would be riding in it, nor that the cargo would be *Sûreté* constables reinforced with bank security. He had no doubt that this would help his political career though.

It was hot as hell in his survival suit at the front of the bomb bay, and dark. Suit running lights traced out the eight guys with their sidearms and crude but effective 3D-printed rifles. Tétreau didn't expect the guns to be necessary. Sheer numbers and tasers should be more than enough.

The plane ran radio silent forty-six kilometers above the surface. If someone radar-pinged them, the plane would show up clearly, but he didn't expect *coureurs* to do that—they skulked, listening, slipping unseen through deep clouds.

"There's a small storm eddy ahead," the bank security chief said. Amanda Copeland stood tall and bulky in a new survival suit and helmet. "We're reading multiple weak EM signals. Some of it is certainly trawler noise from the cables. Some of it is probably machinery and low-wattage station-keeping comms. We've seen this before with *coureur* herds. We have six big passive signals that could be habitat-sized, but we can't be sure without pinging them with radar. One of those passive signals has other emissions, like there's electronic equipment there."

"That must be the *Causapscal-des-Profondeurs,*" Tétreau said.

"That's not the one D'Aquillon is going to," Copeland said. "Which one do we want to hit?"

Four weeks ago, *Présidente* Gaschel had pulled Tétreau away from Félix Lévesque in *l'Assemblée* and onto her staff, ostensibly as an advisor. In reality, he'd become her eyes and ears in the flotilla, and occasionally her voice. The simple question put to him as *la présidente*'s representative felt like a test. If he made the wrong call, would they overrule him? The bank was 'here to help' and yet, from what he'd seen, they were plenty ready to steer if given the chance. The relationship between the state of Venus and the Bank of Pallas wasn't equal; the bank would survive without Venus, but the converse wasn't true, though neither side said it out loud.

"Both," Tétreau said. "Drop two constables after Émile D'Aquillon. The other six can jump to descend on the main D'Aquillon habitat. We can adjust forces as needed."

Copeland's nod gave no hint of what she thought. She never looked happy. Both prepared their people.

FORTY-SIX

THE NAV INFO didn't lead Émile to the *Causapscal-des-Profondeurs*. He arrived at *L'Anse-à-Beaufils,* the old habitat they'd lived in when he was a kid. Marthe and Pascale had been born here and *Maman* had died here. A decade ago, the valves had gotten too woody and couldn't handle the pressure differential anymore. They'd still been maturing new walls in the trawler they would call *Causapscal-des-Profondeurs*, but had to move early. For a time, they'd relied on both, with the *Anse* providing a lot of the oxygen until the *Causapscal* could handle the burden of a whole family. *L'Anse-à-Beaufils* still charged batteries and produced oxygen, but was now used mostly for storage. So it was weird that there were lights on under it.

Émile pulled back on the throttle as he came to the old gantry, now only half the size it had once been. He saw two small figures climbing into the bathyscaphe dangled under a winch. He'd never seen this magical hunk of steel. It pissed him off no end that Pa had never showed it to him and that he'd had to learn about it from Marthe. She'd explained its existence when she'd spilled everything about the family's discovery under the planet's surface. Then, it had just seemed like one more unbelievable thing in a flood of them.

It looked both smaller and bigger than he'd imagined, half-hiding in shadow. They'd shut the light off with his arrival. He was pissed at Pa, but a deeper feeling hit him too. Who the *crisse* was fucking with the family's stuff? They didn't seem to be going anywhere, although it was uncovered and looked ready to go. Normally the family battened everything down under acid-proof tarps and tied them to the main supports.

He pulled himself onto the gantry, clipped the cables of the safe sack to it and unclipped himself. About half a kilometer away, he could see the *Causapscal-des-Vents* pretty well: all dark. He limped over to the bathyscaphe and shone his light through the little back window, then the big front one. The two figures within looked like they were trying to hide. He pounded his fist on the side of the bathyscaphe.

"Get the fuck out of there!" he said.

One of the faces looked up and through the layers of faceplates and diamond porthole, he recognized him.

"Jean-Eudes!" Émile said. He began to laugh and a kind of effortless happiness hit him. "Jean-Eudes! Open up. It's Émile!"

His big brother crawled to the front window and pressed his face against it; Émile did the same. Jean-Eudes's smile widened and through the layers, Émile heard a muffled, "Émile! It's Émile! Alexis! It's Émile." And then Jean-Eudes was laughing too.

"Open the door!" Émile said.

The steel braces on the pressure door released and, in a moment, the bathyscaphe wobbled on its cables as Jean-Eudes came out, wrapping his arms around Émile's chest and back. Even with the helmet, Jean-Eudes's head didn't reach Émile's chin.

"Careful, buddy! I'm covered in acid," Émile said, but he hugged back hard.

"Émile, you're home," Jean-Eudes said.

"I missed you, Jean-Eudes."

A smaller, wrinkly-suited figure came out of the bathyscaphe.

"Alexis?" Émile said. "Holy shit, little buddy! You grew up! Do you remember your uncle Émile?"

Émile pried himself, reluctantly, from his big brother. Jean-Eudes looked so happy. Émile felt his own cheeks aching from smiling so wide. The boy was shorter than Jean-Eudes, looking up at him shyly. Of course. How many people had Alexis seen in his whole life, trapped as he was here with Pa? He didn't know strangers. Marthe had said he was a smart kid. Like Pascale. Through the faceplate, Alexis looked like a miniature Chloé.

"Jean-Eudes. Alexis. What the *crisse* are you guys doing here? Who's taking care of you? Do you have safety balloons? This isn't a safe place."

"*Pa* says someone's coming," Jean-Eudes said. "A plane."

"What?"

"*Grand-papa* brought us over here to hide for a while."

"*Tabarnak*! You might be safest back in the bathyscaphe. I've got Louise and Paul-Égide here. Let me get them down."

"What? Who?" Jean-Eudes said. "Where?"

"Get in the bathyscaphe," Émile said. "I'll bring them over to hide with you. Then I'll see what the *crisse* is happening."

Hesitantly, Jean-Eudes and Alexis went back to the bathyscaphe. Émile looked across the way. The *Causapscal-des-Profondeurs* looked hazy, nestled among thick clouds. Its running lights were still off. Émile didn't hear or see anything, but *Pa* was a suspicious bugger and had long ago equipped the herd with passive listening antennas. As kids, they'd been taught to keep one ear on them, even though frustratingly, the weather set them off a lot. Émile hoped this talk of a plane was just weather.

Émile wrapped the cable around a winch and hauled down hard on the safe sack and balloons. Soon, Louise and Paul-Égide came into view, scraping a bit on the outer waist of the trawler bulb. He wound the cable around a cleat when they'd almost reached the gantry, then opened the acid-spattered plastic, unclipped Paul-Égide and set him behind him. Then he lifted down Louise.

"Come on."

"What's happening?" Louise gripped the gantry railing tightly as she crept, looking uncertainly through the hard cable grille under her feet.

"Get in here," Émile said, holding open the door to the bathyscaphe. They were going to be crowded. Jean-Eudes and Alexis looked a bit frightened at the front of the little craft. "Get in, get in. Come on."

"What's happening?" Louise said.

"This is my brother and my nephew. They're hiding. You hide with them while I make sure everything is safe around here."

"What's wrong?"

"Pa thinks there may be strangers here," Émile said. "Close this. Don't open it for anyone but me or Pa, and don't touch the controls."

Émile closed the hatch and watched as someone sealed it tight from the inside. The gantry rocked and he heard a sound. Émile moved closer, under the habitat bulb, and lifted open the lid of an old toolbox, its contents mostly made of trawler cable and woody ribs. He would have liked something metal, but they recycled everything they didn't need.

A wing-pack engine sounded somewhere above him, but he couldn't see it. It sounded smooth, not the way theirs sounded down here, but his left ear was still messed up and he hadn't been this deep in a long time.

Émile peeked around the curve of the trawler, trying to get a look through the gaps in the grille. Someone was struggling to climb in the netting below. It wasn't Pa; even on his worst day Pa would have climbed that netting like a monkey. Émile crept closer, listening for the other flyer. At the edge, he looked down. The guy looked up and, through the faceplate, he recognized Daigle.

"You're a long way from home, Yvon," Émile said. "What are you doing here?"

Daigle looked trapped, but he didn't take his eyes from Émile's. Then there was a gun in his hand.

"*Crisse*!" Émile yelled, jerking back.

Daigle fired. The report was loud. Émile backed towards the trawler as Daigle clumsily climbed the netting. As Daigle's hand reached the gantry, Émile leapt forward, swinging the rod of trawler cable. He hit Daigle's faceplate, creating a web of fractures all over it, and a hole. The big cop fell, probably trying to leap and fly, but his foot tangled in the netting and he just hung upside down, calling for help as he started inhaling sulfuric acid mist. And then he was screaming.

Tabarnak. Tabarnak. Tabarnak. What the fuck?

How had the constables found him down here? Émile would have heard if they'd used radar pings, and following a balloon through the clouds without radar was a mug's game. In the distance, from the hazy outline of the *Causapscal-des-Profondeurs,* he heard the drone of multiple wing-packs. Émile spun his engine up and leapt from the gantry as someone buzzed past, firing another handgun.

These guys were serious. They'd already tried killing him once, and they'd gotten Marie-Pier. If they got him and Pa, would they take the kids into custody, or just dump them into the clouds? Venus dissolved witnesses and evidence. And if the bank guy he'd tied up in the *Marais-des-Nuages* was right, they knew where Pascale was. Pascale hadn't even had a chance to try to grow up yet. Every part of Émile's body hurt, but he was full of adrenaline, and he was pissed.

Time in the Court of Venus, by Émile D'Aquillon

Her Court pirouettes to her logic.
Day and night are only veils in dance,
swirling between inconstant winds,
collapsing breathlessly in eddies.

Time in her Court marks neither
growing wood nor crumbling stone,
nor counts pendulum swings. Time
corrodes all she surveys, living and dead.

Her time imposes no reason,
does not sunder cause from effect. Her clocks
melt events into a bitter stew,
its ingredients indefinite, doubtful.

Her hours murder lovers, transfiguring them
with acid, making palimpsests
of beaus and belles, erased and etched
by her hand, rephrased by her pen.

Her courtiers measure time in clutched
angers, stillborn mournings, impotent hopes.
Resentments mark clockfaces poorly, melting
not with forgiveness, but with exhaustion.

The officials of Queen's Court minute their records
not with days and dates, nor hours and years,
but in grief, which follows its own
ever-rising entropic logic.

FORTY-SEVEN

MARIE-PIER WAS KEPT in solitary confinement. She marked time by the food deliveries. The trays were brought by young men with *Sûreté* constable chevrons who didn't answer her questions or respond to her attempts at conversation. In the long hours alone, the grim anxiety for her sons felt as close as humid, stale air. Labourière might well be able to separate her from her children, or it might be a bluff. She knew some law: the lack of charges and lack of access to a lawyer was a serious failure by the government, unless she wasn't in a world of rule of law. The little information she had wasn't enough to puzzle out the cards she'd been dealt.

Labourière's story of a mechanical failure in the bay doors was rubbish. A door with missing parts wouldn't have opened or closed. Someone had tried to kill her and Émile. Then someone changed their minds about killing them—or Émile getting out had changed their minds. Labourière could and probably would arrest her brother and put Florian and Maxime into foster care. If Labourière had evidence on her, he could probably convince a judge that her brother was an accessory. Hard knots hurt in her chest, where her lungs still stung.

What evidence did Labourière have? He said he had photographs. How? Who would have taken them? She didn't know whether to believe, but his words were too precise to be guesses. Disassembling the *Causapscal-des-Vents* in the depths? Building on the surface? Correct. A vein of radioisotopes? Wrong.

The frustration of not knowing, of not doing anything, of not being able to make sure her children were safe, stifled her, clouded her mind. She was angry; she hated Labourière; she hated Gaschel.

A key sounded in the door. She sat on her bench. One of the young constables leaned his head in, following it with his body, and a tray. He put it down beside the one with the empty bowl and plate and clean-licked spoon. He met her eyes briefly before turning away. The other four hadn't talked to her.

"You're Oscar, aren't you?" she asked.

He froze.

"I know your mother," she said. "Ursule Jousset, right? I used to trade her oxygen. She always had great vegetables."

He softened nervously. "She's got a green thumb."

"I need your help, Oscar," she said. "Something bad is happening."

He frowned. "You're under arrest."

"If I'm under arrest, they should have told me the charges. If I'm under arrest, they should have let me speak to a lawyer. If I'm under arrest, I should be with the other detainees. If this was just an arrest, the government wouldn't have tried to kill me first."

He frowned.

"I'm not asking you to help me escape. I just need to get a message out. How is Ursule? Does her habitat have enough oxygen? It was a leak in the buoyancy tank, wasn't it?"

She rose, but didn't approach. He stood taller than her by more than a head, but he was skittish.

"You're a good kid, Oscar. I just need a voice recorder. You can listen to me record my message, and then I just need it to get out to some people who can help, the same people who help get spare parts and oxygen and food to people who need it."

"They'll know it's me," he said.

"Five of you have brought me food, so far."

Oscar shook his head and wouldn't meet her eyes.

"Is this what you want for your future, Oscar? I'm not even talking about your mother. This is you. Is this all there is for you? Where will you be in five years? Will your mom's habitat still be floating? Will you be begging for a third-class bunk in ten years? Gaschel is driving us down a path where the bank will own us. And eventually, the bank will want its investment back. Do you think they'll share any profits with you, or that any of it will be for us? We have our own path to walk, and Gaschel can't lead us there."

FORTY-EIGHT

ÉMILE FLEW HARD in a wide bank around the *Causapscal-des-Vents*, the stresses and whine of his wing-pack through the soupy atmosphere feeling powerful. His old home was bulbous, dark, with epiphytes dangling from it like a mop top. It looked worn, sad, older, but a pang of homecoming nonetheless twinged in his chest. A few people buzzed around in the air, with suits a lot like his. Pa was obvious on the gantry, in his endlessly patched suit, worn black with the baked remains of antacid goo.

He heard more gunshots, but couldn't see the shooter. If these idiots thought they could hit anything while flying, let them waste their bullets. If they landed though, he was in trouble. He needed to even the odds, but his only weapon was a goddamn piece of trawler wood.

Some constable flew below him.

Without hesitating, Émile boosted the throttle on his wing-pack, flying upward before jack-knifing his body to pitch into a dive. The maneuver wouldn't have worked in the gasping pressure at flotilla altitude, but down here, he changed angle in a moment, coming in fast to overtake the constable. As he came close, Émile jammed the rod of trawler wood into the guy's air exhaust, all the way to the powerful fans. The constable's engine started grinding. Émile throttled up and away as the man's engine burst, trailing smoke as he fell.

Émile banked, back to the habitat. Two guys stood on the gantry of the *Causapscal-des-Vents,* trying to flank Pa, but they seemed to have stalled. Émile couldn't see why. A third guy managed to do a flare-land in the netting. His partner followed him too fast, ramming himself into the netting hard enough to knock against the cable of the trawler. He must have taken a shock—after a moment, he slipped limply from the netting, tumbling into the thick clouds.

And two guys had landed on the top of the *Causapscal*'s bulb. They were taking axes to the woody roof. *Tabarnak!* They were just going to sink it. Trawlers were tough, but not against axes. Émile swooped up near the top of the bulb, aiming to peak and stall about two meters above one of the axe men. He misjudged by a meter and fell sideways, knocking the guy over instead of dropping feet first onto his head. There were a lot of snapping sounds, and one of them was his starboard wing, fracturing along its leading edge. *Câlisse.*

The guy under him didn't move, but the other cop, coming out of his shock, recognized Émile. And Émile recognized him through the faceplate: Téofil Jalbert, one of the big *Sûreté* guys who'd arrested him. Jalbert raised his axe and swung hard. Émile had already pulled the quick releases on his wing-pack; now he rolled the unconscious guy over himself. Jalbert flailed to turn his stroke and managed not to plant the axe in his partner, but still sliced open the suit and wedged the axe head in the woody trawler bulb.

Émile rolled up, scooping the high pH goop from the depression in the middle of the roof, flinging it at Jalbert. He'd been hoping to goop the faceplate and screw with Jalbert's vision, but he missed and hit his chest and shoulder. Jalbert screamed, like he'd been hit with acid. He was wiping, trying to get to his pathetically inadequate and unneeded neutralizing kit. Moron.

Émile clambered to his feet, yanked the axe from the trawler and smashed Jalbert's wing. Jalbert stumbled back into the goop puddle in the middle of the bulb, still freaking out, but got a good grip on the axe—and he was as big as Émile. Stalemate. Émile held the axe with one hand and punched Jalbert's faceplate with the other. It didn't do anything. Jalbert started forcing Émile back over the slippery roof. If Émile went off the edge, it would be over—his wings were busted. He grabbed for the little velcro pocket on Jalbert's chest, and the hard loop of Jalbert's emergency balloon release.

Émile yanked it.

Jalbert grabbed at his chest in sudden surprise, as the silvery balloon bloomed above him. Émile went for the gun in the unconscious guy's holster. The balloon hissed and tugged at Jalbert as he tried to stop its inflation. The only way out now would be for Jalbert to ditch his wing-pack, but only an idiot like Émile would be stupid enough to drop his wing-pack while in the clouds. The balloon tugged Jalbert off his feet. His arms windmilled before he gave up trying to control his ascent and pulled his gun. Émile had already been aiming, though, and shot Jalbert with his partner's pistol.

Émile shoved the gun into a suit pocket, jammed the axe into his belt and climbed down one of the netting ladders they hung over each quadrant of the bulb. He hadn't done this in a while and climbed uncertainly, cautiously, peeking around his feet to make sure no one would be surprising him. He came down behind George-Étienne.

"Pa!" he called.

The old bastard turned with an unflinching, pitiless look in his eyes, which softened to something almost hopeful. Around the curve of the trawler bulb, one of the two guys was still there, not able to advance. He held a gun out; Émile ducked with George-Étienne. The other way around the gantry would be blocked by boxes. For now.

"I got rid of three of the bastards so far," Émile said. "I brought down Louise and Paul-Égide Phocas too; I put them with Jean-Eudes and Alexis. You gotta get them out of here!"

"Get them where?" George-Étienne said.

"Can you get them to another *coureur*?"

"Not in the bathyscaphe. It's too slow."

"What about bringing the kids down to Pascale?" Émile said. Émile took the gun out of his pocket, leaned around the bend and shot at the cop, who ducked desperately. Émile pulled the trigger three times, but only one bullet fired. Empty.

"The machine is made for one, not five," Pa said.

"It might not matter what it's made for if you don't get them out of here!"

A flyer jetted past, accompanied by a popping sound of more shots fired. Another constable landed properly on the netting.

"Goddamn murderers," George-Étienne said, holding up one end of a cable running back towards the boxes, where a big bank guy was pushing his way through. Pa touched his end to the open junction box where they ran electricity from the trawler plumb line for their various outdoor tools. A blinding blue-white flash sparked near George-Étienne's hand, and the bank guy seized up. Smoke puffed just before his oxygen tank burst. He slumped to the gantry.

"You're a dirty fighter, Pa," Émile said, as close to admiration as he ever got with his father. "Get the kids out of here. I'll take care of these bastards."

George-Étienne looked up at him steadily for a moment, then shook his head. "You go. I'll stay."

The guy in the netting was readying himself to come over the edge. He had a gun out, but he was hesitating.

"My wing-pack got smashed, and yours isn't big enough for me," Émile said. "We can't argue. We'll run out of time."

George-Étienne's salt-and-pepper beard wriggled behind the faceplate, considering. "I'll get Jean-Eudes and Alexis to safety and I'll be right back; and by damn, we'll take you a new wing-pack from one of these assholes."

"Run and don't look back, Pa."

"Nobody fucks with my sons. Even you."

Émile felt his throat constrict.

"Pa…"

"Somebody has to take care of Jean-Eudes and Alexis until Pascal is old enough to do it, and by the devil, you're all I've got left." Mists coiled around them. "You're *coureur* enough," Pa finished, quieter.

He held out the cable he'd used to shock the constable. They didn't shake hands or pat each other on the shoulder. Émile regretted not listening to Marthe earlier, or maybe they would have found common ground before now. Despite everything he'd tried, no matter how far and how high he'd travelled, he was still George-Étienne's son. He pulled the axe from his belt as Pa moved to the edge of the gantry.

The flying guy buzzed by again, fast and close, spraying the gantry with gunshots. Something hit Émile in the arm. It burned differently than acid, a deep, bone-aching pain. His arm hung limp. Pa crumpled to the gantry grille.

"*Papa*!"

Émile crouched and rolled George-Étienne over one-handed. He was so light. The chest of Pa's suit was red on the outside, a discordant, peculiar color for these depths. It was pierced on the side of his chest, and also in the neck, just below the helmet seal. George-Étienne's mouth moved wordlessly, gasping, blood filling it as he coughed once, painting the inside of his faceplate.

"Stay low, Pa," he said around a throat growing tighter. "I'll take care of you. I'll keep you safe. We all will."

His father had so much to say, it was clear in the old man's eyes, but his blood-painted lips made no sound. Pa's hand released Émile's arm and moved almost frantically. It took a moment to recognize the *coureur* signals he'd learned from these very hands.

Family. Trust me. Warning. Danger. Hide.

Pa became a blurry, water-clear image in Émile's vision. "Family," Émile repeated, with maybe more feeling than he'd ever said anything in his life, but Pa's chest had already stopped moving. Émile's hand lingered on the old man's chest for just a second before he swallowed hard and switched on his comms.

"Jean-Eudes, Alexis, can you hear me?"

Émile could move his hurt arm a bit now, allowing him to lift the naked conductor that Pa had strung around the box wall. He shifted his grip and flung one end towards the attackers: the one approaching with the gun and the one struggling over the gantry.

"Émile!" Jean-Eudes's voice came clearly across the half-kilometer distance.

"Jean-Eudes, get out of here. Now! Get that bathyscaphe moving. Drop it and blow all the balloons. Float away and try to link up to another *coureur* family. Pa and I have to take care of this."

Émile touched the other end of the cable to the junction box, like Pa had. The guy half on the gantry spasmed and fell back. Émile got a shock too and yanked the contact away. He'd been too close. His muscles twitched.

"Go, big brother! I'll follow when I can."

The guy with the gun saw that there'd been some sort of short. The grille in front of him wasn't electrified anymore.

"What about *Papa*?" Jean-Eudes said plaintively.

"Go now, buddy. We'll be along. We love you. Don't wait."

Émile rose on trembling legs and ran at the guy shooting at him. He didn't know a lot about guns, but he knew that if your hands were shaking, you couldn't aim for shit. He ran the guy down, the back of the axe-head smashing the guy's faceplate, and his momentum carrying them both crashing into the gantry. He was weak. His chest and stomach hurt. The man beneath him screamed as ninety-degree air entered through the broken faceplate and started to cook his head.

"Go now, buddy," Émile said on the radio. "We love you. Tell Pascale and Alexis."

Two figures in new survival suits came forward on the gantry as Émile forced his aching muscles and lungs to keep working. He was too injured… The decompression damage, and the gunshot to his arm. He had no wings to leave even if he wanted to, but he didn't want to.

He didn't want to die. He felt like he hadn't lived yet, like he'd been sleepwalking. Above the clouds they'd all been sleepwalking and everything they'd hoped was just sleeping dreams. The only real things were down here. Pa was dead and it hurt. Like Marthe. Like *Maman* and Chloé. He was the last adult, the last one who could protect the family. His brother. His nephew. Gabriel-Antoine's brother and sister.

He may have failed at almost everything, but he'd be fucked if he let anyone hurt his family.

One-handed, he picked up a rusty plate of steel and swung it experimentally as he advanced on the two suited figures. They held up guns and he lurched suddenly sideways. It was a game he and Marthe had played, making the whole gantry swing. Pa used to punish them for not treating Venus seriously enough. This was fucking serious. The two figures tried to steady themselves as two gunshots went wide. He ran at them.

More muted gunshots sounded and new stings of pain became part of his mind's map of his body, already a topography of burns and aches, leaking landmarks of insistent mortality, of fragility and failure. The pain didn't stop him; it was just a shroud that couldn't contain the force of his bones and muscles. His piece of steel traced an arc that knocked aside a blocking arm and smashed a faceplate. There wasn't time for lifting the steel a second time, but Émile's momentum drove the second figure into the gantry hard enough for something to snap.

The gunshots kept sounding.

Some were just noise, but bit by bit, the map of his body shrank. His legs stopped obeying and the burning pain ended, like distant signal fires being snuffed out. His breath gasped. There was air in his helmet but his chest had stilled. There was a fading scream near him; the guy whose faceplate he'd smashed. Someone kicked him in the ribs, a remote, abstract experience. In the distance he could see *l'Anse-à-Beaufils,* his old shitty home, a relic of a family's past holding the promise of a family's future. All the constables were here, or dead, he thought with satisfaction.

The bathyscaphe, hanging beneath it so lightly, suddenly plummeted, trailing inflating float balloons.

The constables didn't get them. He smiled.

His family wasn't safe, but they were in the hands of Venus now. Clouds began to smother his vision.

He was in the hands of Venus too. He slowly realized that he'd been in her hands for months, years. He'd always belonged to the violent goddess. The poseurs and amateurs above the clouds helped him delude himself, into believing that Venus wanted something small, something definable. She didn't. She wanted everything. All his failures, all his successes, all his reaching and striving, were insufficient offerings on her altar. He'd always been in communion with her. He'd been speaking to her all his life in the language of sacrifice.

You took my mother and two of my sisters, you bitch, but Pa and I fed you today. We paid your tithe. Now take care of these children who believe in you. Coureurs have always been your children. Make it right.

That was all he wanted. He just wanted Venus to make it right.

A smothering darkness shrank his world, until he was just a small, faltering heartbeat, and his supplication to a goddess something too big to understand. He felt Venus take him.

FORTY-NINE

THE *ANSE* HAD turned slowly in the wind, so that Jean-Eudes could once again see his home from the outside. The *Causapscal* was blurry in the mist. It was ugly and beautiful. The black weeds *Papa* had taught him to dry and pound to make a paste for food hung on the outside like dirty hair. There were lots of dark shapes of people flying. He didn't know them. He knew *Papa*'s suit, though—dark and stained and patched and smelly. And he knew Émile, because he knew his little brother. It was funny. Jean-Eudes was the oldest, but Émile was the biggest brother. Seeing Émile had made Jean-Eudes so happy, except now he was scared for everyone. Little Alexis pressed close and peeked out the big window.

"They're going to hurt *Grand-papa*," Alexis said.

"Émile will stop them," Jean-Eudes said. "Your uncle is big."

Jean-Eudes lifted Alexis straight, like he had when Alexis was littler, when he'd taken care of him more. Jean-Eudes had been his uncle and Alexis had been his nephew. Now it was like Alexis was his best friend. He was smart. He decided things, sometimes. But not now. Alexis flopped over him and when Jean-Eudes looked in his faceplate, he saw tears on Alexis's face.

"Are you hurt?" Jean-Eudes said.

Alexis looked back at him like Jean-Eudes didn't understand something.

"They're going to hurt Émile and *Grand-papa,*" Alexis said. "*Grand-papa* said Émile told him the police killed Marie-Pier. The bad people are here."

"They came to our habitat," the girl said. She was as tall as Jean-Eudes. "Émile barely escaped with us."

"There are too many," Alexis said. "They're coming after us next."

Jean-Eudes's stomach had tickly hurts in it. "*Non,*" he said. "They'll be okay."

Émile and *Papa* were on the gantry. Bad guys fell from it. *Papa* and Émile were beating them. Then *Papa* fell down. Jean-Eudes squinted, trying to see, but his eyes were watery and Alexis was crying.

"Jean-Eudes, Alexis, can you hear me?"

It was Émile's voice on the radio. Alexis was crying harder. *Papa* had taught Jean-Eudes how to use the radio in his helmet. He switched it on.

"Émile!" Jean-Eudes said. He swallowed. His eyes were wet.

"Jean-Eudes, get out of here. Now! Get that bathyscaphe moving. Drop it and blow all the balloons. Float away and try to link up to another *coureur* family. *Pa* and I have to take care of this."

The *Anse* was still turning slow with the wind. Soon he wouldn't be able to see his big little brother. Émile kneeled over *Papa*.

"Go, big brother!" Émile said. "I'll follow when I can."

"What about *Papa*?" Jean-Eudes said. He hugged Alexis close, like Alexis was little and it was a storm. Alexis never knew that sometimes storms scared Jean-Eudes too.

"Go, buddy. We'll be along. We love you. Don't wait."

Émile was getting up and running. Jean-Eudes craned his neck, trying to put his eyes where he could see Émile out the window, but he couldn't anymore.

"Go now, buddy." Émile's voice sounded sad. "We love you. Tell Pascale and Alexis."

"I will," Jean-Eudes said. Émile didn't say anything else and Jean-Eudes turned off the radio in his helmet the way *Papa* had taught him.

He held Alexis away from him, like he was correcting him for not doing his chores when he was little.

"Alexis, we have to go. Émile said to go." Alexis looked at him. His crying made Jean-Eudes cry harder, and his throat hurt more.

"Where? We don't know where the other *coureurs* are. How would we find them?"

"Where's Pascale?" Jean-Eudes said.

"On the surface."

"Can we go there?"

"No," Alexis said, the way he sometimes did like Jean-Eudes was dumb.

"We're in the machine *Papa* and Pascale took to *Papa*'s storm."

"*Grand-papa* knew how to fly this. He knew how to navigate there."

"Do you know where *Papa*'s storm is?"

"Yes."

"Is it close?"

Alexis's face twisted like he was having a hard time. Jean-Eudes remembered Alexis's hard times, when the things *Papa* taught him were hard.

"Sort of," Alexis said.

"You can get us there," Jean-Eudes said.

"Émile said to go to *coureurs*!"

"I don't want to go to other families. I want our family. I want to be with Pascale."

"And Gabriel-Antoine!" Louise said.

Alexis looked at Louise. Then back at Jean-Eudes.

"I don't really know everything," he said. "I might make a mistake."

"You are smart," Jean-Eudes said, kind of strongly. "You can do this. Pascale taught you. Pa taught you. You drove the *Causapscal-des-Profondeurs* with me."

"That was easier. On the surface, one mistake and we're all dead."

"Venus took Marthe in the clouds. Venus took your *maman* up here. You were just a baby. It doesn't matter where we are when Venus wants us."

"I want *Grand-papa*," Alexis said.

"You're smart enough! And if *Papa* were here, he would yell at you and tell you to do it because you're a *coureur*," Jean-Eudes said.

"They're coming!" Louise said, pointing out the window. Shapes were climbing onto the gantry. They weren't Émile and they weren't *Papa*.

"You have to, Alexis," Jean-Eudes said. "You're the only one."

Alexis grabbed Jean-Eudes's hand. With his other hand, Jean-Eudes grabbed the stick *Papa* had said not to touch, and pulled it. Then they were falling and screaming.

JEAN-EUDES HADN'T KNOWN they were going to fall so fast. The gantry of the *Anse* looked like it was flying up. It was scary. Jean-Eudes fell into the air above the bench and somebody's foot was kicking in front of his face helmet. He called for *Papa* and felt like he was going to pee. Alexis grabbed at his arm. They fell for a long time and Jean-Eudes maybe peed, but after a while it was like they were slowing down and they were all over the seat and each other. The four of them were all crying or whining. *Papa*'s secret ship was tipped a little forward. The clouds outside were darker, rising outside the front window.

"Alexis," Jean-Eudes said. "Fly *Papa*'s ship."

"Where?" Alexis demanded. "You shouldn't have touched the switches!"

"The bad men were coming. They hurt *Papa*. Émile said to go. You weren't listening to Émile."

"Émile is a loser!" Alexis said. Jean-Eudes had never heard him say anything like that. Those were *Papa*'s words. "We have to help *Grand-papa*! That's what we should have done!"

Alexis punched the bench and his own legs and a bit at Jean-Eudes. Jean-Eudes grabbed his hands. It wasn't touching. They were wearing gloves. He squeezed, hoping Alexis would feel it.

"Marie-Pier is dead. Émile told us," Jean-Eudes said. His throat started to hurt, like when he found out Venus took Marthe, like when *Maman* died. "*Papa* got… hurt by the bad men. We have to go. You can fly us away."

"Where?" Alexis said like he was angry-crying, like when he was little and too tired.

"Take us to Pascale."

"The surface will kill us! You're so stupid!"

Alexis stopped crying and looked at Jean-Eudes. He'd surprised himself with the words. Alexis sometimes got frustrated with Jean-Eudes, but he never called him stupid.

"I'm..." Alexis tried to say, but he didn't have other words.

"I'm a *coureur*," Jean-Eudes said, the way *Papa* would have said it when he knew other people wanted to use it as an insult. "You're a *coureur*. These clouds belong to the *coureurs*. *Papa* would say to stop whining and do what you have to."

Over the last year, Alexis had grown a lot. He could do things Jean-Eudes couldn't, and they both knew it. And sometimes Alexis got frustrated with Jean-Eudes, and how Jean-Eudes couldn't think of everything Alexis could. And it was hard sometimes. Jean-Eudes couldn't fly on wings or make new machines like Pascale and Alexis, but he'd listened all his life to what *Papa* said about how he had to act. Jean-Eudes knew *Papa* and what he would say. Alexis sometimes needed reminding.

"Even Pascal learned from *Grand-papa* the first times," Alexis said. "I don't know enough about the surface to do it."

"If you don't try, the bad men will get us, or we'll just run out of air," Jean-Eudes said.

The girl behind them wriggled and moved her legs so she could talk to them, but *Papa*'s ship tipped even more when she did, and Alexis and the little boy screamed at her and she moved to the back more.

"We're going to the surface?" she said.

"No," Alexis said.

"That's where your brother is. And Pascale," Jean-Eudes said. "They'll take care of us."

"We'll get squashed by the heat and pressure," she said.

"Not in this," Jean-Eudes said. "Pascale and *Papa* went down in it. So did Pascale and Gabriel-Antoine. To the surface. They touched Venus in this ship."

"I don't know where they are," Alexis said. "I don't have maps."

"You know where *Papa*'s storm is," Jean-Eudes said.

"Yes," Alexis said quietly.

"Can you hear the GPS?" Jean-Eudes said.

Alexis looked at the controls like he didn't want to.

"You know how to do the math," Jean-Eudes said. "You did it when Pascale and *Papa* were on the surface. The winds were different, and you had to use math to find a new way to stay in place. We can't stay here. Only you can bring us to Pascale. You're smart enough. You can do it. I know you can, because you're my nephew and you're a D'Aquillon."

Alexis's shoulders were slumped, and he wouldn't look up. Everyone waited.

"We're not balanced," Alexis finally said. "We're tipping. You have to move back and Louise has to come forward."

He had wanted to watch from the big front window, but Jean-Eudes was proud that his little nephew was smart. Jean-Eudes scrunched back and the girl climbed over him and sat beside Alexis. No one looked happy. Everyone looked worried.

"You can do it, Alexis," Jean-Eudes said.

From the back, Jean-Eudes couldn't tell if everything was okay. Everything outside the front window was misty and brown. Beside him, the little boy was crying. Jean-Eudes tried to put his arm around his shoulders, but the boy shrugged it away and took his sister's hand. Jean-Eudes also felt like crying, and he did a little bit, but quiet, because he was bigger and he didn't want to make the others cry more.

Papa was hurt. He'd seen guns in movies. Jean-Eudes hadn't known that there were guns on Venus, but the bad men had guns. And they shot *Papa*. Émile had gone to him, but in the movies, people only got better from bullets if they went to a hospital or a doctor. *Maman* had died at home because there was no doctor and no hospital. No doctor would help *Papa* or Émile.

Jean-Eudes's belly hurt when he thought of Émile. He'd gotten to see his little brother for just a minute, and he'd hugged him, but then... Émile was with *Papa* and they didn't have a doctor. Émile must have been hurt, or the bad men wouldn't have come to the *Anse*. His little brother would have stopped them. Jean-Eudes's throat was tight and he cried without making a sound. He was the uncle. He needed to help his nephew. Alexis was looking back.

"What's wrong, Alexis?" Jean-Eudes said.

"We haven't got enough oxygen," Alexis said.

"For what?" Jean-Eudes said.

"Getting to *Grand-papa*'s storm will take six hours, mostly at this altitude," Alexis said. "Our suits have oxygen for another two hours. Paul-Égide and Louise will run out in an hour."

Jean-Eudes sat still. Not enough air. Émile had said to go. He wouldn't have said to go if he knew there wasn't enough air. Jean-Eudes had listened even though Alexis didn't want to. But Alexis was smart.

"We can't fix not enough air," Jean-Eudes said.

Louise looked at both of them, worried.

"The bathyscaphe has oxygen tanks to fill balloons to take it to fifty kilometers or even higher," Alexis said. "If I fill the balloons, we'll rise and maybe we can be rescued."

"*Papa* is hurt," Jean-Eudes said, even though he knew it was worse. "Émile is hurt."

"The *Sûreté* might pick us up, or someone who will turn us over to the *Sûreté*," Alexis said. "Rescue ships would reach us."

"We just ran away from the police," Louise said.

They were all quiet as the mists moved softly outside, the way Pascale had always talked about.

"Or, I can take the oxygen from the bathyscaphe tanks and refill our suits," Alexis said. "For six hours, we'd need two or three refills. It would use about half the oxygen."

"So do that!" Louise said.

"If we breathe half the oxygen, we won't be able to fully inflate the balloons anymore," Alexis said. "If we can't make it to Pascal and Gabriel-Antoine, or if something goes wrong, we can't rise to rescue depth."

Jean-Eudes thought about what Alexis was saying. "We can't have both," Jean-Eudes said finally. "We try to reach Pascale *or* we try for rescue."

"What could go wrong?" Louise asked.

"Anything!" Alexis said in his frustrated voice. "This thing doesn't have an airlock. There might not be a way for us to get out safely. I saw Pascal's drawings, but I didn't pay attention to them."

"Why not?" Paul-Égide said.

"I was building chips, and cleaning parts to build things, and learning to fly!" Alexis was angry. "What were you doing? Were you helping?"

"Don't be angry, Alexis," Jean-Eudes said. "Would Marthe be proud of you being angry?"

Alexis's little face got tight behind his faceplate. "Marthe isn't here. If she was, she could decide! Even Émile could decide, if he was here." His voice kind of squeaked at the end and he turned away.

"Marthe isn't here," Jean-Eudes said. He was crying again, and it tickled, and he couldn't wipe. "Émile isn't here. They're together again. With *Papa*." Now his throat hurt and he wasn't sure he could talk. "With your *Maman* and *Papa*. But we're here, Alexis, and *Papa* said we always need to take care of each other..."

It felt achy and lonely to say, like it wasn't enough, just Alexis and Jean-Eudes alone, of all the family. No *Papa*. No Marthe. No Pascale. No Émile. No Chloé. No *Maman*. It wasn't fair.

"If we go for rescue," Jean-Eudes said, "what will happen?"

"They killed Marie-Pier," Alexis said. "They tried to kill Émile. If they don't know already, they'll try to make us tell what Pascal and Gabriel-Antoine are doing on the surface. If they can kill people once, they can do it again."

Alexis sounded grown up. That made Jean-Eudes sad, because he could remember only months ago laughing and giggling with Alexis, playing tickle games and watching movies. Alexis was going to grow up to be like Pascale.

"What should we do?" Jean-Eudes said.

"I don't know!" Alexis said. "I don't want to decide. I don't want to make a mistake."

The bathyscaphe bucked with the wind, surprising Louise and Paul-Égide.

"If you were alone in this ship, what would you decide?" Jean-Eudes asked.

Alexis picked at a bit of the bench that was flaking as he thought.

"I would go down," Alexis said, "to Pascal. I would rather die than let the goddamn *présidente* win."

"Alexis," Jean-Eudes said, with the tone Marthe would have used, for Alexis's swearing.

"Who do you think sent down the *Sûreté*? It was her," Alexis said. "They shot *Grand-papa*. They probably killed Émile too. I'd rather go to hell than give the bathyscaphe or even information to her."

"Me too," Jean-Eudes said. These were *Papa*'s words and he was proud to have them.

Paul-Égide whined a bit and then started crying again. He was only eight. This time, he didn't mind when Jean-Eudes patted his back. Louise looked at him and Alexis.

"Are we going to die down there?" she said to Alexis.

"*Grand-papa* taught me to navigate the clouds and I can fly this thing," he said. "I think I can get us there, even if I don't know what we'll find."

Louise's face scrunched. Then she said, "Let's go."

FIFTY

OSCAR SEEMED LIKE a good kid. He wasn't a government loyalist, but he balked at her request—because it wasn't right, he said. But Marie-Pier saw in his eyes the sort of hunger they all had, the kind of hunger that was the opening for haggling in the black market. They all wanted more, and some were desperate. He finally agreed to some indefinite payment later for letting her record the message. He left her alone for a few hours, and she paced for some of that time, trying to work out some of the stiffness in her muscles. It worked a little, but only a little. Decompression injuries usually sorted themselves out after minutes or hours. It had been longer than that, and her lungs and joints continued to ache. She needed a doctor, maybe more help than *la colonie* could handle.

Oscar finally returned, his manner more furtive. In his outstretched hand was a beat-up old pad with a small green light shining on the side.

"No one saw me come back," he said. "Hurry."

The display lit dimly when she thumbed it on. The voice record function winked open on the main screen. Oscar watched her nervously. Her previous confidence that she'd have something to say faltered. She retreated to the hard bench and sat heavily. Oscar looked away as if she were doing something intimate. She tried to take a deep, steadying breath, but couldn't. She ended up clearing her throat half-heartedly.

"Ovide," she began, "if you're getting this whole message, please give whoever brings it to you something good and worth their trouble. Do what you think is best with the message."

She faltered, long enough that Oscar peeked her way. She centered on the blinking red record light. George-Étienne had made this look easy.

"This is Marie-Pier Hudon of the *Coureur-des-Tourbillons*. I was recently detained by the *Sûreté* for the disappearance of the *Causapscal-des-Vents*. I don't deny that I was involved in its disappearance for parts, and I'm ready to face the legal consequences for that. But I've not been charged, nor been given access to a lawyer."

She heard a new weakness in her voice and didn't like it. She hoped no one took it as a sign of dishonesty. She had to rely on the utter strangeness of her message to carry it through.

"Émile D'Aquillon and I were being held on the *Baie-Comeau* in one of the cargo bays," she continued. "Instead of being charged with a crime, someone opened the door. Faced with suffocation, Émile went outside and up the envelope. I don't see how he could be alive, but he might be. If he is, he needs help. Someone in the government tried to kill both of us. The evidence for this is out there and I need people to find it. If the government can just start killing people in detention, we've become a police state."

Her breath was rattling now, and she began to cough.

"Labourière threatened to take my children and imprison my brother Jean-Marc, even though they have nothing to do with any of this. This is not a government that cares about laws, and it is no longer a government in control of the nation. Any government that commits crimes against its own citizens has no mandate to govern.

"I said in *l'Assemblée*: how many people are currently in detention for trying to survive, for trying to feed their families because the government can't anymore? I call those detentions illegal. I call the false accusations against my brother illegal. Taking away people's children is illegal. This government has shown itself to be unfit to govern, and a new government is needed."

Her chest rattled now with every word, not so loud the recording could pick it up, but she felt it, deep below her sternum. And she felt weirdly feverish, with more than just the adrenaline.

"What can you do? Find out if I'm alive and if I've been charged and had access to a lawyer. Demand that those in detention be released. Demand that *l'Assemblée* review, immediately, the punishments for black marketeering. The government cannot fail to provide the basic necessities, and then punish us for seeking them out ourselves. This should be your government. These should be your laws. They are not, because Gaschel and her people have stolen the laws and the government. Good luck."

She stopped recording and tried to catch her breath. Oscar looked at her wide-eyed, almost frightened.

"I can't carry that," he said.

"No one saw you come in."

"Yeah, but…"

"Did you believe what I said?" she asked.

He gaped for a moment. "I don't know."

"I think you do, Oscar. This is for me. This is for you. This is for your mother. If you're scared, ask yourself why. If we're afraid of talking and saying what we think, isn't that bad?"

"They'll find out it was me."

She rose weakly and nonetheless startled him. She held out the pad.

"Take this to Ovide Dubé on the *Lac-Édouard*. He'll take care of everything, no one will know you were involved. When Ovide hears the message, he'll know what he should be giving you. For you and your mom."

He hesitated.

"Go quick, now, so no one sees you," she said.

He froze for one moment more, then took the pad and shoved it into his suit. He sealed his suit to his neck and left without looking back, locking the door silently. She definitely felt feverish as she lay down on the floor.

FIFTY-ONE

SCRUNCHED AT THE back of the bathyscaphe with Paul-Égide, Jean-Eudes was hot and hungry. He could kind of see between Alexis's and Louise's shoulders. The mist was dark in front of the ship.

"That's battery charge?" Louise asked, pointing.

"Yeah," Alexis said.

"And this is for the propeller thrust," she said.

"Yeah," Alexis answered. "Don't touch anything."

"I'd better learn how to fly this thing," Louise said.

"I know how to fly it, and it belongs to my *Grand-papa,* so I have to take care of it," Alexis said. "And if you break something, we'll all die."

Paul-Égide made a whining sound beside Jean-Eudes.

"I need to know how to fly this in case you get sick or die on the way," Louise said. "We shouldn't have just one person to get us out of trouble."

"My *Grand-papa* taught me, and I can't teach you everything I know right now. I'm busy."

Louise turned to look at Alexis, so Jean-Eudes could see that she was making a face at Alexis, as if he had said something dumb.

"I'm already a good pilot," she said. "My brother taught me. I'm a better flyer than Émile."

"You're not a better flyer than Émile," Jean-Eudes said.

"We played tag on wing-packs," she said. "I caught him and he couldn't catch me. I had better wings, though."

Jean-Eudes wasn't sure if she was just making it up, but she must be good if she could play tag with wings. He finally said, "My little brother is a good flyer."

"Wing-packs isn't the same as piloting this ship or a habitat," Alexis said.

"I did all the navigational corrections on the *Marais-des-Nuages*," she said. "Everything is just buoyancy, lift, drag, thrust and steering."

"So?" Alexis said.

"If you pass out from heat exhaustion or something, do you want to die because I didn't know the controls?"

Alexis was quiet. Jean-Eudes knew these moods that Alexis could have. They were like *Papa*'s quiet, angry moods.

"Louise is family," Jean-Eudes said to his nephew. "Marthe said so. Like Gabriel-Antoine. Like Marie-Pier. Maybe it's a good idea that both of you know how to fly."

Alexis took a deep breath and nodded. Then in a quiet voice he started to explain the controls to Louise. Jean-Eudes was proud and sat still as the heat rose a bit more. Jean-Eudes knew how to just be still and sweat.

"My *Papa* told me to just sit still when it's too hot," he said to Paul-Égide. "That's all you can do until it cools down."

He thought Paul-Égide didn't really like him. He hoped it was because the little boy was scared and not because Jean-Eudes didn't talk as good as everyone else. The D'Aquillons knew how Jean-Eudes talked. This was his first time with stranger kids.

"It's going to get hotter," Alexis said from the front of the bathyscaphe. "Our suits should be able to handle one hundred and thirty degrees."

"I don't think ours can," Louise said.

"What?" Paul-Égide said.

"These are upper-cloud suits," Louise said.

"They're still rated for heat," Alexis said like a question.

Louise was quiet. "At least to boiling," she said.

"The bathyscaphe has Stirling engines to cool it," Alexis said. "Pascal and *Grand-papa* spent time on the surface, and they stayed cool enough. We're going to get down as fast as we can."

The light outside the front window changed. Jean-Eudes lifted his head to look between Alexis and Louise; he could see far away to other clouds and foggy mists, really far away. He'd never seen so far away before.

"Whoa," Alexis and Louise said.

"What is it?" Paul-Égide said.

"Is it *Grande Allée*?" Jean-Eudes said. *Papa* had told him many times about *Grande Allée*. Marthe too.

"No. We're below the sub-cloud haze," Alexis said. "There's Venus."

"What? I want to see!" Paul-Égide said, and he started crawling forward.

"Don't move!" Louise snapped at her brother. "You'll unbalance the ship."

Paul-Égide moved back. In his sweaty helmet, he looked like he was going to cry.

"If I move further back," Jean-Eudes asked, "can Paul-Égide go forward a bit, enough to see?"

Paul-Égide looked at Jean-Eudes and Jean-Eudes smiled. The little boy didn't smile back. He looked away like he was shy.

"That can work if you go back first, Jean-Eudes," Alexis said.

Jean-Eudes scooched all the way to the back wall, but he didn't touch it because it was so hot. Paul-Égide carefully moved forward on his knees until he also said, "Whoa." Jean-Eudes wanted to see it too, but when Pascale was little, Marthe had explained to him that children sometimes didn't have the same patience, and that grown-ups had to treat them special. Jean-Eudes was happy for them. Besides, if he knelt as high as he could at the back, so that his helmet touched the ceiling, Jean-Eudes could see the brown and black stone horizon a little bit between their heads.

"Whoa," he said too, quietly.

"I've never seen the surface before," Louise said. "Only in pictures. It's huge."

"Me neither," Alexis said. "This is something the deep *coureurs* show their children. *Grand-papa* was going to show me when I was older." His voice got tight at the end. After a bit, he said, "This is for us. For the House of Styx. This is for our family."

Paul-Égide's big sister shooed him back, and the boy copied Jean-Eudes and stood beside him on his knees. They both saw a little more of the rocky horizon every minute.

"We're going lower?" Jean-Eudes said. He was pretty sure they were, but he wanted to be sure.

"I've opened the ballast tanks to the outside, so we're dropping a kilometer about every minute or two," Alexis said. "It will still take us about forty minutes to reach the surface."

"Can you see *Papa*'s storm?" Jean-Eudes asked.

"There's no more storm," Alexis said. "Pascal and Gabriel-Antoine capped the cave."

"What storm?" Louise said.

"My *papa* found a storm on Venus that shouldn't be there," Jean-Eudes said.

"It's better to show you," Alexis said. "Even before, we couldn't see the storm because there are no clouds at the surface."

"Can you radio Pascale?" Jean-Eudes said.

"Soon," Alexis said. "This thing doesn't have a directional antenna, so anyone above us could hear, if we were transmitting, right up to twenty-eight kilometers away. When we're within ten kilometers, I can set the wattage low and no one above will hear us."

Jean-Eudes saw the horizon clearer. It had lots of pokey, sharp mountains. They were dropping. He could see Venus growing. Jean-Eudes didn't like the way the bathyscaphe creaked. It sounded like the metal was bending. Sometimes, it even looked a bit like the metal was shaking.

"Will we get squashed?" Paul-Égide said.

"The bathyscaphe will protect us," Alexis said.

"What if it doesn't?" Paul-Égide said.

"Why would it work every other time and not this one?" Louise said.

"My *Papa* and my brother used this a lot," Jean-Eudes said.

There was a harder creaking and then a little squeak, like a long fart. It just kept going on.

"What's that?" Louise said.

"It's probably normal," Alexis said.

They were all quiet, just listening to the squeak as they got closer and closer to Venus. Jean-Eudes hoped that Venus didn't get mad at them for coming down here, but he didn't say anything. If it had been just Jean-Eudes and Pascale, he would have asked, and Pascale would have said, "That's silly, Jean-Eudes."

"Internal pressure's up to six atmospheres," Alexis said. "And internal temperature's up to one hundred and ten."

"Is that bad?" Louise said.

"What's bad?" Paul-Égide said.

Louise shushed him.

"*Grand-papa* said that the internal pressure of the bathyscaphe could hold at four atmospheres," Alexis said. "And he and Pascal didn't get to a hundred and ten degrees until they'd been on the surface for a while."

"Is that bad?" Paul-Égide said.

The long squeaking whine was still going.

"Maybe we have a slow leak," Alexis said.

"Can we still get down?" Louise said.

"I don't know," Alexis said.

"Can we go up?" Paul-Égide asked.

"Not to rescue depth," Alexis said. "And we'd just run out of air unless some *coureur* found us. And it's just as likely that the government would find us."

Paul-Égide started crying, and didn't get upset when Jean-Eudes put his arm around his shoulders.

"What do we do?" Louise said.

Alexis was quiet for a while and Paul-Égide sniffled.

"Going up won't help us," Alexis said. "The longer we stay outside, the longer the pressure has to leak in. And the heat, I think."

"So go faster?" Louise said.

"Maybe," Alexis said. "We're at fifteen kilometers. I can probably signal Pascal now."

"Isn't that too high?" Louise said. "People above will hear us."

Alexis was quiet. "If I keep the wattage just right, someone would have to be at thirtieth *rang* to hear us. Nobody goes to thirtieth *rang*."

"Pascale will know what to do," Jean-Eudes said.

Alexis did lots of things to the controls. Jean-Eudes didn't know he knew so much. He was proud.

"Pascal," Alexis said into the radio. "Come in, Pascal. This is Alexis."

They kept dropping and the squeaking sounded louder and Alexis kept calling Pascale. Jean-Eudes started to get worried when Pascale didn't answer. Jean-Eudes didn't want to die. He didn't want Alexis to die. It was the saddest thing he could think of, even more than *Papa*, or Marthe or Émile. He wanted the squeaking to stop. Something crackled in the radio. Jean-Eudes didn't understand. Everyone talked at once, although Louise and Alexis were both saying, "Shut up shut up."

"Pascal? This is Alexis."

"Alexis?" a crackly voice said. There was more static. "Where are you? Where's *Grand-papa*?"

"*Grand-papa* was shot," Alexis said and Jean-Eudes's chest got tight. "And I think Émile too. Bad men came to the *Causapscal*. A lot."

The radio was quiet and then, "Where are you, Alexis? Is Jean-Eudes safe?"

"Émile told us to run away in the bathyscaphe. I'm with Jean-Eudes and Louise and Paul-Égide. Émile said to find a *coureur* family, but we didn't know how. We're on our way to you."

"Four of you in the bathyscaphe?" There was less static now, and Pascale sounded a bit more like Pascale. "Who's piloting?"

"I am. We're eleven kilometers above you. I think I know how to get to you, but the bathyscaphe is making a weird squeaking sound and the pressure inside is seven atmospheres."

After a few seconds, Pascale said, "You should inflate the buoyancy balloons and go to a safer altitude."

Paul-Égide moaned and Jean-Eudes whispered to him, "It'll be okay. Pascale will know what to do."

"Where?" Alexis said. "*Grand-papa* and Émile got shot. We don't have a lot of oxygen left. We used the buoyancy oxygen to breathe."

The line was quiet so long that Alexis said, "Pascale? Pascale?"

"I'm here, Alexis. Hold tight. Let us think."

Louise hugged herself.

"Louise? Paul-Égide?" a voice said through the static. "Are you okay?"

Louise took the microphone. "Gabriel-Antoine! We're okay. It's really hot, but we're okay. We have about an hour of air each."

"What about *Grand-mère* and *Grand-père*?" Gabriel-Antoine said.

"They were okay when Émile got us away from the police," Louise said.

"And what have you got in the oxygen tanks?" Gabriel-Antoine said. "If you blew all the balloons?"

"Less than half," Alexis said.

"What's the pressure in the bathyscaphe now, and the pressure outside?" Gabriel-Antoine said.

"Forty-eight atmospheres outside, seven atmospheres inside," Alexis said.

"Hold on," Gabriel-Antoine said.

FIFTY-TWO

PASCALE ROTATED AROUND the steel cable, pulling a new sheet of steel towards one of their submarine ships. The stars moved outside her faceplate, drifting along in quiet serenity, each of them at peace with themselves and their place in the cosmos. She thought their harmony resonated with something in her, something she was growing to know.

"Are you playing?" Gabriel-Antoine asked, not unkindly.

"All the stars are out there," she said, not stopping her slow rotation. "All the stars we can see and all the ones that are too far to see. We can visit some of them, eventually. It doesn't make sense that this is the only wormhole that was ever built."

She and Gabriel-Antoine had been verifying the construction work of one of the robots, and setting up a new one to the wiring, something that so far they hadn't been able to successfully program her chips to do. Now he stopped, and she held her breath for his reaction.

"I'd never thought of that. Yeah. Odds are this wouldn't be a prototype. *Sapristi*," he whispered.

In that moment of placidity in the widest of star fields, the call had come in. It was weak and the reception scratchy and unreliable, even discounting the fidelity of the comms wire they'd run through the Axis. A sick feeling roiled in Pascale's guts as they'd answered and suddenly the stars seemed distant and unreachable, almost a selfish want.

Pa and Émile dead… She felt empty. And Jean-Eudes and Alexis were in trouble.

"It's a slow leak," Pascale said with a hint of hopeful questioning as they began scrambling along the cables to lead them from the stars to the hard hot world beneath the fractured skin of Venus. "It might hold all the way to the bottom of the atmosphere. We could bring them through fast."

"If we're wrong, or the leak expands, they'll all die," Gabriel-Antoine said. They emerged into the last chamber of the cave.

"They can't go back, even if we brought them oxygen. The *Sûreté* and the bank would take them. We can't give up after everything everyone sacrificed."

"Do you know where the leak is?" he radioed Alexis. "Is there a sound?"

He didn't wait for an answer, but pulled Pascale to the airlock into the little habitat. "We have to get into our ADS suits fast," he said. "You'll get the outer door open, and get ready to bring them in and lower the outer pressure as fast as is survivable."

The airlock to the small habitat hissed and churned.

"What are you going to do?" Pascale said.

Gabriel-Antoine opened the inner airlock and was already taking off his helmet and vacuum suit as he stepped inside. Pascale kept up.

"We have some silicones that become viscous liquids at three hundred degrees," Gabriel-Antoine said, sitting to get his legs out of his vacuum suit.

"A liquid won't hold back dozens of atmospheres of pressure across the bathyscaphe wall," Pascale said.

Gabriel-Antoine began putting on the lower pieces of his atmospheric diving suit. One of Pascale's gauntlets had rolled under a stool; she grabbed it.

"Right now, the outside of the bathyscaphe will be three hundred degrees at least," Gabriel-Antoine said. "The pressure will extrude the liquid silicone through any crack in the bathyscaphe. The silicone will get to the interior, which is hopefully still only a hundred and ten degrees, where it will harden."

It never would have occurred to Pascale. Not right now. Not in this kind of cloudiness she felt. And Gabriel-Antoine had years of engineering experience on her. The feeling of sudden hope was electric.

While they laboriously pulled on the hard suits, Gabriel-Antoine talked on the radio, telling Alexis to hold the bathyscaphe at ten kilometers above the surface, slightly east of the cave's position in Diana Chasma. The prevailing wind at tenth *rang* was slow, but at forty-eight atmospheres, its push was still considerable on a big surface like the bathyscaphe. Alexis could do it, though.

"*Câlisse!*" Gabriel-Antoine swore suddenly.

"What?" Pascale said.

Gabriel-Antoine struggled with the right arm of his ADS.

"It's still seizing up," he said. They had wanted to take it apart and fix it, but they hadn't had time with everything else going on. Pascale helped bend the elbow. "We can't fix this now," Gabriel-Antoine said.

"I'll go," Pascale said.

"I was going to go."

"You save the day next time," Pascale said. "It's your idea, but I can do this."

The right elbow had to stay at a half bend for now. Gabriel-Antoine finished putting on his ADS while he kept puzzling at the problem.

"The only problem is that we're guessing the diagnosis based on what a ten-year-old is telling us," he said. "There may be more wrong. Or something different wrong. I wish I could be up there."

"I'll stay on the radio with you. I'll get them down safe," Pascale promised.

Pascale and Gabriel-Antoine passed through the caps, and after equalizing the pressure of the outer chamber with the surface, they opened its twelve-meter outer door. The fragmented wall and floor of Diana Chasma came into view, black and gray. At another time, Pascale might have been caught up in the beauty of the view, but Venus was now showing them her other face—the face that played with its food before pouncing. Gabriel-Antoine set the oxygen tank beside her as Pascale untangled the lines.

"Ready," she said.

Gabriel-Antoine turned the nozzle with his left hand and a balloon attached to Pascale's suit started to fill and rise. It didn't take long until it was buoyant enough to lift the propeller drone below the balloon, then the oxygen tank, and then finally tug gently at Pascale. Gabriel-Antoine hung all the tool pockets onto the hooks at her waist, his touch distant. They looked at each other through the faceplates and it felt that they were a tight team again. They were the last ones, the only ones who could protect their family.

"I'm sorry about your *papa*," he said. "And your brother."

"I'll bring the children here all safe."

Gabriel-Antoine plugged the oxygen tank valve control into her suit and opened the valve fully. In moments, her feet left Venus. The plain of forbidding basalt, shattered, blasted and wrinkled, receded as she looked to the yellowy-brown skies. Pascale had thought she'd have a good idea of where to look for the bathyscaphe, but now that she faced the whole volume of empty sky, looking for an object four meters long at an altitude of ten kilometers, her confidence flagged. The hazes beneath the clouds made a kind of ceiling to this underworld, but it was a ceiling thirty-five kilometers high, exposing Pascale's naked mind to the vast scale of Venus. And her brother and nephew were floating somewhere in this enormity. The expansiveness of the world below the clouds hadn't affected her before; every other passage through this world was simply *through*—the lower atmosphere had been an ocean to be crossed, not a gulf that hid and threatened those she loved.

"Alexis, this is Pascale. I'm on my way up to fix the leak. Are you holding position?"

"We're here, Pascal," Alexis said. The radio signal sounded a bit clearer. "At about sixty percent throttle. We're holding in place."

"What's the internal and external pressure and temperature?" Gabriel-Antoine asked, his transmission crackling.

After a pause, Alexis said, "Still about forty-nine atmospheres outside, eight atmospheres inside. I think the outside thermometer says three hundred and seventy degrees. Inside it's one hundred and eleven degrees."

"What about inside your suits?" Gabriel-Antoine asked.

"Mine is at thirty-one degrees," Alexis said. After a moment of static, Louise came on and added, "Mine is thirty-four and so is Paul-Égide's. Jean-Eudes's is thirty-one."

Pascale rose, buoyed by the flaccid balloon. At four kilometers, she thought she saw a speck high in the distance that might be the bathyscaphe.

"Alexis," she radioed, "turn on the running lights."

The speck she'd been looking at didn't light up, but far higher, a dim green glow appeared. *That* was six kilometers higher. The emptiness had fooled her sense of scale. Even in the largest of swirling storms, smaller intervening clouds had always given her perspective. Here, her eye had been tricked by a smudge of volcanic ash that had resisted the faint, dispersing wind. She throttled up the propellers on her drone.

"I'll be there soon," she said.

"Pascale," Gabriel-Antoine said on a private channel, "the flotilla suits aren't as good. On paper, they have similar tolerances, but I don't think the insulation will hold as long as *coureur* suits."

"I'll make the patch fast," she said. "My added weight will bring them down faster. Once they're in the third chamber, we can cool down the outside pretty fast."

"Take care of them, Pascale."

"They're our family," she said.

And she realized that it *was* their family now, shrunken, injured, with only Pascale and Gabriel-Antoine left to protect and raise them. All of Marthe's and Pa's and Marie-Pier's plans, having time to lead this strange arranged family, had been dashed. The hopes of bringing Émile into the fold were gone. Pascale was an orphan with a family to raise, still bound on her own journey, while winds she didn't know how to counter pulled Gabriel-Antoine's heart away. And the government and bank were still hunting them, one by one. Her chest ached and her brain felt like it was fogging; this was too big for her.

She needed to focus. They could mourn when they were safe within Venus. Her rise began to slow—her balloon's buoyancy at fifty atmospheres was much less than at the ninety atmospheres on the surface. She didn't want to overshoot, so she activated the pump, compressing oxygen back into the tank. The bathyscaphe floated five hundred meters above her, its propellers churning behind it. The propeller drone under Pascale's balloon brought her closer and closer. Patches of orange surface corrosion blemished the steel-skinned ovoid.

"I'm coming up behind you, Alexis. Say again where you think the leak is."

Louise came on the radio. "We think we hear it on the right side of the roof, about halfway back."

"I'll look," Pascale said.

She rose level with the bathyscaphe, to starboard, avoiding its propwash. Its surface offered few handholds: a couple of big eyelets along the spine to hang it from a pulley for servicing, some on the sides for roping it to cleats in dock, and a small rudder and ailerons that were too close to the propellers to serve as useful grips. Pascale's buoyancy in the heavy suit was about the same as the bathyscaphe's now, and she steered her drone to bring her alongside, just above the dorsal surface. Her best bet would be to steady herself on one of the starboard eyelets. She pointed the drone fans slightly up to push her closer.

She didn't see it through her faceplate, but her leg must have brushed the bathyscaphe—a snapping sounded, accompanying a bright, blue-white flash. She cried out, but no one heard it because everything in her faceplate display was rebooting. The joints of her suit became stiff and the sound of her drone stopped.

She craned her neck inside the helmet to look up. Her drone's propellers had stilled, and a wisp of smoke coiled from its seams. The leg of her suit dragged slowly along the hull as the bathyscaphe began to pull forward on its thrust. The radio came on again. People were calling for her.

"Alexis!" she said. "Turn off the propellers. Drift! Turn off the propellers."

The power assist in the joints came back online, but only partially. Some of the fuses in the suit must have burnt out. She was such an idiot. In the clouds, when approaching any new trawler, she would have dropped a line to equalize their static electrical differences. All the netting under the trawlers was grounded to prevent shocks. Here, beneath all the clouds, in a different kind of suit, worried about the children, she'd forgotten all of that. She grabbed for the dorsal eyelets, but the power-assist was still slow, and she missed.

"Turn off the propellers!" she said into the radio again.

The bathyscaphe's rusty propellers were turning fast enough to damage her suit if they collided. And right now she didn't trust her control.

"What's going on?" Gabriel-Antoine's voice demanded. "Are you okay?"

"They're off!" Alexis said. "What happened? We got a shock! Are you okay, Pascal?"

Pascale's big gloved hand grabbed the small vertical stabilizer and she stopped sliding. The bathyscaphe propellers slowed to a stop. The loss of the propeller drone meant she couldn't direct herself around, but she was still close to neutrally buoyant.

"I'm okay," Pascale said. "The bathyscaphe had a static charge. I'm okay, but it looks like my propeller drone blew some fuses."

"What's going to happen?" Alexis said.

"Just wait. It'll be okay," Pascale said. "I'm going to examine the seams."

Pascale pulled herself forward, putting her knees around the vertical stabilizer and rudder, so that she could reach the last steel eyelet along the spine of the bathyscaphe. Duvieusart had built the bathyscaphe, forty years before, using as many large pieces as possible, to minimize the number of welds that could fail as she became the first person to reach the surface of Venus. Just three major seams ran around the craft.

She began examining the sternmost seam. She'd thought that the quickest thing would be just to apply the silicone compound along all the seams without finding the leak, but she wasn't sure she had enough—or even how much she would need. They'd just grabbed the jars they had in the habitat. But she had an idea.

She pulled down her buoyancy balloon to reach the propeller drone. Dark smoke still snaked from its little motor casing. She unharnessed the drone and held it close to the rearmost seam, watching the way the smoke moved. It gave no sign that the seam was damaged.

She pulled herself forward until she could put her knees around the dorsal eyelet and reach the next one with one hand. At about halfway along the bathyscaphe length, she had access to the major middle seam. The drone smoke was thinning, but there was still enough to repeat her process. Very, very faintly, about thirty degrees down the starboard side of the bathyscaphe, the smoke seemed to wobble and bend over a segment of the seam. She held the drone closer and the smoke wobbled again, slightly, by the weld there. The effect didn't happen anywhere else. She hung the drone from a hook at her waist.

"Gabriel-Antoine, I think I found it," Pascale said. "I'm going to apply the silicone."

Carefully, so as not to jostle her precarious hold, she pulled one of the jars from the hooks on her ADS and opened its hinged lid. The white goop inside moved like syrup as she tilted the jar. She took a dollop on a finger. It spread messily, up and down the seam, almost *too* fluid at this heat. She covered about two meters of the seam, waited a few minutes, then applied another layer.

"Alexis, do you still hear the sound?" Pascale asked.

After a pause, Alexis said, "No. We don't think so."

"What's the temperature and pressure inside?" Pascale asked as she pulled out more cord and ran it through the dorsal eyelet so she couldn't drift away.

"Nine atmospheres," Alexis answered. "A hundred and twelve degrees."

"Your suits okay?" she asked. "Louise and Paul-Égide?"

"Paul-Égide went to sleep," Alexis said. "Louise's suit is thirty-six inside."

"Alexis, you start up the propellers and drop as fast as you can," Pascale said. "Louise and Jean-Eudes, wake up Paul-Égide. He shouldn't sleep. Go, Alexis."

Pascale heard the pumps running inside the bathyscaphe, compressing the oxygen and letting in heavier carbon dioxide from the atmosphere. At the same time, Pascale pumped oxygen out of her balloon, compressing it into her oxygen tank, adding to her own weight to make the bathyscaphe sink faster.

"He's not waking up," Louise said.

"Keep trying," Pascale said. "We'll be down soon."

FIFTY-THREE

GASCHEL REGARDED THE bedraggled crew in her office, struggling to bring her boiling, conflicting emotions to some sort of consensus. White bandages wrapped the bank security chief's right hand. Her foot was similarly wrapped. The D'Aquillon patriarch had electrified the gantry on the *Causapscal-des-Profondeurs* and Copeland had been shocked. Glove and boot had burned through in spots, exposing hand and foot to ninety-degree sulfuric acid. Beside her, Tétreau was pale and sweaty, wounded in the shoulder by a bullet from one of their own guns, taken by one of the D'Aquillons. None of the survivors had come through unscathed. Gaschel shunned the mystical, animistic superstitions some Venusians needed, but couldn't deny the strength of the perverse, persistent wisdoms those beliefs offered, like the idea of Venus taking her due from those who travelled her clouds. She'd tithed heavily today. Four of the assault team hadn't returned at all, some of Gaschel's and some of Woodward's.

"The primary objective was accomplished," Copeland continued in English. "The insurgent George-Étienne D'Aquillon was killed trying to evade arrest. The fugitive Émile D'Aquillon was also killed. Aboard the

Causapscal-des-Profondeurs, we found all sorts of equipment stripped from the hijacked habitat *Causapscal-des-Vents.* Also found nearby were the last remains of the disassembled habitat and four engineered trawlers made by Marie-Pier Hudon."

She hadn't wanted this, but… two of the D'Aquillons were gone. Short of an accident, being killed beside the goods they'd stolen while resisting arrest was about the best outcome Gaschel could have hoped for.

"Recovery teams are down there now," Tétreau said in French. "They'll bring the four trawlers to the middle cloud deck for use as habitats, as they were originally intended. Teams are also recovering all metals and useful materials from the *Causapscal-des-Profondeurs* and their herd."

"D'Aquillon had family," Gaschel said. "Some children, *non*? Where are they?"

Tétreau shrugged, the movement provoking a wince. "The *coureurs* have been making a lot of small alliances. Family may be living in other habitats."

"In terms of intel recovered from the *Causapscal-des-Profondeurs,*" Copeland said, "we found no useful navigational information about their work on the surface. Radio and GPS databases were programmed to purge daily. Two data pads were recovered. One was a database of open-source engineering specs, the kind freely available anywhere in the solar system. Among the bookmarks were designs for nuclear fission rocketry."

Gaschel didn't know what to make of that. It took a lot more radioisotopes than they'd seen to run a nuclear fission rocket. Had the D'Aquillons found that much, or were they just dreaming? They were the cheapest kind of rocket among the asteroids. Designs were ubiquitous and often simple: some gas to heat as a propellant, the right metals for the engine and frame, and fissioning nuclear materials. If the D'Aquillons had found radioisotopes somewhere, there might be a way to partner with the bank to build their own Venusian rockets.

"What do you think?" Gaschel said to Woodward.

The branch manager woman shook her head. "Even if this… House of Styx group had developed rockets, satellites would have seen them anywhere above the atmosphere."

Gaschel had expected more of an answer, or maybe Woodward was considering the implications of a Venus that had an alternative to the bank's exorbitant shipping fees.

Copeland linked to Gaschel's table and displayed images from the raid. Gaschel moved the images around, unsure of what to make of them.

"The other pad contained engineering designs for several disk-shapes," Copeland said, "ten to fifteen meters in diameter, hinged to open, with embedded wind turbines."

"What for?" Gaschel said. "If they're using these in a cave system, that wouldn't stop the people from cooking. Even the most efficient Stirling engines still need somewhere to dump the heat. And why turbines? There's almost no wind on the surface. Even if there were, windmills would be a more efficient use of metals."

"Maybe they're idiots," Tétreau said.

The silence extended as people examined the designs.

"Maybe," Gaschel finally said, "but they've done some things that show a lot of intelligence. The engineering know-how to catch a falling habitat is at the edge of what any of us could do. And they've managed to get access to radioisotopes from somewhere on the surface, apparently enough to at least investigate nuclear rocket designs. The technical difficulties of extracting anything from the surface are monumental. This small group of *coureurs* did it without any help from us."

"They just needed to steal a dozen tons of steel," Copeland said.

Woodward gave the security officer a reproachful look.

"The neutralization of four senior members of the conspiracy reduces their effectiveness," Woodward said, "possibly permanently. Gabriel-Antoine Phocas and Pascal D'Aquillon are an isolated threat, with Marthe, George-Étienne, and Émile D'Aquillon off the board, and Hudon in a cell."

"The second pad also contained star maps," Copeland said. "Nothing suspicious about that, except we can't figure out where they're from. We ran the star maps through the astrometric databases in the branch office. They don't match any astronomical view."

"A fake?" Woodward asked.

"Maybe," Copeland said. "The metadata wasn't very informative—the pictures were downloaded from a dumb system, taken about six months ago. But why fake star maps?"

"Our astrometric data on Venus is just a fraction of what's held at the head office," Woodward said. "If *Présidente Gaschel* gives her permission, we could forward these pictures to the head office to find a match."

Gaschel nodded, although she wasn't sure that this wasn't just disinformation.

"We may get some answers when we arrest D'Aquillon and Phocas," Tétreau said. "I've been working with Copeland on identifying the location in Mignaud's pictures. We ran it against a joint database of visual-spectrum and radar imagery, and we've found the probable location. It's part of the Diana Chasma in the Aphrodite Terra at sixteen degrees south, one hundred and fifty-four east. We got a drone down beneath the sub-cloud haze: telescopic photography found a metal structure at those coordinates, built into the walls of the chasma, very hard to see from most angles."

Pictures rendered grainy by over-enlargement joined the images on Gaschel's table display.

Gaschel shook her head. "What the hell are they doing with our steel?" she said.

Labourière shrugged. "Neither we nor the bank have any equipment to transport people to the surface, but we've come to a rental and service agreement with the bank for the use of two hardened drones to complete an armed reconnaissance—or a stake-out, if needed."

"Are we sure that's where Gabriel-Antoine Phocas and Pascal D'Aquillon are?" Gaschel asked.

"We're not sure," Tétreau said. "If they are, they've at the very least got to be using hard-shelled atmospheric diving suits, but we have no idea how they'd be cooling themselves or any of their systems."

"How soon can you send the hardened drones?" Gaschel asked.

"We're about twelve hours away from a good glide path," Copeland said.

"Let's sew this up," Gaschel said to Tétreau and Copeland, before turning to Woodward. "I would like this concluded and all the uncertainty sorted out so we can get back to a proper business footing."

FIFTY-FOUR

Jean-Eudes listened to Pascale and Gabriel-Antoine tell Alexis what to do and how to fly the ship down to the surface, which took a lot of work, because they were trying to do it fast with no mistakes. Everybody was worried about Paul-Égide, who wouldn't wake up. Louise squiggled back a bit and Jean-Eudes worried that they would tip the ship again, but Alexis said it was okay. Louise was strong, but Jean-Eudes was stronger, so he held up Paul-Égide. Louise was crying. Her face was sweaty and red too.

"He's got heat exhaustion," Jean-Eudes said.

"What do we do?" Louise asked.

"We have to get him cool," Alexis said.

"How?" she said. Her face was angry and worried, and she shook her little brother. Jean-Eudes was worried. There was no place to get cool here. They couldn't take off clothes or give him water. They didn't have a fan.

"We're going to the surface," Alexis said.

"It's hotter there!" Louise said. Her face was red too. Too red.

"Drink your water," Jean-Eudes said. "Use your straw."

Louise looked at him for the first time, and her face was like she didn't want him to say anything or be there. He didn't like it. Jean-Eudes was bigger, bigger than any of them in here, even though they were smarter. He tried to think of what *Papa* or Marthe would do now, but Louise was already looking away, pulling at her brother, away from him. When *Papa* knew what to do, he would say so.

"You have to drink," Jean-Eudes said, "or you'll get heat exhaustion too. Use your straw."

She did drink from the straw in her helmet. Her face was still patchy red, like when Alexis had first started using his suit outside.

"Get closer together," Alexis said.

"What?" Louise said. "We'll get hotter."

"The air inside the bathyscaphe is over a hundred degrees," Alexis said, looking back. "Our bodies are cooler than the air. Everywhere we touch is a place the heat can't get in more."

Jean-Eudes didn't understand, but he was proud of his little nephew. Louise backed up and scrunched next to Jean-Eudes and Paul-Égide, and this let Jean-Eudes see almost all the front window. It was… big.

Marthe had talked to him about Venus. So had Émile and Pascal and *Papa*. And he had looked at a lot of pictures. He moved his head a little side to side and closed one eye, then the other, and the mountains and rocks and ridges and smashed pieces of Venus were all so… big. Bigger than anything he'd ever seen, more space than he'd ever seen. It was scary.

This was so different from pictures and talking. The clouds were a roof, so high up that he couldn't even think of how high. The ground came closer and closer. The mountains looked like toys, but sharp and dirty, like dust and dirt had fallen on them. They went lower, and the little bits of dust and dirt turned out to be boulders and smashed rocks, and then it was hard to remember them as dust. The ship jerked and jumped a bit, but Jean-Eudes didn't feel airsick. The huge mountains were all around them now, and the sky was an itty-bitty scrap at the top of the window.

"You're doing great, Alexis," Pascale's voice said on the radio. Pascale told Alexis a lot of things about how to fly that Jean-Eudes didn't know, and Alexis was doing them. He wasn't little anymore, not really.

Marthe and *Papa* and Émile would have been so proud of Alexis. Jean-Eudes started crying again, quietly, which made it harder to see, and he couldn't wipe his eyes.

The rocks and rocks and rocks kept moving by, more rock than anything Jean-Eudes had ever thought even the Earth would have. This was what *Papa* had said was going to be theirs. Jean-Eudes didn't understand that. So much rock. Jean-Eudes wanted to see *Papa*'s storm. And he wanted to tell him he saw it, even if *Papa* was only a saint looking over them. They were moving slower and slower now. Then there was a hole in the rocks, a cave, with a metal cover that was open.

"I know that!" Jean-Eudes said. "That's the cover we built!"

No one answered him and he went quiet. Pascale was telling Alexis more about flying. Alexis had to get them into the cave. And there was a man in a big hard suit by the big open door.

"It's Gabriel-Antoine!" Jean-Eudes whispered. He shook Louise, who looked like she was falling asleep. "It's Gabriel-Antoine, your brother," he said, pointing.

She said something, like she was really sleepy.

"Stay awake," he said, and shook her. "We'll be there soon and it will be cooler."

Pascale and Alexis and Gabriel-Antoine were talking almost all the time now on the radio, and the ship creaked and Jean-Eudes felt hot, as hot as he'd ever felt in the worst times on the *Causapscal*. He stayed still and kept Louise and Paul-Égide from falling over. The cave got bigger and darker, like going into a giant's mouth in *Maman*'s fairy tales. Gabriel-Antoine was walking in his big suit and there were some lights in the cave. Gabriel-Antoine caught a rope and pulled the ship in. It got really dark, like they were being eaten by Venus.

Jean-Eudes's heart was still beating fast. Pascale and Gabriel-Antoine each had a rope and they started walking down black stairs in the cave, pulling the ship behind them like a floating balloon.

"Start filling the buoyancy tanks with oxygen, Alexis," Gabriel-Antoine said. "We're dropping the pressure before we get to the second airlock."

Alexis knew so many controls. There were a lot of controls. He could do everything they asked him to do. Jean-Eudes remembered the talk he'd had with Pascale, when Alexis and Jean-Eudes were going to be alone for the first time on the *Causapscal*, and Alexis was going to do all the controls. Jean-Eudes had been upset, but Pascale showed him how he should be proud of his little nephew. He was still proud. More proud.

"You're doing good, Alexis," Jean-Eudes said.

Alexis looked back quickly and smiled.

A big metal door was in front of them.

"I saw that door!" Jean-Eudes said, excited. "In the clouds, being built."

"Watch it open, Jean-Eudes," Pascale said on the radio. "Alexis, more oxygen. You have to make yourself more buoyant as the pressure drops. We're down to sixty atmospheres already. It's going to get cool enough soon for you to feel the Stirling engines making a difference in the bathyscaphe."

They all waited. It didn't feel any cooler to Jean-Eudes, but the big door opened towards them, and Pascale and Gabriel-Antoine pulled on the ropes so that the ship passed through. He wanted to see the door close, but the window at the back was small and it was dark in the cave. The cave was twisty like a throat, and it was deep, really deep. Soon, Jean-Eudes saw another metal door.

"The outer pressure is four atmospheres now, Alexis," Pascale said on the radio. "There's a valve to the left of the pilot console. Open it a bit and keep an eye on the internal pressure gauge. Let the pressure bleed off until you get to six atmospheres, and then we'll wait a minute."

Gabriel-Antoine looked funny carrying a ladder, but then he was attaching a cable to the ship and to the roof of the cave. Jean-Eudes felt like they were swinging a bit.

"How's the inner temperature, Alexis?" Pascale said.

"It's down to eighty," Alexis answered. "It's creaking a lot."

Jean-Eudes didn't feel much cooler, but he did hear the creaking. It was like the ship was cracking.

"The drop in pressure out here has the atmosphere at sixty degrees," Pascale said. "Keep the Stirling engines cooling at full. In about ten minutes we'll drop the pressure more and if no one is suffering from the bends, we'll get you into the habitat."

Jean-Eudes knew they weren't supposed to sleep if they were too hot, and so he shook Louise and Paul-Égide a little. It was getting a little cooler. Louise looked cranky, but her eyes were open.

"Drink more," Jean-Eudes said to her. "That's what my *Papa* taught me."

Paul-Égide was awake again; he was whining and crying and saying he was too hot. He wouldn't listen to Jean-Eudes. He didn't drink. Alexis turned and shook Paul-Égide harder than Jean-Eudes did.

"Come on!" Alexis said in a loud voice, shaking Paul-Égide. "Drink! This is what we do. Your straw is right there."

The little boy listened to Alexis, but then he stopped drinking, and Jean-Eudes told Alexis and Alexis said it again, and the boy drank some more.

"Are any of you feeling any pain in your muscles or joints?" Gabriel-Antoine said. "Any dizziness?"

Jean-Eudes and Alexis said no. Gabriel-Antoine had to talk harder to Louise and Paul-Égide to get them to answer. Louise said no, and at first Paul-Égide said he didn't know. Gabriel-Antoine had to yell at him in the helmet radio to get him to answer, and it hurt Jean-Eudes's ears. Paul-Égide said no.

"It went to five atmospheres!" Alexis said in his worried voice.

"It's okay," Pascale said. "Make sure the valve is closed."

"If a seam is damaged, there might be more than one leak," Gabriel-Antoine said. "We had to make a quick repair."

Everybody was worried, but the inside of the ship kept getting cooler, making more and more snapping and cracking noises that Pascale said were normal. Jean-Eudes didn't like them.

"Bleed off more pressure, Alexis," Gabriel-Antoine said. "Real slow, to two atmospheres."

"The inside of the bathyscaphe is down to forty degrees," Louise said. "That's impossible on the surface of Venus."

"Wait until you see the stars," Gabriel-Antoine said.

They waited more and Jean-Eudes had to pee from all the water he drank. He still felt silly peeing in his suit. He'd done it before, but it felt like peeing in his pants. There was a tube, and he would have to wriggle a bit to make it work. He decided to hold it.

"Is anyone feeling any pain in muscles or joints?" Gabriel-Antoine said again. Jean-Eudes moved his arms and answered no. Everyone else answered no. "Okay, Alexis, open the valve and leave it open and tell me when the pressure reaches zero."

"Zero?" Alexis said with a surprised voice. Jean-Eudes wasn't sure why he was surprised.

The big door in front of the ship was opening and past it was only darkness.

"The outside pressure is zero?" Louise said. "That's impossible!"

There was more hissing and creaking in the ship, but a lot of the sounds stopped. Jean-Eudes's suit got funny too. It stopped squeezing him and got puffy and didn't even touch his skin in some places.

"I'm a balloon," he said, touching one puffy suit hand to another.

A banging sound came from behind him. The metal on the door was moving. He scootched forward. There was more banging and hitting that he didn't hear much in his ears—he *felt* the hitting, through his seat. Then the back door opened and everything was quiet and his suit got so puffy it felt kind of hard.

"Gabriel-Antoine!" he called.

Gabriel-Antoine was in the big hard suit they'd built at home. They were all in a cave, in the body of Venus. She was all dark rock and weird, quiet noises. Gabriel-Antoine reached in and picked up Paul-Égide and pulled him out. Then Pascale was there, and Jean-Eudes hugged her. She held tight for a bit.

"I'm so sorry, Jean-Eudes," Pascale said finally.

"What did you do?" Jean-Eudes asked.

"I'm sorry about *Papa* and Émile. We miss them."

Jean-Eudes hugged Pascale again, until she pulled away, too soon.

"Put these on your feet and come on out, Jean-Eudes."

Pascale had flat pieces of trawler cabling with strings attached. She tied them under Jean-Eudes's boots.

"Pascale!" Alexis said.

"Tie these on," Pascale said to him. "Quick." She stopped tying Jean-Eudes's soles and pulled more of the soles out of a little mesh pouch and gave two to Alexis and Louise.

"What are they?" Louise said.

"We can cool the air in here," Pascale said, "but the rock still has all the heat of Venus. Your boots are no good for four-hundred-degree stone. Don't touch the ground with anything but these. Can you walk, Jean-Eudes?"

Jean-Eudes looked at the little soles. The ground sounded scary, but he slowly climbed out the back of the ship and put his feet down. The rock was hard. And it didn't move at all, not like their home in the clouds. It felt like it moved when it didn't.

"This is the first time you've ever stood on solid ground, Jean-Eudes. And you're only the third person in history to step on the surface of Venus. You're part of history."

Pascale's words made Jean-Eudes feel a little heavier and a little smaller, both at once. Pascale checked the soles on Louise and Alexis and then helped them out. Alexis hugged Pascale and wouldn't let go.

"*Grand-papa*," he said.

"I know," Pascale said. "I'm so sorry. He was a good *Papa* and a good *Grand-papa*, and he wasn't done being either."

FIFTY-FIVE

THE LITTLE HABITAT in the cave had only a standard airlock, so Pascale put in Jean-Eudes, Louise and Alexis together. While they cycled the airlock, she closed the last cap, opened the valves for the wind turbine, and reset the middle chamber to about forty atmospheres. She was running on autopilot, focused on the now, but the pressure of everything, the political and financial isolation, the deaths… It would all overwhelm her as soon as she entered the habitat. She wanted to huddle in a hammock and be miserable, but everyone needed her.

When the light over the airlock greened, she cycled through. Inside, Louise, Jean-Eudes and Alexis were standing, a bit bewildered. Their helmets were off, sweaty hair plastered to their foreheads. Paul-Égide sat on a stool, helmet off, drinking from a cup.

Everyone was quiet and Paul-Égide began to cry as Pascale started laboriously removing the hard dive suit. Alexis was dutifully climbing out of his suit, while his eyes became increasingly red-rimmed and moist. Louise went to her little brother, brushing his hair out of his face. Pascale took Alexis's hand and pulled him close, and then folded in Jean-Eudes. She held them tight and kissed the tops of their heads.

"*Grand-papa…*" Alexis said, his face scrunching tight.

"And Émile," Jean-Eudes said.

"I know," she said. Her chest tightened and she was crying with them. After holding them, Pascale put her hammock across its two hooks and sat down brother and nephew and got them a cup of cold water to share. She knelt before them.

"Pa called and told us about Marie-Pier and Émile's escape," she said. "What happened?"

Paul-Égide looked up miserably, but Louise told them about the bank people coming to the *Marais-des-Nuages* and holding them as hostages, and Émile sneaking in and beating up the security man. It took her a breath to talk about their terrifying plunge into the clouds, the heat, the acid, and the times Émile had just left them. Gabriel-Antoine had a dark look on his face, but Louise defended Émile, and Pascale explained what she thought Émile might have been doing when he left the children.

"They shouldn't have been floating in the clouds on their own…" Gabriel-Antoine said sullenly, putting his arm back around his little brother.

Louise kept up her story to the point she and Paul-Égide were pulled out of the safe sack, onto a trawler, and told to get into the bathyscaphe with Alexis and Jean-Eudes. Alexis took over the story there, explaining that *Grand-papa* had thought that bad people were coming and had brought Alexis and Jean-Eudes to *l'Anse-à-Beaufils* by balloon and drone, because neither of them could fly yet. He'd hidden them in the bathyscaphe and told them to stay put, setting it on a course to leave the herd for a few hours. Then he'd gone back to the *Causapscal*. The bad men arrived around the same time as Émile and then Émile had gone to help *Grand-papa*. Alexis had trouble saying the next part and finally it came out like angry crying. "And then they shot them both!"

Pascale hugged them again and wiped her eyes, remembering Pa in dozens of ways, all the memories playing over each other, all the moments of her life. *Oh, Pa. Poor Émile*. Both murdered for a dream of stars.

"Where can we go?" Alexis said. "They're always going to be after us."

"Can they come here?" Louise said.

"I don't want to do this anymore," Alexis said.

Gabriel-Antoine shook his head. "I don't think so. Building suits like ours is hard, and I bet no one has any. And they have no base to operate from, and we've got air and electricity and a habitat down here."

"What do we do now?" Alexis said. "We're stuck in a cave." He was clinging hard to Pascale.

"We have food for a while," Pascale said. "We'll need to get signals out to other *coureur* families to trade, to get more food. We can give them metals. And we're not trapped. Once we're sure your suits work in a vacuum, we'll show you the stars."

Alexis looked like he was trying hard not to cry.

"*Grand-papa* should be here," he said. "He should have seen the stars."

Jean-Eudes felt cramped in this boxy space *inside* Venus, under the rocks. At first, he was scared, because of what everyone had told him about the surface, that no one could ever live there. He knew Pascale and Gabriel-Antoine had come down here with their hard suits, and in the bathyscaphe, so he'd imagined those things, but not this metal and plastic box. It felt cold and weird. He missed the sound of the wind whistling through the gantry, the way it swayed them. Louise and Paul-Égide were upset. Alexis was upset. Pascale and Gabriel-Antoine looked upset, until Gabriel-Antoine put on his suit and went outside.

In the *Causapscal*, Jean-Eudes had seen when people were upset and tried to make them feel better, but he didn't know how here. He felt upset. He was upset. About *Papa*. About Émile and Marie-Pier. About Marthe. Jean-Eudes spent some time trying to make sure all the survival suits worked, but he didn't really do anything, because he didn't know where the tools were, here, and didn't want to ask.

Louise sat beside Jean-Eudes quietly and Jean-Eudes started moving his hands again, as if he'd been working. She looked at him funny. Pa had always said that when people finally met Jean-Eudes, some of them might look at him funny and not to be upset. He wasn't upset.

"Something's wrong," Louise said, quietly.

"What?" Jean-Eudes whispered.

"Émile said Gabriel-Antoine was Pascal's boyfriend. They don't act like it."

Jean-Eudes hadn't thought of that. He'd thought everyone was sad about *Papa* and Émile and Marthe. She was looking at him like she expected an answer.

"I don't know," he said, quietly too.

"Your brother didn't say anything?" Louise whispered.

"Pascale's my sister," he said automatically.

"What?"

Jean-Eudes felt really hot in his face, like he was embarrassed. He wasn't supposed to say Pascale's secret. Pascale and Alexis looked up, too, in surprise. Jean-Eudes thought he'd said it quiet enough, but Pascale's face turned a bit red. Louise looked from Pascale to Jean-Eudes and then rolled her eyes.

"Dummy," she said quietly, getting up.

"Don't call him that!" Alexis said, standing.

Jean-Eudes felt like a dummy, though, and looked at Pascale. She was looking back. He was so sorry. He hadn't meant to say the secret. Pascale didn't look mad—she looked scared.

"Jean-Eudes isn't a dummy," Pascale said finally, smiling a little. "I told Jean-Eudes a secret before almost anyone else. I'm a girl."

"You're a boy," Alexis said, and Jean-Eudes tried shushing him, but he wasn't looking. "I've seen."

Louise and Paul-Égide looked confused, then giggled.

"What matters is what you feel like," Pascale said. "Sometimes what we are on the outside isn't the important thing. I told Jean-Eudes about it a while ago, that I was his sister, not his brother."

Alexis looked confused and a bit mad.

"Nothing else changed, Alexis," Pascale said with a little hopeful smile. "You'll always be my nephew. Your grandfather was always my *Papa*. I taught you algebra. That doesn't change."

"That's why you wore *Grand-maman*'s dress!" Alexis said, standing. Alexis's voice sounded between a joke and being angry. Was he mad

Pascale hadn't told him? Louise snickered. Paul-Égide looked confused.

Pascale's face got redder and she stood too.

"I've always loved you and I always will, Alexis," she said. "And I'll always protect you, and Jean-Eudes, and Louise and Paul-Égide and Gabriel-Antoine. Family still comes first."

Alexis should have said something, but he just looked upset. He walked to Jean-Eudes and sat down beside him, not looking at Pascale. Jean-Eudes was going to say something, but Pascale held up her hand.

"We've lost family," she said. "We're in a strange place. It's hard." She took a deep breath and then started putting on her survival suit. "Gabriel-Antoine probably needs some help."

Jean-Eudes got up and helped Pascale, even though she didn't need help.

"I'm sorry," he whispered. He felt like crying. Pascale wiped her eyes.

"It's okay, Jean-Eudes," she whispered. "I was going to tell them. I was going to tell *Papa*. I didn't know how. Now I don't have the chance."

"I was dumb."

Pascale put a hand on his shoulder and on his face. "It wasn't dumb," she whispered to him and then kissed his forehead, the way *Papa* used to. Jean-Eudes helped Pascale into the last of her suit. Then she went into the airlock.

Alexis was still sitting where Jean-Eudes had been. He was making the face he made when he thought something was stupid or funny, so Jean-Eudes pulled him aside. The habitat wasn't big, but Jean-Eudes got his nephew into the little side-room they used for the toilet. It smelled a bit funny.

"What?" Alexis said, yanking his arm away.

"Whisper," Jean-Eudes whispered.

"What?" Alexis whispered.

"You were going to say something bad about Pascale being a girl."

"He's not a—"

"Whisper!" Jean-Eudes whispered.

Alexis made a face, as if he were saying that Louise could hear them anyway. He put his lips close to Jean-Eudes's ear, which tickled a little. "He's not a girl."

"She is," Jean-Eudes whispered into Alexis's ear. "You can feel different than your body. Pascale told me. You have a boy's body and you feel like a boy."

"That's stupid. He's a boy."

"You don't understand," Jean-Eudes whispered. "I don't understand. We don't have to understand. I don't always understand things you do, but I trust you. If you love Pascale, you have to trust her now."

"The reason you don't understand this is because there's nothing to understand," Alexis said. "It makes no sense."

"I'm not just your uncle," Jean-Eudes whispered. "I'm your best friend. Since you were a baby. I wasn't ready to trust you when *Papa* and Pascale went to the surface and left you in charge. It would have hurt you if I didn't trust you, wouldn't it? Pascale made me trust you. And if you're a person who wants trust, but doesn't trust back, you're just greedy."

Alexis looked upset, like he was insulted. "I'm not greedy. And there's a difference: I understood what to do then."

"And Pascale understands what to do now."

"There's a difference between understanding how to move in the clouds and saying a boy is a girl."

"Just because you're smarter than me doesn't mean you always understand everything," Jean-Eudes whispered. "It will hurt Pascale if you think she's a boy. It will hurt her heart. She loves you. She loves both of us. We don't have to understand what happened. We just need to trust her."

"It's weird," Alexis said.

"*Papa* said family comes first," Jean-Eudes whispered. "Marthe said family comes first. Pascale is our family. I don't want to lose any more family and I don't have to understand anything more. I just have to trust her. Do you trust her?"

Sullenly, his nephew nodded. He looked sad now.

"Don't worry. Pascale won't be mad at you. You're a good boy, Alexis."

FIFTY-SIX

The habitat in the cave was small. Despite curtains and arrangements of crude furniture and tool benches and equipment, it was like the *Causapscal-des-Vents*, in that privacy was either whispered or pretend. So Pascale knew that after the younger children had gone to sleep, Gabriel-Antoine started drinking. Pascale had packed some *bagosse*—whether for medicinal purposes or outright drinking, she hadn't thought through at the time; the taste of eighty-proof made her gag.

Jean-Eudes sat beside Pascale, threading wires through the stator of a new alternator they needed to build. The slow, boring work seemed to calm Jean-Eudes, who had let on that he was wrestling with his own fear and the deaths of Marie-Pier and Pa and Émile. Pascale missed them all, even Émile, whom she'd only seen once in the last five years: the brother with whom she might have had so much more, if only they'd had time. No. If only the government and the bank hadn't murdered him. Pascale patted Jean-Eudes on the shoulder and passed through the curtain to see Gabriel-Antoine in the crude galley.

The single bulb in the ceiling glowed with a harsh white light—their homemade generators and transformers weren't yet as precise as they wanted, and the current often ran high. Gabriel-Antoine sat at the simple trawler-fibre table with a jar and a glass, his cheeks very pink. Pascale cautiously sat in the opposite chair. Gabriel-Antoine didn't look up, and they sat in silence for a time. There was another glass on the little shelf, but Pascale didn't reach for it.

"Marie-Pier was too young to go," Gabriel-Antoine said softly.

Pascale nodded.

"My 'wife,'" Gabriel-Antoine said, making air quotes. "Your father. Your brother. Probably my grandparents." He shook his head, his eyes wet. "We thought we were doing something small and secret, but we were really doing something big, big enough to be killed for. Now we don't know where Marie-Pier's children are. We said we'd protect them if anything bad happened."

"Émile and Pa told them to get to the House of Faeries. Willy Gallant and Juliette Malboeuf are good people."

"They're with strangers."

"Old lady Malboeuf never lied to Pa. She's a *coureur.* So are the children. They'll be cared for. And we'll pay the government back for this," Pascale said, in a voice suddenly steady, steadier than she'd thought possible. Gabriel-Antoine looked up at her in surprise, in a way that made Pascale feel self-consciously visible.

"How are we going to do that?"

"We're the only ones on this whole planet with access to metal, and huge amounts of electricity," she said. "We don't have designs for new weapons, but in the old open-source engineering books, there's stuff from a century ago that would do some damage."

"Who's 'we'?" Gabriel-Antoine said. "Do you have an army lying around?"

"We're enough. You and me. Alexis would be willing to fight."

"Three of us? Against *la colonie*?"

"We're not the only ones who've been wronged. We're not the only ones who want something different. People haven't been offered another way. My heart was changed. Your heart was changed. We're dreaming of a new future."

"Slow down, Pascale." Gabriel-Antoine shook his head with the deliberateness of the drunk. He poured himself another two fingers from the jar. "Changing hearts is hard. If you ask ten people in the flotillas if they want to live like *coureurs,* ten will say no. The math gets worse. Thousands of people live in the flotillas. There are three adults here. This is not a time to fight. A few constables is all they'd need to end the House of Styx. That's all they needed at the *Causapscal-des-Profondeurs.* Dreams are cheap. Even we can afford them."

He stopped talking for so long, Pascale thought he'd finished, and she didn't know what to say. He wiped a tear from his cheek.

"It's a time to build," he went on. "It's a time to grow crops. We had food for two, not for six. We weren't supposed to be down here without resupply from your father."

His eyes drooped in the silence she couldn't answer.

"I'm going to sleep," he said, rising unsteadily.

She realized that she'd been sitting by herself, staring at the wall, for some time when she heard Gabriel-Antoine's erratic snoring. She went to where Alexis slept against Jean-Eudes, who was staring at the ceiling.

"Are you okay?" her brother asked.

"Maybe?" she whispered. "People will want things from us. We have to know what we want. Some wants can't go together."

Jean-Eudes continued staring at the ceiling as Pascale hooked her hammock into the wall eyelets.

"*Papa* and *Maman* wanted me," Jean-Eudes said in the deliberate way he did when he was constructing a line of thinking. "*La colonie* didn't want me. *Papa* and *Maman* came to live down in the lower decks."

"And that turned out okay."

"Not for Émile."

"What do you know about that?" Pascale asked.

"I heard them argue, when you were little. Émile was angry... about losing *Maman*. About losing Chloé. But mostly about *Maman*. If I hadn't been born, maybe *Maman* would still be alive and Émile would be happy with *Papa*."

Jean-Eudes's eyes shone wetly in the dim light.

"Émile loved you a lot. There's always a cost on Venus."

"Maybe I cost too much," Jean-Eudes said. "It would be nice if *Maman* was still here. It would be nice if *Papa* and Émile talked to each other." He wiped his eyes with the heels of his palms and his voice trembled. "It would be nice if they weren't dead."

Pascale knelt beside him. Her voice sounded surer than she'd expected.

"If you feel bad about the way you were born, then I have to feel bad about the way I was born."

Jean-Eudes thought that through, frowning with the intensity of it.

"You're my sister," he said finally. "You're my last sister. Don't change. Don't feel bad."

"Pa and *Maman* made the best decisions they could with what they knew," Pascale said, wiping at Jean-Eudes's tears, his beard tickling her thumb. "Now we have to make decisions for the family, and for ourselves."

TÉTREAU ADMIRED AND envied the *newness* of the branch office, its resources and tools that pointed out the pathway for technological and industrial development on Venus. What Venusians accomplished piecemeal with their hands or with limited machines, and occasionally with the creative use of the wilderness, the bank automated *en masse*. Computer chips, never very reliable in the heat and acidity below, worked steadily in the branch office. As Tétreau and Labourière followed Copeland into the more secure areas, the scientific and technological experiments were sometimes briefly visible. The bank was doing *real* science, while the colony sometimes struggled to provide food and oxygen.

The image of *where we are* was sobering, but always it pointed to *where we might go*. Tétreau needed to understand all the possible ways new technology and investment could develop Venus, and how to negotiate the future with the bank. Gaschel had done a fair job with the cards she'd been dealt, but her progress felt unsatisfyingly incremental. And she wouldn't be president forever. She was hitting sixty and had no clear successor.

carefully over the edge, towards the main cave opening. Pascale joined him. The uneven surface of Diana Chasma lay blasted and corrugated beneath them, running roughly east-west. Four kilometers to the south, the ground rose like foothills at first, and then into a high steep wall beneath a distant ceiling of yellow hazes.

"Are they still there?" she said loudly, without radio. The thick atmosphere carried their voices, when they spoke loud enough.

"Where are they going to go?" Gabriel-Antoine said.

Pascale moved her head a little further over the edge. The two metal ovoids squatted there on steel legs. Mean-looking tubes were welded to their sides. She didn't know what weapons might work down here, but if those machines could damage the outer door, the pressure change might be catastrophic for the little habitat inside.

She surveyed the slope above them. The incline rose steeply. Deep ruts ran along its length, relatively straight cracks from a breath Venus had taken long ago. A good place to run wires to act as an antenna.

They bent to separate the insulators and ground wires. Their radio transmitter would be crude, nothing more than a long wire antenna attached to a transceiver, the kind of homemade setup many *coureurs* used on their trawlers. In the clouds, they laboriously coated the wire with something to protect against corrosion, but they didn't need to here—not even acid could survive this close to Venus.

"I'll attach the wire as high as I can get it," he said.

"Let me go. I'm lighter and it's dangerous."

"You're the transceiver expert. Trust me. I'm going up and down fast. Get the transceiver ready."

Gabriel-Antoine grabbed the wires and began climbing the rut above them. Rocks big and small skittered down and Pascale backed away. Gabriel-Antoine made good time considering the mass of the suit. In ninety atmospheres of pressure, the suit's three atmospheres made most of it almost buoyant, but he still had to contend with its inertia.

Pascale began setting up the ground wires, and the cabling they would run through the frame of the airlock, glancing up frequently to make sure Gabriel-Antoine's footing was holding. After twenty minutes, he began making his way down. About ten meters above her, his foot slipped in a mass of pebbles and he slid.

"Gabriel-Antoine!" she cried, instead of anything smart or useful. If his suit hit anything hard enough to crack it…

But the thickness of the atmosphere and the buoyancy of his suit deceived her. He fell slowly, as if through water. She grabbed him, tried to slow him, but the mass of the suit barrelled along despite her efforts. His feet landed on the ledge, but not quite under him, and he kept falling, tipping backwards. Pascale grabbed his hand in both of hers and lurched forward, until both her arms were holding him over the sixty-degree slope to the floor of the chasma. They stopped. Movement stopped. She lay on the floor of the crater, breathing hard, arms fully extended, her mechanized hands around one of his wrists.

"I have you," she said.

He tried to reach his other arm to the ledge, but the big shoulder, armored against pressure, could only rotate so far. His glove grasped only baking air. Pascale would have to pull him up. He massed hundreds of kilos. Buoyancy took care of most of that—the trick was overcoming the inertia, getting him moving. And Pascale was still lying down.

"Hold on," she said. "Hold on."

She made certain of her grip with her left hand and then freed her right. Pressing it firmly against the baking surface of Venus, she flexed. Slowly, she heaved him, her, and both their suits up until he could get a handhold with his other hand.

She winced at the sound of his suit dragging across the gritty lip of the ledge. The suits weren't made to grind across hard stone like that. His legs were surely still visible to the bank probes if they looked up. The rasping metal was a terrible sound, but finally, they both lay on the ledge of their little crater, panting.

"Are you okay?" she said.

"I think so," he said, out of breath.

"Let's get inside before they come looking," she said. The LEDs in his helmet illuminated an ashen face. "Rest for a second. I'll finish up."

She stood and pulled taut the wire he'd attached high above, tying it to a solid outcropping of rock. Thin and dully metallic, it was hard to see against the dark basalt. Gabriel-Antoine stood slowly, supporting himself against the far wall of the depression. He looked breathless and a bit bewildered. She wondered if he were in a bit of shock.

"Are you okay?" she said. "How's the pressure in your suit?"

He didn't answer.

And then the world turned strange.

A boom echoed directionlessly, the way sound moved fast in dense air. A dark shape entered her peripheral vision, moving so fast that it seemed out of place in this ocean of carbon dioxide. A bullet the size of her thumb streaked by. Neither of them had time to move. The metal slammed into Gabriel-Antoine's left arm, flinging it back against the rock.

Below the elbow, Gabriel-Antoine's suit shell dented deeply. She could hear him screaming. Pascale felt like she was going to throw up. Her brain shut off. She held his helmet, grabbed at his arm, but didn't know what to do. On the dark chasma floor, one ovoid probe was backing up to get a better angle of fire on their little crater ledge. The other drone lifted its bow, adjusting its angle. Pascale hauled Gabriel-Antoine across their ledge to the airlock.

"Can you operate the lock from the inside?" she demanded. Her voice sounded panicked in her own ears. "Can you operate the lock inside?"

He seemed to hear her words. She shoved him in as another shell hit the wall of the depression. Rock chips spattered off the walls and their suits.

"Use your right hand! Turn the other side!" she said, pointing.

When it looked like he was listening, she slammed the outer door shut and wheeled it tight. Peeking in through the little glass, she saw him wheeling the other door open, gas bleeding into the inner space. He struggled with it, but then its own weight swung it open and he stumbled out. She hadn't told him to close the inner door, but he leaned his shoulder into it and then she saw the wheel lock again.

The seconds needed to open the airlock stretched out. Everything seemed slower and louder and hotter, like Venus's fingers were slowly tightening. The *coureurs* lived in a kind of safety in the clouds, ducking and hiding among Venus's skirts, but this was the surface, her shattered garden, the breathing body of the goddess herself. Venus was a force of terrible, whimsical violence, and there was no hiding here. Pascale's vision refracted through accumulating tears.

Gabriel-Antoine. His arm. His poor arm.

Pascale tumbled out the inner airlock door, scrambling down the channel as fast as she could. Gabriel-Antoine lay face-down on the floor of the cave, just in front of the little airlock leading to the middle chamber. The robots he'd built still chiselled at the cave sides, oblivious to his pain and need. She knelt awkwardly and lifted him. Under the hard white lights, his face was blotchy and flushed. His eyes were closed.

"Gabriel-Antoine!" she said. "*Chéri*!"

She shook his limp body. The hard cylinder over his left forearm was dented so deeply that she couldn't see how an arm could even fit. She dragged him as gently as she could. In forty atmospheres of pressure their suits were less buoyant and Gabriel-Antoine was an uneven weight.

The airlock barely fit the two hard dive suits, but she managed to cycle into the middle chamber where the pressure was down to ten atmospheres. It was much cooler, but their suits were now barely buoyant and only mechanical assistance allowed them to move at all. She finally dragged him to the airlock in their little habitat, and cycled them in. She was crying so much, whispering, "Please wake up, *chéri*."

Jean-Eudes, Louise, Paul-Égide and Alexis were startled by their appearance. Pascale dragged Gabriel-Antoine in and laid him on his back on the floor. Louise ran forward to undo his helmet and cried out when she burned her fingers. Around the crackle and snap of cooling suits, Pascale undid her own neck seals and carefully lifted the helmet.

"Get anything we have for first aid," she said. Alexis ran into the back.

"What happened to him?" Louise said. Paul-Égide was crying too. "What happened to his arm?"

"The government shot something at us," Pascale said. She worked at his neck seals. "Bring a blanket, folded."

Jean-Eudes came back momentarily with a folded blanket.

"When I take off his helmet, you hold his head, Jean-Eudes; and Louise, you put the blanket like a pillow under his head."

Jean-Eudes did as instructed. The backs of his hands brushed the hot metal and he cried out, but didn't pull them away.

"Ow, ow, ow." He winced as Louise slid the blanket under Gabriel-Antoine's head to keep his skin off the neck of the suit.

Pascale touched her ear to Gabriel-Antoine's lips. He still breathed, faintly.

"I think he's in shock," she said. She propped a box under his feet and began unscrewing the two halves of the torso pieces. It was hard to do with her gloves on, but she couldn't afford to burn her own fingers now, when she needed to take care of him. She lifted his chest plate off. Gabriel-Antoine was sheened in sweat, but his chest rose and fell. Louise stroked his damp forehead with a palm. He groaned, and Pascale realized that he'd burned his face. When she'd found him face down, his forehead must have been against the hot glass.

"What medicine have we got, Alexis?" Pascale said. "Painkillers?"

She knew they didn't have much, just the homemade stuff made in the cloud decks. Alexis found a carved box with a little bag inside. Small misshapen pills tumbled into his palm. About a dozen.

They unfastened the arm straps and Pascale pulled off the suit's right arm, careful not to touch his skin to the seal. She didn't know what to do with the left arm. It was so crushed that none of the bones could be unbroken. She couldn't just pull it off—it was like a vise locked tight.

A vise…

"We have a vise, Alexis," she said. "In the back. A small one. Go get it."

It took him a long time, so long that Louise, crying angrily, went back to tell him to hurry. They came back with it. It was a crude iron thing with hard trawler wood for the jaw plates and holes to screw it to a bench, but they'd never gotten far enough in setting up the workshop. Pascale opened the jaws as wide as they would go, but it was still too small to get across the crushed, flattened section on Gabriel-Antoine's suit. Almost. She tore away the wooden plates until she could just get the vise jaws on either side.

"Jean-Eudes, you turn the crank," she said, holding the vise in place.

Her brother put all his force into it and the closing jaws started pushing in the sides of the dent, forcing the middle of the dent out. The hollow gradually lifted away from Gabriel-Antoine's arm; his eyelids fluttered and he whimpered.

"Keep going, Jean-Eudes," Pascale said. "Go fast."

Louise cried harder and kissed Gabriel-Antoine's forehead. Paul-Égide seemed stunned and frightened. Pascale wanted to help them, but any mistake with Gabriel-Antoine right now... She didn't want to think of that. Gabriel-Antoine's face had paled further and his eyelids drooped again. Jean-Eudes turned the screw handle more and more until the dent in the steel sleeve of the suit had almost popped back out. Pascale climbed over Gabriel-Antoine and gently pulled at the sleeve. Gabriel-Antoine moaned, but the shell was coming off, revealing a misshapen limb painted with bright blood. The forearm was unnaturally flattened between wrist and elbow. Pascale clicked open her wrist seals and took off her hot gloves, kneeling over him.

"Get me *bagosse,* Alexis," she said.

She couldn't find absorbent pads, or even old cloth, in their pathetic first aid kit. Alexis slid to a stop on his knees, giving Pascale a jar of *bagosse*. Their moonshine could rot the guts, but it was good for wounds. She poured some over Gabriel-Antoine's arm. It collected in little pinkening pools on the floor. Her gorge rose. His forearm was really crushed. She was crying. She didn't know what to do, or how to fix it. She wanted to cup it in her hands and just shape it back to what it was supposed to look like, as if her shattered lover could be reshaped like clay.

"Do something!" Louise screamed.

The blood kept flowing. Pascale tipped a little more *bagosse* on the wound, and pressed bandages over the shattered bone. Gabriel-Antoine moaned.

"You're hurting him!" Paul-Égide said.

Pascale pressed more bandages and wrapped a cloth snugly around his forearm, with a few scraps of rigid trawler shell. Then she made a soft ramp with more building scraps, elevated the arm and tied it all so nothing would move. Then, she deflated, half-collapsing in her half-removed dive suit. Her hands shook and her head felt thick.

"What else?" Louise demanded.

"He needs a hospital," Pascale said. "We can't take care of this here."

Jean-Eudes moaned. Pascale had been too young to understand, but she knew that Jean-Eudes had watched *Maman* die, far from doctors.

"We'll get him to a hospital," she said.

Paul-Égide slumped against Louise.

Pascale's gloves had cooled just enough to touch, and she snapped them back on.

"If he wakes up, you can give him one of the pills and some *bagosse* for the pain," Pascale said. "I'm going to talk to the government, to make sure we can take him up."

The children looked doubtful and frightened. Alexis took Louise's hand. Her head drooped a little, and her soft crying started again.

FIFTY-EIGHT

PASCALE EQUALIZED THE pressure and temperature of the first chamber with the outside, and then closed the spotlights. The turbine stopped. Each cap in the tunnel had a person-sized airlock; she opened one side of the outermost lock and then unscrewed the other side so both doors were open at once, then peeked her head out. The ovoid drones rested on their struts, their weapons pointing at the airlock door. She retreated and turned on her suit's radio to the common colonial channel, although its wattage wouldn't reach more than a few kilometers. That didn't matter; the drones would be remote controlled, they could presumably relay her signal.

"This is Pascale D'Aquillon," she said. "We have a medical emergency."

The channel crackled with soft static for almost a minute.

"We're prepared to proceed with arrests if everyone exits peacefully," was the reply in accented French.

"Who am I speaking to?"

"This is the Bank of Pallas, security division."

"I want to speak to a representative of the government of Venus. This is an emergency."

"The Bank of Pallas is involved in property recovery operations following the theft of the *Causapscal-des-Vents,* which was collateral against a loan. The bank has been deputized to also make arrests."

"You shot Gabriel-Antoine Phocas! He's gravely injured and he needs medical attention immediately. We have to get him to a hospital. He needs surgery, doctors."

"*After* arrests are made and stolen property recovered, detainees can receive medical attention."

"Is the *Baie-Comeau* positioned properly if we rose from here? Even one of the clinic habitats will work, for now, to stabilize him."

"You'll be taken off Venus and extradited to the Bank of Pallas judicial system," came the response. "If you're in a hurry for medical attention, surrender yourself quickly."

"This is Venus. We should be tried in a Venusian court, under Venusian law."

"In addition to property recovery, we've been sub-contracted for judicial proceedings regarding major economic crimes. After your sentences are served, you may return to Venus at your own cost."

"I'm not here to argue the law with you! This is Venus! He needs a doctor right now. We're going to send up a buoyant vehicle so he can be moved to a hospital right away."

"The Bank of Pallas is authorized to use any force it deems necessary to secure its property rights as well as those of loan-holders. Surrender now."

Pascale shut the outer airlock door quickly. As she spun its lock shut, something hammered from the outside, hard, deafening. The door had to be thick, to hold back the weight of the atmosphere, and it was just as well. In time, the bank could likely shoot down the door, but just waiting for them to starve was probably cheaper.

After a time, Marie-Pier was moved by balloon across starry night skies from whatever habitat she'd been on. Her solitary confinement felt like it had gone on forever, and she wasn't even sure they weren't going to try to kill her again. The guards had all changed after Oscar had taken away her message, and the new ones wouldn't speak with her. She hoped Oscar hadn't gotten in trouble.

She recognized the outline of the *Petit Kamouraska* first, and then the glinting marbled lighting of its hydroponics shiny through the transparent buoyancy envelopes. From the roof, she was brought down plastic hallways to the bay that had been converted into a detention facility.

The two big detention cells seemed even more full than before. Outside those common cells, along two walls, hydroponic equipment was being set up, floor to ceiling. In the finished trays, new shoots reflected bright green on the walls of the somber bay. A few detainees were building a new rack of trays, surrounded by tools and guards. The detention area was becoming a permanent fixture.

Marie-Pier's minder opened the barred door to the women's cell and removed her cuffs. An irritated tickle began again, from raw throat to watery lung. Marie-Pier held down most of the painful coughing fit, leaning against the bars as the constable locked the door. She still hadn't seen a doctor. The kind of fatigue she felt sounded a lot like anemia, whose symptoms would be similar to lung damage.

"Marie-Pier?"

A woman with a baby had neared, with a couple of others.

"Laurette," Marie-Pier said. "How's your son?"

"Good," she said, rocking the bundle gently. "What happened? Where's my father?"

"He's not in here? With my brother?"

Laurette shook her head, blinking new tears.

"I've been in solitary." Marie-Pier wasn't used to talking. She started coughing.

"Your message got smuggled in," Laurette said.

"It got out?" Marie-Pier said with relief.

"I don't know how far it got. They really tried to kill you?"

Marie-Pier nodded. "My lungs haven't healed."

"Did you hear the government messages?"

She shook her head.

"The government put out a statement. They said George-Étienne D'Aquillon and Émile D'Aquillon are dead." Laurette put her hand on Marie-Pier's shoulder. "They killed three or four constables while resisting arrest. I'm sorry."

The world seemed to narrow to a gray tunnel. Marie-Pier gripped Laurette's hand tightly.

"They're gone..." she said numbly. "Those poor dreamers... They were good men. They were flawed, but they were good." She exhaled unsteadily. "There was no news about my children? My brother? They should be with your father."

"No news," Laurette said. "People who bring us things bring news, sometimes. Some of the guards will share too. But I haven't heard anything about *Papa*. I'm worried."

"I am too." More people clustered closer. "If he had warning, Jean-Marc would have been able to hide himself and my children somewhere among the *coureurs*. He would have taken your father with him."

Laurette wiped her eyes and nodded. They needed to believe it was true.

"Did the government say anything else? What did they say about the other D'Aquillon children? Pascale, Jean-Eudes, Alexis? And Gabriel-Antoine Phocas. What about him?"

"There are arrest warrants out for Phocas and Pascal," someone else volunteered. "The news didn't have a lot more. The government recovered part of the *Causapscal-des-Vents*—most of the metal was gone. What did you do with it? You just sold it?" The woman's eyes held some recrimination.

"We didn't sell it," Marie-Pier said. "We basically made mining equipment. We figured out a way to survive on the surface and work down there. We've found some rare elements we've brought to the clouds."

"The government is killing for that?" someone else said.

"They threw you in jail for making liquor. Or trading for oxygen or food. This is just the next step. The government wants to control what we figured out how to do—and us—or sell our discoveries to the bank for pennies on the dollar." The bitter words sounded a little like George-Étienne, but they were her words, her meaning. "That's why we're in here, isn't it?"

The *why we're here* landed with a kind of fatalistic finality. Behind bars and powerless, they could scream and yell and it would be for nothing. Were Pascale and Gabriel-Antoine similarly caged, in the base on the surface? George-Étienne was to have supplied them. Poor George-Étienne. Poor Pascale. And somewhere in the clouds, her brother had to be hidden, with Florian and Maxime.

"We have to be more than this," Marie-Pier said.

Laurette and the other women looked at her questioningly. There were more than a hundred people detained on the *Petit Kamouraska*. She knew from *Assemblée* records that people were detained elsewhere in the flotillas as well. Hundreds. She spoke more softly, forcing them to lean in to hear her.

"We're more than this. The government is wrong. We're not staying jailed."

FIFTY-NINE

PASCALE RE-ENTERED THE habitat to find Gabriel-Antoine feverish. He'd struggled up so that Louise and Alexis and Jean-Eudes could remove the rest of his dive suit and move him to a layered pile of blankets. Pascale knelt and kissed his sweaty lips. The kids moved away, Louise reluctantly.

"How bad is it?" Pascale asked. The bandages on Gabriel-Antoine's arm had reddened, but weren't saturated.

"I was going to ask you the same thing," he said weakly.

She put his lips close to his ear.

"Your arm was crushed pretty bad," she whispered. "There are broken bones. You might have stopped bleeding."

"Where were you?" he said.

"Talking to the bank. That's who's outside. I need to get you to a hospital. They have to let us go."

"Are they?"

"No, but I'll take you anyway."

"What about the children and Jean-Eudes?"

"We can't get a doctor down here."

Pascale stroked Gabriel-Antoine's stubbled cheek.

"The government or the bank killed Émile and your dad, and maybe Marie-Pier. They won't let us go." Gabriel-Antoine sounded more lucid than Pascale felt.

"I'm saving your life," she said.

"I might not be so bad. It hurts a lot. I've never broken a bone before."

"It isn't broken, *chéri*, it's crushed."

"Let's give it a few hours. We don't even have a way up anymore. The bathyscaphe can only get us to forty-fifth *rang*. How do we transfer me? I don't know if I can even wear a regular survival suit."

"In a couple of weeks, the first of our submarines will be ready," Pascale said.

"They're untested and experimental," Gabriel-Antoine said. "If we've made mistakes, those ships will crumple like an old bag or melt when they meet Venus. We don't have weeks."

"Jean-Eudes could adjust the arm of your suit to fit the bandages."

"At best it will take a day or more to get to the high clouds," Gabriel-Antoine said. "A lot of it will be waiting to decompress properly."

"So we should start now."

"They won't let us get out of here, Pascale." Gabriel-Antoine's eyes had a profound, tired sadness in them. "We reached the stars and the magic country, but now we can't get back home. Those are the rules in faerie tales, right? Every step is irrevocable."

It seemed like a strange thing to say. Gabriel-Antoine was not prone to superstition or philosophizing. He'd come from an unromantic world above the clouds. He'd laughed indulgently when Pascale had told him of the faerie tales the *coureurs* made up. He was trembling. She touched his face; it felt hotter. She fetched another one of their pills and the *bagosse*.

GABRIEL-ANTOINE'S FEVER HAD risen and fallen over hours and days, but had stayed high over the last hours. With haunted expressions, Louise and Paul-Égide mopped at the sweat on his forehead and fanned his blotchy cheeks. Pascale sat at their small, improvised radio set. For a time, she just stared blankly, not really processing anything, just looking at the wires and homemade vacuum tubes, feeling the black sadness that seemed to soak all the way to her bones. She was the last one, the last grown-up, until they could get Gabriel-Antoine to a doctor. She'd chased the dream of Venus for nothing, and now the whole family was depending on her, and she didn't know how to keep them safe. She needed help.

She turned the radio set on. Sporadic chatter, some in *coureur* code, sounded. Those frequencies were also listened to by family and friends on flotilla radios. After a time, the transactional conversations faltered and a low hissing lull took over, occasionally interrupted by squawks of far-off lightning. She flipped the switch to transmit.

"I'm... Pascale D'Aquillon. I'm the... daughter of George-Étienne and Jeanne-Manse. My *Papa* used to transmit, but... he's dead. The government and the Bank of Pallas murdered him four days ago. They murdered my brother Émile too. My family was unarmed and the constables and banks came to our trawler with guns.

"Pa and Émile put up a good fight. Three or four of the bank security people and constables didn't make it. Venus took her tithe."

Pascale swallowed hard and wiped at her eyes. Louise, Paul-Égide, Jean-Eudes and Alexis were all standing there, watching her. She smiled at them. Tried to.

"The government and the Bank of Pallas found out that the House of Styx had made a small base on the surface. We're pulling out metal, metal for us, at our own risk, metal we'll trade to the flotillas for far less than what the bank would charge. We built the base out of metals we took from the *Causapscal-des-Vents,* but we've already gotten more than that back.

"I know the *présidente* says we stole it."

Pascale's chest hurt. She didn't know how many people were listening to her. Maybe nobody. Maybe everybody. She felt seen, in the most uncomfortable way; judged. Is this how Pa felt when he and *Maman* had decided to keep Jean-Eudes? And through all the years that followed. She realized in that moment how lonely he must have felt. But he'd had

Marthe. Pascale looked up. She had Jean-Eudes. She had Alexis. Maybe there were more. That was what this message was about.

"It was never Gaschel's to start with. We fought to keep the *Causapscal* afloat for years without any help or parts from the government. We traded away our own food for components. It's ours as much as any habitat belongs to the ones who live in it. Gaschel controls us by holding out the possibility of better bunks or worse bunks, more medicine or less medicine, better food or worse food. None of that is hers to give, or to withhold. She's tied *la colonie* in knots by mortgaging our futures away to the bank. Now government forces murdered my brother and *Papa*, just like they killed Grégoire Tremblay.

"Gabriel-Antoine Phocas and I and our families are on the surface now, getting metals for trading, but the bank sent drones, with weapons. One of the drones hit him and… and his arm is all smashed. I went to negotiate with the bank to try to get Gabriel-Antoine to a doctor. They won't let us through. They're willing to let Gabriel-Antoine die so that they control our mine.

"I don't know what to do. I want to ask the *coureurs* for help, but I know that none of you can reach us. I have to find a way to get Gabriel-Antoine to a doctor soon.

"This government has no right to lead. They're murdering to keep us permanently indebted to the Bank of Pallas. Gaschel doesn't have a plan out of this mess. You may be part of the flotilla, thinking you're not affected by her, that she's only killing a few *coureurs*, and that the bank will never come after you.

"Of course they will.

"Ask yourself who's next. The *coureurs* know that we're next, so we've been forming alliances of families, making houses. The House of Styx has staked out a claim, down on the surface. We're going to hold and mine that claim and trade freely with anyone who wants to trade fairly with us. And we'll remember our friends, because that's what my *Papa* taught me.

"In the flotillas, you should protect yourself against the government too. You're not powerless. You need to put the government on notice that it has lost its mandate. You can take steps to form new alliances to protect yourselves against the lies and the violence the government can bring. You need to rise up and tell the government that the constables can't come to your habitats. You need to tell the government that it can't choose who gets what bunk, who gets what medicine. We don't need a new government copied from every other government that's come before. We need a new way to think about ourselves as Venusians. The House of Styx is ready to work with other houses, to protect each other."

THE *PERCHOIR*, THE Corbeau habitat, rocked in a rough wind, rattling the dishes in their webbing. Fabienne, with Victorine's son Herman, had just finished unloading her cargo and tying down Fabienne's plane while the light storm slowly passed. Félix was coming through the airlock and began neutralizing himself.

"It was while you were flying," Victorine Corbeau told Fabienne with a kind of prying glance, like she thought Fabienne was lying about not having heard the broadcast. "I got a recording of it."

The gray-haired woman retrieved an aged data pad. Fabienne had been far across the vast atmospheric ocean with her herd and hadn't been able to listen to the shortwave chatter. She didn't know Pascale D'Aquillon and hadn't heard her message. Victorine seemed pretty agitated about it. Fabienne finished stripping off her suit, ignoring Herman's interested glance. Victorine was setting out ugly carved cups and a jug of *bagosse*. Fabienne joined her while the boys took their *bagosse* standing on the rocking floor.

Victorine played the recording. Fabienne's jaw dropped, and kept dropping. Victorine refilled everyone's cups as the playback ended.

"What the hell?" Fabienne said. "Old man D'Aquillon, killed by the police?"

"And the bank," Victorine said.

"Shit. I don't think I ever met Émile," Fabienne said. "Did he have a moustache? I know I've never met Pascale."

"No loss on Émile," Herman said. "Asshole."

"So was his Pa, but both were *coureurs,*" Victorine said sharply. "And so was Grégoire Tremblay. If the government and bank are teaming up for open season on *coureurs,* then young Pascale is right that we should be watching our backs. Maybe yours most of all, Fabienne."

"Mine?"

"You *took* those pictures. You found them."

"And Narcisse traded them to Gaschel."

"What's in that mine?" Victorine mused. "Iron is valuable; is it enough to kill for? But government planes haven't been 'mapping' the atmosphere looking for iron mines. I've heard that the police have been asking about radioactives. Radioactives *are* enough to kill for, or even to kill just to tie up loose ends."

The old woman eyed her meaningfully, and Fabienne suppressed a shiver.

"Other than the government, you, your cousins and us are the only ones who know where that mine is," Victorine said. "We'd better hope they aren't going to decide to burn up young Pascale and the Phocas engineer, and then come for us."

"We can go further off the grid."

"I'm thinking of hedging our bets. We've been betting that Gaschel will come out on top, but maybe we want to see what an alliance with Pascale D'Aquillon would look like."

"Playing both sides?" Fabienne said.

"While not getting *caught* playing both sides."

"Do you want me to take this back to Narcisse?"

"You can," Victorine said coyly. "We probably need to move fast, though. And… it's obvious you're smarter than your cousin. He's on a short fuse, and I think we need calmer leadership."

"*You're* partnered with him."

"For now. The alliance is a good idea, but give it some thought. Maybe you'd be a better partner. Narcisse and Liette may not even need to know you're really representing the Mignauds in the House of Crows."

"Narcisse has a real nasty streak."

"You're smart enough to handle him."

The *Perchoir* bucked over turbulence, making the dishes rattle.

"What are you thinking?" Fabienne asked.

Victorine tilted her head side to side, as if puzzling over the thought, but Fabienne had the impression that this was play-acting, and that the older woman already had her ideas.

"Young Pascale's words are a big fucking deal. New government. A lot of people have nothing to lose. It won't take much to set something off: protests, resistance. Once that starts, the government is over a barrel. Venus is not the kind of nation that can be easily pushed around. Every habitat is an island. You know your history? You ever see what fighting over an island looks like? It's not easy for the government, if people decide not to listen. I'm sending Herman and Félix flotilla-side. You should go too."

"What for?"

"Something needs to be set off, and it's better that we're the ones setting it off, so that if it works, the House of Crows is at the front."

"What if it doesn't work? Then the House of Crows is holding the bag."

"That's the nice thing about houses, isn't it? You control who knows who you are. If things go wrong, then it wasn't us, we weren't the House of Crows." Victorine smiled. "But if we find the right spark, things will burn, and when a new government forms, we'll be close to the top."

Fabienne swirled the bitter *bagosse* around her teeth. Victorine thought big. This was dangerous, but *coureurs* did dangerous things all the time for far less.

SIXTY

Pascale brought Alexis and Louise outside their cramped habitat in the last chamber of the tunnel. They'd both cut and mended their suits to fit better. Louise had hesitated leaving Gabriel-Antoine, and now seemed sullen and worried; most of that was for her brother, but some of it was about where they were going.

As the airlock opened to the last volume of the cave, their suits expanded and squeaked for a bit as they became accustomed to the vacuum. Each snapped a cable onto a harness before they stepped out. Centuries or millennia of pouring wind had smoothed the cave walls, which were stippled with millions of tiny craters, some fresh, some new, where gases trapped in the stone had popped chips into the cave. Pascale touched the rock face briefly, staring at the dark circle of the wormhole. Alexis copied her and Louise finally joined them. Through their gloves, the rock was hot, but they could touch Venus for a few seconds, and it felt right to do so as they looked at her soul, the Axis Mundi, the bridge from the mundane to the celestial.

"As soon as we step into the Axis, gravity will disappear," Pascale said, "and we'll be floating. It's disorienting at first."

Three thick cables of bright new steel, each the width of her thumb, were attached to big eyelets drilled into the stone itself. They were taut, leading into the infinite beyond the horizon of the axis. Several thin personal tethers were clipped to the cables, and Pascale attached one to her harness before unclipping the one from the airlock.

"Come on," she said.

They mimicked her actions, Alexis becoming more serious.

"I've never seen the stars," he said.

"You'll be the third and fourth people in all of human history to ever see these ones," Pascale said.

Pascale walked to the edge of the Axis horizon. It was like a dark cave mouth itself, yawning fifteen meters in diameter, parts of its edge buried in baking hot stone.

"I'll disappear because you can't see from inside to outside the wormhole," Pascale said. "Don't be scared. Leave your helmet lights on and just go hand over hand. It'll feel like falling, but it's not."

"I can do it," Alexis said.

"Me too," Louise said.

Pascale found herself holding her breath as she stepped into the weightless, shapeless world. Her gorge rose as if she were in a steep dive on a wing-pack, and she swallowed down the nausea. Arm over arm she advanced, and at about ten meters she stopped and turned to look back. Her helmet lamp touched nothing but the three cables. The axis seemed to have walls, untouchable, unseeable, haunted by ghostly flickers of light. Then, a wobbly light appeared, weaving all around as Alexis clung to the cable like he was climbing a pole.

"If you're going to throw up, go back. But it should be okay," Pascale said. "Close your eyes if you get dizzy, and just remember you're not falling. This is what it feels like with no gravity."

"I'm okay," Alexis said in a thin voice.

Another light appeared, steadier.

"Go on, *épais*," Louise said.

"Just hand over hand, Alexis," Pascale said, "otherwise you might scrape a hole in your suit."

That seemed to settle him. Although young, Alexis was a *coureur*, and puncturing survival suits through negligence was a sin. He moved along. Louise approached more cautiously, but more competently.

"It's just past here," Pascale said. "The whole axis is only about sixty meters long. We're going to follow the cable and you'll see stars."

Pascale resumed her hand-over-hand walk into space. The radio static leapt up in her earphones as the dark sky appeared around her. The stars were hard, distant points. The only real lights were the hot incandescents they'd made themselves by running electricity through fine metals. They were short on glass, but they hadn't needed bulbs—without air, the filaments couldn't burn. The lights showed the half-built hulks of four tubes, ten meters long and about five meters wide. The first was barely a skeleton of shiny new steel, two of them were filled with most of the guts of engine and fuel tanks and maneuvering equipment, the last one was seemingly complete, its thick metal skin whole, its tiny porthole glinting at the prow.

"*Sapristi*!" Alexis swore under a snowstorm of static.

"Are you going to puke?" Louise whispered.

"No," Alexis said. "Are you?"

"That's the asteroid," Louise said to Pascale. In the light of her helmet, Pascale could just see the girl's arm gesture at the hulking mass a few kilometers away.

"We haven't called it anything yet," Pascale said, "but it has about ten percent as much iron and nickel and heavy metals as the asteroid *la colonie* is intending to buy from the bank, which would have kept all of Venus in metals for years. And there are more asteroids. We can bring them all closer."

The glow of electrical arcs shone almost constantly under an obscuring cloud of dust. The dust incandesced a soft red, where lasers and masers beamed power to the mining robots from the slowly growing rectenna, the arrays of antennae absorbing microwave emissions from the pulsar.

One of the safety cables led to the most complete ship, and Pascale brought Alexis and Louise to it. The construction robots had just finished welding the swept-back wings and tail stabilizers to the fuselage. Since

Gabriel-Antoine's injury, since they'd been attacked at the surface, Pascale had also been thinking of how to arm the ships. Venus had no oxygen, and the atmospheric pressure changed so dramatically that a bullet or missile that would work at one altitude wouldn't work at another. But she had ideas she was trying to make work, so that they could protect themselves.

Pascale had given Louise and Alexis a checklist of things to verify. In the habitat, Pascale had taught them all the simple verifications that they had to do and had left the complicated verifications for herself. Louise opened the cockpit hatch and slipped inside while Alexis awkwardly moved hand-over-hand in the zero-g to the engine panels. Between them, they started a radio chatter, sounding earnestly adult, checking each circuit and system, one by one, from the cockpit controls to the engine mechanisms. Their conversation became a reassuring drone in Pascale's helmet.

Pascale unclipped and rode cold jets to the rectenna. The first robots had been chewing through the asteroid, and at first, almost half of everything they'd mined had been turned into antenna to capture radio waves from the pulsar—generating electricity. In the beginning, Gabriel-Antoine and Pascale had been worried about power, but now they had more than enough to smelt, weld, hammer, crush and reshape almost everything on the asteroid. Their next problem had been building enough robots to do all the work. They were three quarters of the way there now, and each day, another robot was built on the asteroid, ready to help build the ships, expand the rectenna, or join the mining effort. They were running out of controller chips, though. In the habitat, Alexis and Louise had quickly learned enough how to make them, but they made small mistakes that required painstaking corrections. If they survived, they would eventually need more people. She reached the back of the rectenna, where she'd put a specialized robot to work building the engines for the ships. One engine, about the size of a chest or trunk, floated beside the robot, ready for inspection, while another was being built. It amazed Pascale that the engine cores were not bigger, but she and Gabriel-Antoine had taken an open-source design from asteroid miners who'd bootstrapped new nuclear engines in the belt between Mars and Jupiter. One day, if they were lucky, the House of Styx would be exploring this star system. The dream, though beaten and injured and lonelier, was still alive. Pascale brought the engine back to the ship Alexis and Louise were checking.

Pascale carefully inserted the engine into its housing. It was finicky, delicate work. She'd just finished tightening all the screws and checking the alignment when she noticed that the radio had gone quiet. She turned up the volume, and when the children's voices didn't grow any louder, she realized that Louise and Alexis, in true *coureur* fashion, had lowered the wattage on their transmitters. As Pascale came forward, she heard crying.

Alexis floated at the cockpit, holding on to the frame. "He'll be okay," he said.

"I'm scared too," she said.

Pascale came close and reached an arm in to squeeze Louise's shoulder. Louise looked at Pascale venomously and shrugged away the hand. "You caused it," she said.

Pascale flinched. All the different fears and blames that had been chasing each other in her thoughts rushed in. She blinked, trying not to cry again. Louise unstrapped herself from the cockpit and faced Pascale.

"If you hadn't come to our habitat and asked for his help, he wouldn't be hurt!" she said. "I would still be with my grandparents, and so would he."

"I know," Pascale said.

"I figured it out," Louise said. "Your sister didn't send your brother, or herself, to ask Gabriel-Antoine. She sent you, because she thought a pretty face wouldn't hurt, right? Was seducing him part of it? And lying to him?"

"Lying to him?" Pascale said, her chest starting to ache.

"The 'walls' are pretty thin," she said angrily, throwing air quotes around *walls*. "We can hear you guys arguing. You conveniently didn't tell him you were going to be a girl, because you knew he wouldn't have gone with you."

It wasn't as if Gabriel-Antoine hadn't flung all these words at Pascale. He had. She just hadn't expected them to come from Louise too, nor to hurt so much.

"I didn't know," Pascale said lamely. "I didn't mean to hurt him."

"You're killing him!" Louise said.

The ache in Pascale's chest became nauseating. This void suddenly felt more empty, the stars very cold and the radio static confusing. This world, like the clouds, had no shape, no direction; it became what they made it. Louise was making Pascale out as a fraud.

"I love him," Pascale said. "I only want good for him."

"He's miserable. And maimed," Louise said, her voice having dropped to a whisper.

"You can hate me," Pascale said, "but we have a chance to get him to a hospital if we can get this ship ready fast."

Louise glared at her for slow seconds and then silently strapped back into the cockpit. She began calling out circuit numbers to Alexis. Pascale felt battered, and retreated, numbly finding more work along the interior of the hull to finish this ship.

Hours later, they were tired and cold, the latter still being a strange experience for Pascale. They winched the first completed ship through the wormhole and into the cave beneath Venus. It felt large, but at meters across the beam, it took up only a part of the Axis's diameter. They had little to cushion the steel against the rock, and so had made makeshift sets of rollers. She and Gabriel-Antoine had been building five, but Pascale had changed the instructions to the robots to focus on the first two, even to the point of cannibalizing the least finished one.

They finally stumbled into the habitat. Louise shucked her survival suit quickly and went to her brother. Jean-Eudes, as if sensing the tension, helped Pascale with her suit, tutted at the wear marks and went to quietly maintain it. Alexis hugged Pascale briefly and went with Jean-Eudes. Pascale sat alone at the uneven table she and Gabriel-Antoine had built. After a time, she took down the jar of *bagosse* from the shelf and unscrewed it. For the first time in her life, she drank alone. Like Pa. Like Marthe. Like Émile.

Everything depended on her; Gabriel-Antoine's life, the lives of all the family's children, the dream they'd had of an independent Venus. She hadn't been prepared for this smothering weight. It ought to have been Pa sitting here, weighing everything, deciding. Or Marie-Pier. Or Marthe. Even Gabriel-Antoine. She and Gabriel-Antoine had laughed about it once, snuggling in a hammock together. Neither of them wanted to be anywhere near the leadership of the families, even though it had always been said that Gabriel-Antoine would take over after Marie-Pier.

"I just said okay to get the deal out of the way," Gabriel-Antoine had told Pascale, who'd been mock-scandalized. "Marthe and I are close to the same age," he had added. "She can be in charge. You and I can have the stars."

Pascale wiped at her cheek. Gabriel-Antoine was hurt so badly. The image of his maimed arm slipped into her mind every time she closed her eyes and she wiped at tears with both hands. She drank. At some point, the bank would lose patience, and with the right equipment they would break in carefully and efficiently, and then Venus's soul would belong to the bank. Pascale didn't know how to stop them, now or in the future. She was just one person, barely grown, with a whole family to take care of.

She closed the jar and walked softly to the curtain walling off the little sleeping space where Gabriel-Antoine lay. She pulled the curtain aside to peek in, and Louise looked up at her resentfully. Paul-Égide snored gently between wall and brother.

"Can I see Gabriel-Antoine for a while?" Pascale asked.

"*Non,*" Louise said.

"It's okay," Gabriel-Antoine said, stirring. "Go on. Come back later."

Pascale's insides, already upset, cooled uncomfortably. She sat hesitantly in the spot vacated by Louise. She stroked the hot, slippery forehead.

"We need to get your fever down," she said quietly. "Can you sit up to take another pill?"

He struggled up, holding his arm higher, but wincing. Despite the shadows, his cheeks showed an unhealthy pallor, and his skin blued beneath red-rimmed eyes.

"We won't have many more pills," he said.

His lips burned against her palm as she tipped in the irregular pill and gave him the *bagosse* to swallow with.

"I have to bring you up to sixty-fifth," she said. "Soon."

Gabriel-Antoine sighed and lay back. "I want to live," he said, "but will I, if we go up?"

"Just hold on a few days, maybe a week."

"What do you think I've been doing?" he said irritably, and then shook his head. "Sorry. Can you get one of the submarine ships ready in a week? Without me?"

"Alexis and Louise are helping."

"I want to see the stars again. If I'm going to die, I want to die floating among the stars, not buried under rock."

Gabriel-Antoine's breathing shook as he trembled in pain. Pascale lay close and hugged him for a time. Little tears at the edges of his eyes hid themselves in the sweat of his temples. He sighed.

"I don't understand why the world is this way," he said. "Venus has a secret beauty, like you said, and it belongs to us, to our people. I want it for Louise and Paul-Égide."

"They want *you* more than the stars," Pascale said. "So do I. I think we can get all of us into two of the ships, maybe one, and then we can escape."

"And leave the wormhole to the bank? And the government? Your Pa was right—they'll never share it with us. We'll be tenants in our own house forever."

"I know. I'm not trading you for anything though," Pascale said.

"They're going to shoot the shit out of us as soon as you open the cap."

Pascale sat again and stroked Gabriel-Antoine's face. After a time, his fingers traced an uneven circle on Pascale's thigh, warm, affectionate.

"I asked you not to change your body," Gabriel-Antoine said, "and mine got changed. It feels like a fairy tale curse."

Gabriel-Antoine shifted his injured arm, trying to lay it across his chest, seeking a comfortable position, but winced and whimpered. Pascale gently guided the arm back to the little pile of cloth they'd made to cushion it. The bandages were not tight, but his fingers were lightly purpling.

"We aren't in a fairy tale."

"Not one with a happy ending," Gabriel-Antoine said. "I'm not a handsome prince anymore."

"You are," she said, kissing his hot lips and cheek. "You are. Always."

"My father loved the old versions of fairy tales, the ones with bad endings. They were always warnings. Fear the wild. Don't be cruel. Don't overreach."

He was trembling again.

"Do you want another pill for the pain? You want the *bagosse*?"

"We came into the wild," Gabriel-Antoine said. "We overreached, setting up a kingdom where we shouldn't have. The throne is cursed, and we still don't want to give it up."

"We'll give up the kingdom for you."

Gabriel-Antoine wiped his forehead.

"No. We'll give this to Paul-Égide and Louise, and Alexis and Florian and everyone on Venus," Gabriel-Antoine said. "Don't let the dragon at the door stop you. Don't let the goddess stop you."

"Us."

"Our fighting doesn't matter anymore," he said.

"We'll win."

"I mean you and me." Gabriel-Antoine's trembling stopped and he reached to touch Pascale's face. "I love you, and it doesn't matter that you're changing. We have days or hours left together, and for that time, you're still the Pascal I love."

Relief came into her heart, accompanied by a vague pain, like she'd been hit sidewise. *She* was changing. That's what he thought. Gabriel-Antoine loved the *him*, not the *her*. Pascal, not Pascale. Gabriel-Antoine talked like there were two people inside her. There weren't. There was only Pascale, and she just hadn't known who she was before. Now she did. Pascale was the same, if a bit wiser. That Gabriel-Antoine didn't see any of that felt cruel. Or he did see it and rejected it, as if this were her choice. She was crying again.

"I love you," she said, and after a time, she retreated, letting Louise sit her vigil.

SIXTY-ONE

PASCALE AND ALEXIS finished a twelve-hour stretch working on the submarine ship and trudged, exhausted, into the habitat airlock. They were getting close. It was incredible how much work was needed to build something that would survive the environmental swings from a freezing vacuum, from the hot supercritical carbon dioxide of the surface, to the corrosive acid of the clouds. And that was not including *protecting* themselves. Pascale had tried making a kind of gun that would work in a vacuum, but the little darts wouldn't feed into the firing chamber. And her clumsy attempt to make a missile had nearly broken Alexis's hand when it jammed in the tube. They couldn't make mistakes. Any flaws under pressure could be fatal.

Pascale had found a way to fit all six of them into the single ship by replacing one of the fuel tanks with a cramped survival chamber. She'd been checking in every hour with Jean-Eudes on Gabriel-Antoine's condition. She wanted to be inside, to be taking care of him herself, but Gabriel-Antoine needed her to devote every hour of her time to getting him safely to the clouds.

The airlock cycled and Jean-Eudes came to help them. Pascale removed her own helmet, but Jean-Eudes helped Alexis. Her nephew seemed smitten with the idea of being grown up enough that Jean-Eudes now helped him take off his suit. Alexis had grown so much, far beyond the subdued eleventh birthday they'd celebrated yesterday. He was growing up at the speed of a boy who'd seen his grandfather and uncle killed. Pascale ruffled Alexis's hair and smiled at him.

"Is Gabriel-Antoine okay?" she asked.

"He's still breathing funny," Jean-Eudes whispered to Pascale. "We haven't got more pills."

Pascale finished removing her suit and pushed aside the curtain. Gabriel-Antoine lay on his little pile of blankets, chest and legs bare, arms damp. The fingers of his left hand were still swollen and red, with purple blotches. Louise pressed a cloth to his face and chest. Her cheeks were a map of dried tears. Paul-Égide leaned on her listlessly.

"Can I sit with him for a while?" Pascale asked.

"No," Louise said numbly. In the last day, Louise's anger towards Pascale seemed to have given up, given way to languishing despair.

"Come on. I've been outside for hours."

"*Vas-y,* Louise," Gabriel-Antoine said weakly. "Be good. There's enough of me to go around." He tried to smile, but there was too much wincing effort in it. Louise absently wiped her dry face with one hand as if new tears had fallen, but held tight to his hand with the other. "Go on, *chérie,*" Gabriel-Antoine insisted.

Sullenly, Louise rose and led Paul-Égide out of the curtained nest. Pascale knelt. Gabriel-Antoine trembled.

"Does it hurt, *chéri*?" she said.

He nodded, tight-lipped.

"I think I can have the ship ready in another day," she said. "Then we'll have you up to a doctor. Two, maybe three days. All of us."

She expected him to argue the Axis Mundi again. He took her hand. She pressed the cooling cloth to chest and legs.

"We're Canto Five," he said.

Canto Five was a shorthand some Venusians—those of a more poetic bent—invoked as a kind of pathway to stoicism. She would have expected it more from Émile than Gabriel-Antoine. Pascale had read that portion of Dante's *Inferno*, but hadn't really been sure she'd understood it. The second circle of Hell was a place of storms that blew lovers apart for all eternity. The parallels to Venus were obvious, and in some ways she'd understood the sense that she'd been pulled away from *Maman* and Chloé permanently. Today, for the first time, though, it hit her the way it could hit a lover.

"No, *bébé*," she said, stroking his cheek. "There are better love stories."

"Romeo and Juliet?" he said, smiling tightly.

She kissed his cheek, his forehead. "Wait for the story to end. Years from now, I'll tell you which love story is ours."

"It's really boring lying here," he said weakly.

"I know, *chéri*."

"I've been fantasizing."

She slapped his chest playfully. "When you get better."

"Fantasies of other lives," he said. "Maybe in another life, you came up to live with your sister and brother. Maybe I would have seen you somewhere, like some mechanics or engineering meeting, or some lame party, and I would have laid on the charm."

"You wouldn't have noticed me," she said.

"I would have noticed," he said emphatically.

"I would have noticed *you* anywhere."

"You would have visited my habitat…"

"Would Louise still be angry?" Pascale whispered.

He laughed briefly. "She's not mad at you," he whispered. "She's mad at all that's happened to us. She's a gentle girl. She was ready for a certain life; now she has this instead, and we don't even know what *this* is. Same with me. We're all blown by the winds of Canto Five, like trawlers in the wind, coming close, brushing against each other just for a moment before the winds tear us apart."

He shook harder. He lifted his crushed arm, which seemed to hurt him more. She tried to help him place it back in its cloth cradle.

"Tell me more," she whispered close to his ear.

He exhaled shakily. "In another life, maybe I visited your habitat to test my wing-pack designs, and we fell in love and got our own trawler, and you taught me how to be a *coureur.*"

"You would be a fine *coureur*," she teased, "flying at top speed around every trawler while I try to get all the work done."

"Flying in loops and spirals and roller coasters in the hot rain," he said around teeth clenched against the rising pain.

"And I would follow you."

"And we'd never change," he said quietly.

Pascale's lips pressed tight. He noticed.

"It's my fantasy," he said, as if by apology, "and in fantasies we can wish for all the things we can't have."

"We could wish that you wanted my change too," she offered sadly.

"I would like to wish that too," he whispered, "if you could be with me."

"Always," she said, running her fingertips tenderly along his forehead. His trembling abated, then stilled, as if she'd taken that promise to heart. It took a moment to realize he'd gone perfectly still.

"*Chéri,*" she said. "*Chéri!*"

He wasn't moving. He wasn't breathing. Then Louise and Paul-Égide were beside her, shaking him, screaming his name.

SIXTY-TWO

TÉTREAU CAME INTO Gaschel's office, trailed by Labourière. Gaschel wanted good news. At first, this situation on the surface of Venus had felt like one sucker punch after another, but Woodward seemed remarkably sanguine about it. She'd sent estimates of what, at minimum, the D'Aquillons might have found on the surface. The bank was reworking its assumptions about Venus and how the colony might industrialize. Woodward was even talking about a licensing agreement with the government. The bank was interested in developing the science and technology of mining at the surface, and pending an on-site survey, might even be interested in a lease. A resource extraction lease and royalties from mining could be a stable, long-term income stream for the colony.

Tétreau and Labourière sat at her invitation.

"Tell me something good," she said.

"It's contained," Tétreau said.

"Is that the good news?"

"Four of my constables were going to arrest an agitator on the *Avant-Guardiste,* when they were swarmed by a mob who flew in," Tétreau said. "Two of my constables were injured, but all four got away. Food, parts and oxygen supplies to the *Avant-Guardiste* have been suspended. The habitat has weekly needs, so within three to four days, they'll have to come to terms."

"It looks bad," she said.

"Appearances only," Labourière said. "This kind of civil disobedience happens on other colonies. It's almost always resolved by waiting the perpetrators out. We have more patience. And Woodward's specialists got back to me. They may be interested in buying the *Causapscal-des-Vents*."

"It's in pieces," she said.

"In pieces right where they're interested in owning it. It was collateral on a loan. Although it's changed shape, they're willing to exercise the foreclosure clause and credit us the original value of the collateral. We'd be selling the junk we can't reach at close to full price."

"And they get a station on the surface."

"That would be a condition. They've got drones to exploit it, and they want to see how the D'Aquillons did it. It could inform the way they mine on Mercury."

She handed Labourière the reports on a surface lease to the bank. "Look at this, too, and give me a recommendation," she said. "What else?"

Tétreau sat straighter. "We're tracking protests, both just to know and to keep traffic and essential services working. We're more worried about sabotage now, intentional and inadvertent. Thieves are getting bolder. We'll probably need more constables, better weapons."

Gaschel rubbed at her temples, trying to head off a growing headache.

"Not yet. Give it another day or two. If we need to buy weapons from the bank, I don't want to do it until absolutely necessary. I don't want them thinking we don't have the situation under control."

LOUISE AND PAUL-ÉGIDE had never seen burial rites before. Alexis knew of them from what Pa and Jean-Eudes had told him. *La colonie* needed every gram of organic carbon, especially nitrogen, hydrogen, calcium and the minerals in a human body. In the heights at sixty-fifth, after a short period of mourning and a service, the coroner would come and dismember the body and take away the pieces for reincorporation into life systems. 'Reincorporation' was an ironic word, as if the dead really became newly bodied, as soil and fertilizer, as water, as minerals. Reincorporation gave some of the life back to the community.

The distance of the coroner, up above the clouds, was important. The *coureurs* had no such detached person who would come, and when someone died gently in the depths, two families of *coureurs* would come together. After the service, the mourning family would wait outside their habitat while the visiting *coureurs* would dismember the body and process it, so that it would decompose more quickly and be incorporated into their anemic hydroponic areas and life support systems. Pa had sometimes left a younger Pascale and Jean-Eudes and Alexis on the *Causapscal-des-Profondeurs* while he and Émile crossed to another nearby habitat to prepare the body of a dead *coureur* for some other family.

Pascale had been too young to really understand what was happening, too young to leave the habitat with Pa and Émile, when it was *Maman*'s turn. Marthe and Chloé were too little to have survival suits, and Jean-Eudes didn't yet know how to use one. So the four siblings had stayed in one room when the visiting *coureurs* had come to prepare *Maman*. Pascale understood now why they'd brought music with them and played it loud. She didn't know what the music had been, but she remembered how it went, and ever since, she'd associated it with death. Its echoes accompanied her now.

Alone here, no visiting family could prepare Gabriel-Antoine. The parsimonious, frugal part of Pascale thought of the loss of all that had been Gabriel-Antoine's beautiful body. He might not be newly bodied, reincorporated like *Maman,* nourishing other life. Sometimes Venus broke that cycle, levied her tithe, and took something vital from the community for her own, like she'd done with Chloé, with Marthe, with Pa and Émile.

Pascale had haltingly explained all this to the weeping Louise and stunned Paul-Égide. Their service had been brief—a yielding to tears, a silent battle of blame—but they wouldn't have time for the burial rites. If they lived, it was something they could do later. So after Louise and Pascale had washed Gabriel-Antoine's body for the last time, Jean-Eudes wrapped him in an impermeable plastic safe sack, and then another sack woven of tough trawler fibers. It wasn't perfect, and he would slowly desiccate, but he would be preserved for a time. Pascale and Jean-Eudes carried him to the airlock, and then Pascale cycled him out and carried his body to the Axis Mundi. The stars, he'd said. Gabriel-Antoine had wanted to be with the stars.

She carried him through the Axis Mundi, to the infinite starry heart of Venus. The still, silent world welcomed them. Starlight lensed through her tears. The robots had brought some small asteroids closer, just pieces of rock and metal and volatiles a few meters across. They would use them all eventually, but Pascale picked an iron-nickel one and used the vacuum cold jet pack that Gabriel-Antoine had built.

This tiny world had no gravity to speak of. She could release him and her handhold and they floated together, slowly orbiting the invisible pulsar at the heart of the system. The projections on the tiny asteroid were awkwardly placed for tying Gabriel-Antoine down, but she had enough cable; after a time it was done, the first real grave for any Venusian. She stroked Gabriel-Antoine's cheek through the shroud they'd made with their own hands. She cried as she thought of her lover's slowly freezing body, destined to eternity in the cold.

"*Au revoir, mon amour,*" she whispered, and touched her faceplate to the weave and pressed her lips to the inside of her helmet.

Pascale moved slowly back to the Axis on the cold jets, moving numbly hand over hand back to the silent cave, with only the rustle of her suit for noise. She still wasn't used to silences. Venus's hot clouds had no silences: the wind or rain would press at the creaking trawler walls, or the pressure pumps would flex like laboured breathing. And *family* made noise, the snoring, breathing, scratching, walking, burping sounds of people. Venus at her heart was different, a lonely reflection of Pascale's heart, now. Venus had been alone for so long, with nothing but the floating, humming trawlers for company, that it might take time for her to warm to the noise of life.

In the last section of the cave, the submarine ship they'd built sat bereft, gleaming metal reflecting dark walls. They'd been within perhaps twenty-four hours of launching, to take them all to the upper clouds, to bring Gabriel-Antoine to doctors, and the rest of them to detention. They were still free, for a while longer—still seeing the heart of Venus—only because Venus had taken Gabriel-Antoine for her own.

She touched her hand to the flank of the submarine ship, as if feeling through gauntlet and hull. It was an ugly engineering marvel. Perhaps not a marvel by the standards of the banks, nor of the other colonies of humanity, but the ship was a marvel for Venus. It was built by Venusian hands within the secret heart of Venus, with no help from outsiders. It owed nothing to anyone. That she'd cannibalized some components from the *Causapscal-des-Vents* didn't bother her or make this any less native-built. The *coureurs* had tithed for Venus. Once, her conscience had questioned, but now she'd come to Pa's way of thinking. The *Causapscal-des-Vents* had been theirs. Venus was a new world, and their home. They didn't need to play to rules imposed by foreign powers and banks for their own interests. She and Gabriel-Antoine had designed and built this together.

The mood inside the habitat was somber and joyless. Jean-Eudes and Alexis helped Pascale unsuit. Pascale found Louise wrapped protectively around Paul-Égide, lying on the bed where their brother had died.

"We need to talk, Louise."

Louise blinked silently.

"I made your brother sad," she said, sitting, "but he made me sad too. He said some things that hurt me, that will probably always hurt, but I forgive him. And he forgave me. I don't know if it ever would have worked, but we were both in love, and my heart feels like it's been ripped out."

Louise grimaced, unable to stop new tears.

"He loved both of you," Pascale said. "He would want me to protect you. I can't do it alone, though. I need your help."

Louise hid her face with a hand.

"The government and the bank killed Gabriel-Antoine," Pascale said. "I feel like I'm shrivelling inside, but I can't, because of Alexis and Paul-Égide and Jean-Eudes. And you. Just like I'm the big sister, you're the big sister too. Paul-Égide needs you. And so do Florian and Maxime. We need to find them—and if it wasn't a trick, Marie-Pier too. You didn't ask to be the head of your family and neither did I, but it happened. The bank isn't done, not until what we made here belongs to them. I need you to help me, Louise, to protect Paul-Égide, Maxime and Florian. I need you to be hard. We need to hit back, for family."

Louise wiped hard at her eyes with a palm and took several deep breaths. "Okay," she finally said.

SIXTY-THREE

Pascale and Gabriel-Antoine had never had time to figure out what to call these tubes of steel they'd built. The vessels could maneuver in the naked vacuum of space. Their retractable fins and wings would make them clumsily maneuverable and somewhat aerodynamic in the winds, and most importantly, their steel skin would withstand the crushing pressures of Diana Chasma. They weren't airplanes or rockets, although they had some qualities of both. They weren't dirigibles, although their buoyancy in and above the clouds was carefully designed. They looked most like submarines, but that wasn't right either, because Venus had only a boiling mockery of an ocean. These vessels were something new and unique to the circumstances of Venus, like the *coureurs* and even the upclouder *colonistes*.

Pascale called the first one the *Sainte-Marthe*. They would need all the angels and ghosts they had, if they were to even hope to survive. In her suit, Pascale lay within the *Sainte-Marthe*, on a bench much like the one in the bathyscaphe, her head near a thick glass porthole. She couldn't see much right now, because beyond the porthole was a second one about two meters out, set within a shield she'd attached to the front of the *Sainte-Marthe*.

The controls were in a little pit where her arms could comfortably rest beneath her while she lay on her stomach. The pilot area was only three meters long, with just the space to turn around and reach into the top of the engines and some limited maintenance access. If anything went wrong, the *Sainte-Marthe* basically needed to be dry-docked—on-the-go maintenance had been too complicated to design. Jean-Eudes scrunched at the back, past Pascale's feet: she and Gabriel-Antoine had only designed the vessel for one crew member.

The robots had excavated the cave system as much as possible in the last weeks, but the channel still curved and twisted. The vessels, each five meters in diameter and ten meters long, could navigate it, but with awkward and worrying bumping and scratching against the hot, rocky walls. The biggest problem was gravity. Manipulating and building them in zero-gravity had been child's play. The caves averaged a forty-degree slope from the mouth of the Axis to the surface, under nearly a full standard gravity the whole way. So the *Sainte-Marthe* rode up a crude winch system to the middle door.

The big door to the axis mouth closed behind her, and she waited as the forty atmospheres of pressure beyond the next door was bled away by the turbine and refrigeration system, until both inner chambers equalized at one atmosphere. The cap opened, and robots hooked up new cables to unceremoniously drag the *Sainte-Marthe* over the rock into the next chamber. The chamber door closed behind her.

They were finally ready. They would test their design against the real pressure and heat of Venus—and against the bank.

Venus's hot atmosphere poured around the *Sainte-Marthe*, filling the chamber. The skin of the vessel creaked as the pressure crept from one atmosphere to forty, the same as being four hundred meters below the surface of an ocean. The temperature quickly rose as well and the Stirling engines activated, surprising Jean-Eudes.

"It's okay, Jean-Eudes," Pascale said. "It's just some engines to try to cool us."

The forty atmospheres of pressure bobbed the *Sainte-Marthe* towards the top of the chamber, despite the ballast they'd attached beneath.

Twice the top of the vessel knocked against the cave ceiling, making Pascale flinch. If the vessel got even a little hole, the pressure would quickly kill her and Jean-Eudes.

Once the pressure equalized, the door to the outer chamber opened and robotic manipulators attached new cables to pull the *Sainte-Marthe* forward. The door closed behind her and the outer cap began letting in pressure from the outside. Sixty atmospheres of Venus's ocean of carbon dioxide pressed hot and tight around the *Sainte-Marthe*.

"It's happening!" Louise said on the radio. "It's holding!"

Louise was two chambers back, in the *Saint-Gabriel* with Paul-Égide. Alexis was out of radio contact, still on the other side of the Axis Mundi but on his way through.

"I'm going out," Pascale said with a hint of a tremor in her voice.

The last chamber equalized with the environment of the Diana Chasma—ninety-three atmospheres and four hundred and forty degrees. Within the open cave mouth, the *Sainte-Marthe* creaked under the pressure of the roasting ocean of super-critical carbon dioxide. Their robots had built it in a vacuum, and they'd sealed several empty chambers within the craft in that vacuum. Most habitats used oxygen as a buoyant gas, but a hard vacuum was even more buoyant. The *Sainte-Marthe* floated against the rock ceiling of the cave as simple robots attached a heavy ballast: part rock, and part crude cannon.

Pascale signalled for the cap door to open. It clanged and swung slowly out, rising to let in more and more of the murky, spectral light from the bottom of Venus. The Bank of Pallas drones waited out there on their steel frames.

The *Sainte-Marthe* emerged from the cave mouth, bobbing like an emergency balloon tied to a heavy habitat. Louise would emerge in the *Saint-Gabriel* in ten minutes; Pascale had to banish the dragons from the door by then. The sharp rocky floor of Diana Chasma was beneath her. The *Sainte-Marthe* swung wildly for a moment, struggling to rise against the ballast. For a moment, she could see the scattered debris fields of dark basalt rockslides in the distance, then the far wall of Diana Chasma, rising to the shoulders of dead volcanic hotspots that had left their immense coronae as tombstones. The crazed wobbling calmed as the ballast dragged the *Sainte-Marthe* down the slope to rock gently in front of the bank equipment.

The drones were blocky metal ovals with small wings on their sides, standing on sturdy struts. They had to be durable to have waited on the surface this long. The bank was most likely controlling them by cloud-penetrating radio from satellites. The range of radio frequencies that penetrated the clouds was narrow, and Pascale switched on her first weapon. The *Sainte-Marthe* filled the key radio bands with loud static, enough to swamp any signal, enough to be heard all the way in orbit. In the frame of her narrow view, the two egg shapes fired at the *Sainte-Marthe*. Metal hammered on metal deafeningly in Pascale's submarine ship. Jean-Eudes screamed.

"It's okay! It's okay!" Pascale called back. "We're okay!" She hadn't wanted to bring Jean-Eudes and Paul-Égide, but she couldn't leave them behind either. This was what the government had forced them to become—the kind of people who could only protect their innocents by bringing them to battle.

The same sharp, thumb-sized metal bullets that had struck Gabriel-Antoine, possibly the only things that could carry any kinetic force in these pressures, hammered them. Two of them punctured the shield hanging on the front of her ship. Debris rattled and scratched the *Sainte-Marthe,* but didn't pierce it.

Pascale aimed carefully and fired her own weapon, one very similar to the drones', affixed to the ballast beneath the vessel. She missed on the first shot, but on the second, pierced one of the egg shapes. It tipped over, a slow spray of fragments falling around it.

The second egg-shaped drone fired insistently, but given her radio-jamming, it would have been acting dumb, running on a simple program. Only the simplest software could run on the few chips that could survive at this temperature.

Pascale aimed the narrow cannon, centering the crosshairs on the egg shape. The projectile struck a glancing blow, deflected by the tremendous weight of the atmosphere, but it was enough to knock the ovoid onto its side. It tried to right itself with its manipulators, but the impact had damaged the undercarriage. A hatch opened and a balloon started inflating, to lift it away. One careful shot by Pascale pierced the fabric, causing the balloon to flop unceremoniously beside the drone, fluttering as the oxygen escaped.

The drones were still.

"Is it all done?" Jean-Eudes asked.

"For now. I'm sorry it was noisy. There'll be more noise."

"I can do it," he said. "Storms didn't scare me much at home."

"I know."

The *Saint-Gabriel* was emerging from the cave, piloted by Louise. Pascale canted the *Sainte-Marthe*'s bow forward. She didn't need the shield anymore, and pulled a trigger. The heavy extra shielding on the bow dropped off, revealing a vista of almost a hundred and forty degrees wide.

"Look, Jean-Eudes," Pascale said. "You probably didn't see it much on the way down. This is Venus. This is our home. You can unstrap and scootch up a bit."

Warily her big brother unbuckled and crawled forward, pressing against her. She put her arm around him. Pa had shown Pascale the real Venus, as he had shown Émile, Marthe and Chloé. Pascale was taking care of Jean-Eudes now.

"It's pretty," Jean-Eudes said, and Pascale laughed. Then Jean-Eudes did too. "She's not pretty."

"Not here, she's not," Pascale said. "This is only Venus's skin. You've seen Venus's heart—you know that it's really filled with stars."

Jean-Eudes's expression, behind his faceplate, was a mix of open-mouthed wonder and forehead-scrunching thought. He was still taking the big idea and making it into something he could more easily hold.

"I'm glad *Papa* got to know it, too," he said, with a little catch in his voice. "And Marthe."

"Me too," she said, squeezing his shoulder.

Alexis's ship, the *Saint-George,* finally emerged from the cave mouth, bobbing on its ballast cables. They lingered for another ten minutes of system checks and verifications, then Pascale signalled the door to the cave to close again, and one by one, the three ships released their mooring lines. They floated rapidly upward, propelled by their tremendous buoyancy. A thousand meters' climb transformed the view, revealing a crumpled, stony Venus reclining in basaltic glory. They ascended through a wispy cloud of lead sulfide at two thousand meters and Venus continued to grow, revealing her volcano-blasted immensity, although the sharp blades of the mountains still framed the horizons. The lowest fringes of Venus's cloudy skirts were still twenty kilometers above them when their ascent slowed. The atmospheric pressure had thinned to fifty atmospheres.

"Are you okay, Louise?" Pascale asked.

"Yes," she said after a moment.

"The controls are okay?"

"It's all so big," she said.

"I was too scared to notice anything at first," Alexis cut in.

Pascal had crude directional cameras on the *Sainte-Marthe,* and she swivelled one down. Alexis floated about a kilometer lower and two kilometers south of her in the *Saint-George*. Louise bobbed about five hundred meters away in the *Saint-Gabriel*, bright and metallic, just a bit north. Around twenty-seven kilometers from the surface, they began to encounter tendrils of haze floating beneath the main cloud layer. The air here was two hundred degrees cooler and their hulls squeaked as they throbbed away the heat of the surface. They needed a little time at this altitude for decompression.

Pascale turned on the short wave, and a common coureur mask, one that encoded text into the sounds of trawler electrical discharges. She signalled Juliette Malboeuf at *La Reine des Fées*. It took about five minutes of trying before Pascale finally received a similarly coded signal.

Are the Hudon children okay? Pascale asked.

All are well, was the response.

Pascale was more relieved than she'd expected. She'd never met Marie-Pier's children, but their mother had spoken of them so often and lovingly that some bond had already been woven.

Merci. It's time. We're starting, Pascale signalled back. *Are you and the other houses ready?*

Oui was the only response.

There was nothing more Pascale could do to prepare. Everything would be decided in the next few hours. There was a grim fatalism in the idea that she might not survive, but she didn't entertain it for even a moment. She *had* to live. For the children of the House of Styx, for Venus, and for her family, for all the sacrifices that they'd made. It had to have been worth something. She had to make it worth something.

She turned off the encoding mask and took a deep breath. Then, with a deep breath, she transmitted into the air traffic channel that most habitats kept on in the background across the entire planet.

"This is the *Saint-George*, the *Saint-Gabriel*, and the *Sainte-Marthe,* armed ships of the House of Styx," Pascale said. "We denounce the current government of Venus, its *présidente*, and its ties to the Bank of Pallas. We accuse the government of Venus of murder and treason. And we declare, on behalf of all Venusian *colonistes*, the overthrow of the government and the immediate exclusion from Venusian space of all representatives of the Bank of Pallas. We're coming up now to arrest all those involved in the government's crimes."

Pascale released the radio and exhaled some of the adrenaline. Then, all three vessels jettisoned the tons of rock they'd carried as ballast, beginning a new, rapid ascent into the haze.

SIXTY-FOUR

Marie-Pier had known of Gabriel-Antoine's injuries for some days, from recordings smuggled into the detention cells. She'd struggled with her grieving for him, with trying to separate the uncertainty of Gabriel-Antoine's fate from the fate of her children, with enduring the persistent injuries to her lungs. Laurette tried to help, but she needed as much support as Marie-Pier, nursing a child in a jail, and Marie-Pier had to use up her nervous energy. She helped Laurette, and others besides: those who got sick in detention, those who began to lose hope, those who would accept arbitration in a conflict.

People treated her with some deference. Her position had become oddly elevated, by fame or infamy, once Gaschel had made her statements about the sinking of the *Causapscal-des-Vents*. Fellow detainees demanded her story, including her dramatic attempted murder by Émile D'Aquillon, which she dismissed as nonsense.

People believed her. Everyone in detention felt like they'd been strong-armed by an overreaching government. The attempted murders of Marie-Pier and Émile was a matter of degree to them, as much as stealing a whole habitat was only different in degree from what they'd been doing stripping parts. They were the same, to them, and the breathtaking ballsiness of her crimes earned their admiration.

They all wanted to know more about what was going on in Diana Chasma, and Marie-Pier stuck to the story of mining with new, Venusian *coureur* technology, and they accepted that she wouldn't spill the secrets. Day by day, she turned her new notoriety into chances to deliver moments of dawning clarity for people who might not have thought before in terms of nations and peoples. This was all part of building their nation, and when people thought about the direction they were being driven, many came to sobering conclusions.

So it was that when Oscar snuck in a recording and handed it to Laurette, it came right to Marie-Pier at the back of the cell, and everyone crowded around her oxygen tank to hear. Marie-Pier listened to Pascale's brief statement with astonishment, with the eyes of fifty fellow detainees on her, looking for cues. She didn't have any. Not yet, but she had a sinking feeling about Gabriel-Antoine.

The *Saint-George* and the *Sainte-Marthe,* both named for dead family.

The *Saint-Gabriel*.

Oh, Gabriel-Antoine. So young and beautiful. So gifted and visionary.

"What is it?" Laurette asked. "The *coureurs* have ships? What ships? They're armed? That's your… step-daughter?"

Marie-Pier had never thought about it that way.

"Yes. Pascale is my step-daughter. If she says she's… armed, then she is."

"She's really going to overthrow the government? Gaschel? All of them?" Claudine demanded.

She was holding hands with her husband Maurice through the bars. They were a beautiful couple, and they'd been here for weeks before Marie-Pier, just two more people trading on the black market to get by. At the bars to the outside, Oscar and another constable waited, anxious, watching her. It wasn't fair. It wasn't fair for any of them. Not for Claudine and Maurice. Not for George-Étienne or Émile or Gabriel-Antoine. Not for Pascale. Not for her children, who were without their mother. She rose.

"Not just her," Marie-Pier said. "I'm from the House of Styx, and Pascale denounced the government on my behalf, too. She did it on behalf of all of us."

Marie-Pier walked slowly to the bars, to Oscar and the other constable. Everyone followed, all the women in her cell and all the men in the cell beside theirs. Oscar and his friend shrank back. A couple of other constables neared.

"Did you hear the message?" Marie-Pier asked them.

Oscar nodded. So did the others.

"Do you know what it means?" she asked.

Oscar shook his head.

"My… my family made it to the surface, by ourselves, despite the obstacles created by the government and the banks. We found metals where people said there weren't any. And because they wanted to control it, the government killed my husband, and my stepson—and they tried to kill me. Do you know that?"

Oscar was frozen. The other constables paled.

"I've always been good to your mother, Oscar. You can ask her. And my family will be good to her, and you, and anyone who's on our side. Make no mistake—Pascale is coming up. She's armed and she's going to arrest anyone who is not on our side. You four need to decide whether you're with Gaschel and the bank, or whether you're with the eighty of us in here. And you're going to need to decide quickly, because things are going to happen fast."

One constable, a nervous twenty-something called Charles, put his hand on the butt of his pistol. Marie-Pier glared at him the way she would stare down Florian. Charles stared back defiantly and drew his gun, his confidence growing. People backed away from Marie-Pier.

"Is that it, Charles?" she said. "Are you going to gun down an unarmed prisoner? In front of eighty witnesses? While the government that protects you is falling to my stepdaughter?"

Charles hesitated, but kept hold of the gun.

"Oscar. You two," she said, jerking her chin at the other two constables. "You're going to stand by and watch a murder happen? Is that why you became constables? Is that what you want for Venus? I said things are going to happen fast. This is your first choice. Are you with Charles, or are you with me and your mothers?"

Neither Oscar nor the other two had guns. Charles ostensibly outranked them. Oscar looked at her pleadingly, and Marie-Pier held his gaze. In a lurch more than a step, Oscar staggered forward, in front of Marie-Pier, and pivoted to face Charles.

Charles face hardened. "Get out of the way, Oscar."

Oscar shook his head. Charles raised the gun. People screamed. Oscar didn't move. The other constables shuffled hesitantly.

"Get out of the way!" Charles yelled. Everyone was yelling.

The gun went off, and Charles was tackled by the other two constables. Oscar staggered back to the bars, knees buckling, to be caught by inmates. Marie-Pier was calling his name, and then her hands were at his belt, grabbing his keys. She opened first the door to the women's cell, and then to the men's. People streamed out.

Charles was still on the floor, and one of the other constables had his gun now. It was going to go badly. Marie-Pier stomped forward and waved her hands.

"Put Charles in a cell," she said. "He's under arrest. Get a doctor down here right away for Oscar. Give the gun to Maurice. He'll hold it for now."

There was a long frozen moment, and then people started moving, even the constables.

"You two constables," she said after they'd thrown Charles in the cell. "You're both deputized constables under the House of Styx. You report to Maurice, who reports to me. Do you understand?"

All three seemed stunned, but after a few moments, they nodded.

Marie-Pier sent dozens of the detainees to take control of the *Petit Kamouraska*. There were fewer constables on board than she'd expected; she soon had access to the radio. She set the channel to the flotilla-wide ATC band and pressed transmit.

"This is Marie-Pier Hudon of the House of Styx. The *Petit Kamouraska* declares itself against the government and the Bank of

Pallas. Those illegally detained have been released, and deputies for the people will be heading to the *Baie-Comeau* to assist the *Sainte-Marthe,* the *Saint-George,* and the *Saint-Gabriel* in the arrest of Gaschel and her government."

A cheer went up behind her, transmitted to the colony.

To the Cutter at the Party, by Émile D'Aquillon

Bright and trembling, round and bloated
on pale skin, red shines in hard sunlight
slicing between window slats.
We wrap ourselves in metal and plastic
and hope, leaving exposed your wrists
and mine.

You're part of the furniture, ornamental,
a drum strike in the pounding chaos
of a party that can't bear
to understand you. Alone in a crowd,
no one talks to you,
but they watch.

You keep coming back, a tiresome rhythm,
an emotional stutter, a totem of our aches,
foreshortened by the dizzy buzz
of bagosse moonshine,
distanced by a half-eaten cake
of sulfur-bittered hash.

We didn't choose to drift on the winds,
grasping for ground like Dante's
lovers, naked thunder deafening our
music. Our parents chose this
in all the ways they choose
all our forevers.

Puzzle pieces seek their match.
We've made puzzles of spinning
clouds, imposed shapes of animals
we've never seen, tilted at windmills

that blow away before we realized
they never were.

Molten red runs wrist to
sleeve, uneven, unspeaking.
Veinous volcanoes write new geographies,
mapping places we suffered, times we couldn't
hold on, lettered in a language of scars
young and old.

SIXTY-FIVE

VISIBILITY WAS ONLY a few kilometers here, so Pascale had to help Louise and Alexis keep a tight formation, but this was her world, so familiar as to be comforting, and it felt easy, until an alarm lit up on her controls. There was a ping in the radar band. Then another burst on the same band. Then another. The government had noticed them, or the bank. She'd expected it, although not at this depth. *La colonie* equipped its aircraft with radar for meteorology, and search and rescue, but few planes were equipped for the acid, heat and pressure at this depth. A frisson of fear snuck up her stomach, but less than she might have expected: fury smothered it, ready to burn something.

Her mind stayed clear. She wondered what the other craft thought when they saw the bright radar echoes. There was no steel in the clouds, nothing hard enough to reflect radar as well as these three ships would, and she could imagine their consternation. The radar pings continued. The planes flew ten to fifteen kilometers above her, approaching from several directions.

The *Sainte-Marthe*, the *Saint-Gabriel*, and the *Saint-George* slowed their rise at forty-one kilometers. They'd planned to wait here, to acclimatize to the pressure while their hulls cooled, but they probably didn't have time. Their bodies hadn't spent too much time at higher pressures, so they didn't need too much time to decompress.

Most of the radio bands were being monitored, so near the end of the dial, at frequencies no one else used, Pascale spoke on a low wattage that hopefully would only travel a few kilometers.

"Are you ready?" she said.

"I'm scared," Alexis said.

"It'll be okay," Louise said before Pascale could say something reassuring. "You have your *grand-père* to think about."

Alexis transmitted his heavy breathing for a few moments of hesitation, before saying, "I'm thinking about Gabriel-Antoine, too."

"Yeah," Louise said.

"Let's make them proud," Pascale finished.

They dropped the last of their rocky ballast and began a new shuddering rise through Pascale's world. These clouds and hazes, these mists and winds and rains and storms, were her home. They'd found the stars both above and below the clouds, redefining the world in wondrous ways, and that reassured her that this was home, and that it was right to feel good here. At fiftieth *rang,* the radar pings became regular and strong, and in the distance she saw the first colonial planes. She ran her radio receiver through the different official channels and finally found their conversation.

"...shape, like a dirigible coated in silver paint. Reading three, still rising. Not sure of design."

Pascale turned to the main colonial short wave channels. They were buzzing with news of UFOs and theories based on Pascale's radio message from days ago, and the real meaning of the House of Styx. Some speakers also mentioned the House of Storms, the House of Crows and the Faerie House with some alarm. Some of the talk bordered on hysterical, as if these alliances encompassed hundreds of people instead of just small families. They'd come high enough to pick up some of the weaker sub-channels, too, those that supported low bit-rate message board communities, conversations guessing at weapons held by the houses, and other topics that might have normally drawn the attention of the government. But there was too much of it. Judging by the comms traffic, the whole *colonie* was vibrating.

A strong signal came on the ATC channel. "Unknown craft at fiftieth *rang,* thirteen degrees south, one hundred and fifty-six degrees longitude, identify yourselves and come to a full drift."

The planes flew in wide arcs around the three rising submarine ships. Alexis's voice came in on a tight-beam channel.

"Should we get them?" he said with a kind of nervous courage.

"Not now," Pascale said. "We only have a few tricks up our sleeves."

"I'd like to," Louise said.

Pascale wanted to make someone pay too, but this wasn't the place or time. These planes were nobodies.

ATC repeated the message about every minute as Pascale, Alexis, and Louise rose. As they climbed through the gaping emptiness of *Grande-Allée* and *Les Plaines,* their rise became slow and stately, and finally stopped just above the buffeting convection rolls of *les Rapides Plates* at sixty-second *rang*.

Pascale peered through her porthole. They were still low enough that the sky didn't appear quite black, but rather a blurred slate, with stars winking through the haze. The patrol planes from the depths had been joined by another four. Above them, figures flew in survival suits and wing packs. The distance made it hard to be sure, but they might be carrying weapons. Three- and four-prop drones, bright and new, hovered in the distance. Those weren't colonial drones; *la colonie* couldn't even afford medicine. Louise's ship and Alexis's stopped a little higher than hers. The steel sheen of their hulls had corroded, sulfuric acid scarring their skins with chalky white rust. Venus's baptism.

"Unknown craft at sixtieth *rang*, at thirteen degrees south, one hundred and fifty-six degrees longitude, identify yourselves and come to a full drift."

Pascale took a breath, trying to calm the fluttering in her stomach, and ignored them. She'd said all she needed to say. The ATC channel went silent for a time until a clamour of overlapping voices called for the arrest of the D'Aquillons, and for the arrest of the *présidente* and *l'Assemblée*. It swamped the channel until air traffic cut in, demanding that only navigational messages be conveyed on this band.

"Start the engines," Pascale said to Alexis and Louise.

She activated her own and watched twin propellers fold out from the hull of the *Saint-Gabriel* and the *Saint-George*. Both ships began to plow along the top of the rolling turbulence of *Rapides Plates*. Her ship shuddered and picked up speed, pulling ahead of Alexis and Louise.

"*Saint-George, Saint Gabriel* and *Sainte-Marthe,*" came a new message on the official government channel, "stand to and prepare to be boarded. If you do not, you will be fired upon."

"Can I answer?" Alexis's voice said on their tight channel.

"They didn't ask Pa for an answer," Pascale said. "Or Émile. Or Marie-Pier."

The *Sainte-Marthe* bucked around Pascale as the propellers built to full speed. She was stuck at sixty-second *rang,* though. Venus wasn't strong enough to lift them past here. Pascale had reached the edge of Venus's influence and protection. The rest of the struggle belonged to her now.

"This is your last warning," the government channel said. "Stand down or be shot down."

They'd reached their top speed, but they were still heavy steel tubes. Their stubby wings and stabilizers and control surfaces weren't meant to steer them quickly so much as keep them straight. There wasn't much Pascale, Louise and Alexis could do to evade the ovoid drones now descending on them.

Two drones came within a few hundred meters, shooting from angry-looking gun barrels. At this altitude, their guns could fire smaller bullets, and they travelled so fast that Pascale couldn't even see them cross the space to hammer the hull. The *Sainte-Marthe* didn't slow, but Pascale's rearward camera seemed to not be working. She couldn't see what was happening with Alexis and Louise.

"Alexis! Louise!" she said into their private channel. "Are you okay?"

"Right behind you," Louise answered.

"Their bullets couldn't do anything!" Alexis said. He laughed.

"We don't know what they have. They might yet have something that will punch through steel. Let's be careful. Are the drones still back there?" she asked, craning her neck to look as far back as the porthole allowed.

"Way behind!" Alexis said.

"Their second try is coming," Pascale said.

The *Saint-George, Saint-Marthe* and the *Saint-Gabriel* ran well, reaching their maximum of thirty kilometers per hour. The winged figures descended, graceful and far faster. One of Pascale's rearward cameras gave a cloudy image as if acid had scored its lens, and the other was just black.

"My rear cameras are busted," Pascale said to Louise and Alexis. "Go past me, so I can cover you better."

She throttled back just a little, and the *Saint-Gabriel* and *Saint-George* drew slowly past. Six flyers, their survival suits slate-black and smooth, their wing-packs sleek, descended. They carried heavy rifles like in the movies. It wasn't the *Sûreté.* One landed on top of the *Saint-Gabriel.* The figure carried some kind of blades, and stabbed them at the hull, apparently expecting to find the typical plasticky envelope material. The blades glanced off metal and the figure slipped off the curved ship, tumbling briefly in the air before righting and banking away.

Pascale couldn't pick up their radio channel, or it was encrypted, but the flyers didn't make the same mistake twice. Two of them flew behind the *Saint-Gabriel* and fired their rifles at the propellers. Their heavy bullets ricocheted in all directions, but Alexis's right propeller began to slow.

Pascale activated the little swivel-mounted gun beneath the *Sainte-Marthe*. It didn't have a real explosive charge in a casing like a bullet—they hadn't had all the chemicals and conditions they would have liked to work with—but they'd designed a small-caliber spring-powered system of flechettes. Pascale aimed and fired. The stream of darts pulled to the right. By the time she adjusted her targeting, the flyers had swept away, probably coming behind her. Pascale took aim at the ones near

Louise's ship. The darts pulled to the right again, but Pascale adjusted, spraying her fire in an arc. She came very close, but the flyers scattered and drew behind Pascale too.

Pascale was no weapons designer. The flyers on their wing-packs could harry the three of them until eventually they damaged something important, or could land with a welding torch or explosives. She didn't know what the bank had. But Alexis had better aim, and some of his flechettes hit a flyer in the legs. As if receiving an order, the flyers retreated towards the branch office, the speck of green floating kilometers eastwards.

The radio filled with whooping shouts and a flight of figures in shabby, patched survival suits flew by, wobbling as if they weren't used to conditions at this altitude. *Coureurs.* The radio channel filled with swearing, directed at the bank, at the government, and at up-clouders in general. Pascale flipped transmit on her radio.

"This is Pascale D'Aquillon of the House of Styx," she said, "to the *coureur* flyers. Stay focused. Let's get to the *Baie-Comeau*."

The whooping continued, but the civilians made for the *Baie-Comeau* in a more orderly way. The formation of the flotilla was also shifting. The sixty or so habitats were spreading out, as if distancing themselves from the three metal monstrosities, or perhaps from the *coureurs*. But their positions also gave them line-of-sight on the *Sainte-Marthe*, the *Saint-Gabriel*, and the *Saint-George*. Other flyers had taken to the air too; people had donned wing-packs and come in for closer views. Some were probably *Sûreté* constables. The radio channels told Pascale that no one knew what was going on. She switched to the colonial emergency channel, one which would buzz in every habitat in a real emergency.

"This is Pascale D'Aquillon of the House of Styx," she said. "I am in one of the three steel… ships closing in on the *Baie-Comeau*. We have no dispute with those Venusian citizens who aren't part of the government. We're here seeking justice. I will rendezvous shortly with the *Baie-Comeau* to take control of it, not in the name of one congregate of families, but in the name of all Venusians.

"We seek the arrest of Angéline Gaschel and her associates for the attempted murder of Marie-Pier Hudon and Émile D'Aquillon on the *Baie-Comeau*. We are also seeking the arrest of Angéline Gaschel and her government, and Bank of Pallas officials and security personnel, for the murders of Émile D'Aquillon and George-Étienne D'Aquillon at the *Causapscal-des-Profondeurs,* the murder of Gabriel-Antoine Phocas on the surface of Venus, and the murder of Grégoire Tremblay on the *Chevreuil*. These victims deserve justice. And we deserve a Venus of our own, one free of the hands of strangers who profit from our poverty."

She switched off the transmit function. Her heart thumped. Her face felt hot. Only the normal static of distant lightning sounded in the emergency channel, like faint, crinkling paper.

"Pascale?" Jean-Eudes whispered.

She looked back. Her brother had dutifully scrunched to the back of the pilot tube as she'd asked. His bearded face regarded her earnestly from under his faceplate.

"Are you okay?" he said.

Her eyes were moist, but she wasn't crying. She'd just listed all her losses. She wasn't just Pascale à George-Étienne anymore. She wasn't floating in the clouds anymore. She'd lost that, lost that life with people she'd loved. Now she spoke for the House of Styx, for the other houses, for all *coureurs*. She'd made demands. She was demanding that the world change. Those things felt like someone else doing them because inside she still felt like Pascale à George-Étienne.

"I'm okay," she said, blinking. She smiled a bit. "Come closer. Come see the sky. We're going to try to go higher, high enough to see the stars."

Jean-Eudes unstrapped and crawled forward to squish beside her. In silent wonder, he craned his head to see the vapor-colored sky and its points of light.

They'd made *Sainte-Marthe* with considerable buoyancy, thanks to the vacuum-filled chambers, but even with that, the vessel could go no higher on its own than sixty-second or sixty-third *rang*. The flotilla bobbed another few kilometers higher. Pascale signalled Alexis and

Louise to inflate their buoyancy balloons. She did the same. Clicks sounded as little plates in the tops of the vessels opened and balloons began to fill.

The *Sainte-Marthe* slowly rose. The *Saint-Gabriel* and *Saint-George* followed gracefully. Pascale came level with the *Baie-Comeau* at first, and then floated above it. Winged figures on the roof were fleeing the habitat, while a much larger number of *coureurs* and normal civilians arrived. No bank security or colonial constables were in sight. Within a few minutes, Pascale brought the *Sainte-Marthe* over the *Baie-Comeau*. *Coureurs* caught cables and drew the vessel to the roof. Although massive, the *Sainte-Marthe* was almost neutrally buoyant right now, and Pascale couldn't feel the touch-down. Outside the porthole, faces in helmets craned up to see her.

"Stay here, Jean-Eudes," she said. "Keep the hatch closed while I'm out, okay?"

"Did we win?" he asked.

"Not yet. I have to talk to people."

Jean-Eudes seemed unconvinced, but didn't say more. Pascale opened the top hatch and cautiously stood. She was in the sky from the waist up, and the *Baie-Comeau*'s envelope curved away on all sides, so that she felt like she was looking down on the whole world. The sun shone hard to the west, in a sky black and starry. Gasping winds puffed around her, the faintest echo of Venus's true strength. A distant cheer sounded, faint on the thin air, almost imagined. Below the *Sainte-Marthe*, a host of *coureur* faces, and many flotilla ones, looked up at her. She made her way down the ladder rungs built into the side of the ship.

Thirty *coureurs* awaited her. Some had clubs, some had knives, some had crude guns. Around them, a dozen up-clouders with cleaner survival suits stood uncertainly, some with badges of the *Sûreté*. A few people, neither constable nor *coureur,* were with them on the roof, and new up-clouders kept landing all the time. Cameras looked up at her from the crowd.

The attention made Pascale feel strange. She'd spoken into the short-wave before, spoken to as many people as would listen, but that audience had been unseen, imagined. These people were in front of her, looking at her, and she was looking back, feeling bewildered. Who was she to tell these people what they should do, or how to live their lives? She was a seventeen-year-old, barely figuring out who she was, still on her journey to being herself. She wasn't Marthe. She wasn't Pa.

She stepped to the deck, and some of the gathered people slapped her back, congratulating her. Their wondering and slightly awe-struck attention focused on the hulking tube of steel. From the deck of the *Baie-Comeau,* it impressed even her. It dwarfed them all, rounded on both ends, with fine steel propellers and small aerodynamic wings folded close to the body. The gaping maw at the stern looked something like a rocket engine. There was as much steel in the *Saint-Marthe* as there had been in the whole of the *Causapscal-des-Vents,* and the *Saint-Gabriel* and *Saint-George* were still in the sky. This was wealth and power to Venusians, one of the most powerful political arguments she could make.

"We've got to go down," Pascale said, "and arrest Gaschel. We need to arrest her staff. Most importantly, we need to get her records."

One of the up-clouder civilians said, "Some of her staff might be down there, but Gaschel left. She flew to the bank when too few constables came to defend the *Baie-Comeau*. Some of her people went with her."

Another up-clouder pushed forward. "The idiots are taking over?"

Some of the *coureurs* turned on him, punching and kicking.

"Stop!" Pascale said.

The man straightened, holding his midsection. "Is this how it's going to be, then, with the mob in charge?" He looked meaningfully at the two cameras recording at the back of the crowd.

"That isn't how it's going to be at all," Pascale said. "That's how it's been so far, except that the government did it quietly, where they thought no one would notice, with the help of the bank. I watched the bank kill Gabriel-Antoine Phocas. My brother saw the bank and the constables kill Émile and my father. The *Chevreuil* was found with bullet holes in it and Grégoire Tremblay missing, after we'd traded him some radioisotopes to build a particle detector. The government and the bank need to be brought to justice."

A cheer went up, and the man didn't seem to know how to react. Pascale detached some of the *coureurs* to go seize the computers and records in the president's office. It surprised her a little that they listened. She called forward the constables, who came nervously in a path opened by the *coureurs*, a few of whom stood beside Pascale protectively.

"I'm Réjean Ayotte," said one of the men, with constable stripes on his suit. "I knew your brother. He was my friend. I'm with you."

"Thank you," Pascale said. "Where are all the people in detention for black marketeering?"

"They've got control of the *Petit Kamouraska*," Réjean said. "Some are still in their cells on the *Détroit d'Honguedo*."

"Go release them. Take some of these *coureurs* to help," Pascale said. "And bring Marie-Pier Hudon here as soon as you can."

"Releasing all the criminals?" the first man said. He still held his midsection. "Criminals releasing criminals! You stole the *Causapscal-des-Vents*, it belonged to all of us!"

People looked expectantly at Pascale; some of them looked ready to start hitting the guy again. Pascale put her gloved hand on the rash of white corrosion over the bright surface of the *Sainte-Marthe*.

"There are about fourteen tons of steel in here," she said. "All of it is new. Not a crumb of recycled metal made up its structure, plating or engines. The House of Styx found enough metals to industrialize the whole of *la colonie*, to make all the machines and habitats and industries we want. Yes, we took the *Causapscal-des-Vents,* because we needed to build the beginnings of an industry on the surface. We took that one habitat and turned it into a mine and foundry. With a little help, we can bring up more and more raw materials. Do you think if we'd gone to *l'Assemblée,* that they would have approved this plan? Do you think they could have pulled it off? Do you think they would have shared it with all of us? Or would they have licensed it to the bank, who would turn around and sell us our own steel at a profit to themselves?"

The man didn't answer, but the *coureurs* did, with swearing agreement.

"The bank isn't here to help us," Pascale said. "They're not a partner. The bank exists only to make money. Gaschel and her predecessors have been partnered with the bank. The House of Styx and the other houses are offering a different Venus. We want to work for ourselves, not investors somewhere on Earth or in the asteroids. The House of Styx and the other houses may need some food and medicines and other things from time to time, but other than that, we can supply you with all the steel, the aluminum, and the heavy metals you need, for whatever you want. The only question is, what do you want to build?"

The *coureurs* roared approval and the constables and up-clouders looked cautiously hopeful. The man holding his ribs eyed Pascale resentfully and turned away.

Pascale recognized Willy Gallant, a *coureur* who had sometimes visited Pa on the *Causapscal-des-Profondeurs*. He was now one of the leaders of the Faerie House.

"Willy!" she said, and he smiled and came close. His grey beard tangled behind his face plate. His suit looked as patched as Pa's had been.

"Your Pa would be proud of you," he said, slapping her shoulder.

Pascale looked away, feeling too seen, too observed. Willy was one of the few people who'd known her before she'd known who she really was. "Are Maxime and Florian okay?"

"They miss their *Maman*," he said. "They're safe, though."

"Thank you. Can you go down to Gaschel's office with another couple of *coureurs*?" Pascale said. "I don't trust that everyone is going to be helpful as we get the documents we want."

SIXTY-SIX

"WE HAD A deal with Gaschel," Victorine Corbeau said in the tight private channel to Fabienne, Angèle and Narcisse. Pascale D'Aquillon was making her way through the airlock into the *Baie-Comeau* with some of her supporters. Victorine stared up at the huge steel airship resting on the roof of the *Baie-Comeau,* its weight straining against the big silvery balloons above it. "It's all gone to shit! Look at all that steel."

"Their ground operation," her cousin Narcisse said bitterly. "All this time the government and scientists told us that there was no metal in the basalt, and yet George-Étienne struck the mother lode. Lucky bastard."

"He's a dead bastard," Victorine said. "Gaschel was going to give us metals and parts, and now she's been chased off the *Baie-Comeau*."

"The Bank of Pallas has a shit ton of money invested in Gaschel and her government," Narcisse said. "It doesn't matter if Gaschel is outgunned. The bank isn't, and they're not going to roll over when George-Étienne's last daughter and her retarded brother say that *la colonie* isn't paying back the loans."

"I don't know," Victorine said. "Either way we pick, we stand to get boned."

"Not necessarily," Fabienne said. Narcisse looked at her as if she'd interrupted the grown-ups; Angèle looked at her in a kind of panic. Narcisse had beaten them for talking, back when they were younger. She didn't care. Narcisse had gotten them into this. Fabienne had been the one to find not just the *Causapscal-des-Vents,* but the location of the D'Aquillon mine on the surface.

"Narcisse, stay in communication with Gaschel, as if nothing's gone wrong with the deal," Fabienne said, "or even better, negotiate for a better deal. She needs us more than we need her right now. At the same time, Angèle and I stick ourselves to Pascale and make sure she sees us protecting her. If it looks like we can get away with it, we should steal one of those steel ships."

Narcisse looked reluctant, but he shared a long look with Victorine.

"Do it," he said. "Get one of those ships."

THE STAFF IN Gaschel's office seemed shocked. They'd never imagined facing an invading mob armed with knives and clubs, and random guns and tasers, nor that the *présidente* would flee. Pascale strode in, but hadn't won anything real yet. Gaschel was more dangerous now that she and the bank knew how much they had to lose.

"Give us the passwords to all the systems," Pascale said to the office manager, one of Gaschel's aides. "Everyone else, get away from the computers."

People backed away, but the man didn't do anything. Suddenly someone in a survival suit pushed by Pascale and punched the man in the face. The punch was awkward—and made more so by the layers of suit—but effective. The man clutched at his cheek.

"Give us the passwords to the systems now!" the woman yelled, holding up her fist. "Hurry up, or there's more of this!"

Pascale stepped close and pulled on her hand. It was Angèle Mignaud.

"Easy," Pascale said. "Our enemies are the bank, and the government. Some of these people have nothing to do with everything that's gone wrong."

"The House of Styx can forgive and forget," Angèle said. "The House of Crows wants to see results before we let up."

The office manager, still holding his cheek, unlocked the computer station so that Angèle could create new accounts. Pascale watched her create accounts for herself, Pascale and Fabienne Mignaud. Then Pascale began copying the databases, so nothing could be destroyed by an administrator. Fabienne Mignaud came close to Pascale and pushed away one of the office staff.

"Look out, Pascale," Fabienne whispered. "You've got a big target on your back. If any one of these people manages to kill you, where's the future then? You don't have any more brothers and sisters to take over, do you?"

Pascale looked at the woman Fabienne had pushed away. She didn't look dangerous, but Pascale had no experience with any of this. If Émile had been here to help her understand these people, she might have felt safe. And loved. As she thought of Émile, she suddenly recognized a face in the crowd: thin, crowned with long dark hair, the woman who had seemed to make being beautiful so easy. Pascale pressed forward, with Fabienne trailing her almost like a bodyguard. People parted until she stood before the woman. Everyone watched her.

"You're Thérèse, aren't you?" Pascale asked.

Austere, poised, the woman nodded slowly.

"We met once. Émile introduced us."

"I remember," Thérèse said.

"I'm so sorry for your loss," Pascale said. Thérèse's face hardened with a kind of grief Pascale knew, and she felt her own eyes begin to moisten with thoughts of Gabriel-Antoine. "I know how much Émile meant to you. He loved you very much. I saw it in his poems, and heard about it in the way he talked about you."

A shade of red crept into Thérèse's face, and then Pascale's face became hot. She felt suddenly stupid for having reached out to her brother's lover now. Thérèse's flush threw into contrast a patch of deep acid scarring above the neckline of her suit.

"If things had turned out differently, we might have been sisters-in-law," Pascale said.

The stiffness in Thérèse faltered, and Pascale saw the woman described in Émile's poetry. His muse. The weeping muse. The drifting child of Venus. The terrible communion. Even the whirling children of Cain. Émile had seen so much depth of soul in this woman, and Pascale felt like it was all a window into the woman's heart.

"Don't stop, Pascale," Thérèse said. "Yours is the only new vision we've had of Venus, of ourselves. This is the only way out before we wither and die."

"The bank and the government will hit back hard. No one is on our side."

"I'll get people on our side," Thérèse said. "Engineers and mechanics. Artists. Even some of the constables. I'll call them."

"I wish Émile were here to thank you too," Pascale said. Thérèse stiffened again and both retreated from curious stares.

SIXTY-SEVEN

GASCHEL DID NOT want to be seen going to the branch office in this moment of crisis. She did not even want to be seen meeting with Woodward, officially, but it couldn't be helped. They met in Woodward's boardroom, where the air felt close. One wall leaned in at a thirty-degree angle, filling the office with reflected cloud light. Woodward and Copeland sat on one side of the table. Labourière and Tétreau accompanied Gaschel on the other.

"Your *coureurs* are making a loud little mess," Woodward said in English.

"They're not my *coureurs,*" Gaschel replied in the same language. "I thought you had this contained. We priced in the cost of the bank keeping them contained while you arrested them."

"They had more tech down there than you told us," Woodward said. "They weren't supposed to have jamming tech. Our deep drones went blind, and we haven't been able to reestablish contact with them. And now—surprise—they have teeth. Surprise is bad for business, *Madame Présidente.*"

"The last D'Aquillon played a weak hand," Labourière said. "We've done the math—there were tons of steel in the *Causapscal-des-Vents,* but between the metal on the planet and the surface area of their dirigibles, they didn't have enough iron to cover them very thickly."

It was difficult to gauge Woodward's thoughts, other than her general displeasure. The security officer spoke.

"We already observed a fair bit of steel on the surface," Copeland said, "almost enough to account for all of the alloy mass of the *Causapscal-des-Vents*. The metal covering their dirigibles had to be strong enough to withstand the pressure at the surface, so it can't just be a veneer."

"Then they did find a vein of iron ore," Gaschel said.

Woodward frowned. "If they did, they're luckier than every other geological survey in the last century. Maybe they found some older, non-basaltic rock just under the surface. But where did they get the energy to smelt it? How didn't they cook down there?"

No one rose to the question.

"What are you going to do, *Madame Présidente*?" Woodward said.

"As far as we know, there are only three of them piloting the metal-clad ships," Gaschel said. "That means they can be besieged and cut off from food and air and fuel. They're entirely dependent on support from others. Tétreau will be leading the best of the *Sûreté,* to deprive them of that support and to get that one off the *Baie-Comeau*. We can track them anywhere in the atmosphere and wait until they run out of air."

"Hardly an assertive approach," Woodward said. "We've been listening to the chatter. Young D'Aquillon is mildly persuasive. I wonder how loyal the constabulary is. Most of the constables are black marketeers themselves."

"What do you want?" Labourière said. "Should we shoot them out of the sky? We already tried that."

"With all due respect, Mister Labourière, the armament on your planes is a low-calibre afterthought," Woodward said. "Among the bank supplies in storage, we could pull out a couple of 50-calibre machine guns. They pack enough force to pierce most sub-tank armor. I'm not authorized to sell arms to Venus, but we could negotiate a service contract whereby the bank is sub-contracted to achieve very narrow and specific police or military objectives. An act of *l'Assemblée* could provide all the necessary legal authorization."

"I'm not weaponizing Venus," Gaschel said.

"Venus has already been weaponized, by your *coureurs*—and they're calling for your arrest on some quite serious charges," Woodward said. "The time needed to wait them out is easily long enough for your legitimacy as head of government to evaporate. You have a guerrilla force looking to overthrow your government, and they might win the public argument unless you deal with this swiftly. You found *coureurs* with dangerous radioisotopes. You found *coureurs* who stole national resources. You haven't hammered home the public security argument because you're *waiting*. And because the government's law ends if the government is overthrown, you have no idea what they'll do to you, whether you'll even have a fair trial."

"I can handle the people," Gaschel said. "Three ironclads with three people aboard can't overthrow a whole state."

A light flashed on Copeland's wrist and she listened to something in an earpiece. She gestured to Woodward. "There are a few calls to the president," she said, "mostly bureaucratic and political calls. There's a *coureur* calling though: Mignaud."

Woodward looked meaningfully at Gaschel. She'd told the branch manager about the intel she'd gotten from Mignaud.

"Patch it through. I'll take it," Gaschel said.

Copeland handed her a palm microphone.

"Yes," Gaschel said in French.

"Gaschel?" Narcisse Mignaud's rough voice said. She turned down the volume.

"I'm a bit busy, Mignaud," she said.

"I bet you are," he said. "You screwed this one up pretty badly."

"Are you calling with anything important?"

"I hitched my wagon to you, and I haven't gotten my payoff yet," he said. "What the hell are you doing to save yourself?"

"Where are you?" Gaschel said. "Could you take out Pascale D'Aquillon?"

"Kill her?" There was a long pause on the line. "I can see why you want to. There are a shitload of people listening to her. There's the makings of a celebration on the *Baie-Comeau*. Even if you jail her ass, she's going to be a lightning rod. Problem is, if I do something to her in the middle of this crowd, I'll get jumped."

"You can hit and run," Gaschel said. "You'll be rewarded."

"You can't afford me," he said. "I want a whole upper habitat of my own. Not one of the chintzy one-family ones, either. A big one, for twenty or thirty people. And it's mine, not on loan to me."

"The *Jonquière* houses fifteen," she said.

"Plus some non-tangible services we can sort out later."

"Agreed."

"And if I manage to take one of their steel ships, it belongs to the Mignaud family. Not yours. Mine. My steel, to do what I want with it, including trading it without you getting pissy about black marketeering."

"Agreed, but that offer is only good for the next hour or two, or until the standoff is resolved," Gaschel said.

"Okay. We have a deal. I'll save your damn presidency." The line went quiet and Gaschel handed back the microphone.

"I will," Gaschel said to Woodward in English, "for the period of this situation, take the guns as long as your crews are officered by my people."

"They're too big to be mounted on any of your planes," Woodward said, "but they could be mounted on the roof of the branch office. As long as *l'Assemblée* authorizes the service agreement, I'm sure we can come to a fair price. It will likely be a good investment for the colony. A few holes in their hulls would set them to sinking, and then planes or winged personnel can follow them down and attach rescue balloons. You'll recover a lot of metal: all that you lost with the sinking of the *Causapscal-des-Vents* and more. And you'll get whatever is on the surface. And people will see decisive leadership."

SIXTY-EIGHT

THE WHOLE FLOTILLA—all the flotillas—were buzzing about the coup, or attempted coup. *La présidente* had made some statements, but they didn't convince Noëlle. Délia said it was a *coureur* mob and kept demanding to know why the *Sûreté* wasn't squashing them. The constables had guns, they thought, and there weren't many *coureurs,* and they were all dirty hillbillies and wouldn't be missed if some of them got shot to make a point. Délia got madder when *coureurs* came up in conversation—Noëlle's occasional dalliances with Marthe hadn't made Délia like them any more. When Délia found out it was actually Marthe's family leading the attempted coup, she flipped out. Nothing Noëlle could say would calm her down, and Délia said some pretty awful things, until Noëlle finally stomped to the roof of the *Saint-Jérôme.* Gaétane Bolduc, one of Délia's cousins, was there with a taser in hand. She glanced up briefly as Noëlle came out of the airlock.

"Are they coming here?" Noëlle asked.

"If they are, I'm going to make them regret it."

"Someone said *la présidente* was killed," Noëlle said.

"I heard she was with the bank, negotiating for weapons. I also heard she was negotiating with the *coureurs* to give them the *Baie-Comeau*."

Angéline Gaschel had been *présidente*, or near the top, for as long as Noëlle had paid attention to anything like that. She didn't care about Gaschel one way or another—she was a part of the environment she didn't need to think about, until now. She didn't know Pascale D'Aquillon, how crazy the family was, or what they might do.

"They made battleships in the depths," Noëlle said. "Imagine if we could get that steel."

"I doubt they're going to share," Gaétane said.

"Pascale D'Aquillon just said on the radio that she would."

Gaétane snorted. Another set of messages came across various channels, many of them contradictory. One said Gaschel had resigned. Another said she'd declared martial law. One said that the detention cells were being emptied and the prisoners being armed. Noëlle knew a couple of black marketeers who'd been nabbed.

"I'm going to go to the *Baie-Comeau*," she said suddenly.

"Why?" Gaétane asked.

"Somebody needs to find out what's going on. This is stupid."

"Your funeral," Gaétane said.

"Do you know Josette Racine?"

"Why?"

"She was detained for black marketeering," Noëlle said. "Message her. If she answers, then the story about detainees being freed is true."

Gaétane shook her head. "This is all messed up. Things are bad, but a coup isn't going to help."

"Unless the D'Aquillons really have found metal on the surface."

"You and the D'Aquillons…"

Noëlle gave Gaétane the finger. "I'll message you as soon as I find out what's going on."

She leapt off the platform, wing-pack keening, wings wide. She swooped and gained speed, then altitude, and headed for the *Baie-Comeau*. The radio traffic and contradictory gossip didn't become any clearer on the way. Gaschel had sent a colony-wide message that there was an active coup attempt and people should stay in their habitats, and that habitats should disperse slightly, for safety. It said the main coup attempt was being made at the *Baie-Comeau* and that government functions were being run out of the bank branch office.

There were pictures too, of the steel ships. They looked big; Noëlle couldn't believe that there was so much new metal. Some people messaged that there was no new metal, that the D'Aquillons had made the three ships out of the *Causapscal-des-Vents,* but Noëlle couldn't see how one habitat would have that much steel. She also couldn't see how those ships could be buoyant at this altitude, so maybe all the steel was on the outside. Someone was transmitting video from the roof of the *Baie-Comeau,* where a crowd had gathered, and Pascale D'Aquillon was offering *la colonie* steel, lots of it.

By the time Noëlle landed on the *Baie-Comeau,* Pascale was already inside, but the roof was still filled with gawkers. Noëlle moved closer to the ship. It was taller than her, and it was long, like a fat cigar. She beat her fist against the rough rusty finish of its side, expecting a hollow echo, but it was hard and quiet—her fist struck too softly to make any noise. Even with balloons, how had they gotten this much buoyancy?

She waited in line to cycle through the airlock to follow Pascale into the government offices, and joined the crowd below. Pascale had her helmet off. She was a pretty young woman who looked like she hadn't washed in weeks. Her face was dirty and smudged and her shoulder-length hair was sweaty and snarled. Noëlle saw the resemblance to Marthe and Émile. Noëlle thought that Marthe had only had brothers, but she'd never paid much attention when Marthe talked about family.

Pascale spoke with a kind of shy certainty, flushing every so often as if suddenly realizing that everyone was looking at her. She didn't seem scary, but sometimes a hard confidence surfaced, reminding her of Marthe. That uncomfortably told Noëlle that she probably missed Marthe, but also gave her a sense that maybe this coup would work. Marthe could have pulled it off, and the littlest sister gave off that same feeling of knowing what she wanted.

Pascale approached a tall, thin woman and the whole crowd listened to them. Émile's girlfriend? People were looking at the woman in a new way, as she said she'd rally the mechanics to the coup. And artists, whatever use they were. Pascale didn't know Noëlle, didn't know that she'd been special to Marthe, and Noëlle was a bit envious that the Thérèse woman was being singled out for some kind of recognition when Émile had been such a loser. Noëlle had sort of been with Marthe for a long time, hadn't she?

Pascale headed back to the roof, flanked by two angry-looking women who looked like they wanted to fight to protect her. Noëlle couldn't get close enough to tell Pascale who she was and who she'd been to Marthe. She sidled closer to the group of people around Thérèse. They were looking at Thérèse with a new respect, like she'd been the girlfriend of a guerrilla leader. Noëlle waited until the conversation and attention died down and people started drifting away, and approached the artist-mechanic.

"I'm sorry about Émile," Noëlle said.

"Who are you?" Thérèse said.

"I was… Marthe was my… We were together."

Thérèse's green eyes felt hard, pinning Noëlle to the spot.

"I only met her once," Thérèse said. "She was a bitch."

"Yeah," Noëlle said with a little smile.

She had been, but she'd also been kindness and danger and excitement, the kind that didn't fit easily with other people who weren't moving as fast as her. Maybe Noëlle understood Pascale and the *coureurs* and the people following her—they wanted to do things, and they just did them.

The D'Aquillons were willing to throw away all the things other people thought were important. Noëlle had thought that was just an irritating quirk of Marthe's, but it seemed to be the whole family. Marthe had once talked about her brother, Jean-Eudes, and how the family hadn't accepted what others thought, and that for that they'd become *coureurs*. Nothing of Noëlle's pleading had ever changed Marthe. Émile was a loser mechanic who wanted to be a poet and he'd just *done* it, written poem after poem, even though no one thought he could do it. And they'd taken the *Causapscal-des-Vents* to get metals from the surface, even though everyone would be against them. With those metals, they'd made steel ships and demanded a new government. She'd thought Marthe had been a bitch, but now that she thought about her as a *coureur,* she seemed kind of inspiring, and Délia seemed a bit flat.

"I didn't really understand Émile's poems," Noëlle said. "I didn't know he had it in him."

"You've read them?"

Noëlle heard a kind of accusation in the question, like Thérèse knew Noëlle had stolen Émile's datapad.

"Marthe needed money and sold me a datapad," Noëlle stammered. "I was just doing it to be nice. It's a good datapad, but it's got some of Émile's stuff on it."

Thérèse's stare made her fidget.

"Those poems were supposed to be left with me," Thérèse said uncertainly.

"You can give me what I paid for it."

Thérèse looked even less happy when Noëlle named her price, way too much for an old datapad, but she'd given up on getting a better bunk assignment out of Labourière.

SIXTY-NINE

Pascale emerged onto the roof of the *Baie-Comeau* with four other nervously excited conspirators. Narcisse Mignaud, concerned about Pascale's safety, had tried to push his way into the airlock, but it had already been full.

"I'm okay," Pascale said, waving to him as someone closed the inner airlock door. He looked intense, like Pa on his bad days, and that made Pascale nervous.

Was Pascale safe here in the airlock, with these people? Alexis and Louise were like chess pieces, covering her descent from the *Sainte-Marthe,* and Jean-Eudes could keep the hatch locked, but Pascale started to feel vulnerable, and wished that maybe Narcisse had been with her. She emerged from the airlock and walked to the ladder of the *Sainte-Marthe.* She rose two rungs and looked at the forty or so people on the roof.

This was the moment of truth; if anyone wanted to shoot her, this was their chance. The crowd of faces looked up at her, or each other. Some filmed with helmet cams.

"The government and the bank murdered to keep *la colonie* dependent on the bank until even our grandchildren are old," she said in her helmet radio. "The government and the bank imprisoned people who were just trying to trade for things their families needed. I lost my family because of the government and the bank. Others lost family, too. We won't leave murderers to decide what we'll be. From today onward, we'll decide."

Many of the people watching her cheered. Others looked nervous. She climbed the ladder and onto the roof, where she key-coded open the hatch.

"Pascale!" Jean-Eudes said as she climbed in. "I was worried. I listened to the radio. The government is mad. The *présidente* is mad."

Pascale sealed the hatch and activated the controls to increase their buoyancy. People outside were unmooring the ship.

"Yes, she's mad," Pascale said. "We want to arrest her. She's done some bad things and doesn't want to be judged."

"Can't she just go?" Jean-Eudes said.

The *Sainte-Marthe* slowly lifted off the *Baie-Comeau,* the bags of oxygen tugging hard.

"She's a little like us," Pascale said to Jean-Eudes. "Gaschel has nowhere else to go. This is her home. This is where she belongs. And we're the ones to put her on trial. She's at her most dangerous now, because she's about to lose everything."

"Don't get hurt, Pascale," Jean-Eudes said. "I'll get hurt for you. You need to look after Alexis and Louise and Maxime and Paul-Égide."

Pascale turned awkwardly in the little space and hugged her big brother. He was silently crying. "We'll both be brave, Jean-Eudes. I didn't want this. I wanted to explore the stars and build things. It should have been Pa, and Marthe, and Marie-Pier leading this fight, caring for all of Venus. They can't, so we'll take care of everyone."

Jean-Eudes squeezed her hard and then let her go, pointing at the controls. Pascale settled back into the pilot couch and checked the portholes and mirrors. A dozen people were following them on wing-packs, even though they were much faster than the steel ships and had to circle to stay close. Most were *coureurs,* but some were up-clouders. Many more stayed behind on the *Baie-Comeau*.

The bank branch office floating ten kilometers behind the *Baie-*

Comeau was changing course. Through the telescope, Pascale saw its big propellers pushing its bulk northward.

PASCALE WAS GAMBLING. If this failed and the House of Styx had to run and hide again on the surface, they would be without food, without resupply, without friends: a family that came from nothing and returned to nothing.

"*Sainte-Marthe, Saint-George, Saint-Gabriel,* the branch office recognizes the Gaschel administration as the only legal authority on Venus," came a radio message. "Any forces approaching the branch office without prior authorization will be considered security threats and treated accordingly. The Bank of Pallas is pleased to continue to work with the people of Venus through their legally elected government."

"That's bad," Jean-Eudes said.

"It's what we expected," Pascale said, before switching to the encrypted channel to Alexis and Louise. "You're doing fine," she told them.

Alexis and Louise gave protestations of confidence, but their voices were tight. Pascale felt anxious. She wished Gabriel-Antoine were here, that they were all here, all the people she'd loved who had died for a dream.

Approaching the branch office took ten minutes. Some figures leapt from the branch office on wing-packs, flying towards them. They carried chest packs with mounted gun barrels. As they came close, they fired. The *coureurs* and up-clouders accompanying the *Sainte-Marthe* scattered.

Pascale swivelled the flechette turret beneath the *Sainte-Marthe* and fired after the bank flyers, but they were fast. Two of Pascale's allies tumbled in the air beside the *Sainte-Marthe,* falling to the ochre cloud tops below. Before Pascale could react further, bullets hammered along the sides of the *Sainte-Marthe,* but did no damage. Looking through the windows and mirrors, Pascale sprayed more flechettes into the air. She didn't come very close to them, but the bank flyers pulled away.

She looked to the *Saint-George* and the *Saint-Gabriel*. The bank flyers were pulling back from all three craft, taking wide paths back to the branch office.

"They couldn't do anything!" Louise said in the radio. "They're running."

Pascale wasn't sure. She looked around, but couldn't see any threats.

Then Jean-Eudes shrieked as heavy blows hammered along the sides of the *Sainte-Marthe*, echoing hard all around them, the way thunder amplified inside the tight woody flesh of a trawler. Alexis cried out on the radio too. Pascale looked out the forward porthole. There were flashes on the roof of the branch office. Figures in survival suits stood behind guns mounted on meter-high tripods. Pascale angled the *Sainte-Marthe* about thirty degrees off a direct path to the branch office and the heavy bullets continued to pound the port side.

"Turn slightly away," Pascale radioed to Alexis and Louise. "Leave the steel to take most of the hits."

Jean-Eudes whined softly behind her.

"It's going to be okay, Jean-Eudes," Pascale said. "Their bullets can't get in."

Jean-Eudes screamed as Pascale heard a strange sound. Jean-Eudes was pointing at the port side porthole, now webbed in cracks. The mirror that had been mounted outside it seemed to be gone.

"Get farther back, Jean-Eudes," Pascale said. "Scootch way down, in case the glass breaks." On the radio, she said, "Alexis, Louise! Aim your flechettes at the roof of the branch office."

Pascale swivelled her flechette launcher towards the machine guns and fired, but her shots fell short. The high-calibre guns just had a much longer range. Alexis was getting closer—he hadn't turned. His flechettes briefly drove back one of the gun crews, but the other gun turned fully on the *Saint-George* at close range and launched rounds so thickly that they made visible shadows against the clouds. Alexis screamed and smoke started issuing from the front of the *Saint-George*. Pascale turned towards the guns and fired a continuous stream of flechettes, forcing the crews to duck while she called into the radio.

"Alexis! Alexis! Are you okay? Turn away!"

Alexis's only response was a fresh volley of flechettes, and then more bullets knocked along the hull of the *Sainte-Marthe*. Louise was nearing the branch office, spraying flechettes. Two bodies lay unmoving on the roof, but five figures still manned the pair of guns. Pascale's flechette launcher abruptly stopped. She hadn't used all her ammunition. Something was jammed. High calibre rounds hammered the port side of the *Sainte-Marthe* again, seeming to focus around the porthole.

"I'm hit," Alexis finally said on the radio. "I can't see anything."

"Louise! Can you fire on those guns?" Pascale said. "Turn back, Alexis. Go back to the *Baie-Comeau*."

"I can stay," Alexis said. "I have to get rid of the smoke. Something's burning."

One of the guns swivelled from Louise to Alexis and more bullets rained along the side. The steel hull deflected most of them, but a spray shattered the side porthole and left a few dark holes along the length of the *Saint-George*. Pascale had helped raise Alexis from a baby. For all that Alexis was smart and capable, he was a child; she couldn't dismiss images of his little body broken by flying metal.

"It's too dangerous, Alexis!" Pascale said. "Go back."

Louise's fire forced the gun crews to duck and they struggled to turn their fire on the *Saint-Gabriel*. The *Saint-George* turned slowly towards the *Baie-Comeau* as Pascale tried to swing her ship about. She had the terrible feeling that after all they'd done, all that she'd tried, she was just delivering the last of her family to their deaths.

"Louise, pull back," she said. "Get out of the range of those guns."

SEVENTY

NARCISSE AND ANGÈLE were among a cloud of flyers on the outskirts of the battle. Without binoculars or a telescope, Fabienne couldn't identify anyone, but a few flyers had been struck by ricochets and had fallen, carrying down good metal and parts with them. Some daring flyers followed them, trying to activate their emergency balloons. They even succeeded in saving a couple of them. The noise of battle rattled and banged loud enough to reach the *Baie-Comeau* across kilometers of eerily thin air.

The radio communication was all encrypted. Fabienne couldn't tell if the squawking buzz in the radio was from the bank or the House of Styx, but what interested her most was that the D'Aquillons hadn't broken through. They'd assaulted the branch office and hadn't gotten aboard. The bank was undefeated and the D'Aquillons were taking hits. Pascale D'Aquillon had overplayed her hand, or underestimated the bank, or both.

One of their steel ships was returning, spilling smoke from its bow. Within short minutes, it came alongside the *Baie-Comeau*. People grabbed ropes to bring it onto the roof, jumping to avoid the barely controlled tons of irresistibly moving steel. Fabienne landed.

"I'm a member of the House of Crows!" Fabienne said. "Tie it down loosely in case its weight endangers the *Baie-Comeau*!"

People listened. Fabienne wanted to be first at the ladder, and Liette had the same idea, but an up-clouder got there first and was scrambling up.

"That's not your ship!" Fabienne said. "Get down."

The figure looked down briefly, a woman, tall, skinny, who flipped her the bird.

"Get up there!" Liette said on their private channel. "Get in and I'll tell people to cast off."

It might not be hard to get people to think the big steel ship was better off floating on its own. Pascale had managed the weight and buoyancy of her ship better than this one—the roof of the Baie-Comeau was now deforming in places. Fabienne climbed up while Liette blocked others from reaching the ladder. The woman on the roof looked at the dorsal hatch, as if she were speaking through it. She was speaking—Fabienne found her voice on one of the common engineering channels.

"…of Émile's. It's going to be okay. Are you hurt?"

"No," a child's voice replied. "Some bullets broke through the glass and smashed some of the equipment, but the buoyancy tanks weren't hit."

"Were you hit?" the woman asked.

"My suit isn't leaking," the child said.

"This is Fabienne Mignaud. Open the top hatch and I'll check your suit and assess the damage inside."

"Pascale said not to open it for anyone," the child responded on the radio.

"That's smart," Fabienne said, "but Pascale probably wasn't thinking of damage to your ship. You're George-Étienne's grandson, aren't you? I'm from the House of Crows. I'm a *coureur* like you. I was an ally of your grandfather's. I met him with my cousins Narcisse and Liette."

The woman by the hatch looked at her curiously. The child was silent for a bit.

"No, I'll check it myself," he finally replied.

The dorsal hatch was locked, but the front window was just jagged teeth of thick glass in its frame. If she cleared the shards and removed her wing-pack, she might be able to squeeze in. She also had a taser that she'd gotten from someone who'd stolen it from a constable during a fight. She could get the kid to open the hatch.

"We're *coureurs*," she said. "You know what it's like in the lower cloud decks. No one can do it all. Sticking together is how we survive. Pascale will need your help soon, and we formed the House of Crows because your grandfather asked us to be his allies."

The child wasn't responding. How was she going to do this? There were lots of gawkers below, but she doubted many would interfere if she poked her head in the front opening. The skinny woman moved towards the bow, as if having the same idea as Fabienne.

"Shove off," Fabienne said, climbing onto the spine of the ship.

Suddenly, a knife pressed at her suit in front of her stomach. Its metal shone in the sunlight.

"Get back," the woman said on the common channel. "And get down. He said no. Let him decide."

"He's a child who needs to be protected, not shot at!" Fabienne said.

The knife point advanced and Fabienne retreated. If her suit got damaged, she'd be in trouble. Fabienne weighed pulling the taser from her pocket. She could get cut a lot faster than she could draw. If she retreated and tased the skinny upclouder from the ladder, everyone would see and ask questions. The knife pressed and Fabienne had to scramble to grab the ladder rungs.

"Watch yourself, bitch," Fabienne said as she descended.

The crowd had grown during the exchange. A woman was at the front, leaning on a constable, as if she were going to go up the ladder next.

"I'm protecting the boy," Fabienne said.

"I'm his grandmother," the woman said with a kind of tired irony. She didn't look like a grandmother.

"Get out of the way," the constable told Fabienne.

"You're out of a job," Fabienne said.

"I've thrown in with the House of Styx," he said.

He put a hand meaningfully on a gun on his belt. A little guy with a badge on his suit pushed through the crowd to stand beside him. Fabienne sidled away. The woman needed help climbing the ladder. On the roof, the skinny woman reluctantly stepped out of the way. The grandmother spoke through the dorsal portal. Fabienne listened closer to the broken bow porthole. The child's voice inside said, "Marie-Pier?"

The dorsal hatch soon opened. The woman carefully climbed in and then it closed again.

"*Ostie*," Fabienne swore.

SEVENTY-ONE

Pascale had retreated temporarily to rethink her plan, but as soon as she and Louise had pulled the *Saint-Gabriel* and the *Sainte-Marthe* out of range of the high-calibre guns, more of the bank security people had leapt into the high winds on fast wing-packs. Pascale's flechette launcher was still not working. Worse, something must have damaged her ship—the *Sainte-Marthe*'s nose canted down about fifteen degrees. Pascale and Louise had maybe thirty seconds before the flyers arrived.

Pascale had one weapon left: a homemade missile. Each of the ships had two that shot straight out of holes on the bow, powered by short-burn rockets. The envelopes of all habitats were toughened against acid, wind, pressure changes, UV and even people walking all over them, but they wouldn't stop several meters of speeding steel. The missiles were crude, though; a haphazard shot might hurt innocents. Pascale and Gabriel-Antoine had talked of winning hearts to their side. Killing innocents and sinking tons and tons of steel and valuable electronics wouldn't win hearts.

About twenty seconds to arrival.

For a moment, the image of being on the surface, outside, setting up the transmitter with Gabriel-Antoine, was as clear as if she were there again. The terrible heat and the noise pressed at her once more as the bank drones maimed her lover, as he died a lingering death because they wouldn't let her take him for help. Her molten anger matched the heat of the surface. The bank had built those drones, had transported them, serviced them, fueled them. Not everyone at the bank had killed Gabriel-Antoine, her father, and her brother, but none of them were innocent, either. And the bank and government showed no signs of stopping, because so far, the House of Styx had not shown any ability to make them.

"Louise! I'm not at the right angle! Can you fire a missile?"

"Where?" the radio crackled back, Louise's voice tight and nervous.

"In the center of the branch office," Pascale said. "We don't know how accurate we are."

"What about the people in there?"

Five seconds to the flyers arriving. Pascale tried the flechette trigger again, but nothing happened. Louise warded the flyers away from the *Saint-Gabriel* with arcs of flechette spray.

"They won't stop until we make them," Pascale said. "They won't hesitate to do to us what they did to Gabriel-Antoine."

Scraping and footsteps sounded over Pascale's head, and Jean-Eudes started with a squeak.

Louise did not transmit, but Pascale saw a small tube open on the front of the *Saint-Gabriel*. A moment later, a meter of steel, narrow and vaned for aerodynamic lift, shot from the opening, a contrail of hot carbon dioxide in its wake. The little missile raced through the thin air, its trajectory fading and slowing, dropping beneath the branch office and heading for the cloud tops.

"*Tabarnak*!" Louise transmitted.

They'd not had a chance to test the missiles in the clouds. They had no guidance—they were more like old-fashioned torpedoes than missiles—and their range and thrust were less than Pascale and Gabriel-Antoine had hoped. The *Sainte-Marthe* seemed to be tilting further down, as if there were more weight on the front than the back. Pascale would never be able to aim the missiles like this.

"Try again!" Pascale said. "Get closer."

Louise neared the branch office as the suited figures climbing over the *Saint-Gabriel* focused their attentions on the locked dorsal hatch. They didn't seem to have the tools to break in, not yet, but eventually they would bring some over.

"When you get closer, they'll have to get the people off your ship to shoot at you, or not shoot," Pascale said.

Pascale turned on the pumps and started draining oxygen from the stern balloon to inflate the bow balloon. Slowly, the *Sainte-Marthe* started tilting. The ship would be level in about thirty seconds, and would start to tilt upward in forty or fifty. Pascale didn't have time to do the math, but she estimated that she'd need about a fifteen-to-twenty-degree upward tilt to get her missiles all the way to the branch office.

Louise fired, from nearer. The second steel rod streaked towards the habitat, its arc dipping. It tore through both envelope layers on the ventral side of the branch office. Water, greenery and debris fell from the gash, but it wasn't a significant hit. Just the thought of hurting people would have made her sick even a few months ago, but now a hot anger fogged her vision.

"Louise, back away!" Pascale said. "You can't do more. I don't want you hurt."

As the *Saint-Gabriel* glided past the habitat, the guns on the roof targeted the propellers and the exhaust funnels at the ship's stern. Most of the rounds bounced off, some even ricocheted back at the branch office, but they did some damage. The *Saint-Gabriel* began to smoke, and the flyers on its roof laboured at something.

Suddenly, the stern balloon cable snapped and the *Saint-Gabriel* tipped upward. The bank forces tumbled into the air, but extended their wings and flew back to the branch office. The balloon flew free, its flaccid skin fluttering. Louise was helpless.

"Pascale!" she called on the radio.

The pumps churned on the *Sainte-Marthe* and the nose slowly lifted past level. She pulled the lever to open the missile tube cover.

"You can't do anything else here, Louise," Pascale transmitted.

"Detach your forward buoyancy balloon and drop. You'll fall for a long time, but the buoyancy of the *Saint-Gabriel* will even out around fortieth *rang.* You'll be safe. *Coureurs* will help you."

"Pascale, no!"

Pascale fired her first missile. It streaked through the thin air, flying true and hitting the branch office squarely in the centre, puncturing the forward envelopes without slowing and tearing deep into the habitat. It stalled somewhere within. Habitat air escaped from the tear, visible as a cloud of rapidly freezing ice crystals. The branch office remained buoyant, though. Pascale pulled the levers to set the second missile into the tube.

"Go, Louise! I just have to hit the office one more time."

The missile wasn't sliding into place; Pascale had to jiggle the levers back and forth before the hollow ring of steel on steel sounded beneath her. The *Saint-Gabriel,* already drifting downward, received two flyers carrying equipment, maybe a welding torch. Pascale couldn't tell from this distance. Then suddenly the men and equipment were scattered as the forward balloon released and the *Saint-Gabriel* fell. The nose of the *Sainte-Marthe* lurched violently down just as Pascale fired the second missile.

Jean-Eudes and Pascale screamed. Even strapped down, Jean-Eudes fell far enough forward to jam Pascale closer to the controls. Pascale watched her last missile vanish into the cloud tops. Nothing would stop or even slow it for sixty-five kilometers. One figure with wings fell past Pascale's view, but caught itself and flew away.

Pascale felt helpless. She'd lost.

"Pascale!" Jean-Eudes said.

"It's okay," she said, although she didn't mean it. "They cut one of the balloons holding up the ship. We're unbalanced."

"I don't like this."

Pascale switched to the rocket engine temperature display. The radioactives, shielded in their lead and steel, were hot. That was another reason they'd designed a few vacuum chambers into their ships—to insulate them from the heat of the engine. Until now, Pascale, Louise and Alexis had been running the ships on batteries. Pascale hadn't intended to need to fire the rocket engines in the atmosphere. She'd thought about that in the designs, but they'd never tested it. She took a deep breath.

"I can fix this, Jean-Eudes, but it's going to be scary. I need you to close your eyes and get ready for a little fall."

"I'm not ready!" Jean-Eudes said in alarm.

"It's okay, Jean-Eudes. I'm here with you and I'm going to take care of you. And *Papa* is watching over us. And Marthe. And *Maman*. We have a house full of saints watching over us."

Jean-Eudes let out a little whimper, and then an uncertain, "Okay."

Pascale unfolded the small wings on the sides of the *Sainte-Marthe* and released the stern buoyancy balloon. The *Sainte-Marthe* plunged. Pascale had felt freefall many times, but always with the accompanying feel of wind and heat and responsive wings on her back. She'd never felt the naked fear of an uncontrolled plummet strapped to the inside of a hollow tube.

As they fell, Pascale turned on the rocket engine and opened the valve to the exhaust cones behind the ship. Cold, compressed gas ran through tubes over the hot radioactives, heating immediately by a thousand degrees before bursting out the exhaust tubes at high velocity. She felt herself being pushed back against her seat as the rocket threw the little ship forward.

The ship shuddered as free fall turned into unstable flight. Their angle of attack was about thirty degrees down and Pascale adjusted the small ailerons and elevators to turn it into a climb. She felt heavy as the ship responded. She wrestled the ship into a rising spiral. At most, they had about a minute of thrust before their carbon dioxide tanks emptied.

Pascale looked desperately out of the forward window for the branch office. They hadn't dropped more than a kilometer or two before she'd engaged the rocket engine, but she might be kilometers away across the sky. In the distance, she spotted the *Baie-Comeau,* big and green. She was west of it, so the branch office would be somewhere behind it. Pascale and Jean-Eudes continued climbing, racing along on rocket power meant to be used in small bursts in the vacuum of space.

Pascale was scared. She didn't know if what she was planning would work. She didn't know if she was a good enough pilot to do it, or if the *Sainte-Marthe* was precise enough, or if it would kill her. If Pascale died, the House of Styx would die. She felt that in her heart. Alexis and Louise were too young to carry it on, and Marie-Pier was hurt. Pascale was the last person who really understood Venus's secret. And yet, in this moment, with all these doubts, surrounded by the saints she'd promised Jean-Eudes were watching over them, she couldn't think of any other way to drive the bank off.

The branch office grew startlingly fast ahead of them. It was higher than them, but the *Sainte-Marthe* was climbing quickly. They had about twenty seconds of thrust left. The bank habitat grew and grew, so fast.

"Hold on, Jean-Eudes!"

Pascale angled the nose of the *Sainte-Marthe* so that it passed just over the top of the branch office, so that the steel ventral surface slammed into the roof, very near where the machine guns had been mounted. The noise of the crash was tremendous, but they were so heavy and going so fast that they smashed through the rigid roof from bow to stern in a straight line, before bouncing up in a bone-bending deflection. Then the crash was over. The terrible noise stopped and the faint wind and faltering thrust sounded.

With shaking hands, Pascale brought the *Sainte-Marthe* around in a wide banking turn, coming just behind the branch office before the thrust gasped its last. Without its balloons, Pascale waited for the ship to sink, but it didn't. She was puzzled before she realized what had happened. She'd thrown about two thousand kilograms of carbon dioxide ballast overboard as thrust. Lighter now, the *Sainte-Marthe* could float along at sixty-fifth *rang*.

They were about two kilometers behind the branch office. Its roof was a field of fragmented solar cells, hard plastic shards and bent steel struts. The tripod-mounted machine guns had vanished in the carnage, and the whole habitat was listing ten degrees to starboard. Water and gas escaped through the many tears.

"It worked, Jean-Eudes," she whispered cautiously.

Her big brother came forward nervously. "What worked?"

"We didn't have any more missiles, so I hit the bank with the *Sainte-Marthe*."

"Marthe hit the bank," Jean-Eudes said, as if tasting the idea. "*Papa* would like that."

"Yes, he would have," Pascale said. She reached behind and squeezed his hand.

"I didn't like that," Jean-Eudes said. "I was so scared I peed my pants."

Pascale laughed. "I think I did, too."

Jean-Eudes gave a little laugh, then a louder one, and Pascale squeezed his hand harder. When he had quieted, she turned on the radio.

"This is Pascale D'Aquillon of the House of Styx," she said, "to the other houses and to our allies from the flotillas: the branch office of the bank is drifting and damaged and her guns are gone. Proceed to the branch office to arrest Gaschel and her officers, as well as the branch manager and her security forces, if any of them survived."

A loud cheer went up on the radio channel. Pascale ramped up the rotation on the propellers, and the ship slowly moved towards the branch office.

"Louise, this is Pascale," she said in their private encrypted channel. "Are you all right?"

That channel sounded grainy static for a time until Louise said, "Pascale, I'm okay. The *Saint-Gabriel* is floating at fifty-fifth *rang*. I have engines and battery, but I can't climb."

"You can dump some of the compressed carbon dioxide," Pascale said. "Right now it's ballast. Don't turn on the rocket engines, just let the carbon dioxide out slowly and you can rendezvous with the flotilla."

She agreed with nervous optimism and Pascale switched back to the common channel.

THE *SAINTE-MARTHE* DREW closer and closer to the branch office from one side while about forty *coureur* flyers with wing-packs approached from the west. A stern cargo bay door on the branch office opened and a strange, flat vehicle dropped out. It had small wings, and hot thrust blew from its tail. The craft shot away, climbing rapidly. Although she could only watch its speeding trajectory for a few seconds, Pascale was pretty sure it was heading to low orbit. The bank had shipping resources in orbit capable of achieving escape velocity. Whoever was on that little vessel was gone.

SEVENTY-TWO

Pascale couldn't catch her breath. The House of Styx had surprised everyone today. Their weapons and ships had been crude and rushed, but had been good enough. Pascale felt queasy and weak. Her heart still thumped hard even though the danger had receded. The cloud tops throbbed an eye-watering yellow-white, misting through the nervous fog of too-quick breaths on the inside of her faceplate. Voices sounded in her radio. Pascale thought one was Fabienne Mignaud's, among some twenty *colonistes* winging their way to the bank habitat.

"Are they leaving?" Louise said, tight and nervous.

Now that her adrenaline was dropping, her brain was starting to work again. The receding bank rocket wouldn't be back, not right away. That wasn't the way fuel and gravity worked. If the bank staff were to return, it would be after having used their fuel to escape Venus's heavy gravity. By then, after reorganizing and refueling, they would have no base of operations to return to if the *coureurs* held the branch office—if it was even salvageable. The bank couldn't return without coming in force, which would be an enormous expense; moving that much metal for weaponry and armor from the asteroids to Venus would be a major undertaking, and not worth the return on investment. It wouldn't be worth it for the bank at least until they learned what the House of Styx had found.

She imagined that when that secret became known, Venus would know all the anger of the bank's greed.

"They're leaving," Pascale said to Louise. "Come around beside the branch office when you can."

Pascale's ship turned ponderously about, matching the branch office's heading. Mignaud's flyers neared. Pascale came close, and flyers tied her ship to a side docking platform of the branch office. She and Jean-Eudes emerged near one of the branch office airlocks. She locked the *Sainte-Marthe* while Jean-Eudes looked about him in wonder and terror.

"That's the sun, Jean-Eudes," Pascale said.

"It's too bright."

"I know," Pascale said, feeling a giddy smile on her face.

The airlock opened easily. The pressure inside was as thin as the atmosphere outside. Emergency lights were on. Smoke hung on the faint air. Nothing Pascale and Louise had done would have started a fire; the retreating bank staff must have tried to burn something, but with the pierced hull, the fires had guttered and died. Loud voices in rough survival suits challenged her. She responded with *coureur* hand gestures and spoke.

"I'm Pascale D'Aquillon."

A smile appeared in one of the faceplates and a woman neared. It was Angèle, the youngest of the Mignaud cousins. No, not Mignaud—Angèle of the House of Crows.

"They ran!" Angèle said with a kind of breathless euphoria and disbelieving excitement. Some of that feeling was in Pascale's chest too, partly smothered under nervousness. Some of them looked strangely at Jean-Eudes, but without malice. Pascale took her brother's hand.

"Cowards!" someone else whooped, pumping their fist.

"It ain't cowardice if they really were getting their asses kicked!" Angèle said, slapping Pascale's shoulder. "Wooo!"

Pascale's cheeks were getting sore and she realized she was grinning. She tasted salt, too. She didn't know what kind of tears they were. She'd had so many kinds in the last year: joy, love, grief, relief, despair. Angèle must have seen the streaks on Pascale's cheeks; her expression softened, her eyes became watery and she abruptly pounced to hug Pascale. Pascale's body shook a bit.

They'd done it. They'd made the dream come true. George-Étienne's dream, and Pascale's. A dream they'd shared with Marthe and Émile, who paid more for it than Pascale. And she'd shared the dream with Gabriel-Antoine, more deeply, more personally, and now that dream was wrapped in a cloak of aching, exciting will-bes and might-have-beens. She should have been weeping for Pa, for Marthe, for the Émile she barely knew, but Gabriel-Antoine crowded out everyone as Angèle hugged her. She hugged back.

After a minute, she let Angèle go self-consciously and waved at the smoke. Their little mob gave her and Jean-Eudes a respectful space and she led them all forward. Some of the computers had been inexpertly smashed, but would certainly be scavengeable. In the disorderly retreat, other servers hadn't been touched. Pascale tried to log on, but they were unsurprisingly encrypted and secured.

"Make sure we don't damage these or lose track of them," Pascale said. "We don't have any decryption tech now, but someday we will, and when we do, we'll want all the evidence of the Bank of Pallas's crimes. They need to be held responsible."

Expressions behind faceplates sobered.

Like any habitat, in case of leaks, the branch office had multiple volumes that could be sealed to contain depressurization. Pascale's collision had damaged the dorsal structure, but it hadn't been deep, nor caused major decompressions. The two missiles had shredded part of the outer layer protecting the crops, and the inner layer of solar cells all the way to the first habitable ring. The core area beyond the airlock was still pressurized, although smoky; the bank staff's attempt at scuttling the branch office had failed when sprinklers had gone off.

They took off their helmets. Jean-Eudes fussed, looking to neutralize as if he were still in the depths. People stared at his features and Pascale wasn't sure if he was self-conscious among strangers, regardless of their behaviour. She certainly was. And then he surprised her, saying proudly to the person nearest to him, "Pascale is my sister." People smiled kindly.

They found the *coloniste* employees of the bank in one of the boardrooms. The twenty of them stood uncertainly under emergency lights, keeping apart from Angéline Gaschel. Pascale recognized her from pictures and videos. The *présidente* looked older and smaller than she'd expected, hardly the fierce and relentless opponent Pa and Marthe had described. Gaschel's expression was nervously resigned, looking from one to another of the mob—of course no one knew what Pascale looked like, the one who had led this. Gaschel's eyes finally settled with some consternation on Jean-Eudes and her expression became unreadable.

"The *Petit Kamouraska* is close," Pascale said. "The people illegally detained by Gaschel's administration rotted there for months. That will be a good place to hold her for trial."

Gaschel's angry eyes settled on Pascale. She was an impressive older woman, accomplished, a doctor, a politician, a president. Pascale had expected to feel small and uncertain before her, unpolished, rustic, undeserving, but she discovered her father's hard pride in her, too much inherited resentment for the way Gaschel had reduced Jean-Eudes's life to cost and benefit. Gaschel was charismatic, with a palpable presence, and Pascale was just a *coureur,* but Pascale felt an immovable certainty inside her now. She knew who she was. She knew what was important to her. She knew what she was willing to do and risk for a dream of stars, for a goddess they couldn't know, for the people of Venus, and for herself.

"Will you go quietly?" Pascale asked her.

"You've ruined *la colonie,*" Gaschel said to her. "Without the bank loans, we're all going to starve and shrivel away now."

Pascale shook her head. "Will you go quietly, or do you have to be taken to the *Petit Kamouraska* by float bag?"

Gaschel's certainty wavered. Her shoulders squared, but only for a moment, then there was an air of deflation. Eugène Ferlatte of the House of Storms was near them. Pascale looked at him and Léo Bareilles of the House of Ghosts.

"Can you place her under arrest on the *Petit Kamouraska*?" Pascale said. Eugène grinned and motioned Gaschel to walk. Reluctantly she followed.

"Everything you're doing is illegal," Gaschel said.

"Many laws are going to change," Pascale said, "but murder isn't one of them."

The boardroom quieted as the *présidente* was led out. Everyone seemed to be waiting on Pascale. She'd become their leader. She felt strangely unworthy. Jean-Eudes didn't seem to understand that everyone was looking at them expectantly. His eyes were wet.

"That was the goddamn bitch?" he asked.

Pascale smiled at Pa's words out of her big brother's mouth. She nodded, and her brother wiped at his eye in a bit of confusion. Everyone else looked at the D'Aquillons, none of them quite understanding. And they couldn't. All of this, all that they'd sacrificed and lost and gambled and won, had not just been for a people; it had been for their family's dream first.

SEVENTY-THREE

Six weeks later

THE ROCKET TRANSIT from Venus to Pallas had been cramped, unpleasant and mind-numbing. Woodward, the bank staff and the security contractors would need a fair bit of radiation therapy; Pallas had a strange orbit, and the only way to make the rendezvous in less than six months had been to take a high-thrust orbit after shucking some of their radiation shielding. The bank directors hadn't called on her in the first hours. There were decontamination procedures to complete, the first anti-radiation meds to take, and her DNA repair systems to amplify.

The directors were no doubt already reading her reports and proposals, the less classified ones that she'd been able to send by encrypted lasers. She'd had no indication yet what her career punishment was going to be—a headquarters job under supervision, maybe a demotion from management. If she were lucky, she might not bear too much of the blame. She might get another assignment as a branch manager where she could redeem her record.

On her first evening on Pallas, she walked carefully on magnetic soles down the insulated hallways in the faint gravity of Pallas, to the offices of Grant Sine, Senior Vice-President. She'd not expected to be talking to someone this far up the food chain. Sine's immense office suites had carpets and paintings from Earth, along with abstract holographic art pieces, and bustled with busy staff and analysts. Sine sat at a polished wooden desk. Rosalind Stickles, the Investment Banking Vice-President that Woodward reported to, was already there. Without rising, Sine indicated a seat opposite Stickles. Woodward carefully pulled herself into the chair and attached the belt. The table in front of Sine was covered in reports and graphs, some of which Woodward had written.

"Not our finest moment," Sine said. "We own a great deal of foreclosed property we can't reach. Venus has just cost us millions." *Venus*. Not Woodward. "Your reports suggest you have something more you didn't want to send, even with encryption."

"A proposal, sir," Woodward said. "A plan of action to isolate the Venusian colony and to grow the bank."

"I have quarterly profit targets to reach, Woodward. The Venusian investment is a lot of red ink before a shareholder meeting." Sine looked pointedly at Stickles. "I'm not looking to throw good money after bad."

"Diplomatically supporting the legitimately elected government of Venus—not the guerrilla forces who have staged a coup—won't cost much," Woodward said.

"We're a bank, not a state," Sine said. "We don't have any role in diplomacy."

"The Bank of Pallas is a transnational power," she said. "If we act like a state, people will treat us like one."

"To what end?" Stickles asked.

"We have investments in Venus, and they're better than we expected, but our return is being held by an insurrectionist power," Woodward said. "Although it's not the normal business of a bank, we're now in a position where we need to show the solar system that it's not wise to screw with the Bank of Pallas. Otherwise other borrowers could get ideas."

"Military action rarely pays for itself, Woodward," Sine said impatiently.

"Earth has international institutions to resolve disputes," Woodward said. "The solar system has just the customs and laws that people agree to, or what they can enforce themselves. What happened on Venus is a loss, but it will be more expensive if others think they can renege on agreements with the Bank of Pallas."

"A bank becomes a state?"

"In the Middle Ages, the Bank of St. George minted its own coins and had its own diplomats and soldiers, alongside Genoese coins, diplomats and soldiers," Woodward said. "Many states happen to have banks. The Bank of St. George happened to have a state."

Sine looked thoughtful. "I have a stakeholder meeting soon," he said. "Draw up this proposal, with numbers and cost projections, and give it to me tomorrow. If my analysts think it's persuasive, Venus *might* not be the end of your career."

When the moment dragged on long enough that Woodward looked to Stickles for some cue, the Senior Vice-President spoke again.

"What do you think of the star map found in that habitat?" he asked.

She saw a print-out of it on his desk, half-covered by another paper. She slid it delicately out with one finger to consider it.

"I'm not sure yet," she said. "I was hoping to see what astrometric AIs here thought. I hope it's not counter-intel."

Sine looked at the star map too, and then hunted for another piece of paper with fine printing on it.

"Astrometric AIs came to an erroneous conclusion that got bumped up to human astronomers for correction," he said.

He put his finger on the star map and rotated it.

"The AIs found the approximate location that would yield the map," he said.

"Oort cloud?" Woodward guessed. Imaging from the furthest reaches of the solar system would be the only way to really change their view of the stars, and even then, how would such an image have gotten to a poor family in the lower acid clouds of Venus?

Sine shook his head. "That image could only have been taken from about two hundred light-years away, in the direction of Corona Australis," he said. "There's nothing out there but a lone pulsar." He passed her the densely printed page he'd pulled out. At the top was an identifier: RX J185635-3754.

"A fake?" Woodward said.

"If it's a fake, whoever made this map had access to astrometric data at least as good as ours," Sine said. "There are only half a dozen centers that would have the AIs and data needed to fake this."

"And none of them have any contact with Venus," Woodward realised.

"Give this a few days of thought," Sine said. "It may be nothing, but if it's something, I want to know about it."

SEVENTY-FOUR

PASCALE FLOATED IN the crackling, radio-filled space, hearing her breathing, feeling like she'd been exhaling forever. Louise, to her right, corrected her own drift with maneuvering jets. The big asteroid, five kilometers long, three and a half wide, had a very slow, almost negligible rotation as it orbited the pulsar. It was too big to bring closer to the Axis Mundi, so they had stretched their thin resources to travel through nearly six hundred kilometers of cold space.

Lazare Jeangras, the newest member of the House of Saints, floated to her left. Beyond him, Marie-Pier was there too, coughing softly. In this new Venusian reality, Lazare's time running a black market hub was done. Before immigrating to Venus, Lazare had spent six years among asteroid mining corporations and had a lot to teach them about exploiting the stars at Venus's heart.

Pascale inhaled deeply, searching for words, searching for the kind of significance and meaning that she wanted for this moment. She hadn't Émile's words. She was just Pascale.

"Goodbye," she whispered.

She and Louise were on a private radio channel. Louise's hand snaked into hers and squeezed. The contact, through layers of gloves, against all the harshness of this system, was real. Pascale wasn't alone. Her heart wasn't better yet—and staring at the cold monument to her lover, she didn't know if it ever would be—but she wasn't alone.

For some time, Venus would be isolated, even a bit of a pariah. During the trial of Angéline Gaschel, the letters had flown in furiously from the Bank of Pallas, enumerating damages, defaults, penalties, and legal and financial threats. The subtext of their communiqués implied that more might be done—Pascale didn't quite know what 'repossession and confiscation service companies' were, but she could guess. *La colonie* had begun arming itself.

The isolation wouldn't matter, not right away. *La colonie* had a whole native Venusian industry to build: foundries, factories, schools, universities, colleges, housing, everything that had been stalled by their poverty. Acid and lack of metals had prevented major automation. The Axis Mundi opened onto a star system that had been cracked open like a nut. As far as they could tell, every planet that might have orbited the original star had been shattered by the supernova that had birthed the pulsar. All the materials of all the asteroids were theirs, a gift from Venus to her children. They would slowly learn. And maybe over time, the House of Saints could make new alliances and bring in experts, maybe astronomers and physicists, to learn new secrets of the cosmos from the Axis Mundi.

Pascale and Marie-Pier had not brought in Lazare's whole family; his daughter Laurette had taken over Lazare's trading operations among the flotillas. The House of Saints was still led by the D'Aquillons, the Phocas, and the Hudons, right now in a kind of weird partnership between Marie-Pier and Pascale. Lazare was a new kind of member of their political family, not a part of the political leadership, but a trusted addition of skills and talent, sworn to loyalty and secrecy, believing in a dream of stars and exploration.

His expertise had helped program their new robots to build the mausoleum for Gabriel-Antoine, a home to keep her lover's body safe for all eternity. Pascale and Louise had worked on the design together.

They couldn't really base it on mausoleums from Earth, where there was gravity. When she came to visit Gabriel-Antoine, Pascale would always be approaching from above, so the sight lines had to take that into account. Even Paul-Égide had given some shy opinions. Louise and Pascale had wanted something with a feeling of weight, something enduring, even while floating in the vacuum of space. They'd started with slabs of silicates, carved from other asteroids, still veined with iron-nickel. They liked the idea that in a thousand years, a million, this monument to Gabriel-Antoine might still be here. In all of Venusian history, no one had ever had a grave. Until now, they'd all been erased, by Venus or by themselves. That would change. Every member of the House of Saints would have a tomb, something to mark that they'd existed, to show that they'd affected history, that they'd been loved.

The government and bank had not had time to finish stripping and scuttling the *Causapscal-des-Profondeurs*. The House of Faeries, the ones who'd been caring for Maxime and Florian Hudon, had found it. The normal *coureur* reaction to finding an abandoned habitat would have been to quietly strip it themselves, but they were all different now. Willy Gallant, Nathan Fabres and Juliette Malboeuf had radioed Pascale, to let her know that the House of Faeries had repaired the habitat, to the point of replacing some of its lost equipment with their own.

The government had taken some things no one ever found again, but some of the most important possessions were still there: a few old photos, dishes, clothes, and knick-knacks that reminded Pascale and Jean-Eudes of *Papa, Maman,* Chloé, Marthe, and Émile. Although their bodies were gone, Pascale and Jean-Eudes and Alexis would make tombs for them, to be remembered. Over time, this asteroid would become a necropolis, a statement that the people they'd loved had lived. It would become a place where eventually, each of them might be laid to rest beside their loved ones.

"I'll be back, *mon amour,*" Pascale said.

Louise turned her head to Pascale, then back down to her brother's tomb.

"I will too," she whispered.

EPILOGUE I

The Son of the Harsh Mother:
a Biography of Émile D'Aquillon
Introduction by Nicolas Duvieusart

The circumstances of Émile D'Aquillon's death, gifted to history by children and the first of *Les Petits Saints*, will never be perfectly known. Whether or not father and son carried their feud to their broiling graves is one of the great lost questions of history, one already extensively explored in books, film, and theatre.

Most of D'Aquillon's poetic corpus survives, complete with drafts, versions and dates, because of the strength of the love between D'Aquillon and his muse, Thérèse Jetté. It is only due to Jetté's loving preservation that D'Aquillon's work came to us at all. Without it, Venusian poetry and culture might have been very much the poorer.

The D'Aquillon corpus allows for a reconstruction of his development as a poet and serves as a window onto pre-Congregate social forces and tensions. His poetic soul, his daring double life as the family's spy within government forces, his astonishing escape from extrajudicial execution, and his tragic sacrifice to save the younger members of the House of Styx elevate his legend in a family already filled with legends like his brother Jean-Eudes and his sisters Marthe and Chancellor Pascale D'Aquillon.

Yet it is not for his actions as a guerrilla freedom fighter, but for his poetry, that he is most lauded. His poems insightfully reveal the soul of not only the people, but of the world itself. His readers share a sense that the complex relationship between Venus and its people reaches its highest and rawest expression within the D'Aquillon poems. Not for nothing are they a standard of the Congregate school curriculum, and widely published in translation, with interstellar, intercultural readerships in Anglo-Spanish, Arabic, Mandarin and…

EPILOGUE II

"Venus on the Eve of the First Chancellorship"
Volume 2, Chapter 47, *History of the Early Congregate State*, Bicentennial Edition, 2456 CE (*Les Presses de l'Université de Vénus*)

PASCALE D'AQUILLON, THE first chancellor of the Congregate and, upon the foundation of the Praesidium, the first Congregate head of state, remained a private, elusive figure, revealing little of her personal life outside of public debates and the duties and functions expected in leading a young government. Her accomplishments during her 18-year tenure as chancellor, especially in the fields of economic development, foreign policy, science policy and military policy, will occupy the bulk of volumes 3-8 of this history. The First Chancellor period also covers the evolution of the complex political systems of the Venusian Houses, including some of the structural flaws that many historians argue led directly to the creation of a rival state under the House of Crows in the Middle Congregate period.

Chancellor Pascale D'Aquillon was succeeded by her nephew Alexis D'Aquillon in 2274 CE. Alexis D'Aquillon's legacy as a successful wartime leader was cemented by the outcome of the Second Congregate-Bank War, the subsequent recognition of Venusian statehood by the Banks, and the Banks' surrender of disputed territory and of all claims to both Venus and Mercury. This period and the postwar period of sustained expansion will be the focus of volumes 9-12. Pascale D'Aquillon's post-political activities as an explorer with Louise Phocas were important drivers of this expansion, and warrant special attention in volumes 13-15, which will bring this history to 2300 CE and the end of the period generally characterized as the Early Congregate State.

Historical scholarship of this period depends in large part on…

The Whirling Children of Cain, by Émile D'Aquillon

Many are the children of Cain,
stained by the acts of dead forebears,
in the dye of ancestral sins.

The children are fated to repeat,
relive, recapitulate, never innocent,
never whole, never home,

Sundered by language,
broken by strife, scattered further
than the eye can see.

They press at hurts and aches,
nursing betrayals and rejections,
deeper than flesh, older than the womb,

dreaming of green fields and blue
oceans imagined in stories,
leached of color,

seeking some kinder god
in some kinder world
for some kinder fate.

The kindest fate might be
for the winds to take them,
never to return, never to see,

nor to touch, nor to smile,
nor to leave any mark at all.
But the many children of Cain

foolishly cling to any anchor,
fight the wind, reaching for one
another, as they blow past.

TIMELINE OF *THE QUANTUM EVOLUTION* AND *THE VENUS ASCENDANT* SERIES

All years are in Common Era (CE)

2201	Beginning of the Colonial Venus Period
2203	Birth of George-Étienne D'Aquillon in the nation of Québec
2210	Generation ships launched from Earth to Epsilon Eridani and other destinations
2212	Solar System Partition Conference in Mexico City
2215	Events of ***Persephone Descending*** (*Analog*, November 2014, reprinted in Afsharirad's *The Year's Best Military SF & Space Opera,* 2015, and in *Flight From the Ages and Other Stories,* by Solaris, 2022)
2255	Events of ***The House of Styx,*** published by Solaris, 2020
2256	Events of ***The House of Saints,*** published by Solaris, 2023
2290	Events of ***Long Leap*** (*On Spec*, 2012)
2298	Interplanetary corporations and banks in the sol system, grown vast and wealthy, nucleate the political mergers that result in the creation of the Anglo-Spanish Plutocracy
2310	Discovery of the second Axis Mundi wormhole by the First Bank of the Anglo-Spanish Plutocracy
2324	Discovery of the third Axis Mundi wormhole by the Ummah
2325	Events of ***Beneath Sunlit Shallows*** (*Asimov's*, June 2008, reprinted in *Flight From the Ages and Other Stories,* by Solaris, 2022)
2331	Discovery of the fourth and last Axis Mundi wormhole in the Sol system by the Middle Kingdom
2352	Beginning of the engineering of the Puppets and the Numen
2379	The first Puppets reach puberty, beginning of what the Puppets refer to as the Edenic Period

2385	Commencement of the interstellar embargo on the Numenarchy
2389	Events of ***Water and Diamond*** (*Asimov's*, Nov/Dec 2018)
2390	The Venusian Congregate offers clientage to Zimbabwe as the hegemon of the Sub-Saharan Union
2435	Rise of the Puppets/The Puppet Revolt/The Fall—80,000 Puppets capture 15,000 Numen
2475	Events of ***Pollen from a Future Harvest*** (*Asimov's*, July 2015, reprinted in *Flight From the Ages and Other Stories,* by Solaris, 2022)
2487	Belisarius Arjona and Cassandra Mejía are born, the 11th generation of the *Homo quantus* project
2503	Belisarius Arjona leaves the Garret at 16 years old, and breaks the ultra-advanced AI Saint Matthew out of the First Bank of the Plutocracy
2515	Events of ***The Quantum Magician,*** published by Solaris, 2018
2516	Events of ***The Quantum Garden,*** published by Solaris, 2019
2517	Events of ***The Quantum War,*** published by Solaris, 2021
2518	Events of ***The Quantum Temple,*** to be published by Solaris, 2024
3120	Events of ***Flight From the Ages*** (*Asimov's*, Apr/May 2016, reprinted in Gardner Dozois' *Year's Best Science Fiction*, Vol. 34, and in *Flight From the Ages and Other Stories,* by Solaris, 2022)
3211	Events of ***Schools of Clay*** (*Asimov's*, February 2014, reprinted in Rich Horton's *The Year's Best Fantasy and Science Fiction, 2015* and in *Flight From the Ages and Other Stories,* by Solaris, 2022)

GLOSSARY OF SOME QUÉBÉCOIS FRENCH

I've used some small Québécois terms, mostly for colour, often for swearing, but often just because they felt right and I really wanted them in. If you can't follow them, you won't miss anything. I hope it's not too much of an artistic indulgence, but I love the Québécois culture and language and sometimes love makes us blind. All the terms are googlable. If you don't want that, here's an incomplete glossary for completists and enthusiasts, in my own words, and possibly with errors or regionalisms that are peculiar to the parts of Québec I know.

Bagosse—a kind of moonshine

Bébittes—literally 'bugs' (I have been bitten by many)

Ca va—literally 'it goes'; figuratively 'I'm okay'

Câlisse!—literally 'chalice,' the cup in which the Catholic priest pours the communion wine; figuratively 'fuck'

Champion des épais!—épais means 'thick' which is like 'idiot' in this context, so 'champion of idiots'

Con/Conne—masculine and feminine variants of a word I literally don't say; figuratively, I don't say it either

Crisse!—literally a variant of 'Christ,' but figuratively equivalent to 'fuck'

Gang de caves—like 'champion des épais'; 'un cave' is a kind of idiot, so 'gang of idiots'

Mange d'la marde—'eat shit'

Minute!—literally 'minute'; figuratively 'hang on a minute!'

n'est-ce pas?—'right?'

Ostie—literally the 'host' wafer that becomes the body of Christ during communion; figuratively 'fuck'

Pas mal, mon p'tit gars—'not bad, my boy'

Prêt—'ready'

Qui s'est emmerdé—'emmerdé' means 'in the shit,' in this context meaning 'annoyed'; figuratively 'the one who got annoyed'

Reste içi—'stay here'

Sapristi!—I don't know the literal meaning, but it's a light curse that my aunts would say in good company

Tabarnak—literally 'tabernacle,' a liturgical furnishing used to house the Eucharist; figuratively 'fuck'

Tord-boyaux—another kind of moonshine

Vas-y—'go ahead'

Viarge—a misspelling variant of 'virgin,' literally referring to the Virgin Mary; figuratively expresses anger, but this is not one of the big Québécois swears

Voyons—literally 'look'; figuratively 'come on'

In Québécois swearing, the meaning is made harsher and stronger by concatenating swear words. It's like building a train. The longer the train, the harder the swear. So *ostie d'tabarnak* is worse than either *ostie* or *tabarnak* on their own. Another example of concatenation is *ostie d'con*, or *maudit câlisse de tabarnak de gros problème* which is even worse, with three swears together. The internet has lots of resources on Québécois swearing, so you can learn to build your own train!

ACKNOWLEDGEMENTS

I WOULD LIKE to thank my agent Kim-Mei Kirtland, my editors Michael Rowley and David Moore, and my writers' group friends Hayden Trenholm and Liz Westbrook-Trenholm for their important suggestions for improvements to this novel. I would also like to thank sensitivity reader Eris Young, who gave me additional, specialized advice on Pascale's journey as well as Dr. Amy Borsuk, who thoughtfully commented on Émile's poetry.

FIND US ONLINE!

www.rebellionpublishing.com

/solarisbooks

/solarisbks

/solarisbooks

SIGN UP TO OUR NEWSLETTER!

rebellionpublishing.com/newsletter

YOUR REVIEWS MATTER!

Enjoy this book? Got something to say?

Leave a review on Amazon, GoodReads or with your favourite bookseller and let the world know!